I0589495

Creative Texts Publishers products are available at special discounts for bulk purchase for sale promotions, premiums, fund-raising, and educational needs. For details, write Creative Texts Publishers, PO Box 50, Barto, PA 19504, or visit www.creativetexts.com

PERCY'S MISSION
by Jerry D. Young
Published by Creative Texts Publishers
PO Box 50
Barto, PA 19504
www.creativetexts.com

ISBN: 978-0-692-53415-1

PERCY'S MISSION

By

JERRY D. YOUNG

Think about the events in this story as you read it. You may agree or disagree on the premise, but think about what you would do if...

CHAPTER ONE

"Percivale George Jackson," said Percivale George Jackson. Pronounced "Per-ci-vail", he said, "not Per-ci-vall". The look on his face brooked no attempt at humor based on his name.

The DMV clerk carefully input the information into the computer fighting to control his grin. Percivale was bad enough, but the vehicle being registered was called a Unimog. What the hell kind of truck was a Unimog? Sounded like a character in Lord of the Rings, or four of them, because Percivale was licensing four Unimog trucks.

Cutting his eyes up to the tall, skinny, middle-aged man, the clerk barely managed not to laugh, again, as he took in the sight of the worn felt hat partly covering the longish, mostly brown hair. The overalls Percivale wore were nearly new and the green plaid shirt looked new, too. He managed to keep the comment a silent statement to himself. "Must be his Sunday-go-to-Meetin' overalls", he said.

He came to the purchase price of the trucks and his eyes widened and he whistled under his breath. "Wait a minute," he said then, picking up the purchase form in his hand and looking once more at Percivale. "Is this some kind of joke? This says the trucks are Mercedes-Benz trucks. The other papers say Unimog. There is no such thing as a Mercedes truck."

"Mercedes-Benz does make trucks. Mercedes-Benz is the parent company that makes the Unimog line of vehicles. Is there a problem or something? It usually doesn't take this long to register and license a vehicle." Percy maintained his calm demeanor despite the smirk on the young man's face. The smirk had appeared the moment Percy had stepped up to the counter.

"I suppose nothing is wrong. I just have to be careful. Registering a vehicle is an important procedure. It must be done correctly. This is a somewhat out of the ordinary vehicle. I've never even heard of one before."

That was enough opening for Percy. He was proud of the versatile vehicle. It had taken him almost six months to get them, once he discovered they were available. Telling someone, especially this twerpy clerk about them, would be a pleasure.

"Sort of a cross between a tractor and a giant jeep," Percy said. He realized his mistake immediately. He stopped the explanation as quickly as he'd started it.

"Tractor?" asked the clerk. "We don't license tractors."

Percy groaned. "It's not a tractor... I... ah... was just kidding." It sounded lame to Percy.

The clerk got even snootier. "I'm afraid the DMV does not appreciate such jokes. This is a serious business."

"Yes, sir. Sorry. Sometimes I get a bee in the ol' bonnet. It won't happen again." Percy heard whispers behind him after he had spoken. He turned around and looked to see what was going on. Percy groaned again.

He touched the brim of his hat. "Mornin' Mrs. Applegate. Lovely weather we're having, isn't it?"

"Percivale, the weather is atrocious and you know it. That sense of humor you just told that clerk you had is just as drab as it's ever been. Please don't waste his time, or mine. I'm in a hurry."

"Yes'm," Percy said softly, turning back to the counter. Mrs. Applegate had been his third grade teacher. She was in her eighties and still scared him.

She scared the clerk even more. He knew her as the wife of a state representative, somebody important. He quickly finished the process for Percy and handed him the four sets of license plates. He was already apologizing to Mrs. Applegate for Percy having kept her waiting as Percy stepped out of the way.

Percy sighed and headed out to the Suburban. At least the task was done. It had been a rough morning. Bernard's wife was sick and he had to stay home to take care of her. On top of that, two of his other hands that were due back the previous day were still in Minneapolis because of yet another terrorist attack security clampdown. It was going to be at least another three days before they could get back from visiting their mother.

"Oh, well," Percy muttered to himself, "such is life. Time to go see if Hector wants that tractor."

He'd sold the Case tractor that one of the Unimogs was replacing to his nearest neighbor for a fair price. Percy began to grin as he climbed into the customized Chevy Suburban. "Old Hector wants that John Deere bad. I bet he'll come across and I got to stop talking to myself. People think I'm crazy as it is."

He touched the brim of his floppy felt hat as Mrs. Applegate walked past, her nose in the air. "Maybe I am. Maybe I am," he muttered before falling silent. He started the Suburban and, just to show off a bit, grabbed the joystick mounted on the special console at his right hand and activated the crab steering on the six-wheel-drive, six-wheel-steer running gear of the truck.

There was plenty of space in front of him so he just edged the truck out, parallel to the curb until he was in the street. Percy straightened the wheels and flipped the switch to go back to normal front steering. As usual, passers-by had stopped to gawk at the event. Percy tipped his hat, grinned, and headed toward Hector's place.

An hour and a half later Percy was talking to himself again. "Yep, Hector wanted that tractor bad." Percy had two more stops after leaving Hector's, before he headed back to the estate. He needed to stop and collect from McAlister for the two bob trucks he'd sold him, then go back into town and deposit the checks in the bank. "And probably should stop at Jimbo's Emporium and pick up some gold and silver out of the accounts."

It had taken Percy a long time to get Jimbo to agree to the arrangement. After Percy had kept track of the transactions he would have done if Jimbo would do them, and Jimbo saw what he would make by doing them, he agreed. With the way the precious metals markets had been for the last few years, Percy was able to withdraw significant amounts of the gold and silver in coin form on a regular basis and still maintain trading stocks to keep accumulating more.

Grouchy old McAlister reluctantly gave Percy the check he'd promised. "Things are going to cost me a fortune with the way gasoline prices are, you know," McAlister complained as he handed over the check.

"I know what you mean, Hiram. Diesel is almost as bad."

"Not telling me anything I don't already know," replied McAlister. "Fuel for my diesel equipment is over a third of my operating budget."

Percy's eyebrows rose slightly. He wouldn't have thought that Hiram McAlister even knew what a budget was.

"According to Cynthia... she's doing my books for me now... I'm going to have to go up on my harvesting prices."

"That explains the budget," Percy thought. "His daughter is doing it for him."

McAlister frowned. "I'm not so sure I should have cut that deal with you on the trucks. Even short as I am on cash, giving you two forty acre harvests, plus what cash I am giving you, I'm beginning to think I should have just done all cash."

"Well...if your prices are going up, Hiram, I guess it's only fair to renegotiate."

Before he could continue, McAlister interjected, "I ain't got any more cash to spare, Percy."

"I know," replied Percy. "I was thinking I'd do the hauling for one of the fields. Would that make up the difference between the old price and new?"

"You'd do that? My pricing always includes haulage. That's why I'm buying your two trucks. I need more hauling capacity."

"You're a good guy, Hiram. I want you to stay in business. We made the deal before you knew you had to go up. I'm okay with absorbing some of the difference."

"Well, gee, Percy... Thanks."

"Sure, Hiram. Tell Cynthia I said howdy."

"Sure thing, Percy. Sure thing."

*****

There was a long line at the bank. Since the federal government had restricted cash withdrawals to no more than ten percent of available balances, people were hitting the bank as often as once a day. Even with additional tellers, the line was usually long. At both banks in town. Percy kept half the money he kept in banks in each one and alternated deposits and checks. When he deposited the two checks, he withheld the allowable ten percent in cash.

"Hey, Percy," called Camden Dupree, the assistant manager of the bank. "I hear you have a real truck farm now."

Percy smiled over as he continued toward the door. "You could say that, I suppose, Camden."

Several people laughed. It had become common knowledge that Percy had sold the tractors, both the bob trucks, and three other smaller trucks and planned to replace all seven units with the four Unimogs. It was a running joke. No one seemed to think the Unimogs would be able to do the work.

"Little do they know," muttered Percy as he went through the glass double doors.

"Hey, Mr. Jackson," said Andy Buchanan. He was a delivery driver for Wilkins Oil. That was his full time job. Andy also did quite a bit of side work. "When you gonna let me bring out the semi and fill up that tank?" With a note of pride in his voice he said, "I've got my CDL now."

Andy was a good kid. "Good for you. And one of these days, Andrew. One of these days. Just my regular load this week. Five hundred gallons diesel, hundred gasoline."

"Sure thing, Mr. Jackson. Be there Thursday as usual. Any oils or anything?"

"As a matter of fact, I was going to call and request cold weather additive. I'm afraid it may be hard to get this winter. I want to get some now in case you can't get treated or blended fuel."

"How much you want? A drum?"

"Enough for... the whole tank, I think, in drums. Whatever it takes to treat ten thousand gallons for thirty below."

"Thirty below? It hasn't been even twenty below since I was a kid."

Andy was twenty-five. Percy remembered the last time it was twenty below, when Andy was ten. Half the equipment in the area had stopped because the diesel fuel gelled. The weather seemed to be hitting extremes the last few years. "I know, Andy. But you know me. Be prepared."

"That's good, Mr. Jackson. I was a boy scout. It's a good motto. I'll let the boss know and bring it when I come Thursday. I guess you'll put it in yourself. You don't want the whole batch in with just a couple thousand gallons in the tank like you usually have."

"Oh, I know. I don't want to waste it. I'll add it as needed."

"Okay, Mr. Jackson. I'll take care of it. Uh... Would you consider loaning me one of your Rokon bikes for hunting season? There's a spot up on Six Point I can get to on foot, but it's too far for me to pack out a deer unless I make four trips. I doubt I'd have time... Susie said the Rokon would handle it easy."

With a stern look on his face, Percy said, "You know I'm not much of a loaner, Andrew."

Andy hung his head. "Yes, sir. I know. I just... uh... never mind. Sorry."

Percy grinned. "But I tell you what. You give me a shank of whatever you get, and a couple of mallards, if you get any, and you can use one of the Rokon's."

"Sure, Mr. Jackson! Sure! And... gee... I always get a few ducks during the season. Two is guaranteed. Thanks."

With a wave of acknowledgement, Percy turned toward the Suburban.

"Oh. Uh... Mr. Jackson? Would you tell Susie I... uh... said hello?"

Another grin split Percy's face. "Sure thing, Andrew. I'll tell her."

"Thanks again, Mr. Jackson." Andy walked off with a jaunty step.

It didn't take long at Jimbo's place. He kept Percy's precious metals holdings in plastic coin tubes. He always transferred enough for his commission to his own set of tubes when he made a transaction for Percy.

"I still can't quite figure why this works," Jimbo told Percy, as he handed him a tube of tenth ounce gold Eagles and a tube of pre-1965 silver quarters and two tubes of pre-1965 silver dimes after Percy had checked the accounts. Percy did his own tally every day when he checked the commodities markets on line. Jimbo's numbers always matched his.

"I'm glad it does, though. I make a nice little commission off you. Plus, it's allowed me to increase my gold and silver stocks quite a bit for the business. I'm selling the occasional bullion coin to other people besides just you. What do you do with yours, anyway?"

It was a very impolite question, but Jimbo was Jimbo. "I just like gold and silver. Do give a few away as presents on birthdays and Christmas." It was the truth. Just not the whole truth. He had given a few away, but not very many. Most were in several different stashes and caches he had here and there.

To divert Jimbo, Percy asked, "What's the future look like, Jimbo? Things going to drop or keep climbing?" It didn't matter to Percy. His system was based on the differential in price between the metals, not the actual price. But Jimbo fancied himself as a gifted predictor of the metals market.

"Up, Purse, up. At least for some time. The way the world is now… well… you see the news just like me."

"Yeah. Well, Jimbo, keep that trading stock stashed for me, if you will. Never know when I might need it to bail myself out. You know what they're saying about me and my trucks."

"Yeah. Well, I don't care if you are crazy."

"Uh… Thanks, Jimbo. I'll see you later."

"Okay, Purse."

Percy shook his head on the way out to the truck, the gold and silver in his pocket. "Jimbo sure is Jimbo, no getting around it."

It was just after three in the afternoon when Percy got back to his estate. He checked in with his housekeeper, Mattie.

"Nothin' going on, Mr. Jackson. Smooth as silk all day. When's the twins getting back? Need a little help with moving the furniture for spring cleaning."

"Another three days. What are you planning for supper?"

"Meat loaf. That okay?"

"You know I love meatloaf. I need to go out and check with Randy. See how those equipment modifications are going."

"Yes, sir. I'll leave things ready for you. I need to leave at five. Susie has to get in to the city to do a little shopping."

"Okay. I'll see you in the morning."

Percy walked out to the equipment barn. A one-ton truck set up as a welding truck was parked amidst what looked like a jumble of equipment. Percy knew the jumble was organized to Randy's satisfaction, even if Percy couldn't quite see the logic. Besides the four Unimogs, a whole array of agricultural equipment was there.

Seeing Percy come up, Randy stopped the motion to drop his welding hood into place and sat down on the piece of equipment he was working on.

"How's it coming, Randy?"

"Fine, Mr. Jackson. I'll be finished tomorrow evening. Most of this was easy. I checked every piece of three-point hitch equipment on all the trucks. Everything works perfectly. I'm almost finished with the adapter for the hoe. No reason it won't attach and work just fine on the 'Mogs, too, like it did on the Case and JD. They have plenty of hydraulic power for it. With the other stuff you bought for them, I'm surprised you didn't just buy a backhoe made to fit 'em."

"Already had this one. No need to buy something I already have."

Randy surveyed the equipment. "Yeah. Right." He'd been very skeptical of using a truck as a farm implement for anything except as a tool to haul things around. But having worked with the Unimogs the past few days, he'd changed his mind. Once he'd installed the three point hitches on the trucks, which had been shipped separately, and tried some of the farm equipment, he became convinced that the combination would work. And work well.

There'd only been a few modifications to make on some of the equipment. Mostly for the PTO powered equipment. Some of them needed lengthened shafts or adapter shafts to hook up properly to the rear PTO on the trucks. Adding big mirrors to some of the implements to improve visibility of critical operations from the cab of the truck had been easy. Just a lot of in and out of the cab to make the angle adjustments after the mirrors had been installed.

Part of the reason everything had been so easy was the Unimog trucks themselves. With the set of attachments Percy had for them, like the front forks to lift things with, he'd never even rigged up the A-frame on his welding truck. And that didn't even consider the contribution that Percy's Utility/Service truck made to the operation.

It had an articulated, telescoping aerial man lift with a ladder back and material handling winch, in addition to all the other normal equipment. The lift could reach almost fifty feet at maximum extension. Not to mention the fact that with the articulation, it could reach below ground level. Randy wasn't sure why Percy might need that feature, but it was inherent in the design of the lift.

For anything the material winch on the arm couldn't lift, there was a fifteen-ton capacity hydraulic boom mounted on the right rear corner of the bed. The bed had significant open area, though that was reduced somewhat with the mounting for the aerial arm. There were plenty of toolboxes and room for the lube and fuel hose rack and barrels of lube. Randy wasn't sure why the diesel and gasoline fueling tanks were so large. They were five times larger than normal for a combination mechanic's and lube truck.

Of course, there was no doubt the truck could carry everything efficiently. It was a long Kenworth chassis with tandem steering axles and three rear axles. Unlike most similar trucks, which had only a single steering axle and, at most, two rear driven axles, this one had driven steering axles as well as having all three rear axles driven, which were also steering axles. Also unlike most similar trucks, that used duals on the real axles, Percy was using the same high flotation single tires on the three rear axles as were on the front axles.

As for power, the big Caterpillar engine developed five hundred horsepower. More than adequate for everything the truck was capable of doing. Even with a full load, Randy was convinced that the ground pressure would be half of normal and the truck still could run at highway speeds.

Percy had several trailers for use with the utility/service truck, including a heavy-duty three-axle equipment trailer. It was equipped with the same tires as the truck. It was a tilt bed, and had a winch. It could be used to haul the Unimogs around, if one of them broke down. That didn't seem very likely.

"Okay, Randy. Keep up the good work. And be thinking about that trade I was talking about."

"I really need cash, Mr. Jackson. But I will think about it," responded Randy. He flipped the welding hood down and struck an arc as Percy headed into the equipment barn.

Checking over one of the four Rokon two wheel drive motorbikes racked against one side of the barn, Percy selected yone, pulled the starting rope and headed out of the barn. He entered the fenced pathway that connected the animal barn with the four pastures that Percy used in turn to feed and work the animals. He rolled up to the gate at the third pasture, opened it, went through, and then re-closed the gate. He could see Susie and the Bobcat 5600T Toolcat utility vehicle she was driving at the far side of the pasture. It looked like the entire pack of Airedales was with her. She must be letting the adults train the pups in stock handling. He noted as he went past that the salt and mineral blocks were in the rack near the pasture entrance to the animal barn.

Since he wasn't wearing a helmet, Percy kept the speed down as he went to meet Susie. He swung wide and came around to approach Susie from the front, stopping next to the pipe fence several feet ahead of her.

Susie swung clear of him and stopped the Bobcat. "Hey, boss. What's up?" The adult dogs and older pups flopped down to rest. The pups cavorted around the Rokon, seeking Percy's attention.

Percy patted each in turn as he spoke. "Just passing on a message. Young Andrew Buchanan asked me to tell you he said hi. So hi from Andrew."

A pretty blush covered Susie's cheeks. "Thank you, Mr. Jackson. I'll tell him you told me. The next time I see him."

"Okey Dokey. Go ahead and knock off early if you want. Your mother said you needed to go into the city. Looks like all your major work is done, anyway."

"Yeah. I was heading out to do some training with the dogs. I kind of wanted the pups to watch the adults do a little herding. The cattle and horses saw me coming and headed for the far end of the pasture. Ornery rascals seem to be able to read my mind."

"I think that's a two way street. You sure have a way with the animals. I appreciate you working for me. I know you could get a much better job in town." Queenie got up and came over to him. He scratched the dam behind her ears just the way she liked it.

"Better is relative," replied the young redheaded woman. "The money is actually very good. Thank you again for that, by the way. But this is giving me great hands-on experience with animals. It's a big help in my studies for vet assistant. And since Doc lives next to you, and you let me go over every time he says he has something interesting that I might like to see, no matter what I'm doing, I'm quite happy here, thank you very much."

Percy grinned. "Okay. Have it your way. I never argue with a woman. Well. Almost never. Just let the dogs' move the animals to the barn end of the pasture and you and your Mom go do your shopping. I'm going out to dig the post holes for the surround for the irrigation pump."

"You want the 5600 so you can take the poles with you?"

Percy grinned again. "No thanks. I'll use the A300. I wouldn't deprive you of the opportunity to learn how to put up a real fence tomorrow, since the boys aren't back till this weekend."

"You are so kind, boss."

"Yeah. I know."

Susie whistled for the dogs, to get them to follow her instead of Percy. The adults would have anyway. They knew they were out to herd the stock. The pups would follow the adults. Percy headed back to get the companion machine to the two Bobcat 5600T Utility vehicles he owned. It was a loader/utility vehicle made by Bobcat. Bobcat also made the utility vehicle Susie was using. Both were four-wheel drive, four-wheel steer units. The Bobcat A300 could also be used as a skid steer, though they seldom did.

Like the Unimogs, the Bobcat 5600T utility vehicle had a dump bed, rear attachment points, and front lift arms. The Unimogs didn't have the lift arms as part of the permanent structure, though he had two sets for the trucks that could be quickly attached and detached when needed to carry part of the variety of attachments useable by the Unimogs. The 5600T was just a lot smaller than the trucks.

The Bobcat A300 was a bit shorter than the 5600T. It didn't have a cargo bed. It could handle a wider variety of attachments than the utility vehicle, though. One of the attachments either could use was a hydraulic posthole digger, which is what Percy quickly hooked up to the A300 when he returned to the equipment barn. He waved at Randy as Randy coiled up his welding cables in preparation to going home.

It didn't take long for Percy to get the holes dug. The weather was fine at the moment, so he hadn't bothered bringing tarps to cover them. By the time he got back to the building complex and put away the Bobcat, then checked on the animals, it was somewhat past suppertime.

But no matter if he was a little late. There was no one there to scold him. He'd almost married once, but the potential wife had decided she didn't want to be a conventional farmer's wife. "I'm not really all that conventional, you know," muttered Percy as he thought about what might have been. "Just ask anyone. Oh, well. Water under the bridge. Man, this looks and smells good."

After his meal, Percy had one pipe of tobacco on the roof deck of the earth-sheltered dome that was his house. He enjoyed a snifter of cognac in the library/den as he watched the news. He turned in early, feeling a bit uneasy at the world situation. Terrorism might have replaced the cold war in most people's minds as the big danger in their lives, but it sure looked like there were still some warlike leaders in a few nations. And the weather wasn't looking too good, either. He wasn't going to be able to wait until the twins got back to start ground preparation for spring planting.

Percy's alarm went off at four-thirty the next morning. Knowing Mattie would be there by six he showered, dressed, and went out to check the animals. An hour later the four milk cows were contentedly finishing their feed after having their udders' stocks of milk reduced.

The milk was in the chiller, ready for pick up by Brian Epstein on his way in to the city. So were the fresh eggs from the hens. Brian got a calf from Percy every year as payment for stopping to pick up Percy's milk and eggs to take to town with his own. He made a daily trip to the local dairy and went right by Percy's place on the way.

Percy had tilled forty acres with the one of the Unimogs before he stopped to have breakfast. There was a big grin on his face when he entered the kitchen of the house.

Susie cut him an impish grin. "Musta' worked, huh, Boss?"

"Like a charm. And you knew it would, just as did I, Missy. Hand me the eggs."

Mattie Simpson and Susie had their breakfast at the main house, with Percy, as was their usual custom. Percy had insisted, since they started so early. "There's no reason to cook for two, then for just one. It's easier to cook for three. I'll supply the food as part of your wages."

"How's that?" he'd asked the day Mattie started working for him so many years before, at the same wages as he'd intended, even without the food thrown in. She was a newly widowed single mother. He figured it was the least he could do, and it had worked well over the years.

The Simpsons lived in one of the three other houses that were part of the building complex of the estate. The twins lived in another and the third was vacant at the moment. Two of Percy's other hands lived nearby so didn't need the third house. Bernard lived in the bunkhouse when he was working. The housing was part of their pay. They took another part of their pay in estate-produced goods, in addition to cash. All the hands did, getting truck farm produce, items from the household garden that Mattie tended, and meat and dairy products from the cattle, pigs, and chickens that were part of the estate animal population.

Percy had fallen into bartering many years earlier, when he was a very young man trying to hang on to the family farm. He was a natural born horse trader, as the locals told him. He'd been quite successful in his barters and other endeavors, pulling the farm out of debt and turning it into the estate it now was.

About the only thing original from the old place was the ground itself. His mother had inherited three hundred twenty acres from her grandparents. He'd traded for and bought more.

Percy now owned a full section that was the estate. One square mile. Six hundred forty acres in one parcel. He had almost another thousand acres in forty and eighty acre plots around the county but he leased them to other farmers for the cash flow and some trading of stud services for his animals. He liked to maintain genetic diversity in his stock and outside stud services was one way to accomplish that. He also traded for products he didn't produce himself.

All the buildings were earth-sheltered structures. Even the six big green houses were bermed up to where the polycarbonate panels started and they were connected to an earth-sheltered barn. His utility bills, except for liquid fuels, weren't that much more than they'd been when he took over the operation after his parents' deaths thirty years before.

Percy was thinking about early retirement now, at only fifty-one. He'd built the place to what he'd dreamed as a young man it could be. He had a good crew and the operation was turning a nice profit even after deducting the operating expenses and the principle and interest of the few loans still outstanding for the improvements he'd been making almost from day one. He also had a very nice nest egg.

His parents had not been into preparedness and self-sufficiency, being more the squandering type. They'd let the farm go to pot, after they'd inherited it. They preferred just collecting income from leasing the arable land. When they died in a car crash caused by his father's drinking and driving when Percy was barely twenty, the bank account was empty.

Percy dropped out of college and came back to the farm with what little money he'd saved from working while he was at Iowa State. Not until he got the first monies from one of the local farms leasing the land was he able to start making the changes he wanted. This included farming the land himself, including cultivating some non-traditional crops for the area.

Percy began a truck farm on the few acres of land not under lease. Then, as the leases expired, he didn't lease the acreage out again. Instead, he took over the farming himself, hiring one, then a second hand. By the time he bought and traded for the additional land he now owned, the estate was beginning to take on the look it now had.

Most in the area considered him totally eccentric. They couldn't fathom how he'd been successful enough to gain some of what they considered his toys, as he'd heard many a time. Things like the customized Suburban. He'd had the axles replaced with heavier ones, and added a third, all steerable, to create the six-wheeled rig he privately referred to as Rufus.

Not that many had even seen the Kenworth truck based motor home he only used occasionally. The vehicle was similar to the mechanic's utility/service truck as far as the chassis, running gear and power train were concerned. Where similar converted motor homes costing millions of dollars were equipped with queen sized beds, marble counters and tubs, fancy faucets and fixtures, Percy's was a lot less luxurious and more utilitarian, therefore much less expensive and very maneuverable.

As one person who had seen his house and the motorhome put it, The Beast was like his home, only without the dirt walls. A bit austere, but very comfortable. And with the custom-built barge trailer The Beast pulled, it was amphibious. It took less than ten minutes to unfold and rig up, back it into the water, un-hook, and then back aboard the barge, ready to go. The wheels of The Beast normally powered the barge, though it had a pair of Mercury outboard motors that would propel it empty at speeds of twenty miles an hour or more.

The Kenworth utility/service truck would also fit. Since The Beast could tow the trailers the utility/service truck usually pulled, at least for short distances, the trailers could be transported on the barge, too. So could the semi-trailers used with the third Kenworth truck Percy had. He had dollies so the utility/service truck and The Beast could pull the semi-trailers using their pintle hitches.

The semi-tractor was set up the same way as the utility truck and The Beast, with five steerable axles with single high floatation tires rather than duals. It had a large sleeper suite and was equipped with an equipment winch, rolling tailboard, pintle hitch, and interchangeable fifth wheel and king pin plates so it could tow any type of large trailer.

Percy had a reefer trailer, tilt deck equipment trailer, flatbed trailer, a stock trailer, two convertible floor trailers that were useable as box trailers or grain trailers, a live floor canvas top box trailer primarily for silage, and a curtain wall trailer. All were three axle trailers with high flotation tires, except the equipment trailer, which had four axles. It too had the same tires the other trucks and large trailers used.

Knowing that the fuel situation was going to get worse, Percy had ordered two additional dollies and two seven thousand gallon tank semi-trailers, set up the same as the other trailers. Both tank trailers were stainless steel, with multiple compartments. It wasn't necessary for the fuel, but Percy intended to use one for water and it was easier to order identical trailers. He'd received a significant discount. Percy had already used his smaller three-axle pull behind water trailer to haul drinking water to both drought and flood victims in recent months.

Percy finished his breakfast and headed out to meet his other two hands while Susie helped her mother with a few chores before she headed to the animal barn. Randy was at work again, but didn't need any of the Unimogs for a while, so Percy trained John Jacobson and Smitty Smith on the use of the Unimogs for tilling. They'd have all the ground they intended to put into cultivation that year ready by the next day, excluding the ten acres they were working with the animal teams this particular year.

Susie would have the ten acres plowed and disked in a few days working the four Clydesdale draft horses in teams of two on alternate days. They wanted to break the teams back in slowly after the light work they'd done over the winter. The plan had been for Jim and Bob Hansen to work the teams together, but the work required doing now, before the weather changed.

The way the weather was shaping up, the Hansen twins might be getting back in the middle of a late blizzard. Somehow, that didn't seem that unusual any more.

Percy took care of the small chore work as the day progressed, lending Randy a hand from time to time, as well. As he'd promised, Randy had completed his work by the end of the day. Percy gave him a check, and the barter slip he printed up on the computer for the bartered items Randy had finally agreed to take in partial payment.

The slip had the value of the items listed for tax reasons. It was up to the people he bartered with to report the income or not on their taxes. He made it easy with the three part barter records. He gave one copy to the barter partner and kept two copies.

When whoever it was redeemed the item in question, Percy signed off one of his copies and gave it to the person for their tax records. He kept the third slip and the one they turned in to claim the barter, if they had it. He'd never reneged on a barter because they'd lost their original copy. That was the reason for the third slip. So he'd have one to keep for his records if they lost the first copy.

Randy had decided to take nine tenths of the pay in cash and the other tenth in produce over the next few weeks. Food shipments were getting sporadic, with everything going on. There was plenty of food, just not necessarily what you might want, especially fresh produce. Most of the farms in the area were production farms, mostly corn, milo, oats, and rye. His was one of the few truck farms still left that sold all its products locally. His greenhouse produce was much in demand during the winter. It all went to the local grocery stores, a specialty store in the city, and the co-op outlet, as did much of his commercial truck farm produce.

Some of his other property was leased out on shares and grew commercial crops, using his equipment. Conventional farming equipment. Each place had a barn and the equipment needed to farm it, except for harvesting. That he contracted for those fields.

The next day, after he'd milked the cows and collected the eggs, Percy tilled the three acre plot that would be this year's outside garden plot. He then prepped the next section of growing containers in the second green house. While things grew year round in the greenhouses, like the open fields of the estate, Percy insisted on rotating use of everything. Some areas lay fallow, others were pasture and hay fields. Other fields were planted with cash crops and estate use crops, mostly animal feed and biodiesel oil crops.

Even the garden plot rotated on four sections of ground, a different three acres being used for the garden; while the other three lay fallow, grew ground cover, or was the recipient of estate produced compost, mulch, and animal waste, each plot in turn, just like the big fields.

It didn't take long to till the three acres using the Bobcat A300 with the tiller attachment. He switched to the bucket and spread the winter's accumulation of compost from one of the three compost bins. They'd start letting that bin accumulate again. The second bin had ready to use compost in it, too. They'd use it as needed. Prepping the greenhouse beds took even less time than tilling the outside garden.

It was barely noon when Percy was done with those particular chores. The rest of the day he spent transferring the animal waste from the barn storage bins to the fallow fields using one of the Unimogs to pull the manure spreader and honey wagon. He also had time to fire up the Kenworth utility/service truck and use the aerial bucket to prune the trees that needed it.

The nut trees needed a little work. Percy kept the fruit trees in good shape, so they needed only minor touch up pruning that spring. It would have been easier with another person to drive the truck after he let the bucket down, but he climbed out of the bucket and moved the truck every eight trees, working four trees on each side of the pathway as he went between two rows of trees.

John and Smitty cleaned up the trimmings afterwards and ran them through the chipper, adding the material to the mulch pile that was building. He distributed the garden goods to the four at the end of the day. Part of Mattie's duties was preparing the bounty for distribution each day before everyone went to their respective homes.

Percy took the dogs up to the roof patio of the house with him for his evening smoke. The adults lay contentedly on the bedding that was set out there for them as Percy and Susie put the pups through their training. They were coming along nicely. The two older pups were essentially fully trained. The four younger ones from this year's litter were weaned and taking to the training as well as their older siblings. Percy had already decided which two of the four he planned to keep, but wanted all of them trained to the best of his ability before he sent them to their new homes.

The Airedales he bred were known far and wide for their intelligence and physical attributes. He kept the best of each litter unless that particular year was an outside stud year. Often as not, he wound up keeping the best of the litter anyway, in his opinion.

The other breeders he cross-bred his dogs with often took a pup that he felt was second best. But they often chose on coloring and confirmation only, as they showed their dogs. His were working dogs. They hunted and worked the herds equally well, in addition to the companionship they provided for those living on the estate.

He'd had to put Eda down the previous year. She'd been a prize dam, throwing good pups. The two older pups were both females, out of Eda, from an outside stud dog. He'd breed one with Rip and the other with Lion when they were ready. That would keep the diversity he liked in his animals. With two females from Queenie, also by a different outside stud, he'd be able to produce several litters before he needed outside stud services for the Airedales again.

Lion, Queenie, and Rip had the run of the estate at night. They kept the pups kenneled at night. Susie took the pups with her to put in the kennel when Mattie called up that she was done and ready to go to their cottage.

Percy passed on the cognac that evening, concentrating on the news and weather channels on the satellite TV system. The world situation sure wasn't any better, and the weather forecast for the Midwest was worse. Percy suddenly wasn't sure the boys would make it back that weekend. On sudden impulse he checked the Internet for car dealerships in Minneapolis. It took only a few minutes to decide on a used Jeep nearly identical to the one the boys owned.

He called them and told them to go down to the particular dealership and pick up the Jeep and just drive back. Percy would pay for it with a credit card over the phone the next morning by the time their mother could drop them off at the dealership. "You should be able to get a refund on your tickets because of the mandated flight shut down," he told them. "Pick up what you need with that money and I'll reimburse you for your expenses on the way down, since I'm asking you to do this, and I'll be keeping the Jeep."

Percy went to bed feeling a little easier about things. It'd be Sunday by the time they got home. At least he knew they would get back. Sunday would be the first day they could fly, and that wasn't a sure thing.

The next morning Percy put on his best suit, the charcoal gray one, after getting the cows milked and the eggs collected. He gulped the juice Mattie handed him, but declined the rest of the breakfast. "Too nervous to eat," he told the grinning Mattie and the giggling Suzie.

"You're gonna do just fine, you old codger," Mattie said, handing him his gray fedora. "This isn't the first time you've spoken before the state Emergency Management Agency.

"Yeah," Percy said dryly, "But this is the first time they might actually be listening. Always before they just thanked me and sent me packing. There's meetings scheduled for after my presentation already."

Suzie quit giggling. "Mr. Jackson, what you've been saying for years… it's starting to make sense to a lot of people. I never think about that stuff very much, because I live here and grew up around you. Everything you do has an element of preparedness to it. I know people still make fun of you for some of your ways, but don't let that stop you. People need to think about this stuff and start doing something. I had the news on when I was getting ready this morning and Pakistan and India are into it again over that border issue. It's scary."

Percy frowned. "I know. I watched several reports early this morning." He forced a smile. "But don't worry, Susie. You're right. We are about as prepared as we can be here." With a bit more of a sincere smile on his face he said, "If you want to talk to Andrew about having a place out here if something were to happen... even weather related, like last winter... feel free. He can stay here if you or your mother aren't comfortable with him staying at your cottage."

Susie blushed, "Oh, Mr. Jackson! I couldn't!" She glanced over at her mother. "Could I?"

"You're twenty-three, sweetie. Old enough to make up your mind about such things," replied her mother.

Suddenly Percy was grinning mischievously. "If there's anyone you want to talk to about staying out here in times of trouble, feel free, Mattie."

Mattie didn't and she wasn't going to let Percy get away with the teasing. "Oh, no one really special. But I was thinking, since you brought it up, about talking to Sara McLain to see if she needs a safe place... just in case, you know."

Again Susie giggled, due to Percy's sudden look of panic and very red face. "I... uh... don't think that would be such a good idea..."

"True," Mattie said, quite matter-of-factly. "Probably should come from you. You being master of the estate and all." She grinned.

"You just make sure you don't annoy her in some way."

Mattie continued to grin. "Of course not, Mr. Jackson. I would never do that."

"Just see that you don't," Percy said, rather gruffly. "I don't need any help with... anything."

Both women were chuckling when Percy headed out the door.

"Are you okay, Boss?" Susie asked when Percy came in a little after noon. "You look a little funny."

Percy did look a bit dazed, Mattie decided.

"Yeah. Yeah. I'm fine. It's just... Well, they asked me to put together some more comprehensive recommendations for the Agency with some other people. They want it within two months. Shouldn't take us that long."

The two women saw a bit of red come to Percy's cheeks.

"And... well... Sara's office was closed because of the rolling blackout so she came to the meeting, too. She volunteered to be on the committee."

"Won't that be a conflict of interest since she's Equalization Agent for this district?" asked Susie.

"Not since she is an official state member of the committee. There are a couple more state employees." Percy sighed then. "A couple more local citizens. Jeb Canada and Abigail Landro."

"Ooh," responded Mattie.

Susie looked at her mother. "What?"

"Jeb's the one that tried to foreclose on the farm right after Mr. and Mrs. Jackson died. And Abigail... just sort of... doesn't like Mr. Jackson."

"That's enough, Mattie. That's all in the past. We're all just citizens, trying to do what's best for the majority without hurting anyone. Now, I need to change and check the fields. It's shaping up to rain."

"Don't you want some lunch?" Mattie asked, not bothered in the least by Percy's minor admonishment.

"Sara and I grabbed a burger after the meeting."

When Mattie and Susie grinned at him, he harrumphed and left the kitchen.

Rain it did, but no snow. Springtime storms, but a notch or two more extreme than what used to be considered normal. Percy was glad he had gone ahead and prepped the fields. Even with the severity of the weather at the moment, the rain was good. There was some runoff into the collection canal that ran along three sides of the property, with each field being graded to drainage ditches that emptied into the canal. There wasn't much water in the irrigation holding pond the canal fed. The fields had soaked up the rain like sponges. It had been a very dry winter.

The severity of the drought had been worse the last few years, interspersed with some of these downpours. Percy didn't waste water. That was the reason for the canal around the property. To capture excess rainwater and hold it in a pond. The irrigation wells were only to supplement rain during the driest times.

Of course, the canal served another purpose, which Percy didn't talk about much. With the pipe fence around three sides of the estate that had blackberry brambles growing along it, just inside the canal, and the thick stand of trees that also bordered the estate inside the brambles, getting onto Percy's property was very difficult. A gated drive on each of the sides and back of the estate cut the triple barrier.

The front of the estate, along the highway, also had a fence, but it was an earth berm, faced with a concrete block and brick wall. Two sets of gates served the expansive circle driveway and parking area. The road ditch substituted for the canal around the other three sides of the estate. The front also had a stand of trees, though no blackberries. Instead, the berm was terraced and planted with strawberries, another cash crop for Percy.

Each of the front entries had heavy rolling gates that closed the driveway. They were on automatic openers, but Percy kept them open most of the time anyway. It would take a concerted effort to enter the property by destroying a gate. To get through the barriers would take heavy equipment, such as a bulldozer, and quite a bit of time. And all it looked like was good farm management. The trees were windbreaks and source of firewood. The blackberries were a major cash crop. The canal conserved a precious resource. Water.

Percy smiled as he surveyed the pond. If they got much additional rain the next few weeks, the pond would be well on the way to being full. He checked the well and pump at the edge of the pond. If need be, he could fill the pond, and the entire canal, with extra water for irrigation if they had another drought year, as they'd had the year before.

By the time Percy had checked everything, spent some time with the horses and dogs, it was evening. He paid everyone, in cash, and let them off early. Two days after the rain stopped they'd start planting.

The Hansen twins made it home on Sunday, the same day the rain stopped. Percy trained them on the new equipment Monday and Tuesday, waiting for the fields to be right for planting. Percy had the first committee meeting Tuesday evening, in a meeting room in the civic center, in town. It did not go well. Even Sara was a bit aghast at the scope of things Percy had in mind.

She supported the idea, but being a state employee, was very budget conscious. A couple of the others simply wanted some pamphlets printed. It was going to take the full two months to work something out among the group, after all, Percy decided.

"You... uh... want to get some dinner?" Percy asked Sara as they gathered up the papers that Percy had worked so hard on preparing for the committee. He put them in his briefcase, closed it, and snapped the latches.

"I can't, Percy," Sara said, watching his face closely. "Jeb needs an appraisal on some property tomorrow. I need to get back to the city and get some sleep. Having dinner will put me too late."

A tiny inner smile formed when Sara saw the quick frown cross Percy's face. It was quickly gone, the usual bland look back, as Percy said, "I understand." There was a moment's hesitation before Percy spoke again.

"I know this is quite a jaunt for you. We will have some of the meetings in the city, instead here in town, you know. It's a shame you need to drive back, especially since you have to come back out tomorrow."

"Well, tomorrow is on the state, of course."

"Isn't this?" Percy asked.

"Committee work like this isn't on the expense account. I use my own car and have to pay for my own meals and things. That's the reason I'm not staying at the motel tonight. I can't spare the money."

The words were out of his mouth before he thought about it. "You should come out and stay at the house tonight. That way you'd only have to make the one drive back and you could get an early start, finish up with Canada quickly, and get back to the city early tomorrow. Mattie's making pot roast tonight." He suddenly looked chagrinned at what he'd suggested. "I mean... you know... but if you need to go back..."

Sara cut him off, quickly. "Why thank you, Percy. That's sweet of you. I'll be able to expense the trip back, since I'm working here tomorrow. That will save me half my fuel expense for this meeting."

"Oh. Uh… Thanks. No problem. I'd… uh… better call Mattie and have her get a guest room and bath ready."

"It'll be nice to see Mattie again. It's been a long time since we've talked. How is Susie?"

"Fine," replied Percy as they headed for the front doors of the small civic center the town boasted. "She is marvelous with the animals. She keeps insisting her ambition is to be a vet assistant, but I think she'll go ahead and go to vet school and get her license. I hate to lose her, either way, but with her natural talent and intelligence, she'd make a fine vet.

"I doubt she'd stay here. The Doc is well established and I don't think the area could support two large animal vets. Susie wouldn't be satisfied with just cats, dogs, and birds. Plus, I think she's getting the urge to get married. She's… uh… never mind."

Sara just smiled. Percy didn't like conversations about marriage. She didn't either, for that matter. At least she hadn't. That was changing a bit now. Her first marriage had not gone well, but that didn't mean all marriages were bad. Not when you had the right partner. When she took Percy's arm as they left the building he didn't pull away or comment.

Percy handed Sara into her car after opening the door and then shut it after saying, "Just follow me out. They're working on a couple of intersections on the way out. Be careful of the construction zones."

"I will, Percy. I will." Sara wasn't going to let anything interfere with this opportunity.

He used his cell phone to let Mattie know they were having a guest. He heard Mattie chuckle as she was in the process of hanging up the phone. "Lord," Percy said, looking up at the roof of the cab of the truck, "don't let Mattie get started on middle age marriages. She doesn't have any room to talk, anyway."

Mattie was the soul of discretion. Not one word was uttered about marriage of any kind during the meal. In fact, Mattie made herself scarce as soon as she served the meal. "Just leave the dishes. I'll do them tomorrow. I... uh... need to do something at home. With Susie. Dessert's in the freezer."

"But..." That was all Percy had a chance to say. Mattie was out the door.

Sara smiled over at Percy and patted his hand where it lay on the table. "Don't worry,

Percy. You're safe. I'm not the pushy type. You know that."

"Yeah," Percy said, visibly relaxing. "That's true. You're the nicest woman I know about stuff like that. About everything, actually."

Percy was putting his napkin on his lap and didn't see the huge grin that split Sara's face. It was down to a smile when he looked up and over at her. "I could tell you were not comfortable with some of my ideas at the meeting, but you expressed your doubts in a very non-confrontational way."

"Unlike Jeb and Abigail," commented Sara, as she started to eat.

"They are just expressing their opinions, just like I was, I know. And I'm willing to discuss everything. I'm not trying to push my ideas on anyone. I just want to help."

"I know, Percy. I know. Don't worry. The committee will come to some type of decision. It's just going to take some conversation and negotiation."

"I'm not too good of a negotiator," protested Percy.

"Don't give me that," Sara said. "You are a consummate negotiator. You have ten percent of the local population bartering, Percy, simply because you are so successful at it. You make good deals that benefit you and the other party as well. That's what negotiation is all about. Both parties getting what they want."

"But everyone basically wants much more than they wind up getting."

"Perhaps, but they are very satisfied with what they get or they wouldn't agree to the barter. Now hush and eat your roast. I want to watch the news. My cousin Cliff is going to Germany next week. He's in an artillery battery. I want to see what the situation is over there now. I keep hearing some bad things are going on in Europe."

"Don't worry. I'm sure he'll be fine. The German situation... well, it's not good, but I doubt anything will happen any time soon."

"I hope so. I'm very worried about what's going on in the world, more so the effects of global warming and the weather. That's why I wanted on the committee. People need to realize the possible dangers.

This time it was Percy who patted Sara's hand. She took the opportunity to move it and grasp his for a quick squeeze. "Thanks, Percy. You always make me feel better about these things."

Percy didn't hesitate. "You know, if things were to get bad, you will always have a place here on the estate. We're fairly well prepared for most situations that are likely to occur."

Realizing what he was saying, Percy quickly added. "There's always the third cottage. It's not being used at the moment."

It was good enough for Sara, even with the slight back pedaling Percy had done. "Why, thank you, Percy. That means a lot to me. I will definitely keep it in mind." Sara wasn't particularly worried about needing to be here because of the situations Percy was referring to, but it was a start to having a place here for other reasons.

The news wasn't particularly good when they watched first one, then another of the news channels. German politics were drifting more to the right. They were becoming much more nationalistic and showing much less enthusiasm for the European Union. France was being even more obtuse than usual about everything.

Sara stopped Percy as they left the study and gave him a quick buss on the cheek after she thanked him for letting her stay the night instead of going all the way back into the city, then coming back the next day.

When she'd gone into the bedroom, Percy sighed and went back into the den. He'd put on a good front, but he was worried about the world situation, both politically and weather wise. There'd been a short report on a new study of the salinity of the North Atlantic. Percy knew the dangers that posed. If the North Atlantic became fresher, the heavier saline waters of the Gulf Stream would sink and Europe and much of North America would lose the benefits of the warm waters it provided.

Percy was a bit distracted the next morning. Sara and Mattie exchanged a quick look when Percy bid them good morning and headed out the door. He made a point to fill Sara's fuel tank with gasoline. She was down to a third of a tank in the Honda hybrid she drove. She would have needed to fuel up in town before she went back to the city. Fuel was nearly seventy cents higher in town than it was in the city. It wasn't much, but he was saving her at least ten dollars. On her salary, every dollar counted.

When he'd finished with refueling Sara's car, he walked back to the estate's tank farm. It was time to pump methane from the number two methane generator to the storage tank. When the transfer was finished, Percy drained the liquid from the generator and added it to the honey wagon, then transferred the solid waste to the compost pile. He was well into the process when he saw the hands head to the fields, ready to start planting. Percy knew the process was in good hands and turned back to his work.

He was transferring the depleted mash from number one alcohol still to a stock feed holding tank when Susie stopped by to tell him she was going over to Doc's to help with a foaling.

"Okay, Susie. Let Doc know two of the cows are coming into estrus soon. We'll need his bull's services in a few days."

"Okay. I'll see if he has any semen ready or will need to get a fresh batch."

"Good. Good luck with the foaling. I know that mare. She's a problem."

"That's what Doc said. It'll be good experience for me."

Percy added the accumulation of animal waste from the barn to the methane generator and lowered the cover into place. It was ready to start generating methane gas again. He checked the number one generator. It was operating nicely. The cover dome was about halfway up. It'd be a few more days before he needed to transfer the methane from it and reload it with fresh material.

He refilled number one still with fresh mash and started it. Like the methane operation, Percy checked the second still. It was producing well and the second stage supplied by the two primary stills was running just fine as well. The thousand-gallon double distilled alcohol storage tank was nearly full. The methane tank, also of a thousand gallon capacity was about half. With the increased waste production from newborn animals, it would be full by mid spring and the compost pit would be full, too.

It was time to make another pickup run to gather the manure and liquid wastes from the dozen farms with which Percy had arrangements. Percy took the accumulated waste from the farms for it, so the farms wouldn't have to deal with it. His only expense was transportation, and he had the equipment, anyway, including trailers to haul the waste. He already had most of the trailers he would be pulling behind the Unimogs from time to time. He'd only bought two new trailers for use with the Unimogs when he bought them.

Both were multi-purpose trailers he designed himself and had a trailer repair shop custom build for him. The trailers he used with the group of trucks he'd had before he bought the Unimogs were numerous. The list included two honey wagons, two manure spreaders, a fifth wheel horse trailer and a fifth wheel stock trailer, fifth wheel tilt bed equipment trailer, one fifth wheel and two pull behind box trailers, a stake bed trailer, and four roadside stand trailers he used to sell some of the produce he raised to tourists.

Most of his products went to local merchants and commercial enterprises, but he still liked to sell from the roadside. He'd done that when he first took over the farm. It had been good for him, and lucrative. He kept all proceeds. There was no middleman between him and the consumer. Many of the locals bought directly from the roadside stands despite the fact that he supplied both the local grocery stores in town and an organically grown produce specialty store in the city, as well as the local co-op.

Percy smiled as he thought of Organically Grown Only, the store in the city, as he hooked up one of the honey wagons to a Unimog. People paid twenty percent more in that store than what the local markets charged, even though everything he produced he produced without chemically produced fertilizers or chemical pesticides or herbicides. His fertilizers, pesticides, and herbicides were all produced naturally right on the estate, or were mechanical in nature.

By Sunday Percy had retrieved all the animal and vegetable waste from the other farms. The early crops were planted. Everyone took the day off except Percy. The animals had to have attention every day, no matter what. The milking and egging done, Percy spent some time with each of his animals. Except the barn cats.

He was seriously allergic to them. They didn't like him anyway. He was a dog person.

He thought they were pampered a bit too much by Susie. He hadn't seen any sign of rats or mice, but still... feeding barn cats went against his grain. Percy smiled. He knew he was just prejudiced against cats due to his allergy. That hadn't stopped him from suffering for three days to help nurse one of them through a difficult birth one time.

Percy was careful to step around one of the kittens that was following him around. The kitten made itself scarce when he got to the hog pen in the barn. Betty Joe, his best brood sow came up to the fence and nuzzled him through the bars for a scratch behind the ears.

"You're a pest," he said softly to the animal, then gave each one of the sows the same treatment when they sidled over to see what was going on. Clyde, the boar, just grunted and lay where he was. He'd just made a new wallow in the deep dirt that covered the floor of the inside pen. Clyde was comfortable where he was. Besides, the human would be over shortly to scratch him anyway.

Percy went through the gate, careful not to make any of the piglets squeal. Despite their chummy appearance, it didn't pay to be around a sow if one of her piglets wasn't happy. "You lazy pig," Percy said, squatting down to rub the boar's forehead, then scratched him behind the ears, too.

With a slap on the flank that brought a grunt from Clyde, Percy stood and headed for the outside gate for the hog pen. He opened the inner and outer doors and most of the sows and all of the piglets headed outside. The sows led the way through the fenced path and turned into the pasture in use at the moment. Clyde considered it, then climbed to his feet and lumbered out. A little sunshine would be good, especially in the wallow by the fence next to the gate. He'd just got it the way he liked it. They'd changed pastures a few days before and he couldn't get to the wallow in that one.

Percy turned out the cattle, milk cows, and then the horses. The horses wanted to play in the bright morning sunshine and Percy indulged them, letting them stampede up to him, stop and nudge him softly with their noses before they turned and ran some more.

One of the saddle mares, Herman's Best, tried playing with a piglet the same way, but the piglet squealed in alarm and the mother sow came charging over. Herman's Best sidled away gracefully, and then put her head down. The sow, placid now, ambled over and the two touched noses for a moment. Both snorted and went off to do their own thing. Percy shook his head and headed for the kennel.

Lion, Rip, and Queenie were lying near the outside gate, knowing someone would be by soon to let out the pups. The dogs rubbed up against Percy's legs, in no hurry to have the pups taking Percy's attention away from them. Percy spent quite a bit of time with each of the adult dogs, individually, before he let the pups out of their kennel runs to do the same with them.

He got out one of the Rokon bikes and took the dogs for a run toward the front gates, turning along the tree line when he reached it. When the young pups began to get tired, he slowed and finished the journey around the four mile perimeter of the estate at a slow pace. Percy gave each of the dogs a treat. The pups took theirs and lay down to enjoy them. Rip went to find a good place to bury his for a while, going to open ground in the kennel runs to do so, having learned as a pup himself not to dig up the grounds except in designated areas.

Queenie and Lion began to chew theirs, but stayed with Percy as he put away the bike. When he told them he was going back to the house the two dogs went to join the pups to enjoy the rest of their chew treats. As he headed for the bee barn, Percy saw Rip out cavorting with the horses in the pasture. The horses seemed to be enjoying it as much as the Airedale.

In the facility they all referred to as the bee barn, Percy checked the status of the hives. Everything was in order. He pulled two supers and cut the combs free. It took him only a few moments to get them boxed and ready to take to market. He added them to the case of other comb honey boxes.

He got one of the Unimogs, attached a box trailer and loaded up the case of honey. He moved the trailer over by the green houses and loaded the boxes of produce that had been gathered and prepared for shipment the day before. The twins were working on their jeep. Percy let them know he was headed into town, then the city with a load. He had the produce delivered to both the stores in town in plenty of time for the after church crowd to be able to pick up fresh items for Sunday dinner.

It was a bit after four when Percy finished unloading at Organically Grown Only. He made a couple of stops to do a little shopping and then headed back to the estate. He was pleased with the performance of the Unimog with the trailer.

CHAPTER TWO

Bernard was back in the bunkhouse early Monday morning. He told Percy his wife was okay for now and he'd start his regular routine of staying in the bunkhouse during the week. Bernard went to his home in the city on Fridays and returned mid-morning on Mondays.

The bunkhouse was used primarily for temporary workers Percy hired for some of the harvesting that required hand picking during the summer and fall. It could house up to twenty-four people in six dorm rooms.

Each dorm room had its own bathroom and there were two more off the common rooms. There was also a bedroom with its own bath for the person in charge of the dorm. Bernard used that room. Part of his duties on the estate was foreman for the temporary help when they were needed. That included being dorm boss.

In addition to the rooms already mentioned, there were two large living/gathering rooms, a kitchen suitable for preparing meals for forty people, and the dining room, which seated thirty at five tables. There was a large library and two entertainment rooms, each with a TV and music system. A game room contained a ping-pong table and a pool table, along with four game tables, and a dartboard. There was a fenced yard

and large patio. The parking area for the
temporary employees had a section set aside
lined for a half-court basketball court with a
mobile hoop stand.

There was a second swimming pool that
had originally served the cottages and the
bunkhouse, but Percy had restricted its use to
just the permanent residents of the estate.
There'd been too many problems when the
temporary employees had access to it. He'd
hated the fact that the rest of the temps couldn't
use it, due to the problems caused by a few, but
the risks were too great. The other pool was
within the main house compound.

It took Bernard only a few minutes to settle
in. All his regular gear was already in the
bunkhouse since he'd moved in a few days
before his wife had fallen ill and then gone home
to take care of her. The Hansen twins, and
Mattie and Susie, worked for him year round.
Bernard, John, and Smitty worked only spring,
summer, and fall. They all three took the winter
off.

Bob, Jim, Susie, and Percy were adequate
personnel to take care of the animals and do the
work in the greenhouses through the winter.
They still were able to rotate extra days off
during the winter, since the operation was so
efficient. Many of the processes were automated.

There were several generator sets on the property so the systems continued to work despite the regular rolling brown outs and blackouts caused by the overloaded power grid. That didn't include the unintentional brown outs and blackouts caused by equipment failures and the weather.

Percy let the others train Bernard on the new equipment and hooked another trailer to one of the Unimogs. This was his multi compartment waste oil trailer. As he did with animal wastes with some of the area farms, he had arranged with several businesses that generated waste oil to recover it at no cost to either party. Quite a few restaurants that used significant quantities of cooking oil saved it for him.

More as a courtesy, since the small places produced only a few gallons at any given pickup, Percy did take the oils from many small operations so they wouldn't have to pay to have it removed. They could no longer dispose of it in the old ways, due to EPA regulations. Percy could use it all. He produced biodiesel for his own use. He didn't produce enough to run everything, but it was part of the reason he only carried approximately two thousand gallons of diesel fuel in the ten thousand gallon tank that Andy kept replenished for him.

Andy didn't know about the other tank farm. It, like the one Andy knew about, contained a ten thousand gallon diesel tank, second diesel tank holding a thousand gallons, thousand-gallon gasoline tank, and thousand-gallon propane tank. He had a supplier in the city that kept those tanks at similar levels to those that Andy kept in the one tank farm. Each of the tank farms had an earth-sheltered storage building for lubricants and other liquids, which he bought and stored in drums.

He had two one thousand gallon biodiesel tanks, the thousand-gallon methane and thousand-gallon alcohol tanks, plus appropriate raw material tanks to make the three products. Percy wasn't to the point of being able to produce all his own fuel, but he did produce a significant proportion. He liked having options. Getting fuel when you really needed it was problematic nowadays.

Producing the biodiesel and the alcohol took significant energy, but it was worth the effort to be able to make the liquid fuels. The methane production didn't take that much outside energy. Much of the methane was used to fire the stills jend the biodiesel process and he still had enough to use elsewhere and keep the tank nearly full.

Scrap wood from several sources in town and the city made up the difference in energy use. He got all the odds and ends of lumber from both lumber yards in the city, and contracted with every tree trimming outfit he could find to take their wood and wood chips. He also had arrangements with several of the builders in the area. He took all the wood scrap they generated, for it, leaving them much less to have to take to the landfills and pay to dump.

There were three sources of wood pallets he relied on. Two of them did not reuse or recycle the wooden pallets they received. He got them all. The other place gave him those pallets that were beyond reusing. Between all the sources, he had more than enough wood to burn to make the biodiesel and alcohol, and not touch any of the wood from his wood lots.

It would take him all day to collect the oils, but he considered it time well spent. He would stop and pick up the chemicals he needed to produce the fuels. He'd been buying ten percent more than he needed for each batch and now had enough of the chemicals he couldn't produce himself to make nearly a hundred thousand gallons of biodiesel.

Percy had done the same with nearly every product and item he didn't produce. There were extra tires for every piece of equipment that used tires. Spare parts for all the equipment were on storage shelves in the equipment barn. Fabrication materials were stored, as well. There was a well-equipped shop in the huge equipment barn.

Much of Percy's equipment was old, though kept in excellent shape. Percy preferred tractor mounted or pulled, or in his current case, Unimog compatible, equipment over self-powered specialty implements. He used mounted and towed implements, including hay balers, combines, corn pickers, and silage cutters. Since his was not a huge production farm the mounted and towed equipment worked just fine for the scale of any given crop he grew.

Unfortunately, that type of implement was no longer common. Over the years, Percy had taken great pains to acquire the best of the types of implements he needed. Like every other piece of equipment he owned, he had numerous repair parts in stock and the materials to make most of the rest he might need.

The equipment used on the leased land was more conventional. He didn't expect others to take the time and trouble to farm production farms the old ways.

Percy was tired when he returned home. It had taken three hours longer to make the run than normal. There'd been a huge accident caused by a car running bald tires. He had been stuck in traffic for over an hour on the way in. It seemed like every place he normally picked up used oil had some kind of beef they just had to get off their chest.

Finally, on the way home, only a mile from the estate, the road was blocked for almost twenty minutes where the DOT was having an intersection redone. A semi had dropped a wheel off the pavement where they'd cut down the shoulder to redo it and flipped the rig, tying up the one lane available for traffic.

Waiting patiently for the workers to clear the road, Percy radioed the house and told Mattie to just put his supper in the warming oven. He would be getting home late. Percy knew that he could have taken the ditch with the Unimog and trailer and gone around, but there was no real need and the authorities would have stopped the attempt, anyway. It just grated a little not to be able to use the full capabilities of the Unimog.

Percy had to grin when the wrecker dispatched to the scene was unable to right the tractor and the State Trooper asked Percy if he thought the winch on the Unimog could. It was the work of only minutes to position the Unimog, hook up, and right the semi-tractor. It didn't even strain the Unimog.

"Okay if I take off now?" Percy asked, since he was now on the estate side of the blockage.

"Sure thing. And thanks. It would have taken us another hour to get a different tow truck."

"No problem," Percy replied, slipping the Unimog into gear and pulling away, a smile on his face. "Unimog to the rescue," he said aloud, and then laughed.

The rest of the week went normally for the estate, everyone working as they'd done for several years now. Susie took two of the cows to Doc's to be serviced. The twins finished equipping the Jeep acquired in Minneapolis to Percy's specifications, in addition to their normal work. It wasn't until the following week that anything out of the ordinary happened.

The second committee meeting turned into a shouting match. Percy wasn't involved, but his revised presentation triggered it. Both of the other state employees walked out. The county Civil Defense Director did, as well. Jeb and Abigail were glaring at Percy and Sara as they left.

"Well," Percy said with a sigh. "That went well. At least no one hit anyone else."

"That was a near thing with Jeb and Stanley. I still don't understand why it all started. Your revised plan addressed every objection that was brought up at the first meeting."

They were gathering up everything as they talked. "I thought so, anyway," Percy said. "It's only a tenth of what I think should be done. Do you think there's any need to try to have another meeting?"

"There's a need," Sara said, taking his arm as they headed for the doors. "But when the planning commission gets all the versions of what happened, I suspect they'll disband us. It's a shame. I'm really getting worried something will happen and people won't be prepared. It was bad enough last summer when the temperature was over a hundred for twelve straight days. People don't know how to cope. I was out of power the last two days of the heat wave, then another day before they got the power back on."

She smiled over at Percy. "I never did thank you properly for keeping me supplied with ice for my freezer, and to cool off with." She leaned over and kissed his cheek. "Thank you, Percy. You are a dear man."

"Uh… Well… uh… anyway, uh… do you have any business you need to do here in town tomorrow?"

"No," Sara said with a tiny smile. She was pleased at Percy's disappointed look.

"I'm off tomorrow. They shifted our blackout day to Thursdays. I hate losing the money for these days off, but I was planning on taking it easy for the day."

"You want to stay at the estate tonight? Sleep in? Mattie could make you a brunch and you could go riding, if you want."

Sara kissed his cheek again before he could change his mind and said, "Why, thank you, Percy. That sounds wonderful. I was going to have to stop and get groceries. Knowing you is saving me bundles of money."

She slid into her car and looked at Percy expectantly. "Actually," Percy said, "I need to come to town tomorrow... You could just leave your car here. Ride out and back in with me. Save the gas. It went up another sixty cents this week."

"You're telling me," Sara said, already out of the car. She pulled a small bag from behind the front seat, then closed and locked the door. When Percy looked at it, she said, "Some of us do listen to your ideas, Percy. Be Prepared is my new motto." She didn't really say what she was prepared for with the bag and Percy was afraid to ask.

When they'd finished supper and were in the den watching the news, Percy suddenly asked Sara, "Would you help me put together a proposal, like the first one, that I can send to Congressman Stevenson? I just have to give it one more try, Sara."

"Why, Percy, of course I will. You've done all the work, anyway, but I'll be glad to look it over again."

"Thanks, Sara. I appreciate it. You are a good woman, you know. Putting up with the likes of me."

Sara decided quiet was the best response to that. She turned her head back toward the TV and they watched a news report of the shelling of Indian positions by the Pakistanis in the disputed border area they had been quarreling over for years. Sara heard Percy mutter, "This could get serious."

The next morning Percy kept himself busy, avoiding Sara the best he could. He talked to her a few minutes when she came out to the animal barn and she and Susie saddled up Herman's Best for her to ride for a while. They settled on a time to go to town, and then Percy headed for the equipment barn to work on some equipment with the twins and Bernard. John and Smitty were helping Hector get his spring planning done. The arrangement was one of Percy's barters.

Percy watched unobtrusively as Sara rode. Percy rode, but really wasn't that good on a horse. He had a good hand with the teams, but let Suzie and the others do most of the horse-based farming since they enjoyed it so. He drew in a deep breath when he saw Best galloping toward the far side of the pasture, Sara's long hair flying behind her.

The other horses were following along, as were the dogs. The adults and two older pups, anyway. The young pups gave up and flopped down to rest. Clarence, Percy's stud bull, watched placidly, chewing his cud as the horse and rider went tearing by. He was calm now, but had been agitated the week before when two cows he'd been kept from for two days had disappeared, then returned, no longer ready for him. The memory had faded, so he was happy with his herd of cows again. He'd caught the first whiffs of another cow that would be ready soon, anyway.

His three hands pretty much ignored Percy and went about their jobs, since Percy was considerably more interested in the activities in the pasture than in the work being done on the hay bailer, replacing a set of bearings.

Percy didn't think to say anything when the appointed time came near to head into town. He just walked out of the equipment barn, still watching Sara on Best. The three men exchanged smiles at the usually unflappable boss mooning just a little over a lady.

"How was your ride?" Percy asked.

Sara's cheeks were bright and her eyes sparkled as she dismounted and said, "Wonderful, Percy! Wonderful." She grabbed Percy in a hug. "Oh, thank you so much for bringing me out here! I haven't had such a nice day in a long time." After giving him a little kiss on the cheek, she stepped back. "I suppose I should head back, though."

"I guess so," replied Percy, smiling at Sara's unbridled happiness. She wasn't as old as he was, only forty-seven, and she was still trim and fit. The jeans she wore fit her like a glove, Percy noted as she turned to Best and helped Susie unsaddle her.

"I should stay and help Susie dress her down," Sara said.

"That's okay," Percy said. "If we're going to get lunch in town before you go back to the city we should probably go. You don't mind, do you, Susie?"

"Of course not, Mr. Jackson," replied Susie. She'd seen Percy's eyes drop to Sara's bottom and was grinning mischievously. "Mrs. McLain sure looks good on a horse, doesn't she?"

Susie was amazed when Percy responded to her comment with one of his own. "She looks pretty good off a horse, too."

"Why thank you… both," Sara said, smiling at Percy. "I was going to change, but I suppose Rosie's will let me in wearing jeans."

"Of course she will," Percy replied. "I go in there all the time in my overalls."

Susie shook her head.

"Well, I am getting a bit hungry. I'll grab my bag and tell Mattie goodbye while you get the truck ready."

Not even seeing the grin on Susie's face, Percy hurried to get the Suburban. He found himself having a nice time. They talked about the project a little on the drive in, then local events as they got a light lunch at Rosie's Café. It was with a bit of reluctance that Percy said goodbye. He'd had to argue a bit with Sara about topping off her fuel tank from one of the cans in the rack on the back of the Suburban. He convinced her, filled the tank, and then told her goodbye through the open window.

He stepped back and Sara drove away, headed back to the city. With a sigh, Percy climbed into the Suburban and headed back to the estate. Before he got to the edge of town, Percy remembered the news report they'd watched the night before. He turned around, went to the local welding supply outlet, and tripled the quantities of welding gasses and other supplies he'd ordered the previous week for delivery this week.

Percy had two complete sets of extra tires for every vehicle he owned, including for the spares carried on each vehicle. He called the tire shop he used in the city and ordered a third set for everything. He also ordered several extra wheels of each type. Then he headed for Wilkins Oil. Percy caught Andy just as he was leaving and motioned him into the office.

"Time to stock up," Percy told the manager of the bulk plant. Andy grinned. "Bring a full semi load of diesel today. Then bring a thousand of gasoline first chance. Three barrels each of every oil I use, and triple the order of greases."

"You usually get taxed diesel, Mr. Jackson," Andy interjected. "You want taxed or untaxed for this load? Big difference on seven thousand gallons."

"Good thought, Andrew," Percy replied with a smile. He'd been about to specify the untaxed fuel, which was legal for use on the farm. The trucks would require taxed fuel to run on the highways. He'd pump what clear fuel he had into the one thousand gallon tanks he had for that reason. It had been simpler getting taxed fuel for everything, considering the quantities. But there would be a significant savings getting seven thousand gallons of untaxed red diesel.

Andy walked out with him. "You didn't do this just because I mentioned it the other day, did you, Mr. Jackson?"

"No, Andrew. Much as I like you, I wouldn't spend money like that, just because you want to use that CDL." Percy laughed, and then turned serious. "I'm worried fuel might get even scarcer than it is, with the world situation being what it is. By the way, did Susie mention it was all right for you to come out if there is an emergency? I know you care about Susie." He added the last to give Andy a good reason to say yes.

"Well, she said something about it. I know you keep prepared, but I told her I have some supplies and stuff at my place, but thanks, Mr. Jackson. I really appreciate the thought."

"Sure thing, Andrew. Just keep it in mind," Percy replied, and then climbed into the Suburban. When he left Wilkins Oil, he got on his cell phone and put in an identical order to his other fuel supplier. The one that came out from the city on Tuesdays and filled the second set of tanks.

It was too late to go into the city now, but he made a mental note to call when he got home and make appointments to see both his medical doctor and his dentist. He needed minor dental work. Percy decided to go ahead and get it done as soon as possible. He'd get an extensive physical, too. Just in case. Percy was smiling when he headed out of town. Maybe he and Sara would have a chance to have lunch or maybe even dinner when he went to the city.

Things went well the next two weeks. Sara reviewed the material Percy wanted to send to Washington, D.C., to the Congressman he knew slightly. He incorporated a few wording changes and the suggestions Sara made to change the order of the presentation. Percy mailed it off and put it out of his mind. As Sara had suspected, the committee was disbanded.

The only negative event was the news from Germany. They wanted the United States troop contingent significantly cut. Only part of the sentiment was coming from the Neo-Nazi party that had gained one seat in the governing body. There were many other factions making the same demand. Percy shook his head when the report was finished and muttered, "Too many things in too many places..."

All the cows had been serviced that needed it. One of the milk cows to refresh her, and the heifers to produce beef for the market. Clyde would service the other three milk cows when they went dry and then went into estrus. The calves from the milk cows would also go to market. Percy usually kept a percentage of the meat the local butcher shop prepared for him. It went into his freezers or other storage. The rest of the meat sold through his regular local outlets, including the butcher shop that did the work.

He spaced the butchering out to have fresh meat available all year long. It was time to send in one of the two year old steers to the butcher shop in fact. Susie hated to do it, so Percy sent the twins in with the steer. It would be a few days before the meat and hide were ready. Percy had learned to treat hides to make leather and would do that with this hide, too. There was a good saddle shop in the city that could turn the hides into just about anything he wanted.

Although he didn't think of it in quite that way, Percy found himself looking for reasons to go into the city so he could see Sara. They'd had a pleasant dinner when he'd gone in for his checkup and dental work, and Percy wanted to do it again. He found an excuse, a very good one, when Mattie mentioned the gossip she'd picked up at the hair salon she visited from time to time. Pretty much monthly, actually.

Mattie was telling Susie at breakfast one morning that the town council had been trying to get a clinic going, with the help of the hospital in the city, for some time. They finally had a husband and wife doctor team interested. Now they were working on a building.

"They know where they'll put it?" Percy asked.

"No. That's part of the deal. The couple wants to be out of town a ways... kind of a back to the earth thing. The council is checking with all the real estate agents in the area looking for a suitable place. But you know how land is here. If it can grow anything, it's being used to do so. Someone is going into the city tomorrow evening to meet the couple and bring them to town to take a look around."

"Who?"

"Abigail," Mattie replied, curious about Percy's interest. "She kind of got roped into it. She's not too happy about it."

"Oh," Percy said thoughtfully. It was several moments before he spoke again. Mattie and Susie waited expectantly. "Can you call someone and tell them I'll get the people. I have a piece of property that... I'm trying to... I have a piece of property that might be suitable. I might be willing to just donate to the clinic if the people like the spot and they build the clinic and a house to live right there by it."

Susie interjected, "Do you mean that forty acres Donaldson was leasing? I didn't know you wanted to get rid of it."

"Uh… Well… I just decided recently…" He left it at that, not specifying that it was as recently as that morning, after the subject of the clinic came up.

Mattie and Susie suspected as much but didn't say anything about it. Mattie did say, "I'll call Tom and let him know. I think he'll be pleased, about not only the land, but also about Abigail not being involved. Her idea of fixing the problem is to buy a bus and haul people to the city at the town's expense."

"Sounds like her," Percy muttered, and then said aloud, "Get it set up and I'll go in and talk to Tom. I'll get the deed to that property out."

When he left the table, leaving the last bit of his breakfast behind, Mattie and Susie exchanged a look. "You think he'll really just donate that land? You know how he is about owning property." Susie looked at her mother quizzically.

"I don't know. He is pretty generous, when it comes right down to it. But this…" Mattie said, her eyes on the kitchen door Percy had gone through. "Sure sounds like it. I'd better call Tom before he leaves for work." Tom was a distant cousin of Mattie's and the town Mayor. Also the only insurance agent in the town.

Tom was pleased with the idea. He asked a question, similar to the one Susie had asked, about Percy really donating the land. Mattie gave Tom the same response she'd given Susie.

Percy did donate the land, with the condition that the clinic be built on the land, as well as the housing for the couple. It would be a few months before the clinic was complete, even if they started immediately. Percy also contributed money to get the building process started. He'd liked the couple right off the bat when he picked them up at the airport.

Sara had taken the day off and gone with him when Percy asked. She was amazed when he offered to let them stay at the estate for the two days they were going to be checking on things in the area. He even loaned them the use of the Jeep the twins had brought back from Minnesota.

She quickly agreed to come out, stay both days, and act as guide for Melissa and Jock Bluhm. Jock was a family practice MD, while his wife specialized in obstetrics, gynecology, and pediatrics. Sara had to agree with Percy that the couple would be a valuable addition to the town. She heard about a few protests that the clinic was going to be a mile out of town, but they were quickly silenced when it was learned that there would be a shuttle bus from town to the facility every day it was open.

Sara looked at Percy a little askance when she heard Percy tell Tom to let people know about the state of the art facility and the clinic's shuttle bus. When they had a private moment Sara asked Percy, "And just how is the town going to afford the clinic and the bus and the subsidized low income treatments you mentioned, pray tell?"

"Oh. That. Well..." Percy was looking down at his boots, hands clenched behind his back.

"Well, what?" Sara prompted.

"Well... that is... you see..."

"You set it up yourself! Percy, you sweet man, you!" Sara leaned over and kissed him on the cheek.

Percy turned beet red when Sara kissed him, right there in public and all. "All I did was offer to set up a little trust for them to use the income from. You know the farm is doing okay, now that I have it the way I want it. It wasn't all that much. And I'll help them get another grant for some of it. The committee already has one small one. You know I got those three to do the experimental growing in conjunction with the high school VoAg club. It's not that difficult.

"And a few more people will contribute, I'm sure. Hector and even old Precious Randolph will pitch in. Precious has been trying to get a clinic in here for years. She hates going into the city. Besides, the clinic will eventually be self-supporting and I'll get the trust money back. I just lose the income from it for a few years."

"I know," Sara said, tucking her arm through his and pressing firmly against him. "I'll not embarrass you again by kissing your cheek, but you are a very sweet man. That young couple will fit right in here."

"I had nothing to do with bringing them here. That was all Tom and the city council and the clinic committee."

"Yes, that's true," Sara said, "But when I was showing Melissa around, she told me that they had a similar clinic offer from a small town in Indiana. Not too far from her folks. The initial deal was much more attractive than what we'd offered. They came out as a courtesy, to let the council down easy, and give them a couple more contacts for doctors that might come out here. If you hadn't done what you did, they would not be setting up shop here."

"Oh. I didn't know that," Percy said. "Well, good, then. That's even better. Means they really want to be here and won't leave as soon as the contract is up, probably."

"With that grove of trees and pond on the property and a place to put a small horse barn, I don't think so. Jock loves horses and this is the perfect spot. You going to give him a horse, too?" Sara was joking.

Percy was serious when he replied. "Certainly not going to give him one, but with Herman's Best ready to take to foal this year, I might just see if he'd trade some medical services for a colt or filly."

"Oh, Percy! You are incorrigible!" The others were turning to talk to them again, so Sara fell silent.

Percy studiously avoided looking at Sara when he offered to rent a mobile home for the Bluhms so they could move to the area and supervise the construction of the house and clinic. They would be able to use the old clinic, such as it was, and the county hospital, to start up the practice until the new clinic was finished.

With the deal finalized, they went back to the estate to drop off the Jeep and eat before Percy took the Bluhms and Sara back to the city. The Bluhms were flying out that evening at ten. Percy said a little prayer of thanks that the situation had turned out the way it had when he saw the news that night. He might not retire early, with twenty percent of his retirement having gone into the trust for the clinic, but that was okay. They were going to have two good doctors close.

The way things were going with the climate, transportation situations, and world politics, it might be important. It was just nice, no matter what. They were a nice couple and the report Tom had on their previous practice, though they'd only been in private practice for a year, indicated that they were excellent doctors. Only a surplus of doctors in the area where they'd done their internships then set up a practice had prompted them to look for a family clinic in a small town. Their patients had not been at all happy they were leaving.

Even if the Bluhms did leave when the first contract was over, with the clinic already built, and with associated housing, finding other doctors to work there wouldn't be a problem.

Percy had a two bedroom, two-bath mobile home delivered to the property the following week. It took only three days to have the utilities installed. The water district line went right by the property, as did power lines. A septic tank and disposal field was installed and would be used for the new house.

It would be several weeks before phone service was installed, but both Bluhms had cell phones and were not worried about landline service until construction started on the clinic and house. They would be transferring their satellite TV and internet service from their current provider. The Bluhms were in residence within two weeks after the mobile home set up was completed.

CHAPTER THREE

"Are you sure you want to do this, honey?" Calvin asked his wife of three weeks.

"Yes, Calvin, I want to do this. I have to learn to drive this thing if I'm going to help out around here."

"You don't really have to, you know. I've got a good job. I know you don't want to just sit around all day, but there are plenty of things you could do in town."

"Calvin Stubblefield! We have already discussed this and you agreed that I could help with our side business. You even said you were looking forward to it."

"I know, I know. And I am. Kinda. But I've been thinking... what if you get hurt or something."

"You know I'll be careful," replied Nan. "And I agreed, just as you did, that we'd do the work together. All of it. So it would be safer. I've practiced at home, with you. You know I can do this."

Calvin sighed. Nan wasn't going to give in. They had discussed it thoroughly, and it had seemed like a good idea at the time. But now, with her standing there with the chainsaw in her hands, he was having second thoughts. Sure, she wore good boots and gloves, had on shin guards, a hard hat with face shield, goggles, and hearing protectors. Still, watching your wife getting ready to fell an old, twisted tree was unnerving.

She was right, he knew. Nan was just as capable as he was of handling the chainsaw. Calvin nodded. Nan pulled the starting cord of the chainsaw and it fired right up. A couple of test pulls on the trigger and the chain whizzed rapidly around the bar.

They'd checked the lean of the tree, and its weight distribution. The lay of the land, and the surrounding trees. Despite the deformity of the tree, it should fall well. Nan shifted the saw and stepped forward, after Calvin stepped back out of the way.

It took less than a minute to cut through the tree. Calvin had to admit, Nan had done both the front and back cuts as well as he could have done himself. The tree landed right where it was intended.

Nan looked over at him, a huge grin on her face. He smiled back and picked up the smaller chainsaw and started it. They began to trim the tree prior to cutting it up into logs. They worked for four hours, taking turns felling trees to thin the woodlot. They stopped often to drink from their water jug. It was hot work, despite the cool temperature, with the heavy clothes and safety equipment they wore for protection.

"That's enough for today," Calvin said. "Let's clean this up and get things ready for loading."

Nan smiled tiredly and agreed. Her arms, especially her wrists, ached from the vibration of the saw. It was a good saw, with some of the best vibration dampening available, but it still vibrated some. She helped Calvin load the chainsaws, fuel can, and axes into the trailer attached to the Rokon two-wheel drive motorbike parked close.

She climbed on behind him after he'd started the bike and seated himself. It was only a few minutes before they made it down to their truck, parked as close to where the trees needed thinning as they could get.

Nan unloaded the trailer and put the tools into the toolboxes of the service body mounted on their heavy duty, four-wheel drive, one ton Dodge truck chassis. Calvin was setting down the log skid from the cargo box of the truck. Nan helped lift the Rokon trailer up into the truck after she'd unhitched it. As Calvin hooked up the log skid to the Rokon, Nan looped a pair of log chains over the rear seat of the Rokon.

They took a few moments to eat an energy bar apiece, and drink more water. When they were ready again, Calvin leaned over to pull the starter cord of the bike. Nan grinned at Calvin after he started the Rokon and she swung her leg over the seat. "I'll drive," she said. "It's only fair. You drove us down."

"Yes," Calvin said, a wry grin curving his lips. "I did. Go ahead. I'll walk."

Nan laughed and began easing the Rokon up the same slight track they'd used to come down to the truck. It was the work of another two hours to skid the logs and all but the smallest of the trimmed branches down to the truck. The branches were bundled with the log chains before being moved with the skid. The very small stuff was piled in nearby small gullies and washes to provide cover for the wildlife in the area.

When the last load was added to the others at the truck, they loaded up the Rokon and skid into the truck. "Ready to go home?" Calvin asked Nan.

Wearily she nodded. "I'll say."

Calvin slid behind the wheel of the truck as Nan climbed in on the passenger side. "You did good today, sweetie. I knew you'd do fine, but you did better than fine."

"Thanks, Cal. I have to admit it was more work than I was expecting. Handling the chainsaw and the log chains and such wasn't that bad. It was all the moving over the rough ground."

They were home in just a few minutes. Old man Peterson's property abutted theirs, making the arrangement perfect for them. They were thinning his stand of trees for the wood, plus cash. Enough cash to pay their expenses plus a little. If Peterson was happy, they'd get a good recommendation from him. His opinion carried a lot of weight in the area.

When they got out of the truck both stopped for a moment to look at their house. Both were smiling hugely as they looked at the front. It had taken them three years to get it built, doing much of the work themselves.

Built back into the low bluff, only the front was exposed. And the front wall was a thick triple wall. An outer wall of reinforced natural rock and an interior wall of four-inch thick concrete were tied together with rebar. High R-factor board insulation faced the inside of the rock wall, with the rest of the area between the two walls filled with compacted earth. Two doors and three series of narrow vertical windows provided light and entry into the home. The doors and windows had heavy shutters to each side.

The front faced almost due south, and boasted a wide patio enclosed with a thick rock wall, four feet high. The second floor balcony deck acted as roof for the lower patio, and was, in turn, roofed by another concrete slab, it being covered with enough earth to act as garden area, as did the top of the bluff. The balcony and balcony roof slab were supported by rock faced concrete pillars.

A stairway cupola pierced the top of the bluff, opening onto a large patio centered over the earth-sheltered house. A weather instrument pack mounted on the top of the stairway cupola was hardwired to the weather monitor in the den.

Like the entry patio, the balcony and top patio sported four-foot high rock walls. The south facing walls of all three were covered with solar panels. Photovoltaic, solar hot water collectors and solar space heating collectors.

A freestanding heavy-duty stepped antenna tower at one corner of the upper patio carried a large log periodic high frequency beam antenna and a VHF/UHF log periodic beam antenna on a side arm mount, both with rotors. A tall aluminum antenna mast with a variable base loading assembly was mounted above the HF beam. Three additional side mounts carried Public Service band vertical antennas The base of the tower also had a variable base loading assembly to turn the entire tower and antenna assembly into a large multi-frequency vertical antenna.

An identical antenna tower at the opposite corner of the upper patio carried a deep fringe TV antenna on a rotor. A side arm mount with rotor carried another VHF/UHF log periodic antenna, specifically for monitoring the Public Service Bands. There were a series of non-rotating beam antennas for specific TV channels and VHF/UHF repeater sites mounted on side arm mounts. As with the first tower, this one also had a loading box so the entire tower and antenna assembly would act as a tall vertical antenna.

A large C-band satellite antenna was mounted at the base of one antenna tower, and a dish satellite antenna with satellite internet capability was mounted near the bottom of the other antenna tower, along with a satellite radio antenna.

"You want to put the truck in the garage?" Nan asked Calvin after a moment of enjoying looking at their dream home."

"I think so. We could get rain tonight."

Nan grinned over at Calvin. "You just want to look at everything again."

Calvin smiled back. "Well... maybe."

They unloaded the Rokon, trailer, and log skid from the Dodge. Nan opened the garage door and Calvin backed the truck inside. He helped Nan bring in the bike, trailer, and skid.

Nan watched Calvin for a moment, a smile on her lips as he lowered the garage door. Like the house itself, the garage was dug back into the bluff. It was impossible to tell, for, like the house, narrow windows provided light, as did the light tubes that came down from their exposed ends along the upper patio wall. With the white painted walls and ceiling, the garage was as well lit as any standard garage, and better than many.

Trailing his hand along the workbench top that was part of the well equipped home shop, Calvin joined Nan near the connecting door between the garage and house. "I'm going up to take a look around," he said as Nan started to enter the house.

She nodded and said, "I'll start supper."

Calvin turned to the other inside door. He took the short hallway that connected the garage rear entrance to the stairway that went up to the top patio. When they'd helped design the house, both he and Nan had insisted on alternate means of egress in case of fire, despite the house and garage both having sprinkler systems installed.

That was why there were two entrances on the front, the stairwell to the surface at the back of the units, plus the ability to exit the second floor rooms onto the balcony and climb down. There were projecting rocks in the front wall extending out to create an adequate emergency stairway down from the balcony.

With more than a touch of pride, Calvin surveyed their property from the top patio. They owned twenty acres of old growth forested land. It had been only a tenth of the cost of adjoining properties due to the nature of the geography of the parcel. There were almost no level spots in the twenty acres. The only ones of any size were the one at the face of the bluff and the small area on top of the bluff. The hill that was the bluff fell off sharply to the north, though it wasn't a bluff like the south side. The east and west side were more gradual, but still steep slopes. The rest of the property consisted of steep hillsides, valleys, and ridges, with many rocky outcroppings.

The surrounding areas were hilly, but nothing like their little piece. The real estate agent had been cooperative in the sale. The owner was making a mint on the other parcels of the three hundred or so acres he owned, so had been willing to let this parcel go cheap, since no one seemed to want to build anything on the up and down landscape.

It was at one corner of the large plot, bordering federal land on the back, the Peterson place on one side. The other two sides bordered the Calhoun property, with no easy way in. The only reason Calvin and Nan took it was the easement they got from the owner to get to it from the county road. They'd checked from the air, and used topographical maps to select the route in. It bordered the owner's property line for most of the distance, and then cut in toward Calvin's and Nan's place.

The Calhoun's had not been too upset, since the easement for the track would service several more parcels, except for the last section, and it was on some more or less otherwise un-usable land. It was up to Calvin and Nan to turn the last section into a road. The section serving the rest of the lots the Calhoun's paid a contractor to run a road-grader along the path to establish a minimal road. Additional work would be done as the properties were developed.

Calvin could see several sections of the road from his vantage point. He'd cleared specific trees during the construction of the house to enable the views he wanted. He turned around and looked down the steep slope that was the back side of the bluff. Quite a few trees and all the brush had been cleared around the house site, to minimized fire danger, though there were still plenty of trees around. Just none within fifty feet or so of the house.

They weren't really concerned too much about actual fire damage, as they were lack of oxygen if there was a forest fire. There was a relatively large gulley that drained the flat area in front of the bluff. It was steep and long, mostly bare rock. It emptied into another wash that ran to the creek on Peterson's property.

They were sure that it would act as a vent, bringing fresh air to almost the front door of the house in the event of a fire up where they were. Also during the construction phase much of the large rock excavated from the bluff to make room for the structure was used to create a series of step dams in the gulley to control the flow of runoff water and slow it as much as possible.

Though there was a good well that provided more than five gallons a minute fresh water flow, they had installed a solar powered pump with photovoltaic panel and battery at the largest of the containments. The pump was on a float switch and would pump accumulated water up to the large cistern under the front patio. The water went through a sand and gravel filter into the sump for the pump to keep the water as clean as possible. The water went through a high grade filter when it was pumped from the cistern.

Calvin walked over to the open garden plot. They'd plant their outside crop in a few more days. The seedlings were doing fine in the green house that bordered the garden plot. The big greenhouse beside the garage door was already providing salad vegetables and they had a good start on berries and melons, too. The greenhouse had been one of the first things finished during the construction.

Looking up, Calvin gave a little prayer of thanks. While they'd worked hard to achieve their dream, there'd been an element or two of luck, as well, and Calvin was appreciative. Finding the property when they were in the market had been sheer chance. They'd been scrimping and saving for five years, with both of them working, to be able to afford anything. Both their families had been willing to present highly unusual wedding gifts, after they announced that they would be married three weeks after the house was finished.

The wedding registry had been a list of wants, rather than a list of stores. While they received a few conventional gifts, the families had come through with many of the things with which they wanted to equip, furnish, and stock the house.

Calvin was still smiling when he went downstairs to the kitchen. Nan looked up, saw the smile on Calvin's face and her own smile broadened. She quickly stepped over to him, threw her arms around his neck and kissed him.

"Hey," he said, after the kiss ended, "what's this all about?"

Stepping away, Nan replied, "Nothing special. I'm just happy. Being together the last few years was good, but being married is better. We have the house we want, in an area we love. You have a good job. We've got money in the bank. A little, anyway. And I just love you, is all."

"I love you too, sweetie. You're all a man could ask for in a wife."

They kissed again, but Nan stopped them from going further. "Later," she said with a laugh, removing his hands from her bottom. "We both need something to eat, and I want to go over the budget with you after that. Then we can get to the fun stuff."

Calvin laughed, too. "Okay, baby. You're right. I am ready for some supper."

"You do the salad and I'll do the entrée."

"Sure thing. What's it going to be tonight?"

The teakettle was whistling on the propane cook stove. "Turkey tetrazzini. It's the last of the can." Nan poured the boiling water over the freeze-dried entrée in the bowl on the counter.

"It's a good one," Calvin replied, taking out salad makings from the Servel propane/electric refrigerator.

"This finishes up the long term storage food that your Uncle Henry got us. The month supply lasted us a little over three weeks. We'll need to increase the quantities when we reorder."

"I know," Calvin said. "I really didn't think it would last us a month. Figured the way it is, for a sedentary person, the serving sizes just aren't enough for active people. But the stuff is good.

"If we get that one-year supply the way we planned, and then add quite a few individual cases of specific items, we would be in good shape, long term. Then we could buy a four month supply... based on the same plan as the year supply... every month. We'll use a fourth and store the other three-fourths and have a second full year supply in four months. We can keep doing that until we have the five-year supply we planned.

"With the supply we have now from the order we put in after we got married, that will give us a fifteen month LTS supply now, plus that from the month ahead."

"Good idea," Nan said. She was setting the table as the meal absorbed the water. "I wish we could do it a little faster," she continued, filling glasses with water from the fridge.

"We have to watch the budget. If I get that bonus for the Tashman job, we can put half of it into LTS food and the rest in savings."

"We need to get our savings back up, but I think we should acquire gold and silver a bit more quickly."

"That's what we're doing with the tree thinning service money."

Nan dished out the turkey tetrazzini as Calvin set the filled salad bowls on the table. "I know, but with the world the way it is, I'd like to increase our holdings."

They both sat down and Calvin reached for his fork. "I don't know sweetie. We really knocked a hole in our savings when we built this place. I'd like to get our cash level back up to at least a one year salary equivalent."

"Me, too. I was thinking more about what you said today. I like helping with the tree thinning. It won't be long before we have a five-year supply of wood stocked up. You were right about me being able to get a job in town. I kind of miss working, actually."

A dazzling smile lit her face as she added, "With the design of this house, it only takes a few minutes a day to take care of it, and you help with that and the greenhouses and garden."

"You really want to go back to a job? We are doing okay."

"I think so. Something that it won't be too difficult to leave, once I'm four or five months pregnant."

Calvin's eyes widened. "You're pregnant?"

"No, silly. Not now. We have to keep trying. But we are trying, and it will happen. But in the meantime, I want to keep busy. I hadn't really thought about it before. I really thought I'd have plenty to do around here, but the place is so efficient it just doesn't take very long."

"Your craft work?"

"We have plenty of afghans. And enough baby things for five babies."

"Well, that settles it. It would let us build up things even faster, if you want to go back to work."

"I do, Cal. I really do. With us doing the woodlot thinning only together, that still leaves me a lot of time when you're at work." She smiled. "As long as it's not too hard. I am supposed to be living a life of leisure now, you know."

Calvin snorted. "Like you ever could. Well, go with me Monday and check around. You can make a day of it and I'll pick you up on the way back from the city. You did want something in town, and not in the city, didn't you?"

"Oh, yes," Nan said adamantly. "I'm tired of the city, except for the monthly shopping runs."

"I know. As soon as we can, we'll start a business in town so we can both work it. Like the tree thinning operation. Just too tight to try that now."

"True. But it won't be long, I'm sure." Nan grinned at her husband. "You still want to do the toy route?"

Blushing just slightly, Calvin harrumphed. "I never should have told you that." Nan laughed delightedly.

"Come on, Calvin. You know I think it is a good idea. If Mr. Anderson retires, there won't be anyone else to do small equipment work. What you have in mind should give you work year round. Work that people need. Especially as the other development around here takes place."

"You don't think it's silly? I mean, I really do want to do that type of work because of the equipment. I loved construction toys when I was a kid. And I liked the construction work when I was in college."

Rather softly, Nan replied. "Honey, I know they aren't really toys, but tough, professional grade tools."

"I know you do," Calvin replied. "But they really are neat, as well as being extremely versatile. And they are expensive."

"But you just said it. They are versatile. And you can start... well, not small... but with just the basics and add attachments as you go."

"You really wouldn't mind?"

"Of course not." Nan grinned again. "And I have to admit, running the equipment does look like fun."

Calvin grinned back. "Yeah. I'll work up a serious proposal. See how good our credit is."

"Good. The sooner you get out of the city, the better."

They finished their meal in companionable silence. Nan had started some freeze-dried sliced strawberries soaking in fresh cream. They had those for desert as they watched television that evening.

CHAPTER FOUR

The next day, a Sunday, they slept in, as was their custom. As they were getting dressed, Nan asked Calvin, "How many trips you think it will take to move what we harvested yesterday?"

"I think four will do it."

Over breakfast, which was granola with blueberries from their LTS food stocks, Nan again spoke up. "That truck. The Unimog. That would make the wood harvesting a lot easier, wouldn't it?"

"Sure it would," replied Calvin. "Especially with a material handling arm. That would be one of the attachments I'd eventually like to get."

Nan nodded. "It would take a lot of money to get started, wouldn't it?"

This time Calvin nodded. He paused his eating and looked over at Nan questioningly. "Where you going with this? You know I don't have plans to do it right now. That plan I was talking about is one of the long-range plans we always try to do for big stuff. Like this house."

"I know," replied Nan. She smiled. "I'm not ragging on you. Actually it is the other way around. I'm thinking we should make it a shorter-range plan. Wouldn't the equipment be collateral for the loan?"

"Sure it would. But like you said, it's a lot of money. And doing the tree thinning for Mr. Peterson, and even the Calhoun's property, wouldn't be enough to make the payments."

"What about working with Mr. Anderson? Getting some experience. You said once that his old backhoe was barely able to do the work here, it was so worn out. Maybe he'd welcome a silent partner with new equipment."

"I..." Calvin started to speak, but closed his mouth and looked thoughtful for a moment. "I always figured that if I did it, I'd do it independently."

"I know you have some experience from when you worked construction when you were going to college, but wouldn't some hands on work with Mr. Anderson be an advantage? Plus, it would be getting your foot in the door of a lot of customers."

"That's true." Again Calvin's eyes lost focus as he thought about things. "And you could learn it just as easily as I. I could continue to work at the bank during the week and work with Mr. Anderson on... say... alternate Saturdays. We could continue to do the tree thinning on the alternate Saturdays and on Sundays."

Calvin looked over at Nan. "That is, if you wanted to..."

"I definitely do want to learn. If I get just a part time job in town, that would leave me plenty of time to work with Mr. Anderson. Do you think he'd take me on?"

Calvin snorted. "He lets Jimmy Hollister work for him. I can't see him not letting you, even with your lack of experience. He was impressed with the work you were doing here when we were building the house."

"Okay," Nan replied. "Then let's think about this a bit more, and check with Mr. Anderson. You can do your proposal for the bank after that and see if we can get the equipment."

"This is a big step, Nan," said Calvin. "As big a step as the house was, and getting married."

Very seriously Nan said, "If something happens in the near future, we'd never be able to do this. You saw the news last night. Wouldn't that equipment be invaluable in the aftermath of a serious disaster?"

Calvin nodded. "That's one of the reasons I wanted to get it. We're in good shape here, now, but as things get worse there are going to be many, many people needing help to get prepared. We need to think about this some more."

"I agree. Let's finish up breakfast and get to work. We can both think about it some more and then discuss it some more. How does that sound?"

"Good. It sounds good."

With the tandem wheel trailer behind the Dodge, they had all the timber and trimmings cut up and stacked along the lower patio west wall. They'd been keeping track of the firewood they were gathering. This load brought them up to forty cords total. They'd only used a few pieces to test out the fireplace and wood stoves after they'd been installed.

For the moment, they were using the propane appliances, but would use wood when they had more time to manage it. The wood-fired appliances did take somewhat more time to use and maintain. It had been expensive to get the wood-fired hot water heater and the dual fuel furnace in addition to the propane/solar hot water heater, wood/coal heating stove with a useable cooking surface, and the fireplace. They felt the security of having the multiple options was worth it.

So was the expense of three one-thousand gallon buried propane tanks and the twenty one-hundred pound propane tanks they had as back up. The earth-sheltered house required very little heat and no real cooling to be comfortable. The thousand-gallon propane tanks would suffice for at least three years of cooking and heating with propane, perhaps longer.

There was already enough wood to last two years at least. They'd have triple, at least, that amount of wood, by the end of the year with the thinning they were doing for Peterson. Also by the end of the month, they would have twenty tons of anthracite coal. They joined with a few others that had coal type stoves to order a semi-load from a rather distant mine. The shipping on the coal was costing more than the coal itself, but the group had wanted anthracite, rather than bituminous coal for their stoves.

That Monday they took one of the two Jeeps they owned on the journey to town and the city. After a quick kiss, Calvin dropped Nan off at the post office. It would be some time before they would have rural mail delivery, even to the end of their road, where it met the county road. Calvin and Nan were inclined to just keep the post office box they originally rented rather than switching. It wasn't that much more of a trip to go into town to get it than picking it up at the county road, when that service became available.

It was too early for the mail, of course, but Nan wanted to check the community bulletin board for potential jobs. When she saw the notice Mr. Anderson, or more probably, his wife, had posted, she couldn't keep the grin off her face. He was looking for some temporary office help.

She headed down the sidewalk jauntily, on the way to the small office space Mr. Anderson kept for his various business endeavors. Nan recognized Mrs. Anderson sitting behind the desk in the office. Mrs. Anderson had brought lunch out to Mr. Anderson several times when he was working out at Calvin's and Nan's. She had enjoyed the trips, and the highly unusual house being built.

"Hi, Mrs. Anderson," Nan said cheerfully.

A smile brightened Mrs. Anderson's face. "Hello, young lady. It is very nice to see you again. How do you like your new home, now that you've been in it for a few weeks?"

"Oh, we just love it! It is everything we expected, and more. It is so quiet out there, and cozy."

"Ah, but such a road!" replied Mrs. Anderson.

"True. The road isn't much, but the service truck and the Jeeps do just fine. Going to be a little harder this winter, I know, but I believe it will be worth the hassles." It just occurred to Nan that the equipment she and Calvin were considering getting would allow them to keep the road in much better shape. A good point to bring up with Calvin. One of his biggest worries was her getting stuck or stranded on the road.

"Well, let's hope so," replied Mrs. Anderson. "And what brings you to the office today. Perhaps an invitation to a house warming party?"

It had not occurred to either her or Calvin to have a house warming party, but Mrs. Anderson obviously wanted to see the completed house.

"Not exactly," replied Nan. "I do want to invite you out to the house, but for a business meeting. Of course, we could do it here, but I thought you might like to see the house now that it is completed. Mr. Anderson was such a big help to us."

"That would be wonderful, my dear! When, may I ask?"

"Why, at your earliest opportunity," said Nan. "Tonight if you're of a mind."

"I'm sure Herbert and I can make it. What should we bring?"

"Not a thing," admonished Nan. "We want to repay your kindness since we moved here." Nan smiled brightly again. "We do kind of want something from you and Mr. Anderson."

"Sit down, dearie, and tell me what this is all about."

Nan took a seat across the desk from Mrs. Anderson. "Well, it's really two things," Nan said. "First, I've decided to go back to work, and I saw your notice at the post office and wanted to apply for the job. Now I know…"

Mrs. Anderson stopped her with a lifted hand. "You've got the job. What else is it?"

Nan wasn't too surprised at the abruptness of the offer. Mr. and Mrs. Anderson were both rather abrupt types.

"Well, Calvin and I are thinking about starting our own business and we wanted your guidance and help. Mr. Anderson had told us he was retiring within a few years and we were thinking about doing some of the things he does." Quickly she added, "But only when he's quit doing them. We would never infringe on his work."

"That's good to hear," replied Mrs. Anderson.

"Calvin has run some equipment before, when he was in college, but he needs more experience. We were hoping Mr. Anderson would let him work with him some, to learn what to do. Of course, we'd pay at least something for the training."

Mrs. Anderson stopped Nan quickly again. "Don't be ridiculous. Herbert would welcome someone to learn the business. He's been worried about what the area will do when he retires." Mrs. Anderson frowned. "No one wants to get their hands dirty anymore. That lay about Jimmy Hollister is about all the help Herbert can get, and he's worse than useless, sometimes."

Her next words echoed Calvin sentiment from that morning. "I suspect you could do the work better than Jimmy," said Mrs. Anderson.

"Oh," Nan said carefully, "I certainly wouldn't mind learning that end of the business, too, especially if I'm going to be working for the two of you. May I ask why you need the help? My understanding was that you took care of all the office work."

"Of course, I do." Mrs. Anderson sighed and lowered her voice slightly when she spoke again. "But I'm not as spry as I once was. I'm going to have to have both hip joints replaced pretty soon. I'm not going to be able to get around much for a time."

"I'm so sorry to hear that, Mrs. Anderson," Nan said sympathetically.

"Don't you fret none, missy. I'll be up and about better than ever when it's over and done. I'm looking forward to it. Well, it being over, anyway."

"That is a wonderful attitude, Mrs. Anderson. I admire you."

"Just the way I'm built, dearie. Nothing special. Now, I'll talk to Herbert about this. Let him know I'm hiring you for the office. He and your hubby will want to discuss it themselves, I'm sure. We'll be out this evening. About six?"

"That would be fine, Mrs. Anderson. And don't you dare bring a house warming gift."

"Never tell an old woman what to do," Mrs. Anderson said without malice. "It just makes things worse. Now. Come around the desk. We need to start your training. You know anything about computers?"

Nan spent most of the day with Beth Anderson, learning the ins and outs of Mr. Anderson's various businesses. She went away somewhat awed at what the couple did in the area. She was waiting outside the grocery store when Calvin pulled up that afternoon.

"How'd it go?" he asked after kissing Nan and loading the few groceries she'd picked up for them.

"You will not believe," she said. "Let's get going. We have to prepare for company this evening."

Knowing he would be thoroughly briefed, in time, Calvin nodded and climbed into the Jeep as Nan entered on the passenger side. They were well on their way back home before Nan excitedly told Calvin what had transpired that day.

"Wow," he replied when Nan had finished. "You sure don't let the grass grow under your feet. I don't know what to say. At lunch time today I checked on all the equipment again and got updated prices and availability. I'll be able to explain it all to Mr. Anderson, even without an official proposal."

"I suspect they'd turn down an official proposal. Just talking it out will be better. What are the chances of getting the equipment soon?"

"The availability is there, except for some of the things I want for the Unimog. The Bobcats and their attachments are no problem, just the money. I made a couple of calls to banks about business loans. They're willing to discuss it. I'll definitely do an official business proposal for them."

As Nan had suspected from Mrs. Anderson's words, Beth and Herbert had a house warming gift for them when they arrived. A nice Home Sweet Home embroidery.

"I'd rather not talk business till after we eat," were Mr. Anderson's first words, after "Howdy, folks."

"That's just fine," Calvin told him, taking the coats to hang up in the entry way closet.

"It'll be ready in just a few minutes," Nan said, coming from the kitchen. "I hope meatloaf is okay."

"Excellent. Excellent," Mr. Anderson said. "I doubt it will be as good as Beth's, but it'd take an expert cook to even come close."

"I must admit I do make a prize winning meatloaf," Mrs. Anderson said. "But I'm sure we'll enjoy yours." She took one of Nan's hands in hers and patted it reassuringly.

Nan took it in stride, turning to sweep an arm toward the living room. "What do you think? Would you like a tour?"

As Mrs. Anderson was saying yes, Mr. Anderson told Calvin. "You can tell a lot about a man from the tools he owns. You got any tools, young man?"

"I do for a fact," Calvin said, looking over at his wife and winking when Mrs. Anderson couldn't see. They went their separate ways, Calvin showing Mr. Anderson the house starting in the garage, with Nan showing Mrs. Anderson the kitchen first.

Both the Andersons seemed somewhat impressed with the house, and the Stubblefield's, too, when they gathered around the dining table. "It will just take a moment," Nan said. "Calvin, could you lend a hand, please?"

It was a rather simple meal. Meatloaf, mashed potatoes, whole kernel corn, and rather than a salad, sliced tomato, cucumber, and onion in peppered vinegar. The Anderson's seemed to enjoy it, Mr. Anderson going so far as saying, "Not as good as Beth's, like I expected, but fine. Mighty fine. What's dessert?"

"Now, Herbert. You know you aren't supposed to eat much sweets." She cut her eyes toward Nan. "But I would be curious as to what you might have prepared."

"I made up a batch of black walnut brownies and a quart of ice cream."

"You made the ice cream?" Mr. Anderson said, his face showing his surprise.

"Strawberry," replied Calvin.

Mr. Anderson shot a pleading look at his wife. She looked thoughtful, but took little time in answering. "Well, I suppose a bit won't hurt you all that much. I wouldn't mind trying your brownies… maybe just a scoop of that ice cream, to see if I can tell which recipe you used."

Mrs. Anderson never really said what recipes she thought Nan had used, but seemed to enjoy the dessert as much as Mr. Anderson did."

"Mighty fine," Mr. Anderson said, patting his stomach as Nan and Calvin cleared the table.

"Would you like to take your coffee to the living room where we can talk?"

"No more coffee," said Mr. Anderson. "Might you have anything stronger?"

"Now Herbert," admonished Mrs. Anderson.

"We have a small bar," replied Calvin, when Mrs. Anderson didn't insist on a no, and looked rather interested herself. Calvin went over to the built-in cabinets flanking the fireplace and opened one.

"We don't drink much," Calvin continued, but we like to keep a selection for guests. Is there anything in particular you would like?"

"I usually just drink sippin' whiskey, but I'm a mind to try something new," Mr. Anderson said, walking over to join Calvin and take a look at the offerings. "What's that rounded bottle with the long neck. He squinted a bit. "Irish something."

"Irish Mist," replied Calvin. He opened the bottle and let Mr. Anderson take a sniff. "It's very good," Calvin said. "Would you like to try a snifter?"

"Yeah. That'll do."

Calvin poured a nice shot of the Irish Mist into a balloon snifter and handed it to Mr. Anderson. He turned to Mrs. Anderson. "Would you like one, as well?" he asked.

"Perhaps some sherry, or something like that," she replied.

"How about an aperitif?" responded Calvin. "We have Galiano, Frangelica, Crème de Menthe..."

Mrs. Anderson interrupted him. "A Crème de Menthe," she said. "That sounds nice."

After pouring the drink he asked Nan, "Honey? What are you having?"

"I think the Frangelica," she said.

He poured her drink and a snifter of Amaretto for himself. Though they hadn't used it except to try it to make sure it worked properly, a fire was kept set in the fireplace. Calvin lit a match and started a piece of fatwood burning. He put it under the tinder and closed the screen.

By the time he took a seat on the sofa, Nan perching on the arm beside him, the fire was already catching.

"Dinner's over," said Mr. Anderson. "The drink here don't count. What's on your mind, sonny? Beth told me a little, but I need to hear it from you."

"Yes, sir," Calvin said. "Well, Nan and I have been thinking of starting a business, similar to some of the business you have. I was hoping you might give me a few pointers. Training, actually. On weekends."

"Don't work on the Sabbath. Ain't right. At least not unless it's a real emergency."

"I meant on Saturday, Mr. Anderson," Calvin replied.

"That would be okay. Don't work many Saturdays, when I can help it. But have to some; because that's the only time some people have to be home for me to do the work. And I bet, even though you haven't got much experience, you'd be better'n Jimmy.

"You gotta understand," Mr. Anderson continued, "my equipment is like me. Old and slow. I can teach you some things, sure enough, but it might not mean much in your own business. Unless you want to buy me out someday. I probably wouldn't sell it to you. Wouldn't be right. I can handle it okay. Wouldn't expect no one else to make a living with that old hoe and the other equipment."

"I appreciate that, Mr. Anderson." Nan put her hand on Calvin's shoulder in encouragement as he continued. "I'm working on a plan to go ahead and get my own equipment. If I can do that, you could train me on it. If you would."

Mr. Anderson took a quick sip of the Irish Mist, thinking. Finally he asked. "Just what kind of equipment? It pays to buy good equipment, you know. My old hoe was a good one once. It was pretty hard used before I got it. Didn't want to invest too much when I got it, 'cause I didn't know if I wanted to do that kind of work for good."

"Actually," Calvin said, "We…" he looked up at Nan for a moment before he continued. "We were thinking about getting a Unimog, and a couple of models of Bobcat equipment. Plus attachments."

"I know Bobcats, but what in the world is a Unimog? And what's this about attachments?" asked Mr. Anderson. "Those little Bobcat spinners got a bucket, don't they?"

"Yes, sir, Mr. Anderson. But they can take a variety of attachments, such as a snow blower, tiller… rototiller that is, backhoes, trencher, rollers, tree transplanter…"

"Whoa, boy! Those little things can do all that?"

"With the right selection of attachments. I do have in mind one of the larger units. Two, actually. An A300. It can be used as a skid steer, but it can also use four wheel steer. Easier on lawns and such. The other one is the Toolcat 5600T utility vehicle. Kind of a small pickup truck with front lift arms to take a bucket or the other attachments."

"Does sound interesting," replied Mr. Anderson. He took another sip of the Irish Mist, and then asked, "New or used. I can take care of old equipment okay myself, but I wouldn't want to deal with any more than I already got."

"I plan to purchase new units, straight from the dealer."

"That's good. That's right good. Now what's this other thing you mention. Moogy something?"

"Unimog. U500 model. It's a truck made by Mercedes-Benz. Where the Bobcat Toolcat is like a small four wheel drive pickup with front lift arms, the Unimog is like a giant four wheel drive pickup with, on the one I plan to get, front attachment points that can handle lift arms and other attachments. Can also mount or tow equipment on the rear, too. It has engine and transmission PTO shafts, as well as hydraulic connections front and rear."

"Didn't know Mercedes made trucks. Here in the US, anyways. Way back when I was in the service I saw some Mercedes trucks over in Germany. But nothing like a big pickup truck."

"I'm not explaining it very well, I'm afraid," Calvin said. "I've got some literature..."

"I'll get it," Nan said, getting up and heading for the den. She was back in moments with a handful of brochures and data sheets. "Here you go, Mr. Anderson."

"That is an ugly sucker, isn't it?" said Mr. Anderson, looking at the picture of the Unimog on the cover of the brochure. "Don't really look like a pickup to me, though. Just a small flatbed..." He squinted a bit at the picture. "Not a flatbed, though, looks like a short sided bed."

"It is," replied Calvin. "The one I would get would have that bed with a three way dump kit. Plus the bed can attach and detach pretty quickly without much trouble. I'd get a couple other beds for specific purposes."

"Hey," said Mr. Anderson, as he leafed through the brochure. "This shows a bucket on the front, and a pair of forks, and..." He fell silent and looked through the brochure in more detail as his wife, Nan, and Calvin looked on.

Mr. Anderson handed the first brochure to his wife and went through the other papers. Mrs. Anderson looked through them with as much intensity as had her husband."

"I don't know," Mr. Anderson said, after going through all the papers. "Sounds like a good idea. But something trying to do everything usually isn't as good as a specific piece of equipment."

"I agree, sir. But for what I envision, I think they would serve the purpose."

"Maybe." Mr. Anderson looked thoughtful again for a moment. "Got to admit, Mercedes makes good stuff. Beth, remember that diesel sedan I traded for back a few years ago? Turned a nice profit on that, after driving it for a year. Really good car."

Mrs. Anderson nodded her agreement.

"And Conrad has a Bobcat out on his farm. He swears by it." Mr. Anderson frowned. "But he never said nothing about extras for it. He just uses the bucket for all kinds of things." He looked at Calvin. "You say they can plow snow?"

"Plow or blow, Mr. Anderson."

"Used to do a pretty good little business plowing driveways and such for people when I had the old Ford with a snow blade on it. Blew the engine and never got it fixed. We had two or three years of mild winters and I didn't see the need. Way winters been the last couple, snow removal could be a big business."

This time Mr. Anderson gave Calvin a hard look. "You really do this? This stuff can't be cheap."

"I'm pretty sure, but I can't guarantee it. I don't want to do half measures, so if we can't do it the way we want, we won't do it." He looked up at Nan and she nodded her agreement.

Mr. Anderson drained the snifter of the last of the Irish Mist and set it down on the coffee table. "I tell you what, sonny. I'll train you, Saturdays, on my equipment. If you can come up with the equipment, I'll help you with it, too. This area can't support a big contractor, but needs lots of work done on a small to medium scale. I been doing it for forty years now, but I'm ready to retire. If you work out, and can get the 'quipment, I'll put in a good word for you with my regular customers."

Mr. Anderson stood, and the others did as well. Calvin held out his hand and Mr. Anderson took it in a firm grip and gave it a good hard double shake.

"Thank you, Mr. Anderson. I appreciate your faith in me. I'll have a proposal for the bank by the end of the week. I should know if I'm approved a week or ten days after that."

"Okay, sonny. I'll see you this coming Saturday at nine at the office. We got a septic job to do for the Widow Hammond."

"Yes, sir. I'll be there."

With that, the Anderson's took their leave. When Calvin closed the door after they drove away, he turned to Nan and asked, "You think we're doing the right thing?"

"I do, honey. Mr. Anderson made it pretty obvious that the type of service we plan on doing is needed. I think he's only still working because there isn't anyone else around here that could and would do those types of jobs."

"I'll get to work on that proposal. Do you think you could get some numbers from Mrs.

Anderson that I can use to show the potential for the equipment?"

Nan put her arm around Calvin's waist as they walked toward the den. "I'm sure they won't mind. Mrs. Anderson didn't show it much, but I'm pretty sure she is excited about the idea. I think she really wants them to be able to retire as soon as possible. She has a cruise line brochure at the office that is dog eared from being looked at so much. It's for an around the world cruise."

Calvin nodded. "Well, we'll do our best to help them accomplish that, if that is what they want." Calvin took Nan in his arms and kissed her firmly. When he stepped back he said. "I love you."

"And I you," Nan replied, stepping away from him. "I'll go clean things up while you start working."

CHAPTER FIVE

Buddy Henderson wrote down the deposit in his checkbook. "Yes!" he said quietly to himself. He finally hit the goal he'd been shooting for. He now had ten thousand dollars in his savings account and five thousand in the checking account. The vendors were all paid off for the job just finished. So were the two apprentice plumbers he'd hired to help. The three thousand dollar final payment had been all profit.

He was going to have to take Charlene out to dinner to thank her for her help with the special orders. She'd done the orders for him and kept on top of deliveries and such while he'd concentrated on getting the job done. It was his biggest contract job to date.

The bank account contents were only one part of the plan he'd been working on for several years. He had paid off the plumbing truck, a large step van, the year before. Buddy owned free and clear the extensive stock the truck held, as well as the contents of the storage building behind the house, and the pipe rack beside it.

The house was free and clear. It was the first thing he paid off. It was a small two-bedroom tract house with a small den. But it served his needs nicely. He used the master bedroom and kept the second bedroom for personal storage.

The only thing left to pay off was his personal transportation. That consisted of a lovingly restored and customized 1977 Chevy three-quarter ton crew cab four-wheel-drive pickup truck. It had taken hours of work, some expert help, and quite a few dollars, to get it the way Buddy wanted it. But it had been worth it. He knew it was 100% reliable, and would go anywhere a wheeled vehicle had any business going.

Only one payment left on the engine work for the truck and he'd get the title. And the money was in the payment file already. He just needed to take it down to Hooper's and give it to them. He just hadn't had a chance this past week. It wasn't even due for another week, but Buddy wanted it paid off.

Most of his emergency preparations were well along. But now he had the opportunity to get a few things he'd been holding off from buying. Instead he'd accumulated some expedient gear. He'd keep it, of course, but it would be regulated to back up status.

Buddy stopped at the house and changed clothes. He started a small load of laundry, and then went to the fire resistant, locking file cabinet in the den. Opening the top drawer, he removed the money from his haircut folder. It was about time for another haircut, anyway, and if he was going to take Charlene out, he wanted to look his best.

Another drawer held last year's tax information. He took it out and put it in a manila envelope. He'd drop it off at his tax person's place on the way to the barbershop. He'd run rough numbers himself and thought he'd get a substantial refund. The jobs had looked pretty good, so he'd paid more each quarter on his taxes than he thought he might need. Let the government use the money for a while and then get it back in a lump sum.

Some of his friends made fun of him for letting the government use the money, but Buddy liked not having to worry about coming up with a large sum to pay his taxes if he shorted the quarterly payments. And getting the refund was nice. He'd always saved money, but this was just one more way of forced savings.

Buddy grabbed his hard hat out of habit, then smiled and hung it back up and picked up his Ditch Witch cap. He'd rented the one machine enough lately that the rental place had given him the cap and a pair of work gloves in appreciation. Though he owned the plumbing truck, rental rates were low enough compared to maintenance rates that he was better off renting some of the necessary equipment as he needed it than he was buying it.

After checking the fuel gauges in the Chevy, Buddy decided to top off the fuel tanks on the way to the barbershop. He dropped off the tax documents first, and then drove down the street to the station he used. He rotated use of all three fuel tanks in the truck to keep the gasoline fresh.

The rear tank, where the spare tire originally went, was almost empty. It held thirty-six gallons. He put twenty-one in it to fill it. The other two tanks, a pair of twenty-gallon tanks, one on each side of the frame, were full. Buddy flipped the auxiliary/main switch to main, then the right/left switch to left. He'd run on the left tank until it was about empty, then fill it and switch to the right tank.

Buddy was whistling softly as he entered the barbershop. He grabbed the paper and took a seat. There would be a wait. The shop was full. His good mood moderated a bit when he saw the headlines. The Department of Homeland Security had shut down the airport again. And gasoline prices were still going up. The two fuel cans on the rack on the back of the truck were full, but it had been a while since he'd emptied and refilled them.

He'd do that while he was running on the left tank. It was time to check with the surplus place and see if they had any more of the cans in stock. There were two more at the house, in the shed, but he'd like to get a few more. But he wanted the good ones. Maybe another water can or two, as well, for the truck.

The barber had to call his name twice before Buddy looked up from the paper, then rose to go to the chair. "Sorry, Bobby. Got caught up in the paper."

"It's a mess, isn't it?" Bobby, eighty, replied as he put the cloth around Buddy's neck. "Gonna be worse than the depression and the big war combined, I'm a'thinkin', when it happens this time."

"You really think so?" Buddy asked. He respected Bobby. Bobby had gone through the depression, and then served in both World War Two and Korea. Lost a finger to frostbite in Korea, but it didn't slow him down any as a barber. Buddy wondered sometimes why Bobby still worked. He knew he didn't have to.

"Do for a fact. Do for a fact. Won't live through this one, I'm a'thinkin'. Was a hellion in my day, but my day is over. First cold night we have without heat and I'm a goner. Yes sir'ee. A goner."

You're tough as nails," protested Buddy.

"Not any more. Doc said it's just a matter of time."

One of the other barbers called over. "We've been trying to get him to retire and take it easy. He's got that property up in the hills just waiting for him. Put in a manufactured home, and he's set."

"Not likely," was Bobby's reply. "With the interstate going the way it did, that place isn't going to get any utilities for years. I bought it more for the investment than to ever use. Ain't no way I'm going be up there with no utilities. I lived enough days in the field when I was in the service. It'll be a nice rest home for me till the end comes.

"I'll find some sucker that'll give me what I paid for it and it'll be someone else's headache. Without the utilities going in and the limited access, no one in their right mind is going to develop that area. I just made a bad call on that place. 'Bout the only one I ever did, I'm a'thinkin'. Yes sir'ee. 'Bout the only one. So I got no regrets. One of these young'uns will want one of them off-grid lock things I hear about. I'll sell it or let the estate sell it if I die first. My kids sure don't want it."

"You really serious about selling it, Bobby?" Buddy asked thoughtfully.

"Sure am. Had it listed now for a year. Nary a nibble. People just don't want in the sticks any more. Take a jeep to get to it, the way it is. Went up there when I bought it. Found the best parcel, in my opinion, they had up there. View for miles, but still lots of trees. Good flat spot for a house. Small one, anyway. Wind blows like the dickens, though. Don't like the wind much. Can't hear enough around you when the wind blows. Wind almost got me killed three times. Once in Germany and twice in Korea. Don't like the wind much."

"I might just be interested in it. Would it be okay to go up and take a look at it this weekend?"

Bobby was putting the final touches on Buddy's flattop. "I'll cut you a deal, I will. I don't aim to go up there, but I got all the particulars and I can let the real estate lady know. She might go up there with you, though I doubt it. I think she just took it 'cause she felt sorry for me." Bobby laughed. "Real politically correct gal, that one. Me being a disabled vet and all. And old." Bobby waggled his fingers, the one obviously missing, and laughed.

"Long as I've got good directions and a map, I can find it," Buddy replied.

"Well, sure thing," said Bobby, brushing the loose hairs carefully from Buddy's face and neck. "Stop by Saturday morn and I'll have those directions for you." He removed the cape and shook it free of hair as Buddy got out of the chair.

"I will, Bobby. Here you go." Buddy handed Bobby the money and waved away the change, as always.

"Stop by the realtors, if you want and ask about the property. They can give you their version of the details." He laughed. "Then me and thee can sit down and discuss it after you've looked at it."

Buddy nodded. "That sounds good, Bobby. Thanks."

One of the things he'd planned on doing when he'd met his financial goals was to obtain a piece of rural property. Like Bobby, he considered it an investment, but more importantly, a place to go if things really got bad. A retreat, so to speak.

Maybe a place to retire. But mostly just a place to get away for the next few years. He'd done a lot of camping when he was younger and he missed it. Hadn't had much chance the last few years, with staying as busy as he could with the business, and saving money, and getting the things he'd wanted. Not much time for leisure. Nor much of a social life.

Buddy thought of Charlene. They were friends. Good friends. Had been since high school. He'd dated her off and on even then. She was a good woman. Straightforward, intelligent. Kind of pretty, though not a flashing beauty. That was partly why he was comfortable with her. They were pretty similar in a lot of ways. He had his plumbing business and she had that little curio shop. She did all right for herself.

Checking the traffic behind him, Buddy quickly turned into the first parking lot he came to. He wasn't about to get a ticket, much less the hassles now attendant with using a cellular phone while you were driving. He called up Charlene. It took only a few moments to arrange to pick her up that evening for dinner.

CHAPTER SIX

Buddy was showered and dressed in plenty of time to pick up Charlene. He was glad he'd started early, for he decided to change into a suit, rather than the sport shirt and slacks he'd initially put on.

Having learned the hard way about suits, Buddy always got shirts and suits that fit properly. No need to suffer with a tight collar when there was no need. He adjusted the tie and flexed his arms in the suit jacket. He was quite comfortable.

Having worn a flattop hair cut for almost all of his life, and having experienced a sunburned scalp at one time, Buddy always wore a cap or a hat. When he wore what he considered to be his bank suit, he usually wore the snappy grey fedora with it. Unaware that he was whistling softly again, Buddy went out to the truck.

He usually preferred to drive, but when he got to Charlene's and saw the nice dress she was wearing, he was both glad he'd worn the suit, and a bit concerned about needing to help Charlene in and out of the truck. The Chevy wasn't like some of the trucks around where you needed a ladder to get in, but it did sport a two inch lift kit and had tires two sizes larger than stock.

"Uh… Charlene…" Buddy said a bit hesitatingly. "Would you mind if we took your car? I'm not sure I want to be helping you in and out of the truck with you in that skirt."

Charlene just chuckled and said, "Why, thank you, Buddy. And we may certainly take my car. You can even drive if you want."

"No. That's okay. It's your car. You should probably drive. And why did you thank me just now?"

Her dimples showing, Charlene smiled over at Buddy and said, "It was maybe a bit left handed, but I took it as a compliment. You didn't want to embarrass me by seeing too much when I climbed in and out of the truck. Right?"

"Well… yeah… I guess so," Buddy slowly admitted.

"Then two reasons. I'm flattered you think I'm attractive enough to want to look, and pleased that you don't want to embarrass me." The smile was now a grin. "Or embarrass yourself."

A sheepish smile curved Buddy's lips. "I guess you know me a bit too well."

"Not too well," Charlene replied, still smiling. "Where did you want to go?"

"I know you like Red Lobster. Let's go there. I'm celebrating, and this is for you for helping me with the Barbarosa job."

"You already thanked me. Lots of times," replied Charlene. "You didn't have to take me out to dinner, too."

"I wanted to. You were a big help. Besides, we haven't done anything in a long time, except for getting together for the job. I need to get out more. You should too, you know. You need to find someone. Start a relationship."

"I'm working on it," said Charlene, without looking over at Buddy.

"Oh. Really?" Buddy looked at her a bit uncertainly. "I... didn't know you were seeing someone."

"It's just casual right now. But I have hopes." Again she was careful not to look at him. She knew the sparkle in her eyes would probably give her away. He knew her pretty well, too.

As much as he wanted to, he didn't ask any more questions. He certainly wanted to know more, but was afraid of the answers. He wanted the best for her, was having a bit of difficulty dealing with the fact that she had someone in her life. He was silent the rest of the way to the restaurant.

Seeing a birthday party group when they walked up to the door cheered him up. He couldn't help but laugh at the antics of the children, waiting anxiously for a table to open.

Apparently it was a very special treat for them to come here.

Besides, it was nice to have Charlene's arm curled around his as they stood near the door waiting to be called. Buddy looked over at Charlene after a moment and asked, "You want something from the bar? No place to sit, but..."

"That would be nice. A glass of Chardonnay. I think I'll wait here."

"Smart woman," Buddy responded with a grin. He had to work his way to the bar through the crowd. He was trying to remember when he'd been in and it wasn't crowded. He couldn't think of a time. But it was always worth it.

He wasn't much of a drinker, but wine with dinner was nice, so he ordered the Chardonnay for himself, as well. He got all of it back to Charlene, though it had been a near thing.

They stood companionably, saying little, sipping the wine while they waited. It wasn't all that long and they were escorted back to their booth. "We're splurging tonight, so get whatever you want. I deposited the final check today. I plan on having lobster."

"It is Red Lobster, after all," Charlene said, perusing the menu. "I think I'll have the same, since you offered." She closed the menu and set it aside. "Something is on your mind. I can tell. What's going on?"

Buddy set his menu aside as well, then arranged his napkin and flatware. "You know I've been thinking about buying a piece of undeveloped property…"

Charlene nodded, and then took a sip of wine.

"Bobby, down at the barbershop, has some he wants to sell. I'm seriously considering it. Oh. After I take a look at it, of course. But getting something."

"Going to sell the house and move?" Charlene asked, slightly dreading the answer.

"Not right away." Buddy looked up as their server arrived. He didn't see Charlene's sigh of relief.

They were occupied for a few moments with the server, and then when she left, Charlene asked. "Just investment property, or something you want to develop eventually?"

"Partly for investment, but primarily to have a place outside the city and suburbs. I miss camping. I'm ready to get away from the hustle and bustle from time to time, now. I'm financially secure enough to do it. Though there are a couple more large expenditures I plan to make right away. But those two apprentice plumbers I hired have a lot of potential. I've got two more large jobs lined up that will give me a similar payoff to the one I just finished.

"I'm more comfortable now handling the purchases of some of the esoteric items people tend to want now, since you helped me recently."

Quickly Charlene cut in. "You know I don't mind helping, any time."

"I know, and I appreciate it, Char. You didn't just help me get what I needed, but taught me how to do it myself."

Charlene nodded.

"If I get just a few more jobs like the last one, over the next couple of years, I will be able to get another truck and put a couple of guys to work, full time."

"That's wonderful, Buddy!" Charlene laid her hand on Buddy's. He didn't pull away.

"That's what I plan on doing, but in the meantime, I don't want to get myself in a bind, with the way things are going in the world now."

The conversation was interrupted for a moment when their appetizer arrived. But Charlene picked up the thread as they began to eat. "I know what you mean, Buddy. I'm worried about things, too. I got hit with the rolling blackout just the other day. I'm glad you suggested storing water. I have some at the house and the shop. And I'm keeping at least two weeks of packaged food all the time now. That was good advice. It didn't happen, but I thought about what could have when they shut down trucking for a day for security reasons. It was only one day, but when I went into the store that evening, the shelves were half empty."

"I know," replied Buddy. "The rolling blackouts haven't affected me much. I'm usually not home when the residential ones happen in my neighborhood. But I went into the store that day, too. There was fighting over canned goods when the store, not knowing when they'd get another delivery, put limits on how much could be bought by one person at one time."

"I think it will get worse," Charlene said, watching Buddy carefully.

"So do I," he said softly, his eyes on his plate for a moment. He lifted them and met Charlene's rather intense gaze.

"That's part of the reason I want to get the property. Have a place to go to if things get too crazy in the city."

Charlene nodded. "I've thought about it some. I don't know what I would do. Since my sister died, I don't have any place to run to if things get that bad. I think I should make more preparations, but the FEMA stuff on line really doesn't get into it all that deep. Would you be willing to help me get better prepared?"

Buddy didn't hesitate. "Certainly. And don't worry about a place to go. If I get the property, you'll be welcome. I've always planned to have enough to take care of my family's needs. There would be plenty for you, too."

"Your brother isn't making preparations?"

"No. I've tried. Betty is inclined, but he refuses to acknowledge the fact that the government might not be able to help everyone if things really do get bad. You know him. He's a horse's behind of the first order. But he is my brother, and Betty and the kids are good people. I still plan on having room for them, no matter what happens."

Again Charlene's hand went to his where it rested beside his plate. "You're a good man, Buddy. I'm glad I know you and that we're friends."

This time he squeezed back, at least a little. "So am I, Charlene. And don't worry too much about things. I'm planning on doing quite a bit more to be prepared. I'll be glad to help you get ready, too."

The rest of the meal was spent in lighter conversation as they enjoyed the food and service. When they got back to Charlene's house, she asked Buddy, "Do you want to come in for a drink before you go?"

Buddy shook his head. "No. The wine was enough. I still have to drive home."

"Coffee, then?"

"I have to be up early in the morning. I'm giving my proposal on the next project after the one I'm starting next week." On impulse, he leaned forward and kissed Charlene on the cheek. "Thanks for going with me tonight. I had a nice time. You're great company. And just figure out a good evening for you and I'll come over and we can start planning on how to get you more ready for the future."

"Okay, Buddy. I'll do that. Good night."

"Good night."

CHAPTER SEVEN

Charlie groaned and rolled over, and then gathered the newspapers on which, and under which, he'd slept, back around him. He was cold. He'd lost his long wool overcoat two days previously when two other homeless men and a homeless woman had taken over the drain culvert he'd been using to sleep in for the most part of the winter. He'd been able to sneak back and get both of his stashes, but the woman had glommed the coat. It would have been a fight to get it back. One he knew he'd lose anyway.

At least spring was here, though it was hard to tell sometimes. The weather the last few years had been more unpredictable than usual. Maybe it was time for him to head somewhere down south, though he really couldn't tolerate high heat and humidity. Maybe he'd go in a year or two, if he didn't find something soon.

Of course, he knew he wouldn't. He really wasn't even trying anymore. He'd cut back the drinking, but he hadn't stopped. A good part of the money he made from odd jobs went for cheap booze. But he had been hanging on to some of it for emergencies. That's why getting his stashes back had been so important.

He was always careful not to have all of his money, little as it was, in only one place, whether on him, or stashed.

"Might as well get up," he thought. He wouldn't go back to sleep now, anyway. The sun was up. At least it hadn't rained. He would have had to leave the culvert if it had rained during the night, or drown.

Bones aching and ligaments and tendons popping, Charlie crawled out of the culvert and looked carefully around. Nothing stirring, except some birds. He put out two rat traps the evening before and he decided to check them. Nothing in one, but the other had killed a pigeon.

Breakfast.

It didn't take long to set up his tin can stove and start a few sticks burning using newspaper as tinder. He contemplated his future as he grilled the pigeon breast. He took a drink from one of his two bottles of water. He'd been able to keep them filled from partially full ones he often found in trash bins.

Things were getting bad in the city. More homeless than ever, and they were getting meaner. So were the cops. Not much tolerance anymore. The shelters were full, and he'd had to shave his head and privates after the last time. He'd wound up with lice from the blanket in the shelter. He'd borrowed a pair of scissors, and used his last disposable razor to do it. At least he'd been able to take a shower afterwards, but he'd immediately left the shelter afterward and hadn't been back.

Maybe along the border between the city proper and the 'burbs. Enough city stuff to keep him fed and housed, but close to good handyman work. He checked his cash. The stash in the hidden pocket inside the sleeve of his jacket, above the elbow, held a twenty in a zip-lock sandwich bag.

He had three dollars in his wallet in his left hip pocket. He never kept much in his wallet in case he got rolled. But he always kept a little in the hope that they would take it and not search much more. There was a five in the bottom of his left shoe.

Two fives were wrapped around his hickory walking staff, hidden under the leather handgrip. A ten was folded and in the palm of his left hand, under the fingerless, skin tight, leather glove he wore to hide the burn scars on the back of that hand.

Not much, but more than what many had. He still had a half of a pint of whiskey in the pocket of his jacket and the water, but no other food left. The others had got what little he'd had when they chased him from his other spot. At least he'd had his bottle of vitamins in one of the stashes.

His kit was divided between two 5-gallon buckets that had once held drywall paste. He'd made a couple of bucks helping clean up that construction job, got the buckets with lids, and a perfectly good closet rod they were going to just throw away. One of the carpenters had drilled quarter-inch holes an inch from each end for him. He bought two quarter-inch J-bolts from a discount store, two extra nuts, four washers, four feet of light chain, and two S-hooks. With the J-bolts mounted and the middle of the rod wrapped with cloth padding and duct tape, he had an over the shoulder carrier for the two buckets. Had to be a bit careful with his pace to keep the buckets from swinging on the chains and throwing him off balance, but it let him carry and use them easily.

There was a pretty decent set of Dickies tan work clothes in one bucket. It also contained an extra pair of underwear and a tee-shirt, and two pair of socks in a gallon zip-lock bag. That bucket also held his tin can stove when he wasn't using it like now, a lidded pot, steak knife, spoon, a zip-lock with his small stash of toiletries, the bottle of vitamins, and one water bottle.

The other bucket contained the two rat traps, a small roll of duct tape, the other drinking water bottle, another pot, several pads of toilet paper in a zip-lock bag, a small box of zip-lock bags, coil of mechanic's wire, multi-tip screwdriver, pair of water pump pliers, a very good carpenter's hammer, and a hacksaw blade. There were a few odds and ends of screws, nails, and bolts. Another one-gallon zip-lock bag held his other change of underwear and socks, two bandanas, and a half roll of quarters for the Laundromat.

Along with the clothes he was wearing, a-bit-worse-for-wear set of Dickies work clothes, tee-shirt, insulated shirt, boxer shorts, insulated long handles, three pairs of socks, insulated gloves, stocking cap, heavy jacket, and boots, with a bandana around his neck and another one in his left hip pocket, and the contents of the buckets were the sum of his worldly goods.

Fed, morning ablutions taken care of, and buckets repacked, destination in mind, Charlie headed out.

CHAPTER EIGHT

Edward Baumgartner had it made, a luxury SUV, a Mercedes sedan, and a Corvette. He had a paid off house with a pool and money in the bank. In two banks, actually, both of which he owned. Of course, he did have a wife and two bratty kids. He grinned as he drove the SUV toward the bank that he considered his base of operations. There were other positives, though. His secretary was ambitious and beautiful. More importantly, she was willing to bargain her way up the ladder. He had a standing arrangement with her for a weekly frolic at an out of the way hotel.

His grin faded as he listened to the news. Things were getting bad. Maybe he should get out of some of his growth stocks and put the money in blue chips. T-bills, too. And that one teller, Angela, was always talking about being prepared. Like she was a boy scout or something. But still... He'd do a search on the internet and see what he could find.

When he saw the hobo walking along, looking like a coolie without the hat, checking trash receptacles as he went, Edward frowned. This was a decent part of town. They didn't need his kind around. Along with the other things he planned for the day, he would write a letter-to-the-editor of the paper and give his opinion on the situation. It was important for people like him to help keep a handle on the goings-on in the area.

He winked at Courtney as he went past, and then frowned at Angela. There were two people standing with her and they were looking at some kind of catalog. Probably one of her survival equipment catalogs.

Edward changed course and headed for the three. Things were set up for opening time, but he couldn't let them just stand around like slackers. "I'll take that. You can have it back after work. All of you find something to do until opening."

Angela didn't protest. She knew it wouldn't do any good. She was looking for work at another bank, but things were pretty tight. The pay was decent here, the working conditions were good, and her workmates were great, except for Mr. Baumgartner and Courtney. She sighed and went to count the money, again, in the till at her teller station.

Dropping the catalog on his desk, Edward went around the desk and sat down. In moments his computer monitor was up. He checked the banks accounts for the night's transfers. Everything was fine. After a look at the clock on the wall, he got up again and made his usual inspection of the bank just before opening.

By ten he'd taken care of all the routine business and nothing special had come up. He picked up the catalog he'd put on his credenza when he was working on bank business. It was a survival equipment catalog. Edward noted that it was listed as preparedness items, but he knew they really meant that survivalist nonsense.

He thumbed through it, stopping here and there as particular items caught his eye. Edward noted a year supply of food for a family of four and whistled. But he thought about it for a moment, mentally calculating how much they spent in a year on food. Not that much difference, he decided. Something to think about. It was getting hard to find some items when he wanted them. He'd had to get on to his wife more than once for not bringing home the foods he liked on what was now a regular basis.

Of course he knew he was too smart to fall for the ads. No way it would be as good as the pictures looked. But still... He tossed the catalog aside and turned to the computer. He pulled up the internet search engine he used and typed survival and shelter into the search bar.

He was amazed at the number of entries that came back. Pages of them. Suddenly one particular one caught his eye and he clicked on the link. This had to be what that banker from Tennessee had been talking about at the last convention to which he'd gone. Edward had forgotten about that until he saw the company name.

The man said he'd bought one of the pre-packaged shelter deals. If he remembered correctly, several of the other bankers had expressed an interest. Maybe this might be the thing to do. If other bankers were doing it, there had to be some merit in it. He'd hate to go to a conference and have to admit he'd prepared for a financial emergency, but not a physical one. "Hum..."

Courtney buzzed him and Edward went back to the bank's business.

CHAPTER NINE

The three weeks went quickly for Percy. Aside from helping get the Bluhms settled, and working on the grant paperwork, Percy also kept busy working in the greenhouses on spring harvest. Two of the roadside trailer stands were set up on the weekends and Percy hired four high school kids to staff them. Many locals looked forward to Percy's early produce every spring.

Percy was tired that Monday evening in late April. He had worked the day as usual, giving the others the extra day off after all the hard work they'd all been doing. Everything was going well, but even with the automated systems, caring for all the animals for two days was still a strain.

He ate a small potpie that Mattie had left prepared for him. Percy ate in the den, watching the news channels. Halfway through the chicken potpie, Percy quit eating, his attention taken by the news report from the disputed border area between India and Pakistan.

The conflict was worsening. There were exchanges between ground troops now, in addition to the artillery exchanges. As yet, no air strikes, but Percy figured that was just a matter of time.

Reports from Germany were continuing to show strong nationalistic bent. The talk of withdrawing from the European Union was stronger than ever. It seemed the talks of individual treaties with Poland and Czechoslovakia were coming to fruition. New talks were beginning with Hungary. US forces were being isolated from the German population, with new restrictions on fraternization being imposed.

France seemed to be going back to the imperialistic expansion ideal from the turn of the previous century. Many of the former French colonies were having troubles. France was sending troops to many of them, apparently not just to assist in keeping the peace. They were not requesting UN help for the efforts and were taking steps to emplace French rule it seemed to many in the international community.

There were talks in the UN about both situations. Great Britain played only a small role. With their new energy independence because of the oil fields in the North Sea, they were becoming somewhat isolationist. There was a move to bring as many of her subjects back to the islands as they could persuade.

The British Navy was in a building phase, with many of the current vessels being used as convoy escorts as the trade between Great

Britain and other nations was more and more being conducted with British merchant marine vessels only. With the problems of piracy and terrorism, the ships needed protection.

There had been several confirmed reports of a rogue submarine preying on shipping in the South Pacific. It was still not known from which country the submarine originated. No country admitted to the defection of any submarine crews. The rogue was stopping lone ships on the high seas. They were taking over the ship and selling the cargos in the small ports of the Pacific. So far, no ships had been sunk, but a few crews had been massacred when they tried to resist.

When the news was over, Percy turned on the computer in the den and pulled up the lists of emergency supplies he had on hand. All the items were up to the levels he had kept for years. The items were all used in rotation, the oldest being used as new stocks were added to the stores. For essentially everything they used that they didn't produce themselves Percy maintained a minimum of a six month supply. He decided to extend that time to a year, minimum.

By the time he went to bed that evening, Percy had a long shopping list. The next morning he went to see the Bluhms. They were doing some minor medical work at the old clinic, but the facilities weren't the best. They were seeing people in the old clinic three days a week, and then working at the county hospital in the city two days a week taking care of patients they couldn't treat in the clinic, which were many.

Percy talked to the couple for a long time. By the time he left and headed for the city, he'd arranged with them to allow him to stock an extensive line of medications, almost a small pharmacy, at the estate. In addition to the medications, they were willing to have him stock some tools and equipment for their use, in case of emergencies. Percy gave them permission to check on the status of all of it at any time, so they would know he wasn't using any of the items. They were strictly for the doctors' use in emergencies.

He'd done something similar with his regular doctor in the city, but to a much lesser extent. The pharmacist wasn't that surprised when Percy took in the prescriptions to have them filled. While that was being done, Percy filled a cart with the over-the-counter items the two doctors had recommended.

Percy added a few choices of his own, plus plenty of standard first aid supplies. He already had an extensive first aid kit, trauma kit, and what he called his Only-Aid aid kit, at the estate.

Each licensed vehicle had extensive first aid and trauma kits as well as a pair of ten-pound fire extinguishers. Bernard was a trained extinguisher service technician. There were supplies and equipment in the equipment barn to refill the extinguishers in the vehicles, and the others placed around the estate.

When he stopped at the medical supply shop, they wouldn't fill the prescriptions for the dozen bottles of medical oxygen, two sets of regulators and masks, and two oxygen concentrators. It took a few calls, but when Jock had called the hospital and the hospital administrator had called the supply house, Percy was finally able to pay for the items and arrange for delivery to the estate.

Percy included a few items that didn't require prescriptions, which the shop was happy to sell him when they saw that it was a legitimate sale for the oxygen supplies. Very happy. Percy dropped a bundle on medical equipment. If things went well, he'd just donate it to the clinic when it was finished and write the expense off on his taxes.

Feeling a bit better, Percy headed for one of the big discount stores, saw the nearly full parking lot and changed his mind. "This would be a good job for Mattie, Susie, and the twins," Percy muttered to himself. Having decided to let the others do some of the shopping, Percy impulsively went by the state building to see Sara. She was delighted to go to lunch with him and insisted on paying, despite his strong protest.

Mattie looked at him strangely when he entered the house that evening, whistling cheerfully. "You sound cheerful, boss. What's going on?"

"Hey," protested Percy. "I'm cheerful a lot. You make it sound like it's a rare occasion."

"You're avoiding the issue."

"Well, if you must know, I accomplished a few things in the city and had lunch with Mrs. McLain."

Mattie smiled. "Well good for you. What should I expect to be getting delivered?"

"How do you know I ordered anything for delivery?" Percy asked.

"You're on another buying jag. Because of the news. I remember what happened when the first Gulf War started. You did the same thing."

Percy had to acknowledge the truth of the statement. He'd had similar feelings of possible trouble at the time and nothing had come of it. They'd just rotated the extra supplies through the normal course of consumption until the stocks were back to the normal six-month supply. He'd started the bee barn and orchard barn at that time, come to think of it, Percy thought.

"I guess you're right," he said. "You know me too well, Mattie. Uh… Try not to give all my secrets away to Sara, okay?"

Mattie's mouth dropped open in surprise. That sounded like Percy was actually getting serious about Sara McLain. He was out the door before she could think of anything to say.

Percy went out and looked around the property. He'd always meant to have another barn and shop. The equipment barn was relatively full now and it'd be nice to have a larger shop area. There was space between the product barn and the equipment barn. Also over by the animal barn. "It wouldn't hurt to have a utility barn to use for whatever," Percy said aloud.

Percy went back to the house and into the den. It took only a single call to order the two reinforced concrete dome structures. Another call got a promise from David Reynolds to start moving sand, gravel, and dirt from his pit to the estate. It would be used to build up the areas slightly, then mound over the dome structures when they were completed. Like the other structures on the estate, a large walled patio would be built atop the mounded over buildings to provide additional useable space.

Percy made another call, this one to a concrete supplier in the city. He ordered enough sections of pedestrian underpass to connect the new buildings to the existing tunnels that ran between all the buildings. He'd get the trenches dug and the tunnels installed before work began on the domes. It wouldn't take long, or much in materials. One tunnel would tee off the tunnel to the equipment barn and the other would tee off the tunnel between the animal barn and the bulk storage barn.

There was no problem getting the financing for the estate additions. Percy had great credit and he was only financing half the cost, as he usually did, for this type of major project. Just a call to the bank whose turn it was this time to get the business and the papers were going to be prepared for his signature the next day.

Percy began the site preparation that day. He attached the big backhoe to one of the Unimogs and had Bernard attach the hoe for the Bobcat. Between them, they had the trenches for the tunnels dug by that evening. There was still a small stockpile of sand from the last project and he and Bernard dismounted the backhoes and attached buckets to the machines. The next morning they had a bed of sand in place when the first sections of the pedestrian underpass arrived.

Jim Hanson had taken one of the Unimogs with the stake bed on it to pick up drainpipe and several bags of Quikrete. They installed it along each side of the tunnel sections and tied it into the existing pipe system that drained off any water from around the tunnels to minimize the chance of leaks. The joints of the sections of tunnel were sealed with bitumen, but Percy wanted them as dry as possible.

The tunnels, besides being access from one structure to another during severe weather, was a conduit for the cabling that linked them with power, phone, computer, intercom, and video. Each structure has its own set of environmental sensors for temperature, humidity, and such. The information was available at any of the networked computers the estate boasted.

Sensors mounted on one of the antenna towers sent data to a central weather station, also tied into the computer, to collect site weather information. The towers also carried, besides the television, business band, shortwave, and amateur radio antennas, four cameras mounted to give three hundred sixty degree views of the estate from each of the three sixty foot tall freestanding towers. Those images, like the environmental data, were viewable on any of the estate's computers.

Bernard and Percy back filled the trenches around the tunnel sections as they were installed, using sand against the tunnels for the drainage and with the rest of each lift of fill the dirt that had been excavated from the trench. Percy had Bernard using the 5600T with a bucket for backfilling while he used a Unimog. Jim used the A300 Bobcat with a sheep's foot roller to compact the backfill.

It didn't take long to build the forms around the ends of the tunnels to form the entrances into the new buildings and the joints to the existing pipe. They had the old forms from previous building projects.

Using the concrete mixer attachment mounted to the A300, they mixed the Quikrete with water and poured it in the prepared forms at the tunnel junctions. They would be allowed to set for two days before the forms were removed and that section of the trench backfilled. The entrance sections would be poured when the small partial basements and the floors were poured for the domes.

The next day they stripped the topsoil from the areas the new structures would occupy and stockpiled it nearby. They used the material that David Reynolds began delivering to build up the areas to two feet higher than the natural ground level. A little water was sprayed onto the fill and

Jim ran the A300 with the compactor over and over each four-inch layer that was laid down.

By the time the dome builders arrived a week later, the sites were ready for their forms for the perimeter ring and floor. Percy had a carpenter come out and install the forms for the small basement rooms that connected with the tunnels.

The ready mix company delivered and poured the necessary concrete. It would be another week before the dome bladder could be attached to the perimeter ring and inflated, in preparation for blowing on the foam insulation. Rebar would be attached to the foam, and then shotcrete would be blown onto the rebar until the dome was complete. The dome builders would leave and Percy would have crews come in to finish the interiors while he and his hands mounded the dome with earth.

Another crew would install the four-foot high patio walls and the slab when the dome was covered, then Percy would add more earth up to the tops of the top patio walls. It went pretty much as planned, except Percy had David Reynolds do quite a bit of the earthwork. He and the hands were too busy with truck farm business to finish the project as quickly as Percy wanted it done.

By the end of May, the basic structures were finished. Percy found himself at a slight loss as to how to finish them out. He did decide to move the shop from the Equipment Barn to the one dome, expanding its scope in the process. The other structure, with things a bit more stable on the world political scene and the weather behaving more or less normally, Percy decided to simply paint the interior and leave it as it was for the moment. The fixtures for the large bathroom were installed and electrical outlets and lights were added near the entrance panel, but that was the limit to the additions.

Construction was well under way on the new clinic and the Bluhms new house. Percy checked on them from time to time and had the Bluhms over at least once every two weeks to get an update on things.

He was beginning to feel a little foolish by the middle of June. Nothing out of the ordinary had happened and he had huge stocks of pretty much everything, a new empty barn, and a fantastic new shop, with more room in the equipment barn than the vehicles required.

Percy was being both lauded and joked about. He was accustomed to the joking. The praise about his contribution to the clinic was not so familiar. The Bluhms made no bones about the fact that they and the clinic wouldn't be, if it hadn't been for Percy.

Despite all that, Percy didn't allow his level of preparation to go back to where it had been. He kept buying at the same levels as he had before, including fuel, keeping the diesel tanks topped off at almost ten thousand gallons of red, untaxed diesel, and a thousand gallons of clear, taxed diesel, in each of the tank farms. They continued to buy household and estate goods at the usage levels, keeping the level of the stocks where they were.

The tank semi trailers were finally delivered, after a delay due to material shortages. As summer came and the droughts started, Percy hired Andrew Buchanan to take one of the trailers to a town across the state with a load of potable water for the residents when their well gave out. Andy stayed in the area and shuttled water for two weeks until a new well, already under construction, was finished. Andy made it back in time for the Fourth of July ribbon cutting dedication ceremony and open house for the clinic.

With the help of Sara, Jock, and, Melissa, Tom finally convinced Percy to make a short speech at the dedication. It was a very short speech. It surprised a few people, not for its shortness, which was expected, but for its eloquence. The main reason Percy had done what he had wasn't mentioned at all, preparedness in terms of the global situation. Instead, he spoke of small town cohesiveness, family values, and the pleasantness of small town life.

Good a speech as it was, it probably wouldn't have been a standing ovation, except everyone was standing outside the entrance to the clinic, anyway. The clinic wasn't finished, but the building was. Some additional equipment required installation, but that was all for the clinic to be ready. There had been a concerted effort to get the clinic finished in time for the Fourth of July Celebration. A brand new big-city-style shuttle van with a wheelchair lift was parked in front of the clinic.

Percy had been instrumental in getting the grant that paid for it, as well as one that helped finance the clinic. He might still be able to retire in another year or so. The trust could be dissolved in a year.

Susie brought up the team of Clydesdales, hooked to the decked out farm wagon, and Tom, the doctors, Percy, Sara, and a handful of the city council and clinic committee members rode back to town in it, with Susie driving. When they arrived back in town, the wagon led the Fourth of July parade from that side of town to the town's park.

Percy took the team and wagon back to the estate rather early. He wanted to see the news. A report he'd heard when he was getting ready for the dedication had him worried again. There'd been nothing on the satellite radio news station, but it had sounded serious.

It was. When the wagon and horses were put away, Percy hurried into the house to check the news. It was India and Pakistan again. The skirmishes had not been going well for Pakistan. They had issued an ultimatum for India to withdraw from the border area and resume talks to resolve the issue. So far, India had not responded to the implied threat of the use of nuclear weapons in the conflict.

Mattie, Susie, and Sara showed up a few minutes later. Percy was already back outside, checking the estate's state of preparation. The city TV station was forecasting severe thunderstorms for that evening and night. This was the first chance of heavy rains since early spring and Percy wanted the gates open on the irrigation canals to collect all the rainwater in the system that he could. The pond was almost empty. They'd used the wells the last time the fields needed irrigation.

"Are you all right?" Sara asked Percy when he came back into the house, her hand going to his upper arm, her eyes searching his face.

He forced a smile. "You know I don't like giving speeches like that. Come on, let's cut that watermelon I've had on ice for two days. It should be a prizewinner. The crops are doing well this year, despite the drought conditions."

Sara could tell he wasn't being completely open with her, but she let it pass. They'd become closer over the past few months. He'd open up to her fully one of these days.

Concerned about the weather, Percy rushed Sara off back to the city early that afternoon. She had to work the next day. As always, now, he topped off the fuel tank of her car. Mattie and Susie drifted over to their cottage a bit earlier than planned when Percy went out to take care of the animals for the night after Sara left.

"He's worried about something, isn't he?" Susie asked her mother as they entered the two-bedroom earth sheltered dome home they'd lived in since Susie was a baby.

"Yes. Did you see anyone say anything to him at the dedication or the park?"

Susie shook her head. "He seemed to be having a good time. I was a little surprised he came back as early as he did. He was having a good time giving rides to the kids with the team and wagon. Everybody loves those Clydesdales."

Mattie had turned the TV on when they entered the house. "Uh-oh," she said softly. "I think I know what has him upset." She motioned to the TV and turned up the sound with the remote.

The two watched a similar report to that Percy had seen. They exchanged a look after the report was over. "I'm glad we live here on the estate, Mother," Susie said. "I feel safe here. I never thought about it much those other times."

"Yeah," Mattie said, pulling her daughter in for a hug like they hadn't shared for a long time. "Me, too."

Before Percy turned in that evening, he checked the news channels again. Things didn't look any better. He wracked his brain for additional preparations he could make. He couldn't think of any. He was as prepared as he knew how, for whatever might come. "Natural or manmade," he said aloud as he climbed into bed.

CHAPTER TEN

Calvin knew the proposal he'd but together for the bank was a good one. He should know. He looked at similar proposals nearly every day. It was part of his job at the bank where he worked. Of course, to avoid any chance of a conflict of interest, though he had an account at the bank where he worked, he went to the other bank he used for the loan. Knowing the banking system, he always kept two bank accounts. Each bank had to be under completely different ownership.

He definitely knew how to put things in the best light, which he did, while keeping everything very straightforward and above board. It took only three days to get the initial okay from the initial loan officer, but it would have to go up a step, since the amount was large.

Apparently his and Nan's backgrounds checked out. So did the worth of the equipment. Nan told him that the bank had called and talked to Mr. Anderson for quite some time one day. The loan was approved and the money deposited in the account he kept in that bank. A few more days and the equipment was ordered.

Since they would be using it mostly in town, and the road was marginal to their place,

Calvin had it delivered to the Anderson equipment yard. The delivery driver unloaded the Bobcats, and then used the A300 to unload the attachments.

The Unimog was delivered the very next day by another truck. The same procedure was used. The lift arms were already in place on the Unimog. The driver used it to unload the attachments he'd ordered with the truck. The other attachments showed up one at a time over the next few days.

Mr. Anderson tried not to show his wonder at the equipment, but was not entirely successful as Calvin tried everything out the weekend after the major pieces had arrived. Everything worked as advertised. They used the A300 with backhoe to install a septic system for one of Mr. Anderson's regular customers. The Toolcat was used to do the backfill work. The Unimog pulled the equipment trailer with the two Bobcats and associated equipment without a problem.

The branch of the bank where Calvin worked was closed for the scheduled rolling blackout. Calvin took advantage of the weekday and he, Nan, and Mr. Anderson made some major improvements on the road, particularly the stretch from their house to the section on which the Calhoun's would provide some maintenance.

Calvin and Nan had talked it over and decided they didn't want it too easy for people to get to their place. As long as the road was passable, that was all they wanted, at least on the county road end.

Even though he'd used it only a few times, Mr. Anderson quickly mastered the A300 and the other two pieces of equipment. Nan had picked up the nuances quickly, as well. It was early afternoon when they called it quits and drove the equipment back to the house.

"You did good, boy," Mr. Anderson told Calvin as they parked the equipment. "You too, missy. We got more work done today... good work... than I could have done with my equipment in a week. You made a good choice."

"Thank you, Mr. Anderson," replied Calvin. "I appreciate your help on this. Why don't you call your wife and tell her that Nan and I are taking the two of you out for dinner in town."

"Well, that would be nice. Diner has fried catfish and hushpuppies as the special tonight. It's always pretty good, considering how far we are from a good catfish river."

"That sounds just fine to us," Nan replied. "We'll meet you there, say about five?"

"That'll be good. Yep. You did good, boy."

With a wave Mr. Anderson climbed into his beat up old Dodge and headed back to town.

Nan put her arms around Calvin's neck and leaned in against him. "Going pretty good, I'd say," she said. "Wouldn't you agree?"

"I certainly would. I knew intellectually how well things should work, but the last couple of weeks have been an eye opener. There is a huge amount of work available for the equipment. Things that Mr. Anderson never bothered to do since he didn't have a good way to do them. There is going to be plenty of work to keep us busy, especially with the woodlot thinning business."

"Why don't you put in for shorter hours now? I know we weren't going to do that 'til next spring, but with what we've seen, I think it will be okay."

Calvin kissed her, his hands on her hips, before he replied. "I think you're right. And I want to help Mr. Anderson. His health is a lot worse than I realized."

This time Nan kissed Calvin. "Good. That's settled. Let's get cleaned up and get ready to go into town."

CHAPTER ELEVEN

Buddy was surprised when Charlene called him early Saturday morning. "I don't have anything planned today, Buddy. I was wondering if you wanted some company when you go up to see the property."

"I hadn't thought about it. But sure, if you want to. I don't mind. I'll pick you up in a little while."

Charlene smiled when she hung up the phone. Her part time clerk had been willing to work one Saturday. The emphasis on one. It took her only a few minutes to dress in jeans and a flannel shirt and her walking shoes. She grabbed a light jacket and hurried out when Buddy honked his horn.

She had no trouble clambering up into the truck on the passenger side. As she belted herself in Buddy said, "Have to stop at the barbershop to get the directions. I got a map from the realtor, but she wasn't much help otherwise. I don't think she cares if it is sold or not."

"Who is the realtor?" Charlene asked.

When Buddy told her she frowned. "That's who I bought my house through. They weren't very good, in my opinion."

"I sure wouldn't use them," Buddy said. When they pulled up in front of the barbershop Buddy parked the truck and said, "It'll just be a minute. I'll be right back." He hopped out of the truck and went into the barbershop.

It took three minutes rather than one, but Charlene didn't mind. Buddy had a sheaf of papers in his hand when he re-entered the truck. He handed the papers to Charlene to look through as he headed out of town.

"Thirty-seven point three acres," Charlene said. "That's a pretty large piece of property. "You really want something that big?"

"If it's mostly wooded, yeah, I think so. It is going to depend on exactly what the land is like. I know basically what I want. I'll just have to see what the property looks like and if I can do what I want with it."

They rode in silence for a while, Charlene reading the next set of directions when Buddy asked. They left the city on the state road, then another, then onto a paved county road. They had been climbing slowly as they went. When they turned onto the graveled county road the climb became steeper for the most part, though there were ups and downs.

"That must be it," Charlene said, pointing to a rather substantial gate in the fence that paralleled the road on their left. The gate was set back somewhat from the road to allow room to pull in and stop to get out and open the gate. Charlene handed Buddy the key that had been in an envelope that was part of the packet.

He came back to the truck without opening the gate. When Charlene rolled down the window Buddy told her, "Locks rusted solid. Bobby thought it might be. It's a cheap lock. He said to cut it and just bolt it back up. The land owner will need to put another on."

"This isn't where Bobby's land starts?"

"Oh, no. Look at that next page of directions." Buddy went to the tool box in the back of the truck and took out a pair of bolt cutters.

When he passed the window on his way back to the gate Charlene told him, "I see what you mean. We still have a ways to go."

Buddy nodded, and then went to cut the lock. When he had the gate open he looked back and motioned to Charlene. She quickly moved over to the driver's seat and drove the truck through the gate opening. She changed back to the passenger seat as Buddy closed the gate and wrapped the chain around the post, fastening a long bolt through the end links and tightening it finger tight.

It was only a few moments more and Buddy had put the bolt cutters away and was back behind the wheel of the truck. "Okay," he said, "Let me take a look at that last page of directions again."

Buddy studied the handwritten directions, looking up occasionally at the heavily wooded hills before them. "Okay," he said, "I see the first landmark." He pointed to a dead tree leaning against another still growing tree. "We jog north just past that dead tree. When we get there, remind me again what the next landmark is." He handed the directions back to Charlene.

There was a hint of a pair of tracks leading to that first landmark, but by the third landmark they had faded to nothing. Even with Charlene acting as navigator and helping watch for the landmarks, they had to backtrack twice before they got to the Bobby's property line. Some of the way had been over grassy terrain, but much of it was bare earth with outcroppings of rocks. The truck had no difficulty with the terrain.

Bobby had insisted on a survey when he bought the property and one of the benchmarks was obvious when they got there. Buddy found a decent place to park and stopped the truck. The two got out and looked around. There wasn't that much to see. They had come through a stand of trees, the path just wide enough for

Buddy to navigate. All they could see was the small open area and the trees around it.

With yet another sheet of paper in hand, this one the plot of the property, Buddy pointed toward what might be another open area in the trees ahead and started in that direction, up a slight grade. Charlene quickly moved up to his side, zipping her jacket as she went. It was cool in the forest.

When they stepped into that next clearing both stopped. The clearing was large and nearly flat. They had to scramble up several feet to get on the meadow proper. Though there was a thin layer of soil that supported grass, it was obvious trees couldn't grow. There were outcroppings of rock all over.

Though the site was relatively flat, as they journeyed across, it was quickly obvious they were on a slope. When they reached the tree line of the other side of the meadow both turned around. "Oh, my!" Charlene exclaimed softly.

"Yeah," agreed Buddy. Almost due south of where they stood, past the drop off, the land fell away quickly. The tree tops were below their line of sight, exposing the vista of the distant river and the city built on both sides of it. A couple of distant small towns were discernable, as was a long stretch of the interstate.

"Is that… is that the gate?" Charlene asked, pointing off along the left edge of the low tops of the trees.

"I don't know. Maybe." Buddy took a pair of compact binoculars from his jacket pocket. "I can't believe it! That is the gate. Man, you have good eyes." He handed the binoculars to Charlene.

Charlene smiled as she took a look through the binoculars.

"Get a little higher and you could see the first hundred yards or so of the trail, as well as the gate and the stretch of road. Man. And look at this southern exposure. And the trees all around. Plenty of firewood for years if it's managed well. This looks great! What do you think?"

Buddy's enthusiasm was catching. It was beautiful up here, for sure. She didn't realize they had climbed so high until she'd seen the vista. "It is beautiful. I'm not 100% sure exactly what you were looking for, but you sure seem like you found it."

"Too true." Buddy turned and went into the stand of trees to the north. There should be another boundary marker somewhere in this direction. Charlene handed Buddy the binoculars and strode beside him as he roamed over the acreage.

She was tired, but exhilarated when they got back to the truck. Buddy had exclaimed about feature after feature of the terrain. It really was pretty, but that had been the least of Buddy's concerns it was now obvious.

Buddy turned the truck around and they headed home. "I know it wouldn't be suitable for most people, what with the lack of good access and utilities, but it has almost everything I want. For me, it would be worth double what it's listing for. I'll gladly pay the asking price."

"Good," replied Charlene. "I'm glad it's what you were looking for. I must say, I haven't been up in the mountains for a long time. I'd forgotten how much cooler it could be up this high. And doesn't the snow hang around well into summer up here? I'm still trying to picture what it looks like here from the city."

"Snow does hang around longer due to the altitude, but it's on the other side of this range that really holds it, because it's the north side. This south facing slope gets lots of sunshine. And Bobby was right about the wind. It'll be perfect for a wind-powered generator. Solar panels, too, eventually. Photovoltaic panels, I mean. I'd build solar panels for space heating and water heating initially.

Charlene sat quietly, responding to Buddy as needed from time to time as he explained what he wanted to do with the property. It was late in the afternoon when they got back to the city. Buddy had brought along a couple of canteens, so they'd had water, but they were both very hungry when they got to town.

Buddy dropped off the papers at the barbershop. Bobby only worked a couple hours in the morning on Saturdays so he was long gone. When Buddy got back into the truck he looked over at Charlene and said, "I'm starving. You want to stop and get something to eat at The Steakhouse?"

"Sure," Charlene replied, content to spend the time with Buddy.

CHAPTER TWELVE

Charlie took the ten dollars from the grounds man at the country club golf course. He'd helped him rebuild a storage shed on the back nine. He'd seen the ad for the job on the community bulletin board at the grocery store where he'd restocked a few food items with his small amount of cash.

There was a construction site nearby in which he'd found several large drainage pipes stacked out of the way with some pallets of stuff stacked at one end. There was a gap in the fence they didn't seem too anxious about, so he'd started sleeping in one of the pipes. There were chemical toilet huts on site so he had a good bathroom. He was careful to only be around after hours. He left before the guys came to work and went back after they left.

The YMCA wasn't too far away and he'd been able to get a shower and change into his good clothes before he went to the golf course. He carried one of his buckets with the few tools he had in it. It was a long shot that paid off. The grounds man had seen his professional grade hammer and hired him for the job.

"Charlie, why don't you come back tomorrow. I've got a couple more projects I could use some help with until my helper gets over the flu."

"Sure, Mr. Cunningham. I'd be proud to. Thank you."

"Okay then. I'll see you in the morning. I'll let the gateman know you're coming so there won't be a problem at the gate. Oh. You won't need your tools tomorrow. We'll be using the course's stuff."

"Okay, Boss. I'll see you tomorrow."

Charlie's steps lagged when he saw the man waiting near the drainage pipes. Maybe he would at least let Charlie get some of his stuff. Charlie stopped a few feet away from the man, in case he tried something. Charlie would have a better chance of getting away with some distance between them.

The man dropped his cigarette to the ground and put it out with his boot. "You the one been staying here?"

The light was beginning to fade, but the man could see Charlie nod. "How long?" the man asked, hitching up his pants.

Charlie got ready to run. "A week. I'll get my stuff and get out of here. I don't want any trouble."

"You take anything?"

Tense, still ready to drop the bucket and run, Charlie shook his head. "No sir. I'm not a thief. I'm homeless but no thief. I even worked today. Out at the golf course."

"I see. You seen anyone else hanging around when we're not here?"

"No sir."

"How long you plan on being here?"

Charlie watched the man for a few moments. "If there wasn't any trouble I was planning on moving on when they got ready to install the pipes."

The man nodded and lit up another cigarette. "I'm not going to give you a hard time. But if anything turns up missing I'm gonna be on you like a duck on a June bug. You understand me?"

"Yes sir. Thank you. But I better just get my stuff and go. I don't want to be in the middle of trouble if something does turn up missing. That's not unusual in an operation like this." Charlie began to gather the few things he left in the pipe each day.

"Wait. You're right, I guess," the man said. "Look. Just don't cause any trouble and I'll leave you alone. I can't guarantee about anyone else, especially the cops, but nobody here will hassle you if you don't cause the problem."

"Wow!" Charlie said softly. "Thanks, man." He held out his hand.

After a moment the man took it in a firm handshake. "I'm Clyde. Keep your nose clean and there won't be any problems. Keep a low profile. I can't say my bosses would do the same."

"You'll barely know I'm around," Charlie replied.

Clyde turned and headed for his pickup truck, parked just outside the gate of the security fence.

CHAPTER THIRTEEN

Having another period of free time, Edward went to the website he'd been in before. He whistled when he saw the costs of the various shelter systems. It wasn't like he couldn't afford it. He could. But it was still a lot of money for something that would probably never be used. Though, with the things he'd been seeing in the news lately, that thought was changing significantly.

When he'd talked to the Tennessee banker, after finally recalling his name, the man had said he had purchased a top of the line six-person model. Edward frowned as he studied the specifications on the computer screen. The six-person would certainly work for him. It was only him, his wife, and the two kids. Even if he took in Courtney... Still... The other bankers weren't anywhere near as well off as Edward. Edward owned two banks and was having a new branch built. The others only owned, at best, one bank. Most were actually just mangers at small independent chain banks.

Edward started to smile. His wife Emily would have a cow when Courtney showed up, if anything ever happened. But that scene would be minor when Doc Cutter and his wife showed up. He played golf with the doctor nearly every week. The last time they'd played, much of the discussion had been about the goings-on in the world.

Doc lived in a luxury apartment building downtown. Edward had been trying to get him to transfer at least a portion, if not all, of the man's inheritance from the bank he was using to one or both of Edward's. With the man's concern about everything, he might just be willing to transfer some of his millions for a spot in the shelter.

Emily despised both the doctor and his wife. "She'll just have to have two cows," Edward thought to himself as he grinned. One for Courtney and one for the Cutters. "The ten-person, deluxe, with all the extras," Edward said aloud. He began entering the information on the website to get an official quote.

CHAPTER FOURTEEN

They didn't feel the effect of storms much in the earth-sheltered buildings they lived in and worked in, but it was obvious when Percy went out the next morning that they were in the middle of a bad storm.

He ran over to the equipment barn to see if the hands were there. They were, dry and secure. Bob Hansen grinned at him. "You're all wet, boss," he said, stating the obvious.

"Yeah," Bernard said. "Why didn't you use the tunnel? We did. That rain is cold!"

"Next time," Percy replied resettling his hat on his head. He'd had to grab it when he ran over. The wind was wicked. Looking out one of the open equipment doors, he saw Smitty Smith and John Jacobson both drive up, then into the barn.

"Mornin' gentlemen," Percy said when the two had exited their respective vehicles. John a diehard Ford driver, Smitty in his Chevy. Bernard stayed with Dodges. His was parked in the parking lot at the bunkhouse. And of course, Jim and Bob loved their Jeep. Mattie had her old Volvo that was a bit ugly but ran like new, and Susie a Subaru wagon.

Quite an eclectic group of vehicles, particularly when you added Percy's Suburban and the car he very seldom drove, a mint condition 1974 Cadillac Fleetwood Talisman. And that didn't include Percy's other light vehicles, the Kenworths, the Unimogs, the Rokon's, and the two Bobcats. Though, the last two, the Rokon's and Bobcats weren't vehicles so much as pieces of equipment, even though the Rokon's were capable of traveling almost forty miles an hour, though Percy had never had one of them up to that speed.

Percy turned his attention back to the group as Susie joined them. She, like Jim, Bob, and Bernard, had used the tunnels. Susie really didn't like using them, but she liked storms even less, and it was storming violently now.

"Considering the weather... and the hail," Percy added as golf ball sized hail began landing on the ground outside, let's go through all the mobile equipment and service it. Rearrange things a little in here. Oh. And exercise everything a little. We haven't used some of the equipment in a while, especially the features of the Kenworth utility truck."

They'd quit using the utility/service truck in the orchards when Percy bought two three-wheel, hydraulically driven cherry picker style basket lifts. They worked much better in the orchards than the big truck. They were equipped with hydraulic outlets in the baskets to power trimming saws, pruners, and similar items used in the orchard. The operator controlled everything from the basket. The machines were mobile enough to travel throughout the orchard easily and quickly using a hydraulic drive system.

The tree fruit crops were going to be large this year, despite the drought, since they'd irrigated heavily. There had been a lot of thinning to do to ensure a high quality crop. Percy had owned a similar machine previously, but it had quit on him and he'd disposed of it about the time he got the Kenworth service truck. While it worked okay in the orchards, it was overkill for the tasks required. The two lifts were much easier to use than the Kenworth, as they only required one operator. The Kenworth really needed two to be effective.

Despite the fact that the greenhouses were constructed with extruded polycarbonate panels, Percy didn't want the hands working in them with the hail coming down the way it was. So they worked on the equipment, having a rather good time doing it. There was no need to worry about the damage the crops might suffer. They were not able to do anything about the situation now. Percy would check the fields when the weather broke.

The forecast and Percy's own weather instruments indicated the same thing. The storm system would continue to dump rain for at least another day. When they'd finished for the day, Percy told everyone they could take the next day off, he'd tend the animals. They'd done pretty much everything that needed doing in the equipment barn.

As he and Susie walked back to the house through the tunnel, Susie asked Percy, "Mr. Jackson, could I talk to you for a few minutes when we get to the house? I need some advice."

"Sure, Susie. Anytime. You know that."

When they were in the den, Susie started pacing when Percy sat down behind his desk. "What's on your mind, Susie?"

"You know, you've been like a father to me, all these years. I kind of wanted to say thank you, besides just asking for more advice."

"Well, thank you, Susie. I've never tried to substitute for your father, just be available when you needed something."

"That's what good fathers do," Susie replied. She sat down on the large button tufted leather Chesterfield sofa, her hands going between her knees as she sat on the edge of the sofa. "It's about Andy, Mr. Jackson."

"Uh… Perhaps you should talk to your mother about this," Percy said hesitatingly.

Susie turned red and said, "It's not about that!" She started again. "It's that I think Andy may ask me to marry him. What do you think I should do?"

"Susie, that is totally up to you. But if you want some advice on the subject, I suggest you make a list..."

Susie grinned. Percy was big on lists. He made lots of them.

"One side, list the positives if you decide to marry him, and on the other, the negatives. It's a little clinical and cold, but since you know full well where your heart is, it's about the only suggestion I can give you."

"Would you help me?" Susie asked. She smiled again. "You're really good with lists."

"I suppose I could, if you want me to do so. Some of the items will be a little personal. You might want to list those after we do our list."

"Like what?" Susie asked, sitting back on the sofa now."

Percy turned pink. "Well, there's sex, for one. Is that going to be a positive or negative? See why you should do this on your own?"

Susie had turned slightly red herself, again. But Percy was right, she knew. Sex was a factor. "A positive," she said after a moment. Percy was careful not to look at her for a while as they continued with the list.

"Do you both want children, or is there a difference of opinion there?" Percy asked next.

"Well, I kind of want to have… maybe two… pretty soon. Andy is more inclined to think a couple should wait until they are well established. Is there an in-between column?"

"If you say there is, there is," Percy replied, adding another column heading to the paper on which he was writing. "What do you really want in a husband, Susie?"

Susie sighed. "I guess what every woman wants. Faithfulness. Someone that will take care of me, but not be pushy about it. Someone that can take care of me. I mean, I plan to work and all, for a long time, but having kids, now or later, is a big financial responsibility. Raising kids is a big responsibility. All those things. Oh, and he has to love me, of course."

"Of course," Percy said. "Do you think he does?"

"I think so," Susie replied. "I know I love him. He's so much fun to be around. He treats me nice, but doesn't insist on paying for everything every time. He lets me contribute to the things we decide to do. And we do decide. Neither one of us just says. We discuss stuff."

"Have you discussed this with him?"

"No, not really. It's just been some signs recently… I talked to Mother, and she said talk to you. You're a guy. You could give me some insights."

"Yeah. Maybe," Percy said with a wry smile. "You do know I've never had much success with women."

"Mother mentioned that things didn't go well with you and Abigail." Susie hurriedly added when she saw the look on Percy's face, "She didn't say much; just that she didn't think it was your fault. That's pretty much all she said."

"Oh. Okay. Well, anyway... You say you can talk things over with him. That should go in the plus side, don't you think?"

"Of course."

"His responsibility. Do you think he's personally responsible and financially responsible?"

"Personally he's very responsible. Financially... Well, he's saving money. I know that. But every once in a while he gets the hots for some techno thing. He gives in to it part of the time. Right now he wants a Rokon so bad he can taste it. Part of the reason he wants to borrow one of yours is to see for sure if he wants it. I think he'll buy one if it works the way I know it will. They are very good machines. And fun. But still..."

"So personal responsibility in the positive. Financial… Negative or in between."

"In between," Susie said immediately.

"What about the other side of financial responsibility. There's spending, but there's also earning."

"Oh, he's really good about finding and keeping jobs. He's had a couple, I know, but he was laid off the one for lack of work, and the other… the guy wasn't honest. He's had the job with Wilkins Oil now for two years. And he got the CDL. He's worked for you a couple of times before that, and since, driving the Kenworth tractor. And he's taking correspondence courses for a business degree. He just couldn't afford to go to college. I mean he's smart, but he missed so much school his senior year when he broke his leg in that football game. He would have got at least a couple of scholarships, except for that. He loves to learn, but he loves working, too."

"I know he's tried really hard to make up for the lack of college. I know how he feels," Percy said. "So that part of financial responsibility in under the positive heading."

"Definitely."

"Now I know you love him, you said so, but he's like me. Not the most handsome of men. What about the looks of the children. You're a pretty girl. You want your daughter, or even son, to look like him?"

"Hey!" protested Susie. "He's not that bad looking. He got his share of dates in high school. I don't think our kids will be that bad looking."

"Okay. Positive or in between."

"Well... in between, I guess."

"You mentioned he had lots of dates in high school. You mentioned faithfulness. Do you think he'll be faithful?"

There was no hesitation. "He will be. He looks at other girls, just as I do guys when a good-looking one passes by, but he hasn't dated anyone but me, since we started going out. I'm sure of it."

"Faithfulness in the positive column," Percy said, marking it down.

They were laughing by the time they finished, the last few items on the list rather silly.

"What should I do based on the list?" Susie asked the laughter fading.

"That's still up to you," Percy said. He tossed the yellow pad to her.

"Oh my," she said softly, seeing the list. "I may just have to marry him, if he asks," she whispered. She looked up. "I need to go talk to Mother. Thanks, Mr. Jackson, this really helped." She jumped up and ran around the desk to give him a hug and a quick kiss on the cheek. She headed out of the den quickly, the pad still in her hand.

"They sure grow up fast," Percy said softly, turning on the TV. The news wasn't good. The situation between India and Pakistan was still in limbo. China was grumbling about the situation now, too. He decided to see what he could find out on the internet, but it was down again. There'd been a report of power outages in Chicago, one of the major hubs for the internet, though there had been no mention of the internet in the report. Percy suspected that the power outage was the cause of the internet being down.

He was quiet through supper, thoughtful, letting Mattie and Susie discuss Andrew. Percy made a mental note to have Andy come out and pick up the Kenworth and the other tank trailer the next day. He'd have it filled and park it at the tank farm. Start using out of it and keep the other tanks full until the world situation became calmer.

Andy was delighted by the prospect. He was there before noon and back with the load of fuel by two that afternoon. He hung around and helped Percy connect the hoses and top off the stationary tanks from the compartments in the trailer. "I'll let you know when I need you to come out and fill the trailer again, Andrew," Percy said.

"You're really worried about that thing going on in India, aren't you, Mr. Jackson?"

"I am, Andrew, I am. I guess I'm pretty obvious about it, like with this fuel, huh?"

"Not to most. Most people think you're a little strange, anyway."

Percy smiled. They headed back toward Andy's five year old GMC Jimmy. "Uh... Mr. Jackson, can I talk to you for a minute? I need some advice."

"Sure, Andrew. What's up?" Percy wasn't surprised at Andy's response.

"It's about Susie. You know her really well. You're almost like her father. I was wondering..." Andy looked down at the ground for a moment then looked into Percy's eyes, a serious look in his. "What do you think Susie would say if I asked her to get engaged? And... Well... Do you think it would be all right if I did ask her?"

"Andrew, I'm not her father. If you wanted to get permission you should be asking Mrs. Simpson. As to what she would say... Andrew there's no way of knowing until you ask. You obviously love her or you wouldn't be asking me this. Would you say yes if she asked you?"

"I never thought about that!" Andrew replied. "I don't think she would ask, unless I just waited way too long. I'm sure she loves me, but I don't want to ask her if she's going to say no."

"Why not?" Percy asked, gently.

"Well, gee, Mr. Jackson! It'd break my heart if she said no."

"What makes you think she'll say no?" Percy asked then.

"I don't think she will. But… I don't know for sure. I think she'll say yes." He looked around quickly, and then pulled a ring box out of his pocket. "Susie is really practical. She'd certainly want a nice ring, but wouldn't want me to get something I couldn't afford. She's good about keeping my head out of the clouds about stuff I think is neat."

Andy showed Percy the ring, hunching over a little, to hide it from any point of view except Percy's. "Very nice, Andrew. I'm sure she would love it. But you're going to have to offer it to her and ask her before you know for sure. You've said you think she'll say yes. Have you talked to her at all about marriage?"

"Well, kinda. We've commented on other people's marriages a time or two. She seemed really non-committal."

"In that case, next time the situation comes up, why don't you ask her a leading question? If she seems inclined toward marriage more than before, that should tell you what you want to know."

"Hey! That's a great idea, Mr. Jackson! Thanks!" He put the ring box back in his pocket and climbed into the Jimmy. Through the window he asked, "Do you think you'll ever need another hand, Mr. Jackson? Susie likes working here and I sure wouldn't mind working for my father in law." He was grinning when he said it, but Percy was sure there was an element of a real question there.

"You never know, Andrew. I don't need a hand now, but I'd be willing to consider you if I did."

Andy looked surprised. "Really?"

Percy nodded.

"I'll keep it in mind," said Andy. "I want to take good care of my family, and this would be a really good place to do it." With that, Andy turned the Jimmy around and headed for the estate entrance in the now gentle rain.

The smile faded from Percy's face when he went back inside the house. Mattie and Susie were in the house waiting for him. Both of their faces were white.

"Pakistan nuked India," Susie told Percy, her eyes wide. "We saw it on the news over at the cottage while you were outside."

Percy flipped on the main widescreen TV, plus the smaller monitors that flanked each side of the big screen. He'd installed the additional monitors to keep an eye on several of the news channels, the Weather Channel, the local TV station, and the networks, all at once. All of them were reporting the same thing.

Pakistan had used two nuclear devices to attack the cities of Jodhpur and Ahmedabad. One of the stations cut to the UN. The Chinese ambassador was speaking. The translation scrolled across the bottom of the screen.

"Oh, Lord!" Percy breathed out. "This is bad. Very bad." The ambassador had just announced a warning to India not to retaliate against Pakistan. "China is just looking for an excuse to go into India. They want the resources to help fuel their building economy."

"You don't think they'll really do anything, do you?" Mattie asked. "It's unthinkable," she added.

"The Pakistanis thought about it," Percy replied. "There's been a fanatic group trying to take control for months. I suspect they have. Holy Mackerel!" One of the news channel screens suddenly went blank and then the main news desk set came into view. The newsreader was just taking his place behind the desk, putting in his earpiece.

It is unconfirmed at the moment, but we have reason to believe that the capital of Pakistan was just destroyed by a nuclear detonation. There was pandemonium in the background as the news staff tried to get addition information. Percy went to take care of the animals as Mattie and Susie continued to watch the news.

When Percy returned, they filled him in on the most recent information. "India hit back with three nukes," Susie told him. "Islamabad, their nuclear power plant, and where the missiles were launched from, in case they have more, according to the experts."

"Any response from China?" Percy asked.

"Nothing yet," Mattie replied. She rarely used Percy's first name, but she did now. "Percy, would it be all right if we stayed here tonight? I know the cottage is just as safe, but..."

"Of course you can stay here." They heard the doorbell and Percy hurried to answer it. It was the twins.

"We just heard the news," Jim said.

"What do you want us to do, Boss?"

"You can stay here and watch the news with us if you want, otherwise go back to the cottage and try to get plenty of rest. Tomorrow may be a busy day."

The two exchanged a look. "We'll go back to the house and make a couple of calls. Our mother is going to be hysterical. She was in Florida during the Cuban Missile Crisis and is terrified of stuff like this," Bob said.

"If you want, make arrangements to bring her down here to stay with you," Percy said.

"Thanks, boss," Jim said. "We'll try to talk her in to it. It might be a little difficult." The two exchanged another look, and then Jimmy spoke again. "We might have to go get her."

"That's okay. Whatever you need to do. We can handle the estate if we need to," Percy replied.

As the two hurried off, Percy held the door open. Bernard was hurrying over. "Boss, I hate to ask, but my wife is frantic. She wants me to come home."

"Okay, Bernard. You know you're welcome to bring her out here. The other cottage is empty."

"Thanks, boss. I'll try, but she's convinced there's no hope once it starts. And it's definitely started now."

Percy waited until Bernard had left the estate, and then flipped the switches that closed the two pairs of heavy entrance gates. This was the first time Percy had closed them in months, except for their weekly test.

No one was hungry, so Mattie just fixed a light snack for them, and then returned to the den with it to watch the news with Percy and Susie. They finally all went to bed just after midnight, Susie and Mattie sharing one of the guest rooms that had twin beds.

As soon as Percy got up the next morning, he checked the news. Things were getting worse. Germany was demanding the withdrawal of all US troops. France had dispatched additional troops to several of her former colonies, stating it was to maintain the peace in these times of trouble.

The main news story however, was the incursion of North Korea into South Korean territory. The United States was warning North Korea to withdraw immediately. China was warning the world to stay out of the local conflicts. The conflicts were local in nature and the locals would handle them.

The UN Security Council was in emergency session, discussing the situations. According to the reports, the Council would make no announcements until they came to a decision. Percy moved a thirteen-inch TV to the kitchen so they could watch the news while they prepared and had breakfast. The twins came over in the middle of the breakfast to talk to Percy.

"Mr. Jackson, we hate to ask, but Mom doesn't want to come. We need to go back to Minneapolis and try to talk her into coming. We hate to leave you in the lurch, but…" Jim's words faded away.

"We really don't want to leave, but it is our mother…" Bob added softly.

"You don't need to explain," Percy told the brothers. "Take what time you need. Try to get her to come here if you can."

"Believe me, we will," responded Bob. "Thanks, boss. We'll get back as soon as we can."

"Okay. Take care. There's a lot of unrest and fear out there right now. Expect some delays."

"Thanks," Jim added as they headed out the door.

"I'd better get out to the barns," Percy told Mattie and Susie. "I'm expecting John and Smitty to show up at their regular time, since they didn't call." He suddenly looked slightly alarmed. "That's assuming the phones are working." He went over and picked up the receiver of the phone in the kitchen.

He breathed a sigh of relief. "Phones are still working."

"Why wouldn't they be?" Mattie asked, clearing the table. It was obvious Percy wasn't going to eat any more.

"Susie, you can stay in here with your mother if you want. Bring out any new information as it comes in." Percy had stopped his hand on the doorknob.

"I'd rather be working," Susie responded immediately. "Mother, could you bring out any news? We won't be able to hear a radio working in the greenhouses."

"Of course," Mattie replied.

"You really don't have to come out, Susie," Percy told her.

"I'd really rather work," Susie replied.

"Okay. Let's go see if the others are here."

John and Smitty were driving up when Percy and Susie went out. They discussed the situation as they walked to the greenhouses to go to work. Mattie came out once to tell them that the UN had passed a resolution informing China not to interfere, the way China had warned the rest of the world, particularly the United States.

They worked through the day with no additional real news, just speculation and reports of the devastation caused by the five nuclear devices detonated in India and Pakistan.

As they were cleaning up, Smitty Smith asked Percy, "Can I talk to you a minute, Boss?"

They stepped away from the others. "I'm sorry, Percy. I'm going to head for the hills. I have that place up by Yellowstone. Not really a real retreat, as in the Seventies survival craze, but I have a good rock cabin up there and enough supplies for a month. Plenty of game and the laws won't matter if things get as bad as they might."

"I agree with you on that last part," Percy said, knowing he was talking a lost cause. "I'm not so sure that's the best area to be. You know you and your family are welcome here, if things get bad."

"I know, Percy. And I do appreciate it. You have the best setup of anyone around here. But I'm just more comfortable with my own preparations. I just hate to leave you shorthanded, especially if nothing comes of this."

"Don't worry about the estate, Smitty. We'll manage with what we have. If the situation goes bad, it's not going to matter much. We'll just batten down and ride it out."

"That's my plan," Smitty replied. After a moment's hesitation he continued. "I'd understand if you said no, but if everything turns out okay, which I think is a good possibility, I'd like to come back to work when things settle down. If you haven't found a permanent replacement. I really think things are going to be okay, as long as China doesn't do something stupid. I just don't want to take a chance."

"I understand," Percy said. "I feel much the same way, except I'm not as confident as you that China won't involve itself in what's going on. They want India's resources. Either way, don't worry about your job. You'll be welcomed back." Percy forced a grin. "You know there aren't that many people that want to work for a crazy old man like me."

Smitty grinned back. "It's not that bad," he said, "but you do have a point. I'm heading out tomorrow, but if things go the way I think they will, I'll be back in time for fall harvest."

The two shook hands. "Stop by in the morning. I'll have your pay for you. In cash, just in case."

"Don't worry about that, Percy. Just hold it on account for me. I'll be back to collect pretty soon. I'll probably need it more when I get back than I do now."

"In that case, have a safe trip and good luck. We'll see you in a few weeks." Percy didn't add the "I hope," he thought.

John came over as Smitty left. "Smitty heading for the hills?" John asked.

"Yes. I can understand. I'm worried, myself."

"Yeah. We were talking about it the other day. He has that place up in Wyoming, by Yellowstone. Lots of water and game. His cabin has geothermal heat from a hot spring. He asked me to go with him to lend a hand, but I don't want to leave you shorthanded. You said I could stay here. I hope that still goes."

"Of course it does," Percy said. "But if you really want to go with Smitty and think you'd be some help to him, which, of course you would, it's not a problem for you to go."

"I really don't want to leave you short, Boss. I know the twins won't be back for a few days and Bernard is gone for the duration. That leaves an awful lot for just you and Susie."

"I've got a couple other options, plus Mattie can lend a hand. She has in the past," Percy replied.

"Smitty really could use my help. You know they have that new baby and the two little ones. Charlie is a good boy, but he's only twelve. And with me, my truck, and supplies, it would give them an extra margin of safety."

"Sounds to me like you need to go, not just would like too. Honestly," Percy said, earnestly,

"I think you should go. We really will be able to manage. Don't worry about your job, either. Smitty is sure this will all blow over. He just doesn't want to take a chance. Don't worry about your job. It'll be here when you get back."

"I'm not as sure of that as Smitty is. Okay. I'll go help Smitty. I'm really sorry about this."

"Don't be. It's a lot more important to take care of a family than it is our produce. I'm assuming Smitty wants to leave early so if you want to come back this evening I'll have cash, instead of a check."

"A check is fine. I should be able to cash it in town without a problem."

"As long as you're sure. Stop at the house and I'll have it ready for you."

"Okay. Thanks."

As Susie and Percy walked back to the house, and John was getting into his truck, Susie said, "They heading out, too?"

"Yes. Can't blame them, though I'm not so sure being that close to Yellowstone is that safe, under the circumstances. Got to admit, it sounds like Smitty has a nice, secure place there, and with John's help, they should be fine as long as the volcano doesn't blow."

"Yellowstone doesn't have an active volcano. I know there are hot springs and stuff, which means some activity, but not a real volcano."

"Much of Yellowstone Park sits on the caldera of a huge past volcano. It's been hundreds of thousands of years since it blew the last time. No reason to think it will again anytime soon. There aren't any nearby targets to draw a nuke that could set it off. I need to get that check for John. I'll be in for supper in the dining room in a few minutes. I don't want to get too far off our normal routine."

"We'll go back to the cottage tonight. There's no real reason to stay here in the house."

"Up to you guys," Percy said, turning into the den. "I don't mind if you stay here."

It took only moments to get John his check. Percy actually had enough cash on hand, but he made it a point to keep his personal books separate from the estate business books. He paid by check the estate debts, plus the bartering when he could, but he kept the same kind of paperwork for the estate barters as he did personal barters.

After supper they adjourned to the living room to watch the news. Things were tense in the Far East, but no additional action was being taken. The confrontation in Korea was at an impasse. North Korea was entrenched seventy some odd miles into South Korea and fighting was intense, but that was the limit of it.

Mattie and Susie were preparing to go to their cottage when they felt the first tremor. The earth sheltered concrete dome home was solid. You would never know a terrible thunderstorm was raging outside it was so quiet.

When they felt the first movement and the lights went out, Percy called, "Get down next to the coffee table!" It was a heavy, rather blocky table, the legs and rails being oak four by fours, with slate tiles inlaid on three quarter inch oak plywood.

While standing in a doorway was probably better than standing in the middle of the room, the best protection was to be beside something that would support anything falling downward. Many earthquake deaths were crushing deaths. Often ceilings and upper floors would fail and fall. The wall thickness of a doorway did not provide much protection from those types of structural failure.

It was common to find survivors in the cavities next to heavy, stout furniture that supported debris and prevented it from pancaking to the floor, crushing anything between. Percy had a heavy structural element or stout furniture in nearly every room in every structure beside which a person could crouch or lay during earthquakes. It might not even be necessary in the concrete domes, they were so strong, but Percy didn't take chances.

Nothing broke or fell as the rumbling continued for well over a minute. When the shaking stopped, it was slightly over a minute more before the automatic switching for the generator that supplied the house in emergencies started the generator and fed power to the key circuits of the house.

The three climbed to their feet and Percy said, "I'm going to check on the animals."

"I'm going with you," Susie said. Percy didn't object.

"I'll check the house for damage," Mattie added, turning toward the kitchen first.

It took a little while to calm the animals. The other generator that was on automatic controls was the one that fed the animal barn. The lights were on when they entered. As they were going from one animal to another, issuing soothing words and dispensing extra rations of feed, Percy called over to Susie, "Dollars to donuts that was the New Madrid fault letting loose. The local quakes here are usually much shorter and feel a lot different."

"That's such a long ways away," Susie replied.

"Some of the eighteen eleven, eighteen twelve quakes were felt all the way to Boston, here, and in Kansas, too. This one just doesn't feel like our locals. We'll find out in a little bit from the news."

When they had the animals calmed down, especially the horses and dogs, they went back to the house. Both were concerned when they saw Mattie. She was white as a ghost. She pointed to the TV in the living room.

A newscaster looking much the same way as Mattie was saying, The reports are confirmed. A nuclear device has detonated on the San Andreas Fault in California, one at New Madrid on the fault in Missouri, and the third at the United Nations complex in New York during another emergency session.

These are believed to have been terrorist attacks. The devices were low yield. They were not missile or bomb attacks. The United States forces have gone to high alert, but no retaliatory attacks are being launched at this time, nor are any pending. The President is asking for calm and restraint. Aid is being dispatched to the affected areas. There is very little fallout from the San Andreas and New Madrid devices, as both were apparently deep underground detonations. It is believed the devices were dropped down irrigation wells.

The fallout from the UN detonation is, at the moment, blowing out to sea. Warnings have gone out to the area around the UN and to ships at sea. More in a moment. The haggard looking newscaster was removing his earpiece. He looked like he was about to be ill.

Percy switched channels, and then said, "I'm going into the den to check the other monitors. I want you both to stay here tonight. Go get anything you'll need for a few days. But hurry."

As the two headed for the front door, Percy headed for the den and its bank of TV monitors. Even the Weather Channel was reporting on the situation, providing prevailing wind and fallout details.

Percy was at his desk, making a list when Mattie and Susie came in. "We put our stuff in the green guest room. Percy nodded but continued working on the list of things he needed to do the next day.

They stayed in the den all night, dozing on the comfortable sofas and recliners the room boasted, watching the rescue efforts that were already ongoing. When morning came around they were still on emergency power. They showered and changed clothes in turn, and then Percy and Susie went out to tend to the animals. They'd accomplished the needed tasks in the greenhouses the day before, so went back to the house after checking the other buildings for damage.

The structures were well designed and well built. There were a few things that had fallen off shelves, but no serious damage at all. The animals were all calm. Percy debated for a bit before he turned them out, which was the normal daily routine. If things got worse, they might be in the barn for an extended period. Better, he decided, to let them have as much outside time as possible.

The dogs stayed close to Percy as Susie and he made the rounds. The horses hovered near the pasture fence, as close to the humans as they could get. None of the animals seemed to want to drift very far from the entrances to the barn, including the chickens.

When Brian Epstein failed to show up Percy debated again before he decided to take the milk and eggs in to the dairy, instead of processing the milk and candling the eggs and putting them into the household stocks.

Then, when Susie asked him, rather hesitatingly, to stop and check on Andy Buchanan, he changed his mind slightly and sent Susie in. She took the Suburban, instead of her Subaru. The power came back on just as she was driving away. Susie didn't have to stop and open the gates manually. The remote worked when she didn't even think about the power being off and used it to try to open the gates.

When she returned two hours later, Percy was up the third antenna tower, removing the cameras from their mounts. He'd left one on an all axis remote control mount on this tower, but had removed all eleven of the other small cameras.

Susie watched him climb down the tower before she walked into the new shop building with him. "Why'd you take down the cameras? I thought you'd want them up for security."

Percy shook his head. "I left the one up on number three tower on the remote control mount. I don't have spares for these and can't get them. They're a discontinued model. If there is an electromagnetic pulse it will probably fry all of these. If I lose the one, I can replace it with one of the ones I took down."

"Oh," Susie said. "Uh… Mr. Jackson, I made Andy promise to come out here if things got any worse. I hope that's okay."

"Of course it is, Susie. I would have done the same thing if I'd gone in. I should have insisted that you do it when I sent you in. Also the Bluhms. I'll go talk to them here in a little bit. Couple more things I want to make sure get done."

"What do you want me to do, Boss?" Susie asked. "I can't stand just sitting around."

"Until this is over, I'd prefer you and your mother to take up residence in the main house. I'd like you and Mattie to bring over everything you might need for an extended stay. Go ahead and take two rooms so you'll each have plenty of space."

"Mother's not going to want to do that," Susie replied. It sounded like a good idea to her.

"I'll talk to her. You might want to see if Doc needs some help."

"I think I will. He has Stevens' bull over there for pneumonia and it's easier for two to medicate him. I'm surprised he hasn't called me to come over and help."

Percy immediately picked up the phone receiver. "Power's on, but the phones are still out, I guess. I never even thought to check them last night."

They both jumped when the phone suddenly rang.

"Hello?" Percy said, feeling a little foolish.

"Mr. Jackson, it's Andy. Andrew Buchanan. I talked to Susie this morning and she somehow got me to promise to come out there if things got worse. I know you kind of said the same thing, but I wanted to check first, just to make sure."

Percy cut his eyes to Susie. "It's fine, Andrew. I was going to ask you again myself, but I sent Susie because I needed to get some things done here this morning. I don't suppose you have time to do a little side work? You're probably pretty busy with fuel deliveries now, though, aren't you? People are going to want to stock up now, for sure."

"They sure are, but that's a real problem. We were expecting deliveries today, but our supplier called and said it could be as much as a month before we get another significant delivery. We're supposed to get a couple tanker loads tomorrow or the next day, but that's all. Mr. Wilkins thinks there'll be some rationing going on by the time it gets here."

"I could use some help out here, if it turns out Wilkins doesn't need you for a while. Three of my hands are making preparations at home and can't work for a while."

"Yeah, I know. Mr. Jacobson stopped to fuel up and said he and Mr. Smith were headed for Wyoming and that Bernard Robert's wife needed him at home again. I was going to see if you needed me to help when I wasn't working here at Wilkins."

"Thank you, Andrew. I appreciate that. I would like you to come out any time Wilkins doesn't need you. We can discuss the pay when you come out the first time."

"I don't really need pay. Maybe some groceries, like you barter sometimes. I think things might get hard to get, with what's happening in California."

"We'll come to some arrangement, Andrew. What about your father? Do you want to bring him out here?"

"No, Mr. Jackson. Whatever happens I couldn't take care of him. He needs to stay in the rest home. I'll do what I can for him there, but the daily care needs... It's just really not possible. I was there last night when the quake hit. He's upset that he can't help, but knows he has to stay there. It's all that's keeping him alive. He doesn't want to be a burden on me. Pop knows I don't have the resources to take care of him."

"Maybe out here..." Percy suggested, knowing the response he would get.

"You know Pop. He just won't go for it. It's okay his veteran's pension is paying for the rest home. He wouldn't take your help or anyone else's."

"I understand, Andrew. I just wish there was some way I could help."

"I know. Thanks. Pop is where he needs to be, no matter what happens."

"Okay, Andrew. Just come on out any time it suits you. Day or night."

"I will, Mr. Jackson. Thanks. Say hello to Susie for me."

"She's right here, Andrew. You can tell her yourself."

"Andy," Susie said, "I'm glad you apparently agreed to come out here. Especially work for Mr. Jackson. But I don't really appreciate you checking with him after I told you what I did."

"I know. And I believed you. It just one of those guy things, I guess."

"Guy thing, huh? It's a good thing I love you or I'd hang up on you for that."

"You love me? Really? I love you, too, Susie. I wish I'd told you sooner."

"Oh, Andy! I do. I wish I'd told you sooner, too. Please, please, come out here if things look bad. Please."

"I promise, Susie. I promise. I love you. Bye."

"I love you. Bye, Andy."

"Well. That's nice to hear," Percy said.

Susie threw her arms around Percy. "He loves me! He really does. He was asking these kinds of leading questions the other day. About marriage and all. But he didn't ask me and I was afraid I gave him the wrong impression. I don't think so now. I've got to go tell Mother."

"Okay. But don't forget about Doc and moving your stuff."

"I won't."

"Tell your mother, too, that I'm headed for the Bluhms. I want to talk to them about coming here if there are more problems. That's a nice house, but not good enough for anything as serious as what this may become."

"Good. I really like them."

CHAPTER FIFTEEN

It didn't take all that much convincing. The terrorist attacks and the resulting earthquake had scared them. They were closer to town, but agreed to head for the estate if things got worse. He gave them a hand held radio and charger for it. "We'll be monitoring that most of the time. If you need one of us, just keep calling until someone answers. It would make me feel better if you called just to check in so I know the radio is okay. A couple times a day would be fine, if you don't really mind doing that."

"No. That sounds like a good idea," Jock said. "Will it reach all the way to the city? We may have to take Judy Franks in. She's had some labor pains, off and on, the last few hours. It's probably false labor, but we're not about to take a chance, considering the circumstances."

"It's on a repeater system. As long as commercial power is on it should work. On the direct link, only about halfway to the city." Percy hesitated a moment, then asked the doctors, "Do you want me to take her in using the Suburban? There's plenty of room, and I do have an errand I need to run there, anyway."

"No..." Jock said slowly, after looking at Melissa for a moment. "It's not like the weather is bad or anything. But... If you're going pretty soon, we might just tag along with Judy and her family. Just in case. You know."

"Sure thing," Percy said with a smile. "I have a few things to do in town, and then I'll be ready. Meet me at Rosie's when you're ready."

"Okay. I'll call Judy now and make the arrangements. She thinks it's false labor, too, but it is her first and she's a little apprehensive. Her mother will take her in and we'll take the Bug. We need to do a couple of things ourselves."

"You know, I have a Jeep I don't use, if you want something besides the Volkswagen and the Taurus. Winters can get pretty severe here, you know."

"I don't really like Jeeps," Melissa said. "I had a friend roll one, one time. We're thinking about trading in the Taurus on something like an Explorer before winter."

"That would do you a good job. Okay then. I'll be on my way and see you in a little while."

The trip went well, until Percy stopped to see Sara. Percy tried to convince her to move out to the estate. He even offered to supply all her fuel to go to and from the city every day to go to work.

"Are you asking me to move in with you, Percy?" she finally asked.

"Of course I am. I thought that was clear. Oh." He turned slightly red. "Not like that... Just stay in one of the extra rooms. I'm not... Sara, I'm just not ready for that next step."

"I understand, Percy. And that's okay. I just want to be sure. And I appreciate you offering to provide my gasoline, but it's not quite proper, don't you see?"

"Yes. I guess I do. But you will promise me to come out if things get worse. How did your apartment fare, by the way, during the quake?"

Sara frowned. "One of the plates my mother left me broke. I had it on a stand and it walked off the shelf and broke. It's not as if I was all enamored of it, but my mother loved Elvis and that plate was her favorite. I hate to have lost it."

"I'm sorry. I wish I could replace it for you. And I'm sorry if I upset you. I just... Well... I guess I'll be going, then."

"Okay, Percy. And Percy I'm not mad at you or anything." She stepped up to him and gave him a long hug. "I appreciate you trying to look out for me, but I'm a big girl. And I will come to the estate if something worse happens." She leaned back, her arms still around him and looked him in the eyes.

"I care about you, Percy. A lot. I want you to promise me you won't do anything stupid if things do get worse." She brought her face forward and kissed him lightly on the lips before he could protest.

"I... I care about you, too, Sara." Then he frowned. "I don't do stupid things. What made you say that, anyway?"

Sara stepped away from him and smiled. "Oh, Percy. Don't worry about it. I was just teasing. Sort of."

"Well... Okay. I guess I really should go. I want to stop and get a couple of things before I go back to the estate."

"'Bye, Percy."

"Goodbye, Sara."

Percy brooded about the exchange a little, but quickly put it behind him when he went to the medical supply shop. There were no delays this time when he picked up several more medical items. They were glad to help him load them into the Suburban.

When he met the Bluhms' at the hospital again, they told him they were staying in the city to have dinner and thanked him again. Judy was doing fine, but was going to stay in the hospital overnight, then stay with a cousin in the city until the baby came.

He made another stop, at the larger of the two shopping malls the city boasted. He spent much of the early afternoon there and left with a dozen shopping bags. He'd made three trips out to the Suburban to take things out, he'd bought so much.

Percy didn't particularly like firearms, though he did use them like the tools they were. He'd ordered a few items almost three weeks before. There'd been a waiting period and this was the first time he'd been in since the waiting time was up.

The clerk helping Percy carry out the ammunition and the reloading supplies and equipment asked Percy, "How'd you know so far ahead this was going to happen?"

"Know?" Percy asked. "I didn't know. I just... like to be prepared."

"Yeah. You're definitely prepared now. You know good stuff when you see it. That is a cool Suburban."

"Thanks. And thanks for helping me load. I need to head back."

"Sure thing. Come back any time. Ask for me. I made a nice commission on this sale."

Percy waved politely. He didn't like that clerk much. He wasn't bloodthirsty and out to hurt anybody. It was just prudent to have the most effective means available to protect himself and those in his care. The clerk was of a mind to just go out and shoot someone for sport, using the situation as an excuse.

With the Assault Weapon Ban not having been renewed for the moment, he decided to get a few things he couldn't get while the ban was in effect. A pair of the old pistol grip, collapsible stock Heckler and Koch HK-91 .308 rifles and thirty twenty-round magazines, plus thirty thirty-rounders. The two collapsible stock versions would give him six of the HK-91s, including the four HK-91A2s he already had in the gun safe at home. He'd had those since well before the ban, along with four of the very rare, and very expensive, G8 50 round single stack drum magazines.

He'd picked up some thirty round Ruger 10-22 magazines. He had three of the .22 rimfire rifles. The shop had two Mossberg Model 590 12-gauge riot guns and a Remington 11-87 semi-automatic. He'd taken all three of the shotguns and an extended magazine tube and folding stock for the Remington. They brought his total combat shotgun count to six, including two more of the 11-87s with extended magazines and a Remington 870 with pistol grip folding stock and extended magazine.

Again, since they were available once more, he'd added another thirty AUG thirty-round magazines to the order for the four Steyr AUG carbines he'd picked up when he got the original

HK-91s. That gave him a total of a hundred AUG magazines.

He hadn't ordered any additional handguns or hunting rifles. He had plenty of both, including five Para-Ordinance P14s, 3 Glock 21s, a Browning Hi-Power, three Ruger 22/45s, four HK-4s with all four conversion kits each, and an assortment of Ruger single actions, some with interchangeable cylinders, to handle a variety of other calibers.

His hunting rifles included Remington 700s in .223, .243, .270, and .350 Remington Magnum. He had a pair of the rifles each in .308, .30-06, and .375 H&H Magnum. Percy didn't really count what he considered his fun guns. He'd grown up watching re-runs of the 1950s and '60s westerns and had Marlin lever action rifles in .45-70 and .45 Long Colt. He had a pair of Stoeger 12-gauge coach guns and three Ruger Blackhawks, also in .45LC. He also had companion American Derringer Corporation derringers in .45LC and .45ACP.

Also mostly for fun, though they did have serious uses, each of his highway vehicles carried a Marlin Camp Carbine in .45ACP with half a dozen spare magazines.

As far as ammunition went, this order included ten thousand rounds each of .308 and .223 to bring his total up to fifty thousand rounds each. Also included two thousand rounds each of 12-gauge slugs, 12-gauge #4 buckshot, and a thousand rounds of various numbered shot. He already had similar amounts for the .45s, and over a thousand rounds each of the other handgun and hunting calibers he used.

When it came to .22LR he was just as well supplied. Another fifty thousand rounds, ten percent of which was BB caps, CB caps, and shorts.

Since he only expended a few rounds a year for practice and to do the little hunting he did, Percy had never really done much reloading. The twins were into it and provided him with some specialty ammunition he liked to keep on hand. They had pretty extensive reloading equipment and supplies and he'd just bought a complete set of reloading tools and components to reload every cartridge and shell he used, except the rimfires. He counted himself lucky to have found another three hundred 12-gauge brass empty shells. He'd ordered two hundred fifty of them once before and paid the twins to load them for him.

His errands accomplished, except for getting Sara to agree to move out to the estate, Percy headed back. He wanted to get there in time to help take care of the animals. He didn't want Susie to have to do it on her own, though she was perfectly capable of doing so.

Percy smiled when, at four o'clock, he heard Jock's voice on the radio mounted in the Suburban. "This is Jock. Radio check. Percy, are you there?"

"I'm here," Percy replied, picking up and keying the microphone. You're loud and clear."

"We're just going in to get something to eat and thought it'd be a good time to do the radio check."

"Consider it a successful check," Percy responded.

"We're checking in, too," Susie said. "Everything is fine. Have you seen the news?"

"Negative," Percy replied. "What's up?"

"Korea is looking worse," Susie replied. "Oh. And we moved. I went ahead and moved the rest of our stuff to one of the rooms in the utility barn. That way the cottage is available for someone else to use if you need to."

There was a hint there that Percy didn't take to let them know if Sara was coming out to the estate. "You didn't need to do that. But it might not be a bad idea."

When he didn't elaborate, Susie said, "Okay, Boss. I can take care of the animals if you're running late."

"Nope," Percy said, activating the gate opener remote. "Be there in a minute. I'll help with the animals."

"Mom didn't argue at all when I said you wanted us to move into the house for a while," Susie said when she met him at the animal barn.

"I didn't think she would, actually," Percy replied as they worked to bring the animals in and get them fed and bedded down. "Your mother is a very practical woman. She knows I'm going to be pretty active 'til this is all over and it'll be easier for her to just be there around the clock to keep me out of trouble."

Susie laughed. "She did actually mention something to that effect."

They were silent after that, until they'd finished. When Susie went to help him move the things from the sporting goods store, she exclaimed, "Geez, Boss! You expecting a war?"

"Yes," Percy said quietly.

"Oh," Susie replied softly. "Maybe you'd better teach me to shoot something besides a twenty-two," she added after a moment.

"I don't want to do that unless you really want to. I don't want you to feel like you have to defend the estate. That's my responsibility."

With a ferocity that surprised Percy a little, Susie replied, "This is my home, too. You've said so, Mr. Jackson. I'll do what's needed to protect it."

"Well, if you're sure, we'll get you started at the first opportunity."

Susie was grinning at him suddenly. "You didn't say after we checked with Mother."

Percy grinned back. "You're a big girl now and can make your own decisions. Your mother said that herself. I should treat you more like the woman and lady you are, rather than the girl I tend to treat you like."

"I don't know. Sometimes it's a lot easier being a little girl than it is a woman."

"You can handle it just fine. Are handling it. You obviously got Andrew headed in the direction you wanted."

With a fond smile Susie responded. "Well, not completely, but... yeah... I think he might just ask me to move in with him soon. Maybe even marry him."

"He's a fool if he doesn't."

"That's so sweet, Mr. Jackson. You sound just like a dad."

"Yeah? Well..." He let the words trail away, slightly pink. "I'll get the rest if you can help your mother. I'd like to eat in the dining room. I can see the TV in the living room from my chair in the dining room."

"Okay," Susie said. "I'll set the table for Mother."

Percy moved the things he'd bought at the mall to his suite of rooms in the two story seven bedroom, eleven-bath earth sheltered dome home. He had a large bedroom with attached bath and large walk-in closet. The suite also included a small den slash home office. It was as nice as the estate office in the big den down stairs, just smaller. What was once intended to be a nursery adjoining the bedroom Percy used simply as a storage room. That's where he dropped his recent purchases. He'd put them away later.

They were all a bit subdued as they ate. The stalemate in Korea seemed to be heating up. China was making noises about the fallout coming from Pakistan caused by the Indian nuclear attack. One report indicated that India was warning Pakistan to withdraw from the disputed area and acknowledge India's sovereignty or they would renew the attack, the implication being with nuclear weapons again.

"This is bad. It might be all the excuse China needs to invade India," Percy said. "I saw a report last night that indicates China is massing troops along their common border."

"If China gets involved directly, there or in Korea, do you think the US will respond?" asked Mattie.

"Yes. Other reports are linking China and or North Korea with the terrorist attacks here. I think they might have been trying to keep the US at home with the disasters to take care of, plus put the UN out of easy commission. Not like they can't meet at The Hague or something, but most of the ambassadors and their staffs died in the attack. Lot of embassies put out of commission directly or due to radiation. The UN is not going to be effective for some time to come, if ever."

Suzie looked at Percy and said, "I'm afraid if North Korea uses a nuke in South Korea, the US will have to respond. Our troops are directly involved in that fighting."

"Carolyn Mathew's boy was killed over there yesterday, apparently. They got word today. I talked to Helen today and she told me," Mattie said.

"Too many people are dying in too many places," Percy said quietly. "Let's just hope and pray it doesn't come any closer to us than that. Uh-oh."

The news channel changed to a shot of another mushroom cloud. There was no audio at the moment, but the words Seoul, South Korea were superimposed over the cloud.

"That tears it," Percy said.

Another news channel was reporting that China was again warning all nations to stay out of the troubles in the Far East. The station showing Seoul now had another mushroom cloud on screen, this one listed as New Delhi, India."

Yet another channel now had a translation of a Chinese announcement that due to the attacks in Pakistan by India, China was receiving fallout and therefore considered the attack by India on Pakistan an attack on China and had retaliated in kind. There were reports that the Chinese were massing an amphibious force on the coast facing Taiwan. Again China issued warnings to leave the Far East to deal with its own problems.

"No way is that going to happen," Percy said. "Okay. It's time to batten down the hatches. Susie, do you think you can use the Bobcat to move straw bales in front of the barn doors?"

"Sure, no problem. But why?"

"I want to put up a dirt berm in front of all the doors of all the barns. We'll use the straw as a vertical backstop. I'll use a Unimog to move the dirt from the stockpiles I had Reynolds build. This is the future construction I was talking about. Mattie, I want you to keep an eye on the news and fix us something to eat about midnight. It'll be that late by the time we get finished."

It didn't take quite that long. Percy picked up speed on each circuit from the stockpiles to the barns. It was the same with Susie. She was good on the Bobcat anyway, but her speed picked up significantly as she took straw bales from their stack near the storage barn and stacked them in a curve in front of each of the barns where the doors were located. They didn't need to do the houses. Susie realized that one of the design elements of the houses was a berm similar to what they were building, but as part of the total design of the structures.

She thought they should go higher, but Percy pointed out that any radiation coming over the berms from ground level would only hit the roof projection that covered the space where the doors were located. Susie had never seen the need for the awnings Percy had put on the projections. They seldom extended them. There'd been a few times when they'd worked under them in the heavy rains when they needed to work on a piece of equipment.

Their use in this situation became obvious when Percy finished the first berm. He'd taken one of the rolls of plastic from the shop barn and tucked one edge under the top layer of straw bales before he started piling dirt. Susie thought it was just to protect the straw. When he piled the dirt on the slope the tiered straw created, then brought the plastic up and over it, to tuck under that top row of bales again she realized that the awning would direct any fallout that would have fallen between the berm and the building onto the plastic covered slope of the berm.

There was enough room to allow the Bobcat 5600T to get through and into the barns. The only one they did differently was the equipment barn. They had to leave enough room to bring out the equipment. On that one, Percy had Susie build a row of bales two high about where the berm was on the other barns. He laid down a sheet of plastic between the berm and the short wall, forming a channel that would catch anything from the awning. With the slight slope he put on it, he would be able to wash any accumulation of particles to outside the area of the berm.

"Clever," Susie said when she saw what he was doing.

"I've been thinking about things like this for years. Let's just hope it's a big waste of time," Percy replied.

"Yeah."

Mattie had the snack ready, despite their having finished by shortly after eleven. "Things still the same," she told them as they ate and watched the news. "Just more posturing on everyone's part." She sighed. "And aid efforts. Everyone that can is sending teams and equipment. Or at least getting them ready to go. No way they can travel at the moment."

"What's the US response to the nuke on Seoul and the activity on the China coast?" Percy asked.

"Nothing," Mattie replied. "At least nothing on the news. I can't believe they're just sitting there doing nothing, though."

"They aren't. Have there been any shots of the President's helicopter landing or taking off from the White House?" Percy asked then.

"Why?" asked Susie after Mattie had indicated there had been.

"Probably means he's headed for an airborne command post or a bunker. I'm glad we got things ready. I guess we might as well go to bed. Nothing we can do and tomorrow may be a long day."

When they got up the next morning they saw the reports. Japan had asked for help, since some of the islands were in the fallout path of the detonation in Seoul. Two carrier battle groups were headed that way to support the one normally stationed in the area. There'd been three communist coups in the Russian republics and more seemed likely.

The Germans were demanding the US turn over the nuclear arsenal within their borders to them so they could protect themselves against the newly communist Russian Republics. France was rattling sabers at everybody. Great Britain had finally ordered her subjects to come back home, rather than the strong suggestions given before. Brazil warned all the involved nations to leave them out of the mix. They all but said they had nuclear weapons and would use them if attacked.

Little additional information came to light that day. The next day was different. They woke up to reports that the US Navy had used a nuclear cruise missile to hit Pyongyang and issued an ultimatum for North Korea to withdraw from South Korea and for China not to interfere further. The ultimatum included a warning that the US would help defend Taiwan if there was an invasion.

Percy was debating on whether to call Sara and try to talk her into coming out to the estate again. He didn't have to. Sara called him. She was excited.

"Percy, have you heard? The federal government has announced a new Sheltering Plan. Information and instructions are in the process of being issued to implement it. It just came in a little while ago in the state offices. We're supposed to start distributing as soon as we can. From the little I saw, it looks like they are following your advice."

"That's good," Percy said, quickly adding, "Not that they're following my advice. The fact that they're doing anything at all. Let's just hope it's in time."

"I know. Percy, would you have Mattie prepare a room for me? I'd like to start coming out there the way you suggested. I'm scared of what is happening."

"Of course I will. She'll have a room ready for you tonight. The gold room."

"Not real gold, I hope," Sara said the humor evident in her voice.

"Just gold colored trim and accessories like the one we refer to the green room has green accessories and the…"

"I know, Percy. I was just making a joke."

"Oh. Okay. Well, we'll see you when you get here. You still have the gate opener I gave you? I'm keeping the gates closed now."

"Of course I do. I should be there about seven. Do not wait supper for me."

"Okay," Percy agreed, fully intending to wait to eat until she got there.

"I heard," Mattie said, after Percy put the telephone receiver down. "I'll get that room ready shortly."

"Okay. Good. I…" The phone rang again.

It was Melissa Bluhm. "Is that offer still good about coming out there? Jock and I are both worried."

"Of course it is, Melissa. Figure on supper about seven. Bring anything and everything you want."

"Thank you, Mr. Jackson. I love my new house, but we didn't put a shelter in it the way you suggested we do. We were foolish. And I'm pregnant." She was crying now.

"Don't think about that now. Just bring what you need tonight, and we'll take a truck over and bring everything else you want, tomorrow. We'll put you in one of the houses here. You can stay until this is all over."

"Thank you, Mr. Jackson. Thank you."

"Another room. For the Bluhms," Percy said. "Plan on supper at seven."

"I heard," Mattie said.

"It sounded almost like she was crying," Susie said.

"She was, there at the end. She's really worried." Percy didn't feel that it was his place to announce Melissa's pregnancy. She could tell the others when she wanted.

Brian Epstein called and said he wasn't going to be able to pick up the milk and eggs again. Percy decided to take the goods in. He was fairly certain there would be plenty of days in the future where he wouldn't be able to do so. They held out enough for their own use for several days, not just the one day they usually did, bringing their stock up to a two-week supply of fresh, rather than the week supply they normally kept. Percy took the rest into town to the dairy.

He didn't stay long. He did stop at one of the grocery stores and pick up a few things Mattie wanted. Then he stopped at Jimbo's place. He was glad he did. Jimbo was closing up shop and headed to the hills the way Smitty had. Only Jimbo was heading for the Ozarks.

"I was going to keep it up for you," Jimbo said, "using my current stocks. Prices have gone through the roof. I've had more business in the last three days than I have the last three months. Gold and silver, anyway. The other stuff isn't moving. How much do you want this time?"

"All of it," Percy replied.

"All of it! But that's most of my stock!"

"Jimbo, you knew this day would probably come."

Jimbo sighed. "Yeah, I guess so. I should have done a little better keeping my own stocks. Yours has been like the reserves in a bank for me. It's yours, and of course you can have it, but I sure need to figure something else than what I had planned."

Percy suspected Jimbo had quite a bit more stashed than he was letting on. Jimbo had a habit of making things sound rather worse than they actually were, at least when it came to his finances. His little so-called coin shop dealt with a lot more than coins. Legal things like alcohol. His was the only source of anything except beer and a tiny selection of wine the grocery stores carried.

He had a thriving business of cashing checks. Doing that wasn't illegal yet. Only the banks were restricted to the ten percent rule. He charged a minimum of a dollar and it was one percent on checks over one hundred dollars.

There were no feelings of guilt for Percy when he took the tubes of gold and silver coins. "Just keep the fractional ounces left and keep trading for me, if you will. We'll settle up when this is over," Percy said. "And just to say thanks for all your help, here's a tenth ounce gold coin and a roll of silver dimes as a tip."

"Well, thanks, Purse. You didn't really have to do that, but I'll sure take it. These are worth nearly eighty bucks now."

"Take care of yourself, Jimbo. We'll see you after this is all over."

"You bet, Purse. I have a good little thing here. I'm stashing my tinkers stuff out back, just in case. Uh… Don't tell anyone, though, will you?"

"Of course I won't," Percy said.

"I tell you what. If you kind of keep an eye on things for me, you can take a few things if you really need them." Percy was probably the only person alive he'd trust with the secret of his stash. Jimbo showed Percy how to get down into the room off the basement of the small shop. It was filled floor to ceiling with all types of household goods. It was obvious why Jimbo had called it his tinkers stuff. They were all items an old time tinker would have dealt with in the historic past.

"Okay, Jimbo," Percy said. You've got a deal. Anything I use, or if I think it'll help someone and I can do a trade, I'll get the best deal I can. If you don't want me to do that, I'll just promise not to let anyone know anything about it."

"I wasn't figuring on you moving the stuff for me. I guess that'd be okay. You're almost as good a horse trader as I am. Whatever you want to do. But I want gold and silver only. I trust you to make the best deals possible."

"I will," Percy said. "Or, better yet. How about I just buy you out? What would it take to buy everything you showed me? You still have time to convert."

A crafty look came onto Jimbo's face. "I've probably got ten grand tied up in that stuff. And to convert to gold, with the price what it is right now..."

"I'll give you a check for twenty thousand, right now," Percy said.

"Done," Jimbo said immediately. The two shook hands and Percy wrote him the check before he left the shop.

He stopped at the clinic on the way back to the estate. Jock and Melissa were both there, getting ready to load some items into their small cars.

"Why don't you just throw that stuff in the back of the Suburban? I'm headed back right now."

"I guess it would be easier," Jock said, looking from their two cars to the Suburban that dwarfed them. "We'd still like to take the cars. We're going to need to get back and forth. And I haven't had a chance to thank you, yet. This means a lot to me, you taking us in at a time like this."

"Think nothing of it," Percy said, opening the rear hatch of the Suburban. "You're a valuable addition to this community. If things get worse I want to keep it that way."

"You don't really think they will, do you? They'll stop this madness some way. Someone will. They have to."

Percy didn't respond, except to say, "I hope so."

He was leading the way toward the estate, listening to the news on the radio. The radio went dead and he saw the two cars following him begin to slow. "This is bad. Really bad," he muttered aloud as he stopped, and then backed the Suburban up to the Volkswagen. He realized that the vehicle that they would have met in a few seconds coming toward them on the highway had stopped, too.

"I don't know what happened," Melissa said, having popped the hood of the small car before she stepped out. "It just died. The radio went off, too."

"EMP," Percy said when Jock walked up, telling the same story. "Hurry. Let's get them moved onto the shoulder and get to the estate. There's nothing we can do about the cars at the moment."

"What's EMP? And can't we at least try to get them running?" Jock asked.

"Come on, Honey," Melissa urged her husband. "I think Mr. Jackson is right. ElectroMagnetic Pulse is what an atomic bomb does when it explodes up high. It zaps electronic stuff like computers. Like the ones in our cars." She looked at Percy. "You must have a different kind of electrical systems."

Percy didn't try to correct the small mistakes in Melissa's explanation to her husband. It was correct enough for the circumstances. "I do," Percy replied. "I switched when I converted the Suburban to three axles and installed the diesel engine. Let's get these moved. Melissa, you get behind the wheel. We'll push."

It took only a minute or so to move each car. As they were hurrying back to the Suburban, Melissa suddenly stopped. "Oh, my God!" She moaned. "I just realized! We've been attacked with atom bombs!"

Again, Percy didn't try to correct the errors. "Yes," he said. "Let's get to the estate and into shelter. We're not near a target, but you never know what might happen."

They'd barely settled themselves in the vehicle when Melissa looked down at her stomach and wailed. "My baby! What will happen to my baby?"

"Your baby will be fine," Percy reassured her. "The houses at the estate... barns, too, are earth sheltered, as you know. A protection factor of well over a million. Any radiation we might get would be less than one millionth of that we'd get out in the open. There are several places inside the houses double that protection factor.

Percy held up a meter so Melissa could see it from the rear seat. "We aren't getting anything and I have it on the most sensitive range. That occasional tick is background radiation we get all the time. Normal."

Percy put down the meter and put both hands on the wheel. The driver of the vehicle ahead of them was flagging them down by waving his arms in the air. Percy stopped and rolled down his window.

"My car just quit and I guess we're out of range of the cell system. My phone doesn't work. Could you call someone for me when you get where you're going? You are local, aren't you?"

"Yes," Percy said. "Normally I'd just turn around and take you to town, but this lady is ill and I need to get her home. What's the name and number? I'll try it when we get home. Can't promise anything. We lose the phones out here occasionally."

The man gave Percy the number of a hotel in the city and a room number. "Ask my wife to call Triple A and order me a tow truck."

"I'll do what I can," Percy said.

"Why didn't you tell him what was going on?" Jock asked.

"I doubt if he'd have believed me. And I've never tried to save the world, just my little piece of it. Your wife is more important to me. I'll come back after I drop you off and take him into town."

"Oh," Jock said, looking at his still distraught wife. "I'm not thinking too straight right now."

"I don't like leaving someone like that, but I have my priorities. You two come first. You three."

"I'm not going to argue your priorities. I'm not sure what we'd be doing if it wasn't for you."

"Don't worry about it. Things are going to be fine. Don't you worry. Either of you."

Percy dropped them at the estate, leaving them in Mattie's capable hands and headed back to where he'd left the man on the side of the road. The car was there but the man wasn't. Percy assumed he'd been picked up by someone with a car that hadn't been disabled by the EMP. He'd tried the phones at the estate and they weren't working.

He tried the radio and told Susie he was headed back. He stopped in the act of turning around when he saw a yellow and black dirt bike approaching, the rider wearing the same colors. Percy was sure it was Randy Phillips on the bike. He'd seen him race at the Fourth of July Picnic.

"I'm glad I caught you, Mr. Jackson," said Randy. "I was on the way out to see you. Look. I'm willing to give you free welding service for life if you'll help me dig in my shelter. I converted an old tank into a shelter, but Reynolds is booked solid and can't help me. I don't know anyone else that can. I'd never get it done with a shovel. I've got to get my family into shelter, Mr. Jackson."

"Calm down, Randy. I'll help you. You go back home and get everything ready. And don't worry about that for life welding thing. I'll be in with one of the Unimogs to take care of it. It'll take me maybe an hour to get there, but I will be there," Percy assured the young man.

Percy radioed Susie and had her go out and mount the backhoe on the Unimog Percy had used to build the berms. The front bucket was still on it. He told Susie how to swap out the computer with a spare if the Unimog wouldn't start. He breathed a sigh of relief when Susie radioed back and told him the truck started all right.

He had EMP protection on all his electronic equipment and it seemed everything had survived without damage at the estate except for the tower mounted camera and a couple of other minor items.

Susie was almost finished with the attachments to the Unimog. Percy checked with the Bluhms. They were settled in all right. Melissa was calm, cool, and collected now, all signs of her previous moments of panic gone.

"I'll go with you," Jock said when Percy explained what he was going to do.

"Your skills," Percy said, "are too valuable to lose if something were to happen. I'd rather you stay here and help Mattie and Susie. You are a free agent and I won't say no, but I'd like you to think about it. If things go the way they might, doctors are going to be of prime importance."

Jock looked at Percy for several long moments. "Okay, Mr. Jackson. I'll stay here. But I have to be doing something."

"I expect you to lend a hand here, in ways that won't jeopardize your ability to be a doctor. Susie knows what she's doing on the estate. Just follow her orders, and speak up if she asks you to do something you can't do, or shouldn't do."

He turned to Susie. "I don't expect many, if any, people to show up at our doorstep. If it is someone we know, or someone with important skills, let them in. Unless it's a really good vehicle, have them park in the field across from the gates. We can take up to thirty additional people. But we are not a public shelter. If this goes the way it might, this place is going to be very important to the community and I intend to protect it."

"Yes, sir," Susie replied. "I'll do my best."

"I know. I need to get going. Randy is good people. There's a chance someone else will want some help. I have my dose and rate meters. I'll work as long as there is no radiation. If we do start getting any, I'll head home immediately. Mattie, you know where the meters are. Keep an eye on them and let Susie know if we start getting fallout."

Mattie nodded.

"Doctor Bluhm," Percy said then, looking over at the young woman. "If you could help Mattie, I would appreciate it. The same stipulation that I gave Jock goes for you, too."

"I understand," she replied

"I'll see you all later. Oh. Mattie, Sara should be showing up around seven. I doubt if

I'll be here. Make her comfortable and reassure her I'm okay. She should be able to get me on the radio. I'll have one of the handhelds with me when I'm out of the truck. Keep an eye on the news and let me know of anything important."

"I will. Good luck and take care of yourself."

Percy was just pulling up to the gate when it opened. He'd added the circuit for the opener to the ones the generator for the house fed. Sara had opened the gate with her remote. Percy hopped down out of the truck. "You're here. Thank God. I'm off for a little while. Mattie will see to your needs. I'm really glad you came out early. I take it the EMP didn't fry the hybrid's computers in the agency's parking garage."

"All I know is when I tried to start it, it did. When the power went out they sent us all home. There was no reason not to come on out. Where are you going?"

Percy was holding Sara's hand through her open window. "Help out a couple of people. I'll be back... when I'm finished."

"Oh, Percy," Sara almost pleaded. "Be careful. You like to help people. Don't let that get you hurt."

"I won't," Percy replied, "I promise."

"I love you, Percy," Sara said softly, looking into his eyes.

She saw it there before he said it. "I love you, too, Sara. I'm glad you decided to come. If you want, have Mattie put your stuff in my rooms. But only if you want. I want to marry you."

"I want to marry you, too, Percy, but let's wait until things calm down before we jump into anything."

"I guess you're right," Percy said. "But the question, such as it was stands. Will you marry me?"

"When you ask me again, after we know what's going to happen, Percy. Now go help someone. I want to get settled so I can help Mattie."

"Okay. Bye. I love you."

"Bye. I love you too."

Despite the slight delay, Percy made it to Randy's within the hour he'd specified. It took only a few hours to dig the hole, place the converted set of tanks, bolt them together, then backfill and mound them over with three feet of earth dug from the trench.

"I owe you for life," Randy said. I would never have got this done in time. It's only a matter of time before we get some fallout from somewhere."

"You don't owe me for life. Just trade me some labor sometime in the future for this.

That's all I want. Do you need help getting your stuff into the shelter?"

"No. You've done enough. We can handle the rest. Thanks again, Mr. Jackson."

"Don't worry about it. I'll be on my way, then."

He'd barely hit the edge of town on his way back to the estate when someone was flagging him down. "Hey! You for hire? I'll give you five hundred bucks to dig some dirt and pile it around my basement walls."

"No money but you'll owe me twenty hours of labor on my farm sometime."

"Sweet. You got it. Just knock down the fence. You'll have to pile some dirt at the one corner after you move what you can, and I can move it the rest of the way on the back of the house with a shovel."

It took less than an hour. The man and the rest of the family stayed busy shoveling some of the dirt into emptied out dresser drawers and cardboard boxes to stack over one corner of the basement.

Neighbors were coming over to see what was going on. It was close to midnight before Percy got back to the estate. He'd done various excavations and earth moves for a dozen people.

Mattie and Sara were waiting up for him. They had insisted the others go to bed. "Any additional news?" Percy asked as Mattie handed him a sandwich.

"Not really. Just snatches here and there. The satellite seems to be working, but only a few channels are up, and that is intermittent. All we know for sure is that at least one device was detonated almost right over us."

Before Mattie could say anything else they felt the dome vibrating. It was different from the quake caused by the nuke on the New Madrid fault line. It was enough to bring the Bluhms and Susie running into the kitchen. They were all in their nightclothes.

Percy hurried to the den and the others followed. He flipped a switch and a hollow rumble sound filled the room. The room began to shake even more and everyone crouched beside the heavy desk until the shake passed.

"Was that an earthquake, a bomb, or what?" asked Jock.

"Earth tremor, I think. But it's different from the others. The roar became louder for a moment then faded away. The TV screens were all tuned to the same channels as they had been for the last several days. All were blank.

"I don't know for sure, but it kind of felt like the movement was from the west. I'm going to take a look outside." He checked the radiation meters first, then went to the front door and stepped outside. The others followed. All they could see was the night sky.

253

CHAPTER SIXTEEN

Calvin had been a bit worried about trying to cut his hours at the bank, but there were no problems. The bank actually welcomed it. They needed additional tellers with the heavy traffic due to the new banking laws. There were less of other types of bank work, so mid-level staff was being cut back, anyway.

Tuesdays and Wednesdays Calvin would work at the bank. At a significantly reduced salary, of course. But he did still receive enough to cover what few monthly payments they had with that salary. Everything they made with the equipment was available for anything they wanted.

The Stubblefield's essentially took over the equipment based portion of Andersons' businesses. It was easy to just continue getting many of the jobs through the Andersons and give them a cut. They got business on their own, too. Even Herbert was amazed at the additional work they were able to do with the new equipment.

There seemed to be a backlog of work that had accumulated, due to the fact that Anderson simply didn't have the equipment needed to do the work. Fortunately, Anderson was willing to teach Calvin and Nan how to do most of the work that he had not been able to do due to lack of equipment.

One thing Anderson wouldn't do was use the aerial bucket. One of the beds Calvin had purchased for the Unimog was a utility bed with a forty-foot reach aerial lift with material winch. Herbert didn't like heights. He would direct the work from the ground, but refused to get into the bucket.

"Okay, Nan," Calvin called up to his wife. "That looks good. You can ground."

Nan let the hydraulic powered chainsaw rest on the edge of the bucket as she lowered the boom to bring the bucket to the ground. She unhooked the chainsaw hydraulic hoses and the safety cable and handed it to Calvin.

"This is cool, Calvin. I like the high work." Nan parked the boom and bucket on the rack and climbed down.

Calvin grinned at his wife. "I know. You've mentioned it a time or two. But there is ground work, too. Come and help me with the chipper." He walked over to the Toolcat. A limb chipper was mounted on the front. He fired up the machine and began feeding the limbs Nan had trimmed from the tree into the chipper.

Since the homeowner wanted the chips for mulch, Calvin had aimed the discharge to form a pile just inside the property line. With hardhat, face shield, and earmuffs on, Nan began to help. Calvin was likewise outfitted; including similar gloves to those Nan wore. It went quickly with both of them working.

"I love these toys!" Nan said, her enthusiasm obvious. They had loaded the Toolcat onto the trailer now attached to the Unimog. When they started to climb into the cab of the truck, a car stopped beside them. Nan walked around to join Calvin.

"Hi. My name is Joe Brenderman. I live on the other side of town. I was wondering... Do you install fallout shelters?"

"I'm sure we could," replied Calvin, without hesitation. "Do you need one buried?"

"Yeah. Stubby said he could reinforce a shipping container and equip the inside. Now I need someone to dig it in. I was going to get Anderson with his backhoe, but he recommended you guys. He told me you were working over on this side of town."

Calvin looked at Nan. She nodded. Turning back to Joe, Calvin said, "Let's go take a look."

They followed Joe back to his house. There was a forty-foot long shipping container sitting in Joe's back yard. "Stubby said it would be better to wait to fix up the inside until after it was buried. He just finished the reinforcing yesterday. Can your stuff handle the thing?"

"I'm sure we can," Calvin said. "How deep do you want it?"

"Two-thirds. We can use the dirt out of the hole to mound it over."

Calvin shot Joe a price and Joe eagerly accepted. When Nan and Calving were headed home, Nan asked, "Are you sure the truck will handle it?"

"Sure," Calvin replied. "The material hoist won't, but the crane will be here tomorrow. It'll handle it easily."

"Oh. I'd forgotten the crane. I'm glad we ordered it, too."

"This has gone a lot better than I ever imagined," Calvin said. "Thanks for encouraging me for us to do it."

Nan rested her hand on Calvin's shoulder for a moment. "No need to thank me. This is good for me, too." Her hand slid away. "It's been helping me keep my mind off the world situation. Until today. That fallout shelter. I never think of our home that way, but it is, I know. We planned it that way. But it's just home to me."

"We are lucky ones, I guess," Calvin replied. "Being able to do the things we've wanted."

"Luck played a part, I admit. But it was our hard work and foresight that put us where we are today. I feel sorry for those that simply can't see what's really happening."

"I know," Calvin said. "The people around here have been good to us. Maybe we should thank them in some way. Say special discount rate for anything survival related. Like digging the shelter in for Joe. Other things. I'm not sure what. But there are bound to be things people will be doing. You're right. The way we did things, I don't think about individual aspects."

"We can't make people do things, but we could print up flyers say something like 'for your preparedness needs.' We could even order food and supplies for people. Where we're getting the stuff we could even buy retail and make a little on it and it'd still be cheaper than what little you can find around here."

"That's true. Retail is a lot of work. You sure you want to take that on with the woodcutting and the equipment work?" He chuckled. "Of course, you don't have to do much at the Andersons' anymore."

Nan smiled. The job hadn't lasted very long; since they had started doing most of the work almost immediately after Mrs. Anderson had hired her.

The day didn't start at all well. Pakistan nuking India was all over the news. They talked it over, and Calvin and Nan decided to go ahead and do the job they had scheduled for the day. When they got there, they kept the radio on all the time, to get updates on the situation.

They were stopped often, by people anxious for them to help with getting a shelter dug. There was plenty of work lined up for the next several days now. They were tired when they got home, both mentally and physically.

The next day was better. No additional bad news, just the ongoing situation with Pakistan and India. Not all the work was preparedness related. Most of the septic tanks had been installed at about the same time, as the area developed. There was a lot of heavy clay, and those that had not taken good care of their septic systems needed new drainage fields.

Shortly after they sat down to have their dinner Nan looked up and asked, "Did you feel something?"

Calvin responded questioningly. "What? Feel something? No, Did you?"

"Yeah. Something... I don't know." Nan got up and turned on the small TV in the kitchen. "Oh my God!" she exclaimed. Calvin hurried in to join her.

Supper out of their minds, they hurried to the living room to watch the reports of the terrorist attacks on the larger screen TV it boasted. They looked at one another. Calvin said, "It must have been the New Madrid quake you felt." Nan could only nod. They watched the news coverage late into the night.

They were up at their usual time the next morning. The phone rang as they were having breakfast. Calvin opened his cellular phone. "Yes. Yes. We'll be there this morning to take a look at it."

"We're getting the crane delivered today at the Andersons' yard," Nan said.

"I know. That was Audrey Blankenship. She wants us to berm up around their house. They're going to build a shelter in their basement. I told her we'd take a look."

"Oh."

Calvin's cell phone rang again. He had a conversation almost word for word like the first one. "That was one wanting a hole dug to build a shelter."

They didn't need to print any flyers. Calvin and Nan stayed busy in the area helping people prepare shelters. From digging trenches and cutting timber for people to build expedient shelters as illustrated in Nuclear War Survival

Skills by Cresson Kearny, to setting factory and home built shelters from the simple to the elaborate. The library had a copy of the Kearny book. The librarian was kept busy copying the various plans for people. She wouldn't let the book out of the library.

After a short discussion, they took half of their assets and converted them to gold and silver, and bought a huge order of LTS food. They had planned to sell most of it to those who were having difficulty getting ready for whatever might happen. Only the fact that they'd been a regular customer did the company they used agree to send even a fourth of the food they wanted. The company wouldn't guarantee delivery, but would not charge them if they didn't ship.

Every other company they contacted refused the order. Like the company Calvin and Nan used, the other companies were only filling orders for regular customers. There were vastly more orders wanted than all the LTS food companies combined could now fill.

Nan was on the backhoe on the A300 digging a pit for Harley Jacobson to bury a septic tank he was converting to a shelter when the ground began to move. She saw Calvin and Harley both fall down then try to climb back to their feet, without success.

With the bucket curled and resting on the ground, Nan clambered down off the hoe. She wished she'd stayed on the Bobcat. The ground was still shaking and it was making her nauseous. The Bobcat had been moving, but somehow feeling the earth move under your feet was worse. She almost fell, but managed to keep her feet as Calvin and Harley finally scrambled back onto theirs.

"Crimeny!" exclaimed Harley. That was a hell of a..." The words faded, either because he quit talking or they were drowned out by the massive sound that throbbed in their ears.

All three covered their ears with their hands, the sound was so intense. It seemed beyond loud. Almost like a living being. And it lasted, like the shaking had, seemingly forever.

But fade it did, finally. Calvin took his hands from his ears, and when Nan did the same he asked, "Can you hear me?" He was worried he might be deaf, the silence was so total.

When Nan responded in a normal sounding voice, he was relieved. "I can hear, but that was loud enough to hurt. What was it? A nuke?"

Calvin was looking around. "Felt like it could have been, but I didn't see any kind of flash and there's no mushroom cloud. A nuke would have been close to cause that much shaking. Try the radio."

Nan ran to the Unimog and climbed into the cab. "Nothing. Not even static."

"Nuts!" Calvin called out. "See if the engine will start!" He breathed a sigh of relief when the engine turned over and started with nary a grunt. He looked over at Harley. "Harley, try your Ford."

Harley went to his pride and joy. A brand new Ford F150. He tried to start it. It didn't start, even after several tries. There weren't even any clicks you're prone to hear when a battery is just weak.

"EMP," Calvin said. "There was a nuke." He continued to look around. "But there is no sign."

"Oh, my God!" Nan said quietly. What if it was a nuke at Yellowstone?"

Nan saw Calvin blanch. "That wouldn't account for the EMP. But if there was a general attack there would be at least one high altitude blast as an EMP bomb." He'd been staring off into the distance as he'd talked. Now he looked at Nan. "We need to get home."

"But what about my shelter?" wailed Harley. "I'll die!"

Husband and wife looked at one another. They'd read up on fallout and studied the possibility of Yellowstone blowing. "We have time. But that's it." Nan said. "We do this, and then go home." Calvin nodded.

Working quickly but carefully, Calvin and Nan set the two piece septic tank into place. They took enough extra time to help Harley knock a hole in one end to act as the entrance. With the dirt from the hole mounded over the septic tank and the used railroad ties that were leaned against one end to make the right angle entrance they were finished.

Again, working quickly but carefully, they loaded up the A300 and Toolcat onto the transport trailer and headed home. Both were tense, afraid that someone would want them to stop and help. But no one did. They'd barely left town when dust began to rain down.

"Had to be Yellowstone," Calvin said. He slowed down even more than usual. Volcanic ash was highly abrasive. He didn't want any in the engine through the filters. He even preferred stopping occasionally to clear the windshield by hand rather than run the wipers and risk scarring it.

They began to breathe a little easier when they got to the section of road they'd improved. They'd be home in a few minutes. A few seconds later the NukAlert on the Unimog key ring began to chirp. Just one chirp, then another a few seconds later. But then the chirps came much more rapidly.

"Fallout, too," Nan said softly.

"We're almost home," Calvin said, equally softly. "We'll be okay."

They were silent the rest of the way. It only took a few minutes. The NukAlert was chirping continuously when they pulled around the circle drive and stopped. Both jumped from the truck and ran to the house.

"Wait!" Nan said. "We need to decontaminate. The hose." They stripped and took turns holding the hose for the other to thoroughly wash off the small amount of ash and fallout that had accumulated on them during the dash from the truck to the house. Leaving the clothing where it lay, Calvin unlocked the door and they entered the house, shivering slightly.

Nan went to get them some clothes. Calvin turned on the TV. The power light came on, but it wasn't working. "Crap," he muttered. "The EMP." He put on the robe that Nan handed to him, and then hurried to the garage. There was the box.

Calvin took down a storage box from the shelves lining one side of the garage. He opened the box and took out a 5" battery operated television. Carrying the TV he returned to the living room. Nan was using their survey meter to check areas in the room for radiation.

"We've got radiation coming through the door. Not much, but we need to stay out of the line from the front door to right here by the door out to the garage.

"Okay," responded Calvin, going over to the big screen television. He swung one edge of the entertainment center away from the wall. It took only moments to unhook the antenna cable and connect it to the portable. "Get me some D batteries, Nan." They didn't have an AC cord for the little TV.

Nan hurried to, then back from the kitchen, carrying the batteries. Another few moments and the TV was on. It had been a waste of time. Calvin ran the dial up and down. Not a single channel was working. Nan went back to the kitchen and tried the radio in there. Also nothing.

Calvin joined her in the kitchen and they looked at one another for a few moments. "Finding out what is going on will have to wait. I could be wrong, but I think Yellowstone has blown, maybe because of a nuke. That'd be the ash. And the missile silos have probably been hit. The winds are right for them to be the source of the fallout. We in for some rough times, but if we're careful, we'll be all right."

Nan stepped over to him and put her arms around him, her head on his shoulder. "I know. Thank God we've done what we've done. Let's sit down a minute and think this through."

Nan's hands were shaking as she got water from the refrigerator for both of them. She had to hold her glass with both hands to be able to take a sip.

"Okay," Calvin said. "You do what you were doing before. Survey the whole house and find where we're safest from the radiation. We built this house with this in mind, so we have a pretty good idea where those spots are. Just confirm them.

"I want to go ahead and disconnect all the antennas from everything in case there is another big EMP blast. At least we've been keeping the other gear disconnected. I'm afraid to hook up the Shortwave receiver and other monitors. I think the one scanner we have hooked up is dead. It's not scanning. Neither is the weather radio. I just hope some of the antennas are still okay."

"We do have the backup antennas," replied Nan, sipping her water as she tried to calm herself.

"True, but we won't be going out for some time. Not with the radiation and ash coming down the way they are. I suspect we're going to be cooped up in here for some time to come. You up to continuing? I want to check the rest of the communications gear and the power system. We've still got electricity, but I want to see if the rest of the gear is okay. At least we had thyristors protecting the power systems."

Nan nodded and stood. She picked up the survey meter from the table and headed for the living room again.

CHAPTER SEVENTEEN

Buddy didn't waste any time. He wasn't fearful someone else would buy the property. Buddy wanted to get to work on it. Every minute he wasn't working, eating, or sleeping he spent on getting the place ready for whatever might come. The news seemed worse every day.

The plan was to build a nice place in the large clearing, to take advantage of the view, but he wanted something to live in while he was working there. So Buddy bought a thirty-foot fifth-wheel travel trailer. He thought about paying cash, but decided on the spur of the moment to finance it in order to conserve his cash. Besides, he got a zero-percent-interest loan on it.

He was a little worried about there being enough topsoil for an easy septic system, but it didn't turn out to be a problem. Buddy went ahead put in the system so it could be used for the house when it was built.

For the things he was concerned with, living in the trailer as is would not be adequate. It was far too vulnerable to nature's ravages and human kind's efforts. He was going to need a garage and shop, anyway, so he built one to house the trailer and his truck.

Before he started work on the building, he contacted a well driller friend he'd worked with a few times on rural homes. He cut a deal with him to add a basement bathroom in the driller's home to offset a portion of the cost of the well. The well was rather marginal at only five gallons per minute production, but the driller assured Buddy that, though low producing, the wells in the area were steady producers. He could pump five gallons a minute all day, every day, if he wanted.

"How is this going to work again?" Charlene asked when she got out of the truck and stood beside it.

"Okay. These arched pieces I brought up last week will be bolted together to form a Quonset type structure. I'll build walls on each end, and then mound earth over the whole thing."

"That's a lot of dirt!" Charlene said. She followed him over to the stacked arch panels.

Buddy laughed. "I've got a lot of it! I just have to pull it from several spots on the property. It's pretty thin in spots." He'd had a loader delivered to the gate and roaded it to the site the previous week. It had taken a week of evenings to prepare an area the way he wanted.

The footings and floor were poured and cured enough to erect the structure. Getting the concrete truck up had not been difficult, though he did have to cut a few trees to widen the track. The cut up wood was stacked handy for the woodstove that would heat the building.

Like the loader, a small truck crane was rented and sitting ready for use. Buddy had used it and a trailer to tow a man lift up to the site as well. He gave Charlene a hard hat and showed her how to use the crane. It would all be simple work. Buddy was sure she could handle it.

Charlene wasn't as sure as Buddy, but when he helped her lift the ends of the first two arch panels into place so he could bolt them together at the top, she realized she could, in fact, do it. And do it safely. She merely had to be careful and take her time.

They shifted the bases into place on the foundations and Buddy fastened a timber to it to act as a brace when they lifted it up. Charlene lifted the center of the arch into the air. Buddy spotted the brace, fastened it to the ground with a stake, then quickly added nuts to the bolts now projecting up through the base plates of the arches.

It took a while, but they had all the arches up by the time they finished that day. Buddy used the man lift each time they erected an arch panel to connect it to the previous one. When they were done they had a fifty-foot long, thirty-two foot wide, sixteen foot high tunnel.

Buddy drove the crane truck and towed the man lift back to the rental place while Charlene drove his pickup.

Over the next few days Buddy erected reinforced concrete block walls at each end of the tunnel, using scaffolding he had rented for that reason, and to do the high interior finish work. Charlene helped him when she could. She even took a few turns in the loader, when the task was simply moving dirt or gravel. When the end walls were done, Charlene helped him install the drain system consisting of perforated pipe laid in a gravel bed and covered with more gravel.

It took well over a week of loader work to do the mounding. Buddy didn't want the berm too steep, so the berm was very wide. Though he lacked huge amounts of good dirt, he had plenty of rock available. There was one bench he had a powder monkey come up and blast. That provided more than enough fill rock.

The actual soil was only used next to the arches, on the roof section, and to fill in gaps between broken rock. The mounded structure then had sod laid on it. He'd built a four-foot wide tunnel with a right angle turn in it as a rear entrance and exit.

He did the same with the person-sized door on the front. The windows on each end of the garage he had heavy steel shutters made, and a shelf inside on which he could stack solid concrete blocks to provide radiation shielding. The garage door was different.

The trailer he simply parked inside before he put up the front wall. But he wanted to be able to bring the pickup inside, too. Buddy framed and built a heavy steel sliding door for the opening. Next he built a five-foot high concrete block wall, the width of the structure including the earth berming. It was out ten feet from the edge of the berm against the front wall. Then he built a thick berm in front of the wall.

The section between the wall and structure berm was a concrete slab with a shed type metal roof covering the section in front of the garage door. Between the wall, the half-inch metal door, additional solid concrete blocks to stack inside the door, and the sloped roof, which could be sprayed to keep fallout away from the door area, Buddy was sure he had made the structure as radiation resistant as was practical.

There was still plenty of room to get the truck in and out. Though he didn't attempt it, Buddy was pretty sure he could actually get the trailer out, if he wanted. He wasn't sure about getting it back in.

Buddy breathed a sigh of relief when he put the finishing touches on the building. There was time to get some shelving built to hold the extensive supplies he'd ordered earlier.

"Holy cow, Buddy!" Charlene exclaimed when she saw the rental cargo trailer hooked up to Buddy's pickup. "You say that thing is full of food?" The trailer was a sixteen-foot tandem-wheel box trailer normally used for moving.

"Well, almost. There's some water barrels and some other bulky stuff, too." Buddy looked over at her as they belted themselves in for the trip up to the property. "You sure you want to help with this? We'll be getting back late."

"I'll help. But you're sure going to owe me a major dinner at Red Lobster.

Buddy smiled. "Sure thing. I'll be getting a bargain."

"Don't be so sure. You know I love lobster."

They talked companionably after that on the way up to the property. Buddy had picked up the load at the trucking terminal that morning. He wanted to get it into the shelter as soon as possible. The bed of the truck was filled with additional material he wanted to get up there as well.

There was plenty of room on the shelves for everything, with plenty of room left over. They stacked case after case of long-term storage food. Food grade fifty-five-gallon barrels were lined up on the wooden deck Buddy had made when he built the shelves. He'd bring up the generator and fill the barrels with water the next time he came up.

Charlene had brought a picnic lunch up and they had it sitting on the wall berm, watching the city. But it was a light lunch and they more than made up for it at the restaurant that evening.

The next morning Buddy was on the way to the driller's home when the first news report came on the radio about Pakistan and India. A few minutes later Charlene called. She was obviously frightened at the implications. He was able to talk to her for a few minutes and she was calm by the time they hung up.

The driller kept a radio on all day as they worked. The driller was acting as Buddy's helper on the job. When the report came in that India had retaliated, Buddy called Charlene.

"Charlene. Yeah, it's me. You know that bug out bag I helped you put together? Yeah. I want you to go get it and keep it with you all the time now. Okay?"

Sure now that if something worse happened, Charlene had the means to get to the shelter. Buddy had insisted on giving her a set of keys to the locks that secured the place. If need be, she could get there and into the safety of the shelter on her own.

That evening he went over to her house and helped her select things to go ahead and take up the first chance they had. He added a few things to her bug out bag and went over a few procedures in case she did have to go up by herself.

Buddy sweated out the next couple of days. He'd ordered a windmill generator and a solar photovoltaic system. With the things going the way they were, he wasn't sure if he'd get them before something else happened.

People were postponing jobs on him right and left, though there were a couple of rush jobs. Buddy had the time to do a little more shopping himself. Stores were running out of many things, but he was able to pick up most of what he wanted. Most of it was things that he would wind up using anyway, even if nothing more serious happened.

Charlene wasn't getting much business so she took the day off when Buddy was ready to take another load of things up.

On the way home that evening Buddy was explaining the whys and wherefores of some of the items that Charlene had helped him shelve that afternoon when the radio station they had on, low, announced a special bulletin. Buddy quickly pulled over to the side of the road when the first announcement came of the tremendous earthquakes in California and Missouri and Illinois. Buddy turned up the volume and they listened to the report.

Charlene gasped when the reporter stated that terrorists had used nuclear weapons to create the earthquakes and destroy the United Nations building. She looked over at Buddy, her alarm obvious in her face. "Buddy..." she asked tentatively.

"It's okay. Doesn't sound like it's a general attack. Just terrorists." Buddy shook his head. "Did I just say that? Just terrorists? I want to get home and see what the news networks are reporting. I'll drop you off so you can..."

Charlene cut him off. "Buddy, I don't want to be by myself. What if there are more attacks?"

"Okay. You can stay at the house tonight. I'm not sure how much sleep we'll get. Because you're right. This could be the start."

Buddy took Charlene home the next morning when there were no reports of further terrorist activity. He made her promise that if something really bad happened and she couldn't get hold of him she would go up to the shelter by herself.

Buddy was finishing up a job, literally putting the final polishing on the sink he'd just installed when the lights went out in the house where he was working. Suddenly the room was flooded with light. When he hurried out of the room he yelled for the lady of the house to get away from the windows, but it was too late.

He dove back into the bathroom, into the bathtub. He heard the glass breaking and the woman's scream, then the loudest sound he had ever heard. He gave it a few seconds, and then carefully made his way out of the bathroom.

There was nothing he could do for the woman. She was obviously quite dead. The blast wave from the nuclear explosion had shattered the window through which the woman was staring. The broken glass literally shredded the flesh from her bones before it threw her against the far wall. Buddy heard the house creaking. The blast and wind had damaged it severely. Buddy hurried out.

The mushroom cloud was still glowing with heat. None of the houses seemed to have been destroyed, but all looked like they had received moderate to major damage. Buddy tried to start the plumbing truck, but the starter wouldn't even click. "EMP," Buddy muttered.

It took only a couple of minutes to get out the mountain bike he'd taken to carrying in the truck. The bike was equipped with a handlebar bag, and panniers hanging on either side of the rear tire from a stout rack. On the rack was strapped a medium size duffle bag.

There was enough equipment and supplies on the bike, Buddy hoped, to get him to the shelter. However, when he climbed on the bike he headed for home, rather than the shelter. The bike would get him to the shelter, but if he could get there with the truck, and more supplies, so much the better.

Buddy cut his eyes toward the mushroom cloud. It was still growing. He stopped long enough to feel the wind on his face. It was from him toward the cloud. The weather pattern should keep it that way. But Buddy was unsure how the nuke blast itself might affect the local weather pattern.

It was a good bike, with good tires. Despite the occasional plea for help from those milling around outside their houses, Buddy knew that if he stopped to help anyone, much less everyone that might be helped, he'd never survive. He changed to a higher gear and sped up, weaving around obstacles.

It took a while, but he was only six miles from home. An hour later he was at the house. Buddy crossed two fingers of his left hand, and turned the key of his truck with his right.

He breathed a sigh of relief when the truck started right up. The EMP had not destroyed the ignition components. He wasn't worried about any of the other electrical components. As long as the truck would run he was happy.

Buddy quickly set the bike into the back of the truck. It took only a few minutes to add the equipment cases he'd packed and stored in the garage. Just in case. He added the fuel cans from the shed, along with a few other items he kept there.

He heard the survey meter sitting on the seat of the truck began to tick occasionally. He saw some activity at his neighbor's house on his left. Buddy ran into the house for the last few items he was going to take to the shelter and ran back out. He was glad he had. When he came out his neighbor was just starting to get into Buddy's pickup.

One of the things Buddy had retrieved from the house was a Stoeger double barrel Coach shotgun. "I don't think so," he said forcefully, striding up and blocking the man from closing the door of the truck. "Get out!"

Hands in the air, the man slowly slid out of the truck and stepped away. A few steps, and then he turned and ran back to continue loading his car with what looked like to Buddy, totally useless household items.

Buddy took another moment and strapped on the UM-84 holster rigged tanker style for his primary handgun, a Colt 1911A1. He set the shotgun and the rest of his small collection of weapons in the cab, along with a musette bag with ready ammunition for the pistol and rifles. He added four fifty-caliber ammunition boxes full of additional ammunition to the truck.

He tried to reach Charlene on the FRS radio. No response. Buddy put the truck in gear and pulled out of the driveway, headed toward Charlene's shop. It took only a moment to read the note taped on the front door. "Gone to the house to get Big Bob."

She done the identical thing that he had done. Her car wasn't in her regular parking slot so Buddy assumed the EMP hadn't damaged it. He drove over to her house and found another note. It was simple. "Shelter."

Wishing she were with him, instead of on her own, at least Buddy knew she was alive and heading for the shelter. He headed that way himself. The survey meter was still clicking, but Buddy took a moment to glance at the meter.

Still under 0.5 R/hr. If it didn't get much worse for a bit he would be okay.

The roads were jammed. Like quite a few others Buddy put his rig in four-wheel-drive and left the pavement. He'd made careful observations on several different routes out of different parts of the city toward the shelter. He knew where he could stay off pavement and get somewhere and where he had to use the regular roads.

Once he had to use the truck to help push three vehicles off the road that were not working. He didn't ask if it was lack of fuel or EMP damage. He and another man in a pickup just used their front bumpers to get the vehicles out of the way.

Buddy did a double take when he saw Charlene's car up ahead. Charlene was taking a bike similar to Buddy's off the rear rack where she carried it when Buddy got up to her. As horns honked, Buddy stopped and jumped out of the truck to help Charlene load the bike into the truck.

It took less than a minute and Charlene was climbing into the passenger side of the truck and Buddy was moving again. Traffic on this section of the interstate was moving well, but Buddy saw what was shaping up to be a major traffic jam ahead.

"Thank you, Buddy!" Charlene finally managed to say. "I wasn't sure if I would make it on the bike. My car just quit as I was driving. I was having trouble keeping it running since this all started. I thought I was going to just have to take the bike up from the shop, but I finally got it started."

Buddy reached over and squeezed Charlene's hand for a moment. "Yeah. I had to bike from the job home. I'm glad I started unhooking the electronics in the truck. If you'll notice, it's mostly really old vehicles still running."

Charlene looked around at the traffic. Buddy was right. There were a few new models, but the majority was older models.

"Time to take route B," Buddy said and took the next exit. Traffic was backed up almost to the interchange.

"What do you mean?" Charlene asked.

"Road ahead is blocked. We're taking the railroad right of way past the blockage. If we can we'll get back on the Interstate. If not, the railroad will take us all the way to the county road. I know we can get off there. Just keep your eyes peeled for an oncoming train."

Instead of crossing the tracks that paralleled the Interstate and crossed the intersecting road, Buddy turned onto the tracks.

It was something of a rough ride as the tires went over the ties supporting the track, but Buddy was afraid to try to run on the tracks themselves. It would be hard on the tires, for one thing. He didn't think he could keep on the tracks, anyway. At least not at speed.

Apparently someone had seen what he was doing and tried to emulate his actions. Unfortunately they were in a car. The width between the wheels was enough to get the tires on the tracks, but as soon as a little twitch of the wheel bounced them off the track onto the ties the car slid to a stop. The car underside was resting on the tracks. The tires were touching the ties, but there wasn't enough traction for the car to move.

Buddy kept checking the rearview mirror, to make sure a train didn't come up on him unexpectedly. He was sure that the car would be moved off the tracks by someone else wanting to use the tracks the same way he was.

Fortunately, the only time they did have to get off the tracks to allow a train past, there was a good place in which to do it. From the looks of the front of the train someone else had been on the tracks and didn't get off them in time. There were pieces of an automobile hanging from the front coupler of the engine.

The next train was still some distance ahead when they reached the county road and turned off the tracks. The top of the mushroom cloud had broadened significantly. There had been a bit of very fine dust coming down, with the survey needle slowly creeping up from 0.5 R/hr to 0.6 R/hr during the time they'd traveled.

The railroad tracks had been a much more direct path toward the shelter than the roads they normally had to use. It was fortunate because much heavier fallout began and the survey meter jumped up to 200 R/hr. "Hang on," Buddy said. "I'm going to speed up. It was only another mile to the gate.

Charlene started to get out to get the gate, but Buddy said, "The radiation. Stay inside. I'll get it." She didn't argue, just hopped over and drove through the gate when Buddy opened it. She noted that he took the time to close and relock it. He brushed off as much of the fallout that had accumulated on him as he could, then climbed back into the truck.

Charlene held on tight as they bounced over the rough terrain that was the road to the shelter. Buddy pulled onto the concrete under the roofed area between the barrier wall and the shelter. This time Charlene got out of the truck before Buddy could protest. She ran to the entrance of the shelter and went inside to open the garage doors.

Buddy hopped out as well, and as Charlene struggled to open one half of the sliding doors, he pushed open the other. As soon as there was clearance, he got back into the truck and backed it inside.

When they had the doors closed again Buddy called over to Charlene to get a water hose. He washed down first Charlene, then himself. Then he, with Charlene's help, washed down the truck and its contents. The contaminated water ran to a floor drain near the garage door and ultimately to the gully.

It was cool in the underground shelter and Charlene and Buddy were both shivering by the time they were finished. Buddy hustled Charlene into the trailer, grabbed a robe from a closet, handed it to Charlene and pointed to the bathroom.

When she'd had a hot shower and had changed clothes, she went out and continued stacking the concrete blocks in front of the windows and doorways that Buddy had started. He hurried inside the trailer and got his shower and changed clothes. He came back out carrying the damp clothes, holding them well away from his body.

"I'm quarantining these till we have a chance to decontaminate them better."

Charlene nodded. Buddy got the survey meter from the truck and went over to Charlene. "Hold up a minute. Let's see how we're doing, radiation wise."

He ran the survey meter all around Charlene. There was the occasional click and the needle of the meter would wiggle, but it was doing that anyway. There was no appreciably greater intensity of radiation on either of them than the background radiation.

Charlene rested as Buddy checked the rest of the shelter for radiation leaks. Only at the big door and the windows was there any appreciable radiation. Buddy helped Charlene finish stacking the solid concrete blocks to increase the shielding at the big door and the windows. The personnel entryways, with their shielded right angle turns and heavy lead lined steel doors were fine.

When all the additional shielding was in place they took another break. Charlene just looked at Buddy for a moment, and then stepped into his arms. He held her for a long time as she cried. He shed a few tears himself. How was his brother and his brother's family faring?

CHAPTER EIGHTEEN

Charlie was only able to stay in the stacked concrete pipe for another few days. The ground was excavated and the pipes placed and buried. But that wasn't such a bad thing, it turned out. Though the piping was installed, it would be some time before the pipe would be in use.

As it was, Charlie had access to one end of the line. He also had access to the freshly poured basement of the building. He was cautioned about being caught in the building, but Clyde didn't run him off when he started using both places. With the work at the golf course, and the occasional clean up job there at the building site, Charlie was doing okay.

He was able to get a package of disposable razors to replace the single one he'd been using for a couple of weeks. Though he didn't need it at the moment, he found and purchased a nice woolen overcoat at a thrift store nearby. He used it as extra padding for his bed, which was still primarily discarded newspapers, of which he had a good supply.

The previous winter had been a rough one on him. Something else he stocked up on was some extra food. Like the coat, he didn't particularly need it at the moment, but one never knew. Ramen noodles were light and didn't take up all that much space.

He bought another bottle of vitamins and some protein bars, too. All in all, he was feeling pretty good. He always read the newspapers before he added them to his bedroll and the reports he was reading were the only thing bothering him at the moment.

Several of the workers were leaving partial lunches behind, which he scavenged every evening. He was getting more than enough food. He checked the dumpster carefully for things other than food, and found a few more items it contained from the construction site to make his life a bit easier. He'd need to move on before winter, as the building would be mostly complete by then. The dumpster was emptied every morning for the next round of cleanup from the site.

Since the dumpster was outside of the fence, some of the locals had begun using it to get rid of trash after the construction shut down each afternoon. Charlie was able to cull a few useful items from those things that had come from other than the construction site.

When Charlie went down into the basement that evening he noted the tiny trickle of water leaking in at one of the joints of the drainpipe. He'd told Clyde about it and Clyde had asked

Charlie to keep an eye on it. If it got worse, Charlie was to let Clyde know.

Clyde wasn't concerned with the water coming in the drainpipe. He was worried about where it was coming from. There was a twenty-inch main water line running just four feet from the drain tile. If it was leaking, the construction company was going to wind having to pay for the repairs. They'd be blamed for sure, no matter what actually caused the leak.

Charlie shook his head and smiled. The leak wasn't bothering him. Actually it was to his advantage. It had not been hard to work a soda straw from a discarded fast food cup into the crack where the leak was. It didn't divert all the water to the container he placed under the end of the straw, but it did catch most of it. He wouldn't drink it, but he did use it to wash with.

He counted up his money. He had more things now than when he'd first got to this part of town, and even had more money left than when he'd arrived. Charlie was tempted to go back to the thrift shop and get a suit, shirt, tie, and shoes to try to find a job in the area. But it would take all the cash he had at the moment and he was reluctant to do that. Things were just too uncertain.

He might have to leave at any time if those having the building constructed found out he was living here. Charlie sighed. Things were definitely better than he'd had it in a long while, but they were far from perfect. He hadn't had a drink since he finished the bottle when he first got here.

Charlie went out the following morning, to take a long walk as was his usual practice now that he wasn't walking most of the day, dumpster diving. He studied the building as he walked back toward it. It was definitely coming along. When finished it would be five stories. They were working on the second floor steelwork now. Upon seeing the group of fancy cars parked at the gate, Charlie changed his path and skirted the construction site. The bigwigs were there to do an inspection.

Charlie stayed out of sight, out of mind, for most of the day. He wound up making a few dollars helping clean out a burned out store. He'd gone past and seen some men working and asked if they needed help. They hired him on the spot. He was soot and ash coated when he got back to the construction site late that afternoon. Clyde was just locking up the gate.

"I was a bit worried about you. That chintzy banker was here today, looking things over. You'd think the building was his. He is going to have a small branch facility on the first floor, but he acted as if the whole thing was his. You doing okay? You're a mess."

"Helped clean up where they had that fire last week."

"Oh. Come on over to the truck. My wife was cleaning closets and was giving stuff to Goodwill. I thought you might want a few of the items. What you don't want I'll drop off down there."

"Clyde, you don't have to do stuff like this. I still think it was you started leaving those partial lunches behind." But Charlie went over to the truck. He was a practical man. There were several items of clothing he could use, but that was about it. Charlie thanked Clyde and headed to what he was referring, at least to himself, as his lair.

It was cool, as always, in the drain tile, but Charley stripped, washed himself thoroughly, shaved, and put on some of the clothing he'd received from Clyde. Feeling a new man, he sat down to work on a project. He'd been accumulating pieces and parts to construct a handcart to carry his stuff. He had quite a bit more stuff than would fit in just two buckets. He had several more, now, but there was no good way to carry more than two...unless he had a cart.

CHAPTER NINETEEN

Edward really didn't need to be at the meeting, since they wouldn't even start on his part of the building until much later. But he wanted to be there. It was exciting to be involved in the construction of a new multistory building.

He definitely would be here often when they started constructing the vault. It would be a small vault, but it would be brand new. Both the banks he now owned had all been built before he acquired them. They were nice, of course, but even though this was just a branch facility, it was new. And he loved new.

Just as the ten-person shelter was new. He'd been a little surprised when Emily had not put up a fuss about digging up the back yard on the other side of the pool. When he found out how big the hole needed to be he threatened to sue if excavation of the hole for the shelter damaged the pool. It hadn't. They'd even done a decent job of restoring the lawn damaged by the equipment.

He'd only been in it a couple of times. Once to check out the installation when it was completed before he signed off on the bill. The other time was to show it to Doc Cutter. He'd picked a time when Emily was off to a seminar of some kind. No need to have a scene with Emily unless it was needed.

Doc had been ecstatic. Edward smiled at the memory. He'd transferred a third of his assets to each of Edward's banks. Those thoughts faded as he pulled up and stopped at the fence of the new building.

He was careful of his clothing, but he made a show of questioning everything he could about the construction. The others might not care, but he intended to be in one of the best new buildings in the area.

The construction foreman calmly answered each question. He satisfied Edward that he knew what he was talking about and what he was doing. Edward was looking forward to that evening with Courtney. This building was exciting.

CHAPTER TWENTY

Charlie was feeling pretty good, despite the news in the papers. He'd just made fifty dollars working for Clyde on a big cleanup. The hotshots were coming back the next day to do another inspection. Charlie hid his smile when Clyde groused about the banker.

"Thanks for the work, man," Charlie told Clyde as Clyde paid him off. Charlie knew just what he would do with half of it. The thrift store had a really nice bike he could use to tow the cart he'd finally finished. Twenty-five bucks would get it. He would add the other twenty-five to his winter stash. He was trying to put twenty to fifty percent of everything he made away to help him through the winter. The winters seemed to be getting worse.

Charlie stopped at the hardware store the next day to pick up a few items to make the two parts of a hitch so he could tow the cart with his new bike. It wasn't fancy, but it was durable. It made him much more mobile.

He was almost back to the building when everything in front of him brightened. He felt some heat on his back, and then heard a terrifyingly loud rumble. He took a quick look over his shoulder and began to pedal for all he was worth.

The crews on the jobsite first tried their vehicles, and when they wouldn't start, began to run. Charlie assumed they were headed home. He'd just dragged the bike into his tunnel home when the earth shook. A sudden wind pushed him a few feet down the tile, and then pulled him back.

Suddenly he felt of his ears. There was blood coming from the left one. He wiped it away. As he was doing so, he noticed yesterday's paper. It had some rules to follow in case of a nuclear attack. He had not read it yet. The earth still trembling, Charlie dragged his stuff down to the middle of the long pipe, sat down on a bucket, and began to read by the light of a small candle.

After reading the first few paragraphs of the article, Charlie hurried out of the tunnel, and went to the stack of plywood near the building. Working quickly, but carefully, he leaned several sheets of plywood against the end of the piping.

Figuring if he got into trouble, so be it, Charlie climbed up on the skid steer loader the construction outfit used around the building site. Fortunately the bucket was attached. It was the work of only a few minutes to push enough dirt into the hole, against the plywood, to provide shielding.

That done, Charlie checked the site over carefully; taking everything he thought he might need into the basement of the building, then into the tunnel. That included several wheelbarrow loads of dirt.

By the time he was finished he was aching and the fallout was starting to come down heavily. Making up a new bed, Charlie lay down, lighted the candle again and finished the article. After that he pulled his light blanket over himself and tried to fall asleep.

CHAPTER TWENTY-ONE

Edward's wife Emily was in Edward's bank, talking to Angela about the shelter at the house and getting advice on what books to get and read, just in case. She never came to the bank, except on the days that Edward was out golfing. It had been sheer coincidence that she'd run into Angela at a nearby restaurant a few weeks previously and recognized her. Emily had struck up a conversation with Angela and they became friendly.

Like Angela, Emily was worried about the world situation. Emily had been totally amazed when Edward told her it was too bad that she would lose her prize azaleas, for he was putting in a survival shelter.

The only person she felt confident in confiding the news to was Angela. Edward and that scurrilous doctor had not played golf the week before, so Emily had to wait until today to see Angela. She wasn't worried about Courtney seeing her and reporting it to her husband. Courtney always disappeared for several hours when Edward golfed during the week.

Angela and Emily were talking in the break room when they felt the building suddenly shaking. "Oh My God!" cried Emily. "An earthquake!"

"I don't think so," Angela replied. Both women hurried toward the bank lobby from the break room. The mushroom cloud was visible in the distance through the front windows of the bank.

Emily repeated herself. "Oh My God!"

"I don't know about the rest of you people, but I'm heading home to find shelter," Angela called out. She'd thought about the vault as shelter if something like this happened while she was here. But the building and vault were both old. The vault had neither a means to ventilate it, nor an inside lock release. Anyone using the vault for shelter would probably die of asphyxiation.

"No! Wait!" Emily said, grabbing Angela's arm. "Come with me to my house. That shelter is big enough for ten people for months. I don't have a clue how to survive, and I know Edward doesn't either."

"I doubt Mr. Baumgartner would welcome me," replied Angela.

"I don't care! I welcome you. I don't care how many supplies we have. Neither Edward nor I have any clue what we should do. Edward just bought the shelter for a status symbol among his banking cronies. Please. I'm begging you, Angela. Help me."

Angela thought about it and her own chances for survival at her apartment complex. She had a few weeks worth of supplies, but that basement was going to be crowded beyond belief.

"Okay. But you have to deal with Mr. Baumgartner. If we're going, we'd better get started. We'll probably have to walk."

"Oh, no. I have the Mercedes."

"I doubt it will run, but let's check."

It took all of a minute to decide the car wouldn't start. Another minute and a very surprised Angela was urging Mrs. Baumgartner into her old Chevy, which started right up. Angela had not thought it would, due to the EMP.

They did have to walk the last few blocks. The streets were gridlocked within a half hour of the attack. Angela got Emily out of the car and hurried to the rear of the car. Angela opened the trunk. It contained a fold up cart, a large backpack, and three large duffel style totes. There was also a moderate size waist pack with belt. Angela put it on first.

It took only a few moments for Angela to set up the cart, add the three duffels to it and shoulder the pack. At Emily's amazed look, Angela said, "My BOB. Bug out bag. I've been expecting something to happen."

Angela was doing fine, even with the load, but Emily was breathing heavily by the time they made it to the Baumgartner house. Emily nearly fainted when she found her daughter and son alone in the house. The babysitter had left immediately after the blast.

"She'll never work for me again!" declared Emily.

Angela simply responded with, "The fallout has started. Let's get the children into the shelter and see what we need to come back and get."

Emily herded the frightened children before her, Angela following as they made their way to the smooth, rounded entrance hatch of the shelter. Angela opened it without difficulty and had Emily go down first. Next Angela sent Catherine down, and then John. She lowered her bags to Emily. Finally she climbed down herself and closed and dogged the hatch.

Angela took a few long moments to inspect the shelter and decided they really didn't need to go back out for anything.

Edward let Doc tee off, and then Doc's wife. He was feeling good today. The building was coming along nicely. They would start constructing the vault the latter part of next week. The vault door was scheduled to arrive the day the rest of the vault was to be finished. The last independent bankers' meeting had gone well.

Some didn't like the new restrictions on withdrawals, but it suited Edward. And those that had made preparations other than strictly financial had been suitably impressed with his ten-person shelter with just about all the options.

He had food for ten for a year and water for six months. A generator that would provide full power for the shelter with fuel for two months. Battery capacity with a solar panel recharger that could stretch the generator use to four months or more. Every whiz-bang gizmo he'd been able to find to ensure his survival in style.

Once he started buying he found the subject of preparations rather fascinating. As much as he distained it, he'd bought some gold and silver, though his portfolio of paper assets was much greater. He'd even bought two guns. He refused to buy a handgun, but the Steyr AUG had been irresistible. So had the Benelli police style shotgun. Oh, yes. Let the world bring what it might. He was ready.

Except Edward happened to be playing golf on the north side of town. The side closest to the military base fifteen miles away. The three weren't the only ones blinded by the brilliant flash of light. Nor were they the only ones the blast wave sent tumbling along the ground, their bodies bruised and battered beyond recognition. They weren't the only ones to die, just three of millions. Some quickly, like them. Some slowly, over time.

CHAPTER TWENTY-TWO

Percy and the others didn't find out the sequence of events or the identity of most of the targets hit until months later.

China launched a nuclear attack on the US Fleets near Japan and Taiwan after the attack on Pyongyang. The US retaliated with a single nuke in an isolated area of China and a demand to cease hostilities. China responded with an all out attack on the US and Democratic Russia. This began the full-scale exchange by the nuclear powers.

Every nuclear power in the world began launching ballistic missiles, tactical missiles, and cruise missiles, all with nuclear warheads. Nuclear bombs were launched from aircraft. The few artillery pieces that could fire nuclear shells were put into use, until counter battery fire put them out of commission. Several nations and terrorists alike detonated many in-situ nuclear devices emplaced over the years.

Democratic Russia retaliated, primarily at China.

When the exchange began between the United States and China, after China's first EMP blast in subspace over the Midwest United States, the newly communist Russian Republics launched the missiles now under their control.

They targeted mostly Germany, France, and Great Britain with their medium range missiles, and the United States with their long-range missiles. Spain, Italy, and Turkey also took hits on American bases in those countries.

Several additional Russian Republics suffered Communist coups. They too turned their nuclear weapons on the West, including France and Great Britain.

Those countries with the capability retaliated in kind. Germany seized the US missile forces within their borders and launched retaliatory strikes. The US forces also struck back with the nuclear forces still under their control.

Israel struck nearly every Arab nation after Tel Aviv took a hit with a nuke from Iran and chemical and biological weapons from several other Arab nations.

Israel was not the only nation to suffer chemical and biological attacks. Besides the few terrorist nuclear devices detonated, most traditionally Western nations had terrorist planted chemical and biological weapons activated. Some had been in place for years, their sleeper agent handlers just waiting for the appropriate time to activate them. China also launched some missiles with chemical and biological warheads.

Many places took hits with multiple devices. Some intentionally, others because several countries targeted the same place for the same reasons.

Both China and the United States, with the openly available information on potential earthquake and volcanic problem areas of the world, targeted their respective enemies' tectonic weak spots. Targeted as well were nuclear power plants and hydroelectric dams. For the most part, China and the United States were the only two nations that targeted geological formations. Both used the geological targeting heavily.

The geological attacks worked as hoped. One of the missiles in the first wave of ballistic nuclear missiles from China targeted the Yellowstone caldera. The nuclear device triggered another massive super volcanic eruption similar to the one that had created the caldera previously. The local devastation was total. Massive waves of lava spread out for miles. Lava bombs, thick ash, and toxic gasses sprayed for miles more.

The westerly winds carried huge quantities of ash for hundreds of miles across the northern tier of states and southern Canada, all the way to the Great Lakes. The ash mixed with the radioactive fallout, from not only the warhead that created the volcano, but the series of attacks against military, industrial, resource, and population targets in the Northwest and Northern Rockies.

The Yellowstone caldera wasn't the only tectonic weak spot hit. Many fault zones and dormant volcanoes took hits. Volcanic eruptions took place on a massive global scale, as did earthquakes.

The Great Rift in Africa was hit with five small devices, unleashing gigantic tectonic activity at the point where one plate overrides another.

The San Andreas Fault was only one of several fault complexes hit along their lengths. Destroyed dams flooded the river systems that lay downstream from them.

The volcano on La Palma Island in the Canary Island chain was hit. As intended, the western side of the island slid into the ocean, creating a mega-tsunami. The tsunami caused great damage to the southern portion of Great Britain and a few other places. However, the major damage was to the entire eastern seacoast of the United States, already reeling from the nuclear, chemical, and biological weapons being used.

A series of huge waves, the largest of them towering over one hundred feet high when it hit the coast, devastated the entire eastern seaboard. Much of Florida was literally washed into the Gulf of Mexico. Other places were also devastated. The waves traveled inland as much as twelve miles in places, destroying nearly everything in their path.

Many of the Caribbean Islands, like parts of the state of Florida, were scoured clean. Some disappeared all together. The eastern coast of Brazil also suffered massive damage from the tsunami.

A new outlet channel for the Great Lakes opened when the New Madrid fault system and the fault system that includes the Saint Laurence Seaway received nuclear hits. Each of the Great Lakes was hit at least once, causing huge seiches. The combination of factors allowed the Great Lakes to begin draining from Lake Huron to the Ohio River at Cincinnati to the Mississippi at Cairo, Illinois and thus to the Gulf of Mexico, creating a new bay which now extended northward up the old path of the Mississippi River to just south of Memphis, Tennessee.

In addition to the geological targets, China targeted military, industrial, resource, and population centers, just as most of the other nations did, except, of course, in the areas where China wanted to take over in the Far East.

Part of China's goal was to cripple the United States' ability to respond to China's expansion plans. Therefore, they targeted not only the oil fields and refineries the US controlled directly, but also those in Mexico, Central America, and Northern South America to deny the resources to the United States. Brazil also took several nuclear hits with the aim being to destroy the industrial capacity it had developed, to deny its use by North America.

China targeted all major cities in Australia and Japan to keep the Aussies and Japanese from interfering in China's now much broader expansionist plans for not only India but all of Indochina as well.

The US targeted China, North Korea, and the Russian Republics that launched against the US, with some limited strikes against those nations that attacked Israel. South Africa used her small stock of nuclear devices to decimate regional tribal rivals.

Nuclear powered submarines and ships were sunk in several locations during the battles. Most were destroyed completely. A handful were sunk with reactors still mostly intact. When the controls failed, the reactors began to run out of control, pumping megajoules of heat energy into ocean shallows and a few seas, off several coasts.

Some fires started from the thermal radiation caused by the blasts, but most were put out by the blast waves and their reversals. Others succumbed to rain in areas with high humidity as the dust in the area mixed with the moisture and formed gigantic thunderstorms near many of the targets. Ash and smoke from fires still burning, and ash and gasses from activated volcanoes filled the air, mixed with radioactive fallout. Huge storm systems developed over the sites of the still active sunken nuclear reactors.

Huge amounts of fresh water dumped into the Atlantic from the storm systems. This added more fresh water to the North Atlantic, already freshened by the melting sea ice and glaciers caused by global warming. The warm, heavily saline Gulf Stream began to sink beneath the less saline water of the east coast of the United States.

CHAPTER TWENTY-THREE

"I don't know," Percy said, watching the western sky for a few moments before ushering the others inside. "But I don't like it. If it's nukes, we're in for some bad fallout. If it is another earthquake, there probably will be more aftershocks. If it's a volcano, we're in for ash, And probably fallout."

They heard the blast of an air-horn over the outside monitor speaker. Percy ran for the door again, then to the gates. It was Andrew Buchanan driving the Wilkins Oil semi-tractor. He had a seven thousand gallon trailer with a three thousand gallon pup behind it.

"When it all hit the fan they'd just delivered the fuel trailers," Andrew told them after Percy had him pull into the estate and park the trailers by the number one tank farm. "The guy dropped the tanks and took off like a rabbit. I guess he was lucky his truck was an old one. There's a bunch of diesel trucks that aren't running. I didn't think EMP would get diesels."

"Not just the ignitions system that get fried," Percy responded automatically. "How'd you wind up with the tanks out here?"

"Mr. Wilkins was scared. He headed for the shelter some of the city employees made in City Hall for the townspeople. I was afraid something would happen to the fuel. Fuel is going to be really important. I knew you'd give it back if that was the best thing to do." Andy looked hopeful.

"Of course I'll give it back. I'm not sure bringing it here was the best thing, but it is safe. You were thinking on your feet. That's good. But why did it take you so long to get here?"

"I couldn't get the truck started. It took me a while to find another Freightliner computer that wasn't fried. Pete Broomhouser's truck is down. Literally in pieces. The computer was in an old fridge he's using to store some of the delicate parts while he's working on it. I had to give him all the money I had and a check for everything I had in the bank. But I think it was worth it. I can always make more money."

Susie had worked her way over and had her arm linked with Andy's. "That was smart and brave," she said, looking up at his face. "You didn't know what might be happening. You were thinking of the community, not yourself. That's real responsibility."

Andy turned a little red and replied. "Aw, it's nothing. There wasn't any fallout kind of stuff, and I thought, 'What would Mr. Jackson do?' So I did what I did. It's really no big deal."

"I think it is a big deal," Percy said softly. "Be that as it may, from now on, I want you thinking about yourself, just as much as others. Did you bring anything else with you?"

"No. I just thought it more important to get the fuel to a safe place. I'll walk back to town and see if my Jimmy will run. Not very many cars are running, except really old ones. If it doesn't I'll figure out something. I can still stay here, can't I, Mr. Jackson?"

"Of course, Andy, I'll run you in tomorrow or I should say today, because it's after midnight. So, get some sleep everybody. Mattie, put Andrew in the beige room. I'll bring you some clothes and things. Everything else you might need will be in the room."

Andy was dressed, sitting quietly in the kitchen when Percy came down at four-thirty. "I couldn't sleep any longer. I wonder what's going on."

"We'll find out," Percy replied. "at least locally. After we take care of the animals I plan to hook up a shortwave receiver to see what we can find out. May be too early for it, but I'm willing to risk one cheap radio."

Andy followed along as Percy headed for the basement steps. "What do you mean risk the radio? Do you think there could be more EMP?"

"It's possible," Percy replied. "There's no way of knowing what attack scenario has been used. There could be nukes for hours more.

Maybe even for several days. But there will be survivors. Just like us."

"Yeah," Andy responded, taking the dosimeter Percy handed him. He clipped it in the pocket of his shirt, the way Percy was wearing his. Then he uttered a soft "Wow!" when they entered the tunnel.

"The survey meter wasn't showing anything, but I wanted you to see the tunnel. We can get to every major building on the property through these tunnels. It'll be critical when we start receiving fallout."

"Do you think we will, Mr. Jackson? Get fallout?"

"If there was a full attack, we will. If it's just been a few, maybe not. I'm just not willing to take a chance. That's why I want to get the animals taken care of and go get your things. I can't see us having more than a few more hours without fallout."

It didn't take too long to tend the animals. They were restless, however, when they weren't allowed outside.

When they returned to the house, the others were up. Percy told Susie, "The animals are restless. Work with them some in the barn. I want to get Andrew's stuff as quickly as possible and get back. No radiation yet, but use the tunnels, anyway. There is some stuff coming down, but it's not radioactive. Almost has to be ash from a volcano. We're just going to grab some juice and coffee and be on our way. If the ash keeps up it'll start clogging the air filters on the pickup."

Like the Suburban, Percy's Chevrolet one-ton extended crew cab pickup was stretched and equipped with three axles, all steerable. It had a ten-foot pickup bed with a retractable bedcover. It used the same tires and had many other components in common with the Suburban, including the same diesel engine. "Figured we might need the open space of a pickup," Percy said to Andrew as they went into the large attached garage.

"Wow," Andy said again. The garage boasted a pair of sixteen foot wide double garage doors, but was large enough to easily hold the seven vehicles in it with room for a at least three more. Besides the Suburban and the one-ton pickup, there was a lengthened Chevy one-ton van, converted, like the pickups to six wheel steerable drive. The Jeep the twins had picked up in Minneapolis was behind the Suburban.

Two other trucks had been moved from the house garage to the equipment barn after the Jeep had been added to the mix, to provide more space, just in case. One was a second pickup, identical to the first, except with a high shell on the bed, rather than the retractable bed cover. The other truck that had been moved was another one-ton extended crew cab, stretched, with three steerable driven axles and diesel engine, like the pickups. It had a twelve-foot long flat stake bed with a light crane.

The '74 Cadillac Fleetwood Talisman was behind the pickup. Beside the Caddy were two motorcycles. The first a World War Two era Indian motorcycle with sidecar, equipped with a reverse gear.

The other bike was a customized Harley-Davidson. Not really a chopper, but with moderately raked forks and handlebars. The drop style seat rode on springs for comfort. Percy could straddle the bike and stand, feet flat, with comfort. The bike boasted a sliding, padded sissy bar, carrying a large pack. The bike was also equipped with huge leather saddlebags.

"I knew you had the Rokon's," Andy said. "I didn't know you had a Harley!"

"I don't ride much. I just always wanted one, and when I could afford it, I got one. That Baby Boomer thing, I guess. The Indian was my dad's. It was in poor shape, but I had it restored. It was a military dispatch bike and has a reverse gear so you can back it up with the sidecar. Really stable and can carry lots of gear. I have trailers for each bike… see there in the back?"

"Oh. Yeah. Cool." Earnestly, Andy added, "I really appreciate you taking me in to get my stuff. I hope the Jimmy runs, but even if it doesn't, I want to get the other things."

They climbed into the pickup and Percy started it and then opened the garage doors. They were doublewide doors and there were two doors for each opening. There was an inner door and an identical outer door, separated by the five-foot thickness of the outer dirt and concrete vertical wall that fronted the garage section of the house. Both sets of both doors were on electric openers with manual overrides.

Like much of what Percy owned they were custom units. The panels were three-eighths inch thick steel. The panels overlapped when closed. The doors were counterbalanced with weights and pulleys and could be opened electrically or manually. When closed they provided significant fallout protection. With the two layers of steel, separated by four feet of space, they were proof against most types of forced entry when locked. The man doors were also three eighths inch steel and doubled.

Percy activated the door closer when they pulled out and around the berm that had been put up in front of the garage, similar to the ones at the barns. "Are the berms for radiation protection or defense?" Andy asked.

"They'll work for both. I hope we never need to use them for the latter. We did the same thing for the barns. We can wash down everything and still get outside after any radiation level falls to a safe point. Even if there is still some radiation beyond the berms for a while, we will have a safe place to work outside."

"You've thought of everything," Andy said with admiration. They were headed toward town on a deserted highway.

"No one can think of everything," replied Percy. "I'm always worrying about what I might have neglected to get... or do... even now."

They rode in silence. It was cloudy and a fine ash was falling. Percy ran the wipers to keep the dry material cleared. When the first faint scratch appeared he quickly turned off the wipers, remembering that volcanic ash tended to be highly abrasive. He would stop occasionally and dust off the windshield with a cloth.

He checked the survey meter often. They saw not a soul on the way into town. They began to see some movement behind windows as they pulled up to where Andy's Jimmy was parked, near the door to his first floor apartment, in an old two story converted house.

"Good," Percy said, "I thought I remembered you having a tow bar. Even if it doesn't start we can get it out to the estate. Give it a try right quick. We'll hook it up if it doesn't run."

It didn't. It took a couple of minutes to get the Jimmy attached to the back of the truck. As they began loading the things Andy wanted to take with him, a couple of people came out, standing under the roof of the porch.

"Aren't you afraid of radiation?" the first one asked. It was Andy's neighbor, Pamela Johnson. "We've been staying inside, behind piles of books and drawers full of dirt."

Percy quickly showed them the survey meter. "You did the right thing. You've still got time to add more protection. I wish we could stay and help, but the fallout could start any minute. If you see any change in the look of the ash falling, get back into shelter. Do you have water?"

"A little," Pamela replied.

"Again, there's time to get some things. Andrew and I will go see what we can find and bring back, but take the time now to gather up whatever you can and improve your shelter."

They finished loading Andy's belongings as more people came out and Pamela explained what Percy had told her. Percy looked over at Andy when they got back into the truck. "As long as there's no radiation I can't not help."

"I know," Andy replied. "I feel the same way. I'm lucky you're letting me stay at the estate. It's probably the safest place in the state, except for the shelters for government officials. I hope Tom Nesmith and his family have good shelter. They were helping get the shelter at city hall and one at the old granary set up for people when I was out looking for the Freightliner parts.

"We'll stop at both places and see if there's anything we can do. But Andrew, we have to be careful about becoming sidetracked or encumbered with too much. We have people at the estate depending on us. There could be some people that might want to take from us what we have. Just so you'll know, there's a Marlin semi-auto Camp Carbine in .45 ACP under the cover behind the rear seat. I want you to get it out the next time we stop and keep it handy. There are extra magazines there, too."

"Yes, sir," Andy responded, hating the fact that it might be a necessary precaution, but knowing they must be careful.

Percy shifted the bottom of the windbreaker he was wearing. "And I have this." Andy saw the grip of the Para-Ordinance P14 extending from the holster on Percy's belt.

Fortunately they didn't need the rifle or pistol at any of the stops they made. Steven Gregory, the owner of one of the small grocery stores, was in the store, rationing items out. He was letting people take a limited amount, without paying. He told Percy and Andy that the other store had mostly sold out, then been looted. He'd started rationing, at regular prices, until people had more or less run out of money. He quit asking and just handed out what was left, a little to each person that came in.

"You have any water left? The people at Andrew's apartment house could use some," Percy said.

"I'm giving everyone two bottles and two cans of food of their choice. You can take the same for however many are at his place. I trust you, Mr. Jackson, not to cheat."

"Thank you, Steven. You're doing a great thing here." Percy looked around, and then took two coin tubes from his pocket. "Here's a couple of tenth ounce gold coins and a roll of silver dimes."

Pulling a pad of his small barter sheets from his pocket, he wrote quickly, tore the top sheet off at the serrations, and handed the piece to Steven Gregory. "Here's a barter for a week's food, when things settle down. We seem to be okay at the estate and so far the green houses and animals are okay. Use some discretion, but let people know you'll be able to barter for food when the danger of radiation is over."

Steven's eyes brightened. "Really? I didn't know what I was going to do when my personal supplies ran out. I didn't think about the farms around here. Maybe some of the others will trade, too. Could I get some of those barter sheets you use?"

"Sure," Percy said. "Andy, there's a pad in the pocket of the truck. Would you get it for Mr. Gregory?"

"Sure, Boss." Andy was back in a flash with the pad.

"Please don't promise people too much," Percy said, "Or be too specific. I'll do what I can, but until we get together and see what I can supply, I wouldn't do any bartering. I wouldn't even say anything until we know we will be able to do it at all. I could lose everything if we wind up with a nearby detonation."

"I understand. But you'll come through. I know it," Steven said, his voice filled with awe. Percy was the first person he'd seen that had any hope at all. Everyone else was just desperate to survive the next few hours or days. It was a rural area and people tended to keep a few groceries in the pantry, but that was usually a week or two's worth. He'd not been able to think past when the store was empty.

When they got back to the truck, Percy looked at the survey meter. "Andrew, go tell Mr. Gregory the fallout has started."

"Geez!"

Percy turned the truck around and loaded up the items Steven had indicated. Andy jumped into the truck and Percy headed back to Andy's apartment house. "I was afraid we wouldn't have much time," Percy told Andy. "It's just barely above background, but we're definitely getting fallout now.

They quickly unloaded the water and food, leaving them with Pamela to distribute. They told her the radiation had started. Pamela quickly called to the others as Percy and Andy drove away. It took only moments to check in with those sheltering at city hall. They seemed to have what they needed, including a survey meter.

Percy took a moment to take Tom aside and tell him much the same as he'd told Steven Gregory and asked him not to mention it until things settled down. "We might get some help from the state or the feds. I just don't want to get peoples' hopes up then not be able to follow through. I just wanted you to know there are some possible options for food in the foreseeable future."

"Okay, Percy. Thanks."

Percy started to turn away, but then said, "Is Patrick Wilkins here?"

"Yeah. He's a real problem. Feel free to take him with you," Tom said dryly.

Percy grinned. "Not a chance, but I would like to talk to him."

It took only a couple of minutes for Wilkins to sign over the ownership of the trailer loads of fuel to Percy for an ounce of gold and a barter slip for a week's worth of food sometime after the next two weeks.

Andy looked on as the two men had talked privately. He couldn't hear, of course, but when Percy and he walked out to the truck, Andy asked, "Did you just buy that fuel from Mr. Wilkins?"

"Yep. Greedy devil but he's not too knowledgeable of the real value of things. I would have given him a month's food for that fuel. He took a week's worth and an ounce of gold."

"What good is gold? The food I can sure see. Not going to be many reefer trucks with fresh food for a long time."

"He took gold. Others will. We're still going to need a medium of exchange. I don't think paper currency will do it. People won't trust it. I think they will gold and silver, just like people have since the very beginnings of modern civilization. Barter is great, but you still need a medium of exchange. A means to acquire things when you don't have the trade goods the other party wants. Some means to set values that people can understand.

"You've heard me refer to a couple of, quote, weeks' worth, unquote, of food. There's bound to be a difference of opinion on what that is. Since it will appear that I have so much, my definition is going to be considered a lot less to those that are hungry, with their hand out. I'll be more specific in the future, but we're in a hurry right now."

It took a few more minutes at the other shelter. They didn't have a survey meter, just a couple of dosimeters. They did have a hand held radio and plenty of batteries. They would be able to stay in touch with those in the town hall and coordinate activities.

"We're not going to do this again," Percy said, glancing at the survey meter as they headed back out to the estate. Percy had to swerve almost off the road to avoid a SUV rocketing toward them on the way back to the estate.

"That guy's crazy!" Andy exclaimed when Percy had the rig back fully on the road. "He could have killed us and him."

"Scared," Percy said, calmly.

They backed the Jimmy into the garage of one of the cottages, and then returned the pickup to the garage at the house. They washed down both vehicles before they went into the garages. Then Percy called Mattie on the intercom and had her bring out a change of clothes for him. Andy took out a change from one of his suitcases that they'd washed down.

"Not much on these," Percy said as he changed clothes in the garage, "But we do not carry any fallout into the houses or barns. We decontaminate every time from now on. We'll deal with these later." Percy showed Andy where to put the clothes they'd removed, for later cleaning.

"We were getting worried," said Sara, when the two entered the kitchen of the house. She gave each a quick hug, and then stepped back. "We've been watching the meter. There's radiation now."

Percy showed them all how to read the dosimeter he insisted they each now wear at all times. He used his as the example. "See, it's not even a measurable amount. But as I told Andrew, we don't take any chances. From now on, until the radiation falls back to the background level I have recorded for here, we wear the dosimeters and track our accumulated dose, as well as taking readings with the survey meter regularly. We limit our outside trips to those absolutely necessary. And for the immediate future, only Sara, Mattie, and I will go outside, unless there is a major emergency."

All the rest immediately protested that they should share the risk. Percy raised his hand to quiet them and explained. "We three are the oldest. We'll be close to the end of our lives before a low dose of radiation will usually result in cancer or other problems. Like thirty or forty years from now. Even if it's twenty, we'll still be old. You all would just be in the prime of your life, even still in the childbearing years for some. There is no reason for you younger people possibly to suffer during the most productive part of your life, if it can be avoided.

"It's not that you won't get some exposure. It's bound to happen. We won't be in shelter forever. We will limit the exposure more, the younger you are. We're talking long term planning here. We have to think of accumulated dosages over the next twenty, thirty, forty years. Even after it's safe to go out... relatively speaking, each and every time you do, you will be getting a little radiation.

"We'll decontaminate here. Things are set up to make it relatively easy. But the radiation will be decaying after the detonations stop and the dose rate peaks. By the seven ten rule, radiation should be one tenth what it is an hour after the peak dose rate, seven hours after that first hour, then one-tenth of that 49 hours later, then a tenth of that about two weeks later and so on. For each seven fold increase in time the dose rate, assuming no new radiation, the dose rate drops to a tenth of what it was.

"So, if we were to peak at… say… one thousand Röentgens it would be down to zero point one Röentgen in four months and down to zero point zero one Röentgen after about two and a half years.

"While the fallout is building, then the first two days are really dangerous. Then the next two weeks, still dangerous, but should be okay after that to go out for decontamination and necessities. After four months, it will be a matter of sleeping in shelter, but working in decontaminated areas should be okay for a regular daily schedule. In less than three years, there won't be much to worry about, except the weather."

"Nuclear winter?" Melissa asked.

"Possibly, more likely climate change for other reasons. We've been staring at the possibility since the North Sea started freshening up from melting ice. We might get colder, warmer, or stay the same. One thing is for sure, the weather will be unsettled for a long time. As much ash as we are getting, and the different varieties, makes me think that a lot of volcanoes let loose. A couple of big volcanoes can put more debris in the air than all the nukes that could be used.

"If the trend is warmer, we're looking for lots of rain. If the trend is a lot cooler, then we should expect drier weather. Either way, the storms will be worse with really heavy rains and snow, even if it's cooler and drier over all. If it's warmer then we'll just get lots and lots of rain and that's if we're really lucky... Geez!"

The dome shook yet again. Percy ran to the den and flipped on a TV, flipped another switch, then worked a remote control. "This camera is in a grounded steel housing out by the towers. I opened the cover. Look."

There was an ugly glow in the distance to the west, illuminating the clouds and falling ash. "Probably thirty miles, possibly more," Percy said. "No target there. It could be one that just missed or there's something there that we never knew about but they did." Percy didn't specify who 'they' were.

"I just thought!" Jock exclaimed. "What about chemical or biological weapons?"

They all looked at Percy. "They both have very localized areas of destruction. If any were used... are being used, the effect will be right there. They are primarily tactical weapons. They can be used for denial of territory, too, on a strategic scale. We should be fine. The house HVAC system has appropriate filters. So do the animal barn fans. There is a danger of biological weapons spreading diseases from locally affected populations, but I doubt there'll be much long distance travel for a long time.

"Most of the biologicals I know about are virulent and would kill off those exposed quickly. It wouldn't be able to spread without fast transportation. And chemicals should dissipate pretty quickly. Nor are they mobile. They'll stay where they are, except for some possible runoff problems.

"There is always the possibility. We will just have to watch for signs of them as we go about our business. I have suits and respirators for the decontamination. They're good for NBC. We'll be wearing them when we first go out anyway, so if there was something biological or chemical we'll be protected until we can detect it.

"Since we're on the subject, when we do start going out, without the protective suits, I want everyone in long sleeves and no shorts. Everyone wears a wide brim hat, or at least a cap. There's going to be a lot of UV exposure, probably. Even when it's cloudy. A person could pick up a burn without realizing it. Try to wear

UV coated glasses, sunglasses or clear, whenever it's daytime, to protect the eyes from the UV exposure.

"Now, I want to go check the animals after this tremor. They'll probably be agitated and upset anyway about being cooped up."

Everyone except Mattie went with Percy and helped calm the animals. The horses and dogs were the most agitated, but calmed down quickly with the human presence. The cattle and chickens didn't seem to be affected. The pigs showed signs of having been, but were happily rooting around the dirt floor in their area of the barn.

The dirt areas in the barn had raised quite a few comments from people that learned about them. Percy never really explained why he had them. He just told people he was too cheap to buy concrete.

In actuality, it was for the animals' health that he had put in pits in the barn floor and filled them with dirt. The surfaces were kept raked clean of wastes, which went into the compost piles or the methane generator, or both. Each animal had an individual stall, if needed, but were allowed, for the most part, to stay in designated areas in groups.

The barn was a series of connected domes, creating plenty of space for the animals, with a generous area for work and another for feed storage. There was even a well-equipped veterinary area so they could do much of the vet work themselves. Doc usually came to the barn to do what he needed to the animals. Only if one needed isolation did Percy take the animal over to Doc's hospital. He could isolate three animals in the barn if he needed to, it was just labor intensive to take care of them. Doc had a couple of hired hands that did it for him.

The stalls were equipped with individual automatic feeders and waterers. The compounds were equipped with group feeders for each type of animal. Percy, as he did the crops, rotated the animals on the different areas yearly to minimize the chance for disease organisms building up. The occasional complete emptying and refilling of the pits also helped.

The studs were usually stalled when a female of the species came into estrus, when Percy wanted outside breeding. There were separate birthing areas for the horses, cattle, and pigs. The chickens had their yard and coop in the barn. There was a separate sitting coop for when he allowed a brood hen to hatch eggs.

Most of the cattle came to the edge of their pen to watch as Percy and Susie put the horses and dogs through their paces. The pigs pretty much just kept rooting around or sleeping. The humans seemed to enjoy the activity as much as the horses and dogs. They returned the dogs to their indoor kennel. Several went to the doors through which they normally went outside, but made no fuss when they were told they had to stay inside.

Percy showed them the rest of the tunnels and the utility rooms of the various barns before they went back to the house, staying in the tunnels. Mattie had a late lunch on the table when the others returned.

"Reading is up," Mattie said when they all gathered in the dining room after having washed up. "A lot."

Percy went to look at it before he sat down to eat. "Three hundred and climbing," he said when the others looked at him. Percy wasn't particularly religious, but he asked Sara to say grace before they ate.

She did, and included Percy in the thanks for giving them shelter from the storm. They all said heartfelt amen's to the sentiment, knowing the storm Sara meant. As the meal neared its end, Percy said, "I'm going to hook up a shortwave receiver and see what I can get. I've tried the regular broadcast bands and there wasn't anything. Satellite services seem to be out, too. Anyone want to listen in?"

When the others all gave resounding versions of 'yes, of course they wanted to listen,' Percy muttered, "Stupid question, I guess."

They spent the rest of the afternoon listening. There was a great deal of static. There were also some conversations going on in the amateur radio bands, which brought sighs of relief from most of the others. Percy had expected it, but the others seemed to think they might be the only survivors, after the radiation levels began climbing.

They felt several more shocks, though they were very weak. There was much speculation of what was causing them. Nukes, volcanoes, or earthquakes. There was simply no way to tell. Percy checked the camera occasionally, always closing the protective cover after a quick look around. It would be several days before he went out and installed another camera on the antenna towers.

The next few days were spent the same way. Sleeping, eating, tending the animals, and listening to the shortwave. Things were more or less normal, except they couldn't go outside and there was no live TV.

Percy had a vast library of books, music, and video. There were days when there was quite a bit of activity on the shortwave, others when there was little but static. Those days the library got a lot of use. Percy was convinced that the war was still raging in some places in the world. The radiation spiked three times, the last time at six hundred Röentgens per hour, then began a steady decline.

At the end of eight days after the last peak, the dose rate was under two Röentgens per hour. Percy would go out the next day and put up a camera. Mattie and Sara would begin the decontamination.

CHAPTER TWENTY-FOUR

It took Percy less than a half an hour to mount the camera, return to the house, and decontaminate. He'd put a time limit of a half hour on all of them. He paced while he waited for Sara and Mattie to finish their half hour. They seem determined to stay the full length of time, though both had seen him go into the garage.

Percy managed to wait for them without calling them on the radio and telling them to come in. He was waiting by the door when they came through, each woman not starting to remove their respirators, rubber boots, or Tyvek suits until they were in the mudroom. Percy had a simple decontamination shower in the garage that drained to a dry sump in the yard. They'd hosed each other down thoroughly before going inside.

"Barely getting a tick now," Sara said, handing Percy her dosimeter. He checked it, then Mattie's. They picked up only a tiny dose, as had he. He made a point to log it on the chart he'd printed for each person. He'd enter the data in a computer later to keep a running track of accumulated dose over given time periods.

The Doctors Bluhm had been reading up on radiation sickness in the library and were now familiar with the symptoms. At the doses the three had been exposed to, there was no danger. The doctors, as well as Percy, intended to keep it that way.

"Just a tick," Sara repeated. "Inside the berms of the house. Outside, of course, it's still over one. Do you think we can do the animal barn tomorrow and maybe let the animals out, one at a time?"

"Not yet. They're going to want to run free a bit. I want to use the sweeper on at least one of the pastures first. I'm debating whether or not to strip the top soil. I want to look at the crops, too, and decide what to do about them. I'll do what I can in the greenhouses, too. The automatic systems are okay, I saw the watering system go on as I was coming back to the house. We should be able to recover quite a bit."

"Whoa!" Jock said. "Even if all that needs to be done, you can't do it all. Not in one day. It's low enough that a couple of us can get just a little exposure the next couple of days. It should be below zero point six in less than a week, if my calculations are right. We'll be able to do a lot then."

Percy frowned.

"Come on, Boss. We spray the outsides of the greenhouses, and then I can go in and work the greenhouses for half an hour," Susie said.

"Yeah. I know you and Mrs. McLain, and Mrs. Simpson will do most of it right away, but we can risk a little exposure," Andy said. "Except Doctor Bluhm, of course, since she's still pregnant."

"And I will be for another eight months. I don't want to go out much, but a few minutes of fresh air, in the decontaminated zone won't hurt, will it?"

Jock looked reluctant, but his studies told him that the risk was minimal. They had to wear the respirators while they were stirring up dust, but a few minutes without one in the area that Sara and Mattie had cleared today should be okay. He said as much.

Melissa smiled. The others frowned. "Tomorrow," Jock quickly added. "After the area is tested again."

"Well, okay," Melissa said. She touched her belly and said, "I don't want anything happening to junior here, but I really need to get outside. I could stand it when I had to. Now it's hard."

"We all feel the same way," Percy said. He hung up the suits and racked the boots, gloves, and respirators for their next use.

They had the entrances and work areas decontaminated by the end of the week, including the patios atop each of the buildings. It hadn't occurred to Percy to do it sooner. As soon as they were hosed down, and the slopes of the dome, there wasn't even a tick on the survey meter in the center of the patios, being as high as they were and with the mass of the earth covering the domes between the remaining fallout particles and those at the patio center. The radiation was very little higher even at the edges.

Percy decided, for the first pasture to be decontaminated, to till it very shallowly and scrape the tilled soil up. He dug a pit just outside the pasture and buried the dirt he scraped up. Percy had washed three large patches of grass near the barn. He'd used a fire hose run from the barn to wash any fallout from the patches to the surrounding grass. He left the washed patches when he tilled the rest of the pasture. When they turned the animals out the horses and cows went immediately to the three grassy areas. The hogs and chickens were happy with the large expanse of bare ground.

Percy debated about trying to reseed the pasture. The occasional rain they were getting was washing some of the high flying, very light fallout particles out of the sky, but the radiation levels were so low, and Percy knew it would continue for months, if not years, that he decided to go ahead and get the pasture reseeded. He waited until the next day and used a broadcast spreader on one of the Unimogs to get the seed distributed.

They were still limiting their exposures, keeping the time outdoors down, and wearing the exposure suits and respirators whenever they were doing decontamination work, which was at least a little every day it wasn't raining. Percy decided the field crops were going to be a total loss, except as feed for the methane generator and the alcohol still. They would be cut down at ground level, raked into windrows, collected, and then fed to the stills.

After the alcohol content was extracted the material would go into the methane generator. The remains would be buried in a pit. Percy knew it would be useable as compost eventually, but decided to let it wait a couple of years in the pit. Then the compost would be used on fields set aside to grow crops not for human or animal consumption. Those fields would be used for fuel crops for the biodiesel operation.

There was some loss in the greenhouses due to the lack of attention the first few days when radiation levels were too high to go into them from the earth-sheltered structure to which they were connected. Sixteen days after the radiation had peaked at six hundred Röentgens, Percy decided to make a run into town with the produce from the greenhouses.

Susie loved the animals and could not help when Percy butchered a dozen chickens, a calf and two of the yearling pigs to take in, too.

He'd always sent the animals in to the butcher shop, but had everything needed to handle the job at the estate. Percy was a bit surprised when Jock offered to help. He wasn't surprised when Andy did. Andy wanted to learn everything. With the meat and fresh milk on ice from the large ice machine in the product barn, they headed into town with six dozen eggs, the produce, milk, and meat.

Percy was both pleased and disappointed with what he found in town. He, Jock, Andy, Sara, and Susie went. Percy and Sara were in a Unimog with the products, the others were in the van, with Susie driving.

Percy and Andy were both armed with HK-91 rifles and P14 handguns. Susie carried one of the HK-4s in .380. Jock declined, as did Sara.

What pleased him was that those that had stayed in shelters until the worst had passed had come through with flying colors. It had been crowded and uncomfortable in both the public shelters, but they had worked. What was disappointing was the number that had forgone shelter or left it early.

They had stopped at the clinic on the way in to pick up some of the medical supplies that had been stocked. The clinic was still intact and everything was okay. Jock took everything he thought he might need for those in town. He gave the care to the injured, sick, and dying that he could. There were many in the last two categories. Only a couple of injuries were sustained while cleanup and decontamination were being done. He treated them as well.

Like Percy's group, people had been rotating outside work, with everyone still sleeping in the crowded shelters. Progress had been good. David Reynolds had run out of fuel for his backhoe and there were several still unburied bodies. Percy transferred most of diesel that was in the tank of the Unimog to cans for Reynolds to use.

Word was sent around the town by runners that Percy was at the town hall with food. Patrick Wilkins had already made his demand for his week's supply of food. And as Percy had told Andy right after the deal had been made, there was a difference of opinion as to what a week's worth of food was.

As people began to gather, Percy put it up to them. "There's going to be lots of trading and bartering going on. Think about this. I'll let what a week's worth is be decided by vote. Remember, many of you will be growing gardens and trading labor, so think about what's fair for all parties.

Should there be more than I'm offering Mr. Wilkins for our agreement of a week of food?"

Quite a few hands went up. Wilkins demanded a lot more. Percy, pretty sure he'd be handling it like this, had shorted the pile somewhat from what he normally would have given. He added six more eggs and cut off another small piece of beef.

People looked at the quantity of food for the one person. They'd just gone through over two weeks of food rationing and knew what it took to get by. Patrick Wilkins was not a well-liked man. He'd been a constant source of trouble during the entire shelter stay and after. The consensus was that the pile of food was adequate for a week.

"You want to take it all now, or a little at a time as I come in occasionally?" Percy asked Wilkins.

"I want it all, right now," came the growled reply. "And don't none of you think you're getting any of this. It's mine. I traded for it all legal and square." Wilkins gathered up his bounty and disappeared.

As Sara, Susie, and Andy began handing out the food, asking for an hour of labor out at the estate at some point, but not doing any barter slips, Percy talked to Tom and some of the city council.

"My field crops are pretty much a washout," Percy told them. The greenhouses are okay and I think most of the fruit will be all right. But things are going to be short." He waved Steven Gregory over. "I'll get you that food in a minute. We were just discussing the situation."

"Nothing to discuss," Abigail Landro replied. "The city council will take over the farm and handle the distribution.

"I don't think so," Percy said. His temper suddenly was close to the surface. He'd expected something like this, but not this soon. Another of the town council was nodding in agreement with Abigail.

"I'm willing to share, but it will be on my terms," Percy said, rather forcefully. "I have the means and the willingness to protect what is mine." He made no move for the rifle slung over his back or the handgun on his hip, but several pairs of eyes took in the sight.

"Let's be reasonable about this," Tom quickly said. "We can work out something. Percy is a fair man. Always has been. He's managed that place for thirty years and knows how to get the best out of it. He'll help where he can, but has to have the resources to do so."

"Oh, he has resources," Jeb Canada spoke up. Wilkins told me he stole that last load of fuel that came in before the stuff hit the fan."

"That little scene a few minutes ago was part of the pay off for that fuel. Wilkins was more than willing to sell it."

"Yeah. For food to keep from starving and twenty pieces of silver, Judas."

"Judas is the one that took the silver," Percy said. "Not the one that gave it. Now, are we going to discuss this or do I pack up and leave you to your fate?"

"Come on, Percy," Tom said placating. "We will work something out. You do have a right to get for give. What is it you want?"

"For the moment a day's food for one person for one hour of labor at the estate. I'd figured to have Steven Gregory here act as my agent. He knows how to run a store."

People were beginning to gather around. "I want a piece of that action," said Rodney Stalinsky. He'd been the manager of the other grocery store in town. "I can run a store, too."

"Not for me, you can't," Percy replied coldly. "I heard what you did when things started getting tough. You won't be handling anything for me." Percy looked back at Tom, ignoring the crowd around them.

"Steven did a good thing, rationing out what he had, even giving it away. I plan to bring in things as we can produce them, and let Steven run a store just as he has before. We'll work out something between us for his doing this for me. The food will be bartered, at least for the moment, for future labor. I'm decontaminating my fields, but the fuel will eventually run low. I'll have to farm with the animals and by hand labor.

"I'm going to need lots of hands. Everyone will have plenty to do, and not everyone can do that much physical labor. I'll need people to watch the hands' children, others to help cook for them, and so on. So just about anyone can provide an hour of labor from time to time. Steven will give everyone a barter slip. I'll have a record of who owes me labor and work with the individual to pay it off. I'll do all I can to work it out to the person's best time, but some things on a farm just have to be done at a certain time. I'll expect the town council's help on seeing that people follow through on their agreements."

"That's forced labor, bub," Jeb said. "We don't go for that around here."

"Shut up, Jeb," Tom replied. "It's not forced labor. This is still a free country. People still own their property and have the right to price it the way they want. I know for sure I'm willing to work for an hour picking corn or slopping hogs to get a full day's worth of food."

Tom had turned slightly and was addressing the crowd as he continued. "We're scavenging from houses of those that died or abandoned them. If anyone comes back we'll give the individual the equivalent of what we took. Everyone is helping, that can, to start the recovery. And everyone is receiving a share. This is America. We're not inherently socialists. Many people will want to start selling or bartering whatever they can to have the things they want, in a free market. Mr. Jackson is just already ready to do it. What do you say? Do we strike a bargain with Mr. Jackson?"

Not everyone left in town was there, but a majority were, and there was an overwhelming yell of approval of what Tom and Percy had discussed. Percy asked Tom if he could say something else and Tom nodded.

Percy turned to face the crowd. "I'm going to need lots of things myself and I'll barter food for them. For some things I'll pay hard cash. I'll also take hard cash if anyone has it, for food and fuel."

Someone call out, "You mean gold and silver?"

"Yes," Percy replied.

"What about bills?" someone else called out.

"Not right now. I don't know about the future. For now, for me, it's labor, gold, silver, and specific goods. Anyone that wants to convert large denomination gold to smaller denominations or silver, to make trading easier, let me know. Most of the gold I have is the one tenth ounce coins. I also have silver dimes and quarters. A few halves, but not enough to count.

"I'm figuring on converting using the ratio of thirty six ounces of silver to one ounce of gold, just to keep it simple. Two hundred pre-1965 quarters per ounce of gold, or five hundred pre-1965 dimes. That's twenty quarters for a tenth ounce gold coin, or fifty dimes."

"What about gold rings and diamonds and such?" yet another person asked.

"That'll be strictly a negotiated deal. If I take any jewelry, I'll probably remove the stones and melt down the metal. That goes for platinum and other precious metals and stones. Each case would be negotiated."

The additional questions had caught Percy a bit by surprise. In order not to take undue advantage, or get peoples hopes up, he quickly added, "I'll be back day after tomorrow. Anyone that wants to discuss this can see me then, here."

Jock Bluhm came up to where Percy was standing on the steps of city hall. "Mr. Jackson, I need to talk to you." They stepped away from the others.

"What do we do about the injured, sick, and dying? Some of the people I can help, others… Don't have much hope. We don't have that large of a stock of drugs. I guess the pharmacy was picked pretty clean sometime after this started. I talked to the pharmacist. He said there's nothing left."

Percy rubbed his face with his hands. "Okay. Let's go talk to Tom and the council. I have a couple of ideas. But let me talk to Steven first."

Jock nodded and moved over to let Tom know he and Percy needed to talk to him again. Percy went over to join Steven Gregory. "You heard what I told the others. You willing to be my agent? Handle the food distribution? Maybe with Claude's help?"

"Sure. I bought meat from Claude. Some of yours at times, I suppose. I think he'll go for it. Of course, we don't have refrigeration."

"I know. I can do the butchering at the estate, but I prefer to bring them in for Claude to do it. We'll bring in the animals as needed. Keep the meat on the hoof until butchering day. Say Saturdays. The other stuff, two, maybe three days a week. I thought perhaps providing you and your family with the minimums. Anything over a basic amount, you'd have to buy with labor or whatever."

"It's tempting to ask for a percentage, but I know what would happen. Just like with Wilkins. If it is thought I get more than a fair share for doing this, people are going to be really upset."

"Right," Percy said. "If they see you and your family working to get extra, that should mitigate any problems like that."

"Yeah. Okay. You've got a deal. I'll talk to Claude. Same deal?"

"Yes," Percy replied. "I'll have a price list when I bring in the first load."

Steven nodded, and Percy headed back to the steps of city hall.

"Jock said you had something else?" Tom asked.

"Yeah. I just had an idea, after people started asking the questions about jewelry and stuff. Look. I'm set up okay at the estate. We can make it just fine. But I was sincere about needing help, in order to help the community.

"What I have in mind is to buy up some things, to get some circulating currency to make it easier for trading to take place. If people start accepting the coins, it'll make it a lot easier. That's why money was invented in the first place.

"What I'm thinking, is that I'd buy the clinic shuttle bus from the town. I'll use it to run workers to and from the estate, with stops at the clinic. Kind of like it was planned anyway. There are probably a few more items I can use that I'll use gold and silver to buy. That way the city will have a treasury."

Percy smiled. "I'll even pay my taxes in advance in gold and silver. That should be enough of a base, with what I'll buy from individuals, to get the coins flowing. How does that sound?"

"You know good and well the town can't tax you for anything." Tom frowned when Percy just shrugged. "We're going to have to talk this over," Tom said. "We'll let you know when you come in day after tomorrow. Is that okay?"

"Of course it is," Percy responded. "I want to get everyone back to the estate. And Dr. Bluhm needs to take care of some of the people that need help. I'll also trade some fuel for a few things. I know you need to get some bodies buried. I transferred some from the truck to Reynolds, but I imagine you need some more."

"We sure do. We'll make a list of what we need and want. One thing we do need, that I don't think you'd charge us for anyway, is water. Without electricity, we can't pump. The boys are dipping some, but it's a struggle."

"I'll bring some in when I come. Have everyone keep their empty water bottles and bring other containers. We'll figure out how to get the supply back here in town."

"Okay. Then we'll see you day after tomorrow." Tom and the rest of the city council headed into the building to discuss things. Percy joined his small group. They were just handing out the last of the food.

"What now?" Susie asked.

"We check with the doctor. See what he needs."

"Until it's safe to stay at home," Jock said, "I'd like to take a few of these people out to the estate so Melissa and I can take better care of them. I think they'll all be okay, if we keep them from catching something. A couple can be treated and brought to town in a couple of days. The rest... It's only a matter of time. There are eleven more that I don't think will make it, even with the best care I could give them.

"I feel cold and heartless not offering them more than some over the counter stuff that the pharmacist managed to save. If I use more effective measures, it'll only treat the symptoms. It won't save them. Won't even make them that much more comfortable. Except maybe at the end. All of the eleven are okay at the moment, but their first symptoms indicate that they received lethal doses and are in that period where things appear pretty normal. They'll start losing hair and teeth, bleeding at the gums and under the fingernails in a few days. They'll only have a few days after that."

"It's up to you, Dr. Bluhm. I don't mind bringing some out to the estate, even the dying ones, if you think that best. We're making sure those that die will be buried quickly. I'd just as soon not start a cemetery at the estate, though we can, if necessary."

"No. The ones that are sure to die should probably be with their families, even if it is hard on them. I'll talk to the families. We might need to take one or two that don't have anyone to care for them."

"Okay." Percy had noticed Andy sitting off by himself, and then saw Susie go over and sit down beside him, taking Andy's hand in hers. He went over to them.

"Andrew, are you all right?" Percy asked, looking at the tears shimmering in Susie's eyes.

"It's Pop. He died three days after the power went off. I was sure it would happen. He knew it too, when I talked to him the other day. If the facility lost power, he wouldn't last too long without his machine. I thought I was prepared, but..."

"We'll see to it that he gets a proper burial," Percy said.

Susie stood and took Percy a few steps away. "They've already done that. For all those that died at the care facility. He's beating himself up about not trying to do more, even though his father didn't want him to, and there wasn't anything he could have done, anyway."

Percy nodded. He went and sat down beside the young man. Andy was trying to hide his tears, without success. "Whatever you want to do, we will," Percy said gently. "Your father loved you very much. He knew you would not be able to help him and I'm sure as can be he wants you to go on and help as many others that you can."

Andy, tears still streaming down his face looked around at Percy. "I know. He even said, 'You can't help me. Help someone else.' That's part of why I did some of the things I did. We can help people, can't we? Me, at least? I'll work for my share at the estate, but I want to help those here, too. This is my town."

"I know," Percy said, fighting back his own tears at the anguish Andy was in. "We'll all be helping, in whatever ways we can. The city council has a few plans we can help with. I imagine you'll be part of that. At the very least, you'll be driving workers back and forth, and delivering food to the town."

"Really?" Andy said, the tears slowing. "More food like this?" He motioned to the food that was already gone.

"Delivering to the store. It will be distributed from there. Might as well make that the pickup point for the laborers, too. What it amounts to is you're going to be my transportation captain."

The tears stopped now, Andy nodded. "Okay. That sounds like a good plan to me. I can drive pretty much anything with wheels. And drive a team, too. Pop taught me when I was little and we had a pair of old horses for fun. I guess I should check the rigs. Make sure everything is ready for the trip back."

When Andy had turned and begun walking toward the truck and the van, Percy found himself encased in a bear hug from Susie. "Oh, thank you, Mr. Jackson! You made him feel a lot better. A useful human being again. You know just what to say, every time. Thank you." She released him and ran after Andy.

Sara was smiling at him, standing a couple of feet away. "Not you, too?" Percy said, frowning.

"No, of course not," Sara said softly. "I won't add to your embarrassment."

"Good," Percy said. He turned to go help Jock and Sara followed. "Oh," he said, absently,

"I need you to figure the value of my property. I need to pay taxes to the town. Figure it in gold."

CHAPTER TWENTY-FIVE

Calvin couldn't find anything else wrong with any of the electronics. It looked like only the one scanner and the weather radio in the living room had been damaged. And the big screen TV. The radio in the kitchen seemed to be working, and it had been connected to a small wire antenna. None of their receivers worked very well without external antennas due to the shielding effect of the earth-sheltered construction. At least they'd had EMP protection on everything, even though not all of it had worked adequately.

Nan met him in the kitchen a few minutes later and said, "It's like we planned. The kitchen, this bathroom, and the pantry are showing no radiation at all for the moment. There aren't any places where there isn't some reduction, based on the CD V-717 remote meter. But, like the area from the front door toward the hallway, there are a few places where the protection factor is only a hundred or so, rather than much higher."

"We're in good shape then. What was the outside reading?" Calvin asked.

"Only fifty Röentgens/hr, but I swear I could see the needle creeping up as I watched it."

"Probably is. Let's get a few things and set up for an extended stay in here." He hugged her and said into her hair, "We're going to be okay. We just have to hunker down and deal with it."

"I know," she replied, slipping from his embrace. She gave him a quick kiss, and then hurried off to the bedroom, Calvin following quickly behind. It took only a few minutes to bring down enough clothing and toiletries to last for several days.

It was several days and more before they ventured outside. It was two days after things started before the radiation peaked. Calvin assumed it was the massive fallout from the Dakota missile sites. That was about the same time that he and Nan began to cough. Calvin suddenly looked at Nan and said, "I forgot to put the filters in line with the HVAC system!"

He ran for the garage and quickly diverted the air intake through the filter pack and hurried back to the kitchen.

An anxious look on her face, Nan asked, "Do you think it's poison gas?" She coughed to clear the burning sensation in her nose, mouth, and throat. The smell was fading.

"No. No. It's obviously gas, but it had a sulfurous smell. I'm thinking its fumes from Yellowstone or some other volcano. But it could have been poison gas, or lethal fumes from the volcano. I should have switched in the filters immediately. Actually, several of the really bad volcanic fumes are odorless. I could have killed us both!"

"It's all right, Cal," Nan reassured him. "It worked out okay." She added, lightly, "Just don't do it again," to try to make him feel a little better.

"You can count on that. I guess we should eat."

They pretty much ate, read, and slept, with some time spent listening to the shortwave radio from time to time. They heard enough to know that the situation was essentially worldwide. There had been a nuclear war. And Yellowstone had blown. But there were plenty of survivors in some locations. Survivors like themselves.

After a week of being closed in, they began to lose power from the solar cells. It was often cloudy with volcanic ash, which continued to fall steadily. Calvin surmised that the panels were probably covered with the ash. They had several LED flashlights and lamps, with plenty of batteries for them, so they had plenty of light. The stove was propane and they also had plenty of that.

They were getting anxious to get out after the first fourteen days, but the radiation level was still too high. But it did rain and Calvin checked the battery charger the next day. They were getting current again to the batteries. Nan suggested they wait for a couple of days to let the batteries recharge before they began to draw power from them. Calvin agreed.

"I think I should come with you," Nan insisted on the twentieth day after the attack. "It will be safer if we both go out."

"But I don't want you to get any more exposure than you absolutely have to."

"Well, is this trip absolutely necessary?"

"I can't say its life and death, no. But we... I need to check on some things for my own peace of mind."

"I have that same need, Calvin."

Calvin knew better than to press it any longer. Nan had a mind of her own, and when she was right, he had to admit it. They both put on Tyvek footed and hooded coveralls, put on respirators, gloves and boots. They taped the joints for each other, and then ventured outside. Everything had come through with flying colors. They took a little time to wash off the U500, after looking around the place. After that they opened the garage and brought out the A300 and the Toolcat. Both had buckets on them and were used to good effect to clear the parking area of its accumulation of ash.

"That's enough for today," Calvin said. "Let's go in the garage and decontaminate and wash the residue back under the garage door."

Nan had had enough. The sight of the new accumulation of ash, even after the rain had knocked much of it off the trees and down the ravines rather got to her. It was a drab, gray-brown day, even with the sun shining.

But it rained again that night. When they checked the next morning the sky was still hazy, but without falling ash and the trees had been washed clean. They checked the survey meter. Down just a little from the day before. They could risk a quick trip to town. "We turn back at any sign of trouble," Calvin said. "We can't afford to be out of the shelter for more than four hours.

After checking the U500 with the survey meter, they decided to wash it down again. There wasn't much accumulation of fallout, but there were still fine particles of fallout coming down. It was low levels of radiation, but it was better to reduce the risk as much as possible.

They didn't get very far. And it wasn't just the effort to clear the two foot accumulation of ash from the road with the loader bucket mounted on the Unimog. Only halfway down their drive and they came upon a truck they recognized. It was Herbert Anderson's old truck. The truck was off the road. "Oh, no!" Nan said softly, seeing the two forms inside. The bed of the truck was piled high with cardboard boxes.

It was obvious the two were dead, their bodies already decomposing. "What do we do, Calvin?" asked Nan. "We can't just leave them here."

"No, we can't. Let's go back to the house and get something to wrap them in. Or wait. Let's see what they might have in the truck. Every single manufactured item that exists is going to be precious from now until industry is back on its feet. We can't afford to use anything we don't have to, unless it's for a very good reason."

"This is a pretty good reason," Nan replied.

"I know, honey. It is. But let's just see what they have." They went through the boxes in the truck. The rain had washed the fallout off the boxes. It had also ruined many of them. They contained mostly canned and packaged food, some of which was ruined from the exposure to the elements. It also looked like squirrels or birds had been into some of the packages. Most was salvageable.

One large box contained sheets, blankets, and a folded up air bed. Nan stared at the contents. "They were coming out to stay with us," she said.

"From the looks of the ground under the truck they waited quite a while and got caught in the worst of the fallout. I'm thinking Mr. Anderson had a heart attack on the way out and she just stayed with him until she died from the radiation."

"You're probably right," replied Nan. "I guess we can use the bedding to wrap them in, can't we?"

"Yes." Calvin looked over at Nan. "I could use some help doing that, but I can bury them by myself."

Even through the faceplate of the respirator, Calvin could see Nan's face go even paler than it already was. But she nodded and turned to get out the bedding.

It was an ordeal, but they got the bodies out and wrapped up in the sheets and blankets. Nan stayed with Calvin as he took the truck back to the house and fired up the Toolcat. A few more minutes and they had the backhoe attached, and were on their way back to the Anderson's truck. It was the work of only a few minutes to dig a large grave for the couple.

Nan helped Calvin lower the bodies inside, but couldn't watch when he refilled the hole. Silently they loaded the goods from the back of the pickup to the bed of the Toolcat. Nan climbed back into the passenger seat of the

Toolcat and they went back home. The trip to town would have to wait a couple of days.

CHAPTER TWENTY-SIX

Buddy wasn't sure how long he held Charlene, but she finally quit crying. He held her for long moments more, and then gently disengaged himself. "We need to survey the place with the meter. Find out if we have any radiation leaks."

Charlene rubbed her face for a moment with both hands, and then nodded. "Thanks, Buddy. I'm sorry I lost it like that."

"Don't worry about it. We were entitled, I think."

"What do you want me to do?" she asked.

"Go ahead and get the things you brought up put away. I'm going to check the radiation."

Charlene took the few things she'd brought with her and put them away in the trailer's second bedroom where she had stored the stuff she'd already brought up. She hesitated for a few moments, and then quickly began to move everything to the other bedroom. The one Buddy was planning on using. If he argued about it, she'd just have to convince him.

With that thought, Charlene felt herself relaxing a little and she smiled. She stepped out of the rear door of the trailer and walked over to Buddy. "What's it look like?"

"Well, the berm and steel door are keeping most of the radiation out, but we need to avoid the area in front of the big door. Everywhere else is fine."

"What about the truck?" Charlene asked. "It's parked right there, in front of the door."

Buddy shook his head. "The radiation won't hurt it. But I think I'd better get everything out of it that we may need before the radiation level gets any higher."

He handed Charlene the survey meter and went to the truck to unload everything. When Charlene started to help he motioned her back to the safer area of the building. "I'll take care of it. No need for you to increase your exposure any more than necessary."

As he worked, Buddy continued to talk. "I checked the power system. The EMP protection worked, or we wouldn't have the lights. We could have dealt with it, but having power is going to make things so much easier. We won't have to run the genset as long as the solar power and wind systems hold up."

Buddy frowned. "Maybe the fallout won't build up too much. The solar panels are slanted pretty good." Like her short crying jag had helped her, Buddy seemed to need to talk, at least for the moment.

"We should be just fine, even if the photovoltaic panels can't get enough sun. The battery bank is charged and we do still have the wind turbine and generator. We also have alternative sources of light and heat for cooking. Warmth shouldn't be a problem. The temperature stabilized at fifty-five degrees after I closed the place up. Need a jacket or sweater, but it shouldn't be too bad. We can turn the heat on for a bit when we take showers and all."

"What about nuclear winter?" Charlene quickly asked when Buddy fell silent.

"I don't think it will happen... Well... Not nuclear winter. But I've been seeing things about the Gulf Stream. If it fails, we're going to have bad weather for sure. Not like it hasn't been strange, anyway. I'm not sure whom to believe. The global warming people or the new ice age prophets. I just hope there weren't too many nukes used. Like I said, I don't think that would cause nuclear winter, but I'm worried about some of the nukes setting off volcanoes or something. A big volcano or two, on top of the stuff in the air from the nukes might just cause a cooling trend. I just don't know."

"Well, we'll weather whatever the weather does. You've got us pretty well set up here. How long could we stay in the shelter if we had to?"

"Easily two months. But the stuff I've read, we should be able to go out after a couple of weeks after the last nukes go off in this area. We'll just check with the meter every so often and when the radiation is down, we go out and take a look.

"I wish now I'd put some kind of camera system in, but I was afraid the EMP would get it." Finished with the unloading, Buddy walked over to the side of the structure, near where Charlene was standing. "We do have the periscope, such as it is."

Reaching down, Buddy grasped the handles of the hand-built device. It was made of heavy pipe and pipe fittings, quality mirrors, and throttle control cable. It was counterbalanced with lead weights suspended by steel cable. With a grunt he lifted it to viewing level and took a look around. Other than the particulates that were the fallout, everything looked normal. It was still bright and sunny.

"Amazing," he said, stepping away from the periscope so Charlene could take a look.

She had the same take on it as Buddy. "But it looks normal, except for the fallout!"

"That's what I mean," Buddy replied. "It just seems like it should be different, somehow."

Charlene took another look. "Yeah. It is weird. I don't know what it should be, but a bright sunny day with dust in the air isn't it."

"Exactly." Buddy helped Charlene pull the periscope down and secure it. "Not much left to do, except maybe get a bite to eat, maybe read, and wait for the radiation to peak, then fall to a safe level."

Buddy didn't say anything when they went into the trailer and he saw that Charlene had put her things in with his in the one bedroom.

Their days were much as Buddy had said. Sleep, eat, read, watch DVDs. And check the survey meter several times every day.

It was boring, but they got through the two weeks. Buddy checked the periscope, and everything looked the same. It was a clear, sunny day. There was no ash in the air. But when they began checking with the survey meter at the door, the level was just below one Röentgen per hour. The fallout had peaked at 988 Röentgens per hour.

"We can go out for a few minutes," Buddy said, looking at Charlene. "Just to check things. We're going to need to stay sheltered most of the time for three months. But barring a renewed attack, we can at least get out and do some things."

"Three months! Oh, Buddy!" Charlene went into Buddy's arms. He held her for a while, but she calmed herself. "I'm sorry, Buddy." She managed a small smile. "It just I've never been through a nuclear war before and don't quite know how to act."

"It's all right," Buddy said. "I'm not too thrilled with the situation, myself. But I plan to live to a ripe old age, and that means avoiding increasing the risk of cancer any more than I have to."

"I'll cope. As long as you're willing to hold me from time to time."

A soft look came over Buddy's face. "You know I will." He took her in his arms again and kissed her.

Then, stepping back, he added, "Let's at least go take a look around. And I want you armed, just in case."

Charlene nodded. One of the things they'd done to pass the time was firearms training for Charlene. Buddy was no great shot, but he knew the basics and taught them to Charlene over the two weeks. They were able to shoot the pellet pistol and rifle Buddy had, to familiarize her with shooting. One of the things they'd do once they were outside was get a bit of target practice, with the firearms, so Charlene would be comfortable with them.

Buddy was by no means a serious gun collector, nor had he stocked up on "survival" weapons. He had an old M1 Garand his father had picked up, along with the Colt 1911A1 .45 ACP that had belonged to his father as well.

In addition, he owned a Marlin 336 .30/30 for deer hunting; Remington 870 12 gauge pump shotgun for upland birds and waterfowl; a Ruger 10/22 .22 rifle and a Ruger Mark II .22 pistol for small game and for fun; and a Beretta Tomcat pocket pistol in .32 ACP. And because he once thought about getting into Cowboy Action Shooting, he'd bought a cowboy model Marlin 1895 .45-70, the Stoeger 12 gauge Coach gun, a Marlin 1894 in .45 Long Colt, and two Ruger New Model Blackhawk convertibles chambered for .45 LC and .45 ACP, along with an ADC .45 LC double barreled derringer.

His only real "survival" related firearms purchases were his "bug-out" rifle, a Savage 99A in .308 with Williams peep sight, a thoroughly modern Glock 21 in .45 ACP, and a ten round magazine extension for the 870 pump.

The weapons practice would have to wait. For the moment the main concern was just being outside for a few minutes. Despite the radiation exposure, Buddy and Charlene were glad to go out for a little while. They both donned Tyvek hooded coveralls with attached booties, slipped on dust masks, gloves, and rubber boots and went outside. Buddy had the tanker holster on over the coverall with the 1911 in it.

For the first few seconds they just enjoyed the sunshine. Then Buddy lifted the binoculars looped around his neck and looked toward the city. Charlene saw him blanch. She looked in that direction. Even without the binoculars she could see the smoke. Silently Buddy took the binocular strap from around his neck and handed the binoculars to Charlene.

When she used them, she could see what had affected Buddy. There were signs of numerous fires, some long burned out, but others still smoldering and smoking. A large part of the city had been destroyed by the blast and shock and the resulting fires.

Buddy walked up onto the top of the shelter and surveyed the rest of the property. He also checked the gate with the binoculars. The gate was still closed. He doubted if anyone else would be up here, but he couldn't be sure. Many people were fleeing the city that day and probably in the days afterward. With the radiation levels dropping, they were going to have to keep an eye out for things.

The next day they went out again for a little while. Besides checking on things, they began to decontaminate the top of the shelter and the area around it. That became the routine as they waited for the time to pass and the radiation level to fall.

CHAPTER TWENTY-SEVEN

Charlie didn't think about it until a couple of days later when he went to wash up. He hadn't decontaminated when he'd come back into the drainage pipe after sealing the end of the pipe and bringing everything in. He took everything and shook it out and brushed it off in the furthest corner of the basement, then stripped and washed thoroughly at the same spot, then hurried back into the tunnel.

When he began to feel nauseous a week into his shelter stay, Charlie reread the series of articles in the paper, concentrating on the ones about radiation sickness. The best he could determine he must have got a dose somewhere between fifty and two-hundred Röentgens. He would probably be sick, and might have bleeding gums and loose some hair, but it shouldn't be fatal…at least not according to the paper.

Though he didn't feel like eating, he heated water at least once a day and made a meal of the food he had on hand. He had no way to purify the water seeping into the shelter, but it stayed clear and did not seem to be adding to his distress. Charlie ate when he knew he should, and slept most of the rest of the time, his body in the process of repairing the damage done by the early radiation damage.

The simple plan he came up with was to stay in the shelter until there was evidence of activity outside, or his food ran out. Already ill from the radiation sickness, he wouldn't be able to afford to wait very long, if any, to find more food after his accumulation ran out. He'd be too weak to do anything if he waited longer.

He had a little diarrhea during the second week, but there was no way to tell if it was the radiation, the water, or just the overall situation. He had to take the bucket he was using for a toilet, adding some of the earth to cover the waste after each use, to the garage and begin using another. But that was all right. He had plenty. Charlie felt pretty good about the fact that he had enough energy to load it into the wheelbarrow and move it without collapsing.

At least he was getting some exercise moving the water buckets he kept filling from the seep. A little exercise seemed to help, though he did spend the majority of time lying down, much of that time sleeping.

Between the food the workers had left behind the day of the attack, plus the Ramen noodles and other foods he had on hand that day, Charlie was able to stay in the tunnel for twenty-seven days. He had not heard any sounds of activity outside the basement in that time.

He had his last package of Ramen noodles, and put the last energy bar in his pocket before he readied the bicycle and cart to set out to find more food, at the least. Perhaps better shelter, too. Maybe even a relief operation.

CHAPTER TWENTY-EIGHT

When it became obvious that night that Edward and the others would not be coming, Angela thought Emily took it rather well. Angela told her that the radiation was already over two thousand Röentgens per hour. Emily seemed clueless, so Angela explained that if Edward, the Cutters, and Courtney weren't in shelter long before now, they would die of radiation poisoning within a few hours.

Angela decided not to mention it to Emily when the day after the attack she was checking the area using the camera and saw Courtney stagger into the back yard, look around hopelessly and fall to the ground. She didn't move again. Angela shut down the camera.

Fortunately, whoever equipped the shelter for Edward, for it certainly had not been Edward himself, Angela was sure, had included plenty of activities for the children to occupy them.

Despite the toys and games, the DVD player and movie selection, the children got restless not being allowed to go outside. Angela said a little prayer, hoping the person that had stocked the shelter had made it through. Besides the activities, and the long-term storage food, plenty of "comfort" food had been stored, too. The adults, as well as the children, were much the better for it.

Emily let Angela take charge. She took care of the kids and what little housekeeping was involved. Angela took care of the operation of the shelter, monitoring the ventilation, power, water, and sewage systems. Angela used the camera a few times a day to check on their surroundings. Several times all she could see was thick smoke. She saw a pack of dogs one day, early on, and the next time she checked, Courtney's body was gone.

They fell into a relatively easy routine for the weeks they stayed in the shelter. For they did stay in the shelter until the radiation had dropped to under one Röentgen per hour. It took over two months.

CHAPTER TWENTY-NINE

They took two of the eight people they taken to the estate with them to town when they went back. They were the two men that had been injured during the decontamination work in town. The doctors had treated them at the estate and released them. The other six were in the cottage that had not been in use. Two each in the two bedrooms and the other two in the living room on beds brought from one of the other houses. Melissa was caring for them. They all had relatively minor cases of radiation sickness.

Again Melissa stayed at the estate when the others went in to avoid exposure. This time Sara stayed with her to help, to allow Mattie to go in to see Tom and check on a few of her friends. It was raining this first day of August. A light rain, but cold. The temperature was in the mid sixties. Everyone was bundled up as if it was late fall.

It was still raining when they reached the town. There was a small crowd at Steven Gregory's store when they arrived. Percy was glad to see that many people were carrying empty containers for water. He'd filled his second tank trailer with seven thousand gallons of water at the estate and had Andy bring it in with the Kenworth tractor. Andy began filling water bottles immediately.

They'd mounted one of the two box beds Percy had for the Unimogs on one of the trucks and brought the estate products into town in it, with Percy driving. He was pulling a stock trailer with another calf and two pigs, plus half a dozen chickens in a transport crate.

Susie had brought the stretched van with Jock, Mattie, and the two townspeople. Susie let Mattie and Jock out at the store, and then went to drop off the other two at their homes. She pulled the small tank trailer with fuel.

Besides those waiting for food and water, there was a small group of people to see Dr. Bluhm. He'd brought what he thought he might need and began seeing people in the office of the store.

Claude was with Steven, and they helped Percy begin unloading the food from the Unimog. When the food was unloaded, Percy and Claude took the animals to his butcher shop. They unloaded the animals into the holding pens behind the shop. Claude would coordinate the butchering with Steven, to make the meat available for the orders Steven would take ahead of time.

When Susie and Percy both returned, Percy and Mattie walked down to the city hall to see

Tom and the council. Percy had come prepared. Several people were waiting to see Percy there at the city hall. He asked them to wait until after he'd seen the council.

Mattie checked in with Tom, and then went off to find her friends. Percy hitched up the straps of his overalls and went into the council meeting room with Tom and the rest of the council. Several others crowded in to watch the proceedings.

"We can do this in private," Tom said, surveying the group that wanted to watch.

"I'm okay with it," Percy said. "In my view, this is their town and they have a right to know what decisions are being made, just like before the war."

"That's the way I feel, too," Tom said. There were some murmurs from the council members, but Tom ignored them. He addressed those that had taken seats in the observers' section of the meeting room.

"It's okay to observe, but this is official business. Unless we open the floor for questions or comments, I expect everyone to keep it quiet while Mr. Jackson and the council discuss the matters before the council."

Tom sat down at the head of the conference table and the members of the town council did as well. Tom motioned for Percy to take a seat.

Percy took the proffered seat and opened the portfolio he'd brought with him.

"I guess we should let you know what's happened and what we've come up with, before we start negotiating," Tom said.

Abigail interrupted before Tom could continue. "We don't have to explain anything to him. Just let him make his demands and we can do what we have to do. And I still think we should just seize the property and do what we want with it." Her words brought some whispers from those observing.

"He's not even close to the city limits," Tom said, rather harshly. "We have no authority to seize anything outside the limits, and we may be on shaky ground doing what we are doing, if someone ever takes it to court, once the court system is up again. It's just easier for everyone to know what is going on.

"Now. As I was saying, Percy, what we've done, based on what you indicated you'd be doing is assumed that the town owns everything in town that doesn't have a local owner or local resident. Things like the Jiffy Quick store. It's part of a chain and Rodney doesn't own it. He was just manager. So it's part of city property now. Not that there's much use for it. It's just an example.

"There are a lot of people that headed for the hills when this all started. We figure anything not tenanted is public property. We'll keep track of everything, and if someone returns or has a claim, we'll do something to correct the situation. There's been quite a bit of scavenging already, but we've pretty much got that organized now, using your system of barter.

"We're using Johnson's warehouse to store things and Betty Lou is keeping track of where everything came from and where it goes. Most of us never realized how important some simple things are. Old newspapers have become very valuable, if you know what I mean."

Percy smiled. "Toilet paper," he said.

"Exactly. People are not throwing much of anything away and some are cataloging even little things that they have, with the intention of trading for things they need, just like you said. We figure to use the warehouse as a trading post for city property goods. The other businesses will do business as usual, just trading, bartering, and using gold and silver, like you said.

"Clarence, our mechanic, figured a simple way to get water, we just need more fuel. Alfred had a small deep well submersible pump in stock. We moved the generator from the phone company substation down to the maintenance building by the well and hooked it up. We can pump water and there's enough power to use some other electrical stuff. We set up Howard's big ham rig there and he keeps an eye on things while he monitors the radio during the day."

Tom looked at Percy questioningly. "We're giving him food credits, based on you saying you'd be buying some stuff the city has, to handle the well and generator."

"It won't be a problem," Percy said. He pulled two plastic coin tubes from the pockets of his overalls. He removed a pad of his barter slips from the portfolio. "I'm prepared to make a few offers." There were a couple of gasps and whistles at the glistening gold and silver.

The room was crowded with spectators by the time Percy and the council had concluded their deals. The city now had a treasury of ten one ounce gold coins, a hundred tenth ounce gold coins, a hundred twenty silver quarters and five hundred silver dimes. They also owned barter slips for a hundred gallons of gasoline, five hundred gallons of diesel, and food for two hundred individual meals.

In return, Percy now owned several items of town property, including the clinic shuttle bus, and the town's agricultural museum and all its contents. No one seemed to understand why Percy wanted the museum, but Percy had offered what seemed a generous amount for it.

Reasons why he wanted some of the other things weren't quite clear to most, either.

He also gave the town additional gold and silver as his tax contribution for the following year. "We just figured an ounce of gold for each section, and an ounce for the improvements. I've got the six hundred forty at the estate, and then the other nine hundred sixty spread out," Percy said, adding one one-ounce gold coin, five tenth ounce gold coins, a hundred silver quarters and two hundred fifty silver dimes to those already on the table. "We can adjust it next year, if that's okay."

"That's fine, Tom said. "Geez," he added staring at the gold and silver. "How we going to handle this?"

"I was figuring on opening a deposit account with Camden Dupree. I figure his bank is as safe as it ever was. You might consider doing the same."

Tom saw a hand go up in the crowd. He smiled and acknowledged Dupree. Camden stood and said. "I'll be glad to handle the money. For a fee." Most of those in the room laughed.

Percy wasn't sure what Tom intended to say, but Percy spoke first." I'm okay with one tenth of one percent per transaction, accumulated until it is redeemable in round figures."

It was obvious that Camden was figuring in his head. "That's okay by me." He looked around. "I'll do the same with anyone. Gold, silver, and barter slips for labor, food, and fuel, like Mr. Jackson was talking about." He looked at Percy.

"You said before the exchange rate for silver to gold is thirty-six to one. What is it for labor and food?"

Percy had figured to let that work itself out. He had a rough idea in mind. Since it had come up this early, he decided to voice his thoughts on the matter. "To keep it simple, what about a silver dime for a meal, a silver quarter for a day's food, an hour's labor, or a gallon of fuel. Would that work?"

Camden thought another minute. "That'll work for me. Fuel seems high, but there is a limited amount available," he said.

"Some will pay more, or won't pay as much, but with a set conversion rate, at least for the meantime, people have a basis to make deals," Percy said.

"I'll post a chart at the bank. Mean's I'm going to need to hire a teller and a clerk back," Camden said, looking around for his former employees. None were there. "I'll be down at the bank in just a little while to set up the accounts." He left the room, a determined look on his face. He'd been wondering what he'd be able to do, with his back the way it was. Percy had just probably saved him from starvation. He wouldn't be quite as ornery to him as he'd been in the past, he vowed to himself.

"If we're done here," Percy said, turning back to Tom, "I need to make arrangements for some other things."

"We're done. Chief, can you take this down to the bank?" Tom asked the town's Chief of Police and town barber.

"Sure, Mayor. Me and Deputy Jones will get it there safe. Come on, Mark. You're younger. You carry, I'll guard." Mark Jones gathered up the tubes of coins and the filled out barter slips and the two headed for the door.

"Well, then, I'm headed back to the Gregory's and then the bank," Percy said, standing up. He turned to face the now milling crowd. "I'm in the market for a few things. I'll be ready to deal when I get to the bank. Randy, I see you're here. Could you meet me at the bank, in, say, half an hour?" Randy waved an acknowledgement and agreement.

"And if anyone sees Mark's father, let him know I need some stuff from the hardware store."

"He died, Mr. Jackson," someone called to him. "Mark sold the store to Mr. Gregory for the promise of food for a year."

Percy recognized the young man as a friend of Andy's. "Thanks. Are you staying busy or do you need some work?"

"I could use some extra food and stuff for the family. Mom's kind of sick. This ash and stuff has her asthma kicked in really bad. The kids could use more milk."

"Okay," Percy replied, "I recognize you, but I don't know your name.

"Henry Bradshaw, Mr. Jackson. I'm Henry Bradshaw. Me and Andy's good buddies. I'm a hard worker, just like him. I know a couple other fellows need work, too, if you need some good hands."

"I do. Come on with me. You can help Andrew with the water tanker." Besides Henry, several others followed Percy back to Gregory's Grocery. People were lining up to get food. Percy was a little surprised at the number that had silver coins. Most were signing barter slips for labor.

Steven had someone helping, so took a minute to talk to Percy, when Percy asked. "Things going okay?"

"Yeah. I've debated how young to let them sign up for labor. I've kept it at sixteen. What do you think?"

"I have things that can be done by someone as young as twelve. I don't think I'd want the responsibility for anyone younger than that. And no more than four hours for them. Sixteen for adults sixteen and over."

"Men and women the same?"

"Yes. I'll put the person on a job they where they can be effective, no matter what the abilities." Something caught his eye. "Has Jorge Ramirez bought anything?" Percy asked, nodding over to a man sitting in a wheelchair, watching the proceedings.

"No, he hasn't," Steven replied. "I offered him a little, even though he didn't have anything to trade. He said he was okay, just wanted to see what was going on."

"Make sure you make an offer for labor, like for the others. He's as good as they come with horses, even with only one leg. His hour of labor would be just as effective for me as anyone else's."

The rain, which had dropped to a drizzle while they were in city hall, now stopped all together. The clouds were breaking up and the sun was peeking through. People began to shed jackets.

"Steven, I was told you bought the hardware store from Mark, after his father died."

"Yes. I felt sorry for him. The city council wants him to stay on as deputy chief, but they can't provide enough to take care of his family. With what I'm getting from you, I can afford to feed at least him for a year for what's left in the store."

"You want to sell it?"

"What are you offering?" Steven asked.

"That year of food, plus something more. What would you like, in addition to the year's food for one person?"

"People are showing up with their coin collections. It's easier than bartering. Some hard currency would be best for me. People are already willing to take it for things. Abigail baked some bread and will only take silver for it."

"How about a ten rolls of silver dimes? That's five hundred dimes, thirty-six ounces of silver. I know it's not that much."

"That'll do," Steven said. "This store is going to be all I can handle, anyway. Lot more labor intensive with the bartering and all. I'd have to pay someone to help me with the hardware store. I'd rather have the silver."

"Okay," Percy said, handing Steven a plastic roll of dimes. "You trust me to bring in the rest next trip?"

"Of course I do," Steven said, pocketing the roll of coins.

Percy found Randy waiting patiently at the bank for him. "Be right with you," Percy told him, then went into the bank. People were standing around, but there didn't seem to be much going on.

"Okay," Camden said. "Mr. Jackson is here. We're open for business." Percy didn't say anything about them waiting for him before they did anything. He just handed Brittney four coin tubes and three pads of barter slips. One pad was for a gallon of fuel on each of the slips, one was for one meal on each slip, and the third was slips for a day's food.

Camden stood behind Brittney as she tallied up the deposit, wrote it on a deposit slip and handed it to Percy. Camden was beaming. He took the bank's copy of the slip and turned, to hand it to Arthur Lang. "Set up a new account for Mr. Jackson. This is his initial deposit."

Quite officially, his hands clasped behind his back, "We will deduct our one tenth of a percent from your account, Mr. Jackson, and credit the bank. And remember, all withdrawals must be made in person, or by your authorized agent."

"I understand," Percy said. "I'll thumbprint any checks I write on the account, as well as sign."

Camden looked a little startled, but quickly suppressed it. He'd only considered direct deposits and withdrawals. But what was in the bank was in the bank. There was no reason not to allow checks to be written on it."

"Of course, Mr. Jackson," Camden said quickly. "Just mark out the word dollars and write in the currency on which you're paying the debt and initial it."

Percy slid the thumbprint inkpad forward and pressed his thumb against it. "I'll stamp my account sheet, if you like, for latter comparison purposes."

Arthur quickly handed the paper to Camden, who laid it on the counter. Percy pressed his inked thumb on the top of the page, rather with a flourish. He picked up the counter pen and signed, then initialed beside the thumbprint.

"There you go, Mr. Dupree. I assume you will check each transaction against the print, signature, and initials, as appropriate, to verify authenticity." Percy winked just slightly at Camden.

The tiniest of smiles lifted the corners of Camden's lips. "Of course, sir. This bank has always verified identity and authenticity. We will continue to protect our customers' interests, just as we always have."

"Thanks," Percy said and stepped away from the counter. The next person stepped up, a coin collection folder in hand. "I want to go ahead and get my silver in here so I can't lose it," she said.

Percy went out, a smile on his face. "Randy," he said.

Randy stood up from where he'd been sitting on the steps. "Yes, Mr. Jackson?"

"I need to use a little of that labor credit I have with you. I'll supply the fuel, rod, and such for some items I need you to make for me." He pulled a sheaf of papers from the portfolio in which he'd put his deposit slip.

"I need two primary stills and a secondary still to double distill alcohol. I also need another pair of methane digesters built. Here are the drawings. I'd like them twice as big as the originals. Can you figure how to do that?"

Randy studied the drawings for some time. "Yes, sir, I sure can. These are basic. Just a matter of scaling things up. The design can be the same, with some additional reinforcement elements." Randy looked up from the drawings. "Do you have all the materials?"

"I do, but I'd like you to scrounge everything you can. Here's a roll of dimes. Buy as much as you can. Check the rates in the bank and just ball park a price for the things you want. I want as much coin spread around the community as possible, so get a little from each person that has something that will work. Anything you can't come up with, I can supply. I want to conserve the easy to use things as much as possible."

"Okay. I have probably enough fuel to get out to your place, but I'll need some to get back."

Percy nodded. "If it is okay with your family, I'd like you to stay there overnight, every other day, to conserve fuel. I'll provide meals while you're there."

"Okay, Mr. Jackson. You have a deal. I'll still owe you after this. I appreciate you letting me pay off some of that debt."

"Being the greedy man I am," Percy said, "I'd like to extend the time you owe me a bit and pay for part of this with current currency. Food and fuel for you. Is that okay?"

"Well, sure! But you don't really have to do that."

"I want to," Percy said. "You're the only professional welder around. I'm going to need your services from time to time."

"You've got them, guaranteed," Randy replied.

Percy made several more deals that day on the steps of the bank. Some were executed immediately. Some were deals that would be transacted in the future. He hired six of the neediest to go to live at the estate and work full time for room and board, and some spending cash. The six included Henry Bradshaw and one of his friends. It also included Jorge Ramirez.

The fourth and fifth persons were the Jenkins. Ellen and Hank. Ellen would cook, clean, and act as bunkhouse boss. Hank would be working in the shop, mostly. They'd share the bunkhouse boss' bedroom.

The other two were a pair of sisters, aged seventeen and eighteen. They'd be helping Mattie with the house duties, the gardens, and some work in the greenhouses. They were from a large family and were going to help provide food for them. Everyone's belongings for a lengthy stay at the estate were loaded in the Unimog and the six rode out with Susie in the van.

Andy moved into the bunkhouse with his two friends, taking one of the four person bunkrooms. The sisters shared another. As those that were recovering became able to manage for themselves, they were taken back to town, to their homes. Three chose to stay. Two men and one woman. Still weak, Percy made a deal with them to do limited work, as they were able, for the time being, while drawing similar, but slightly less in wages than the others were. Mainly, they got plenty of good food, and the rest they needed to finish their recovery.

The trips were working out well. Percy began culling the animals he'd bought from several locals. He kept Doc and Susie busy taking care of ailing animals. Doc had a good basement and survived just fine, though Percy had to help him bury some of the animals he lost that he didn't have adequate shelter for. They'd all been ill to start with and many didn't survive the exposure of the radiation and the volcanic gasses that wafted through a few times with the ash.

They couldn't save all the animals that were ailing that Percy bought. The carcasses, like those Doc lost, were buried on one of Percy's noncontiguous fields that was close. As they decayed, they would enrich the soil.

A few of the animals that had been fed clean feed, but had been exposed to radiation and would die, were butchered for the meat. The meat wasn't contaminated, but all the organs were processed through the methane generator, just in case. The hides were cleaned and used as rawhide.

Percy managed to be able to take in at least one good-sized animal for Clyde to cut up and Steven to distribute each week. The people that had sold Percy the animals had not been able to care for them properly. They would not even be able to transport them, except to walk them to town. Some of them were ten miles or more from town. Animals and humans alike couldn't afford the additional dosages of radiation it would entail to travel that distance on foot.

People finally figured out why Percy had bought the town's museum. It had an extensive collection of old farming implements. Many were horse drawn versions. Many more were early conversions of horse drawn styles to the then newfangled mechanical tractor. Percy had Randy and Hank convert them to horse drawn.

He got enough horses to have at least six teams that could work the fields, and another half dozen additional saddle horses. There were two sets of four steers each that took to harness and could do the heavy pulling like the Clydesdales. They wouldn't be used to harvest much, but they were ready to work the ground the following spring. Percy used the mechanical equipment to harvest the failed field crops to avoid exposing the animals to the additional residual radiation.

The crops all went into the stills and methane generator, the remains buried with the animals on the other plot to enrich that soil for future use, when the radiation had finally decayed to a point where it could be used safely. The oily crops had been pressed for oil first, to feed the biodiesel conversion process, and then the cake was processed further in the still, then the methane generator.

They finally made a trip into the city. Percy had Susie go with Sara. The state government was functioning, Sara knew from the shortwave and amateur radio reports they were getting. A call had gone for former state employees that could, to report to their local offices.

Sara would eventually do her old job, but for the moment, she was census and report taker. Percy loaned her a laptop with extra batteries and a solar charger to make the work easier. She was one of the very few so blessed.

Percy made a similar arrangements with the city, county, and state government officials as he had with the town. It had taken quite a bit of negotiation, but between Sara, Tom, and Percy they avoided confiscation of Percy's resources. That was despite Abigail's and Jeb's attempts to get Percy kicked off the property and it be taken over by the authorities.

It became obvious to the powers-that-be that Percy could produce far more running the place the way he had been than what the immediate confiscation and use of all his supplies would supply. They could always seize it later if Percy reneged on his agreements or made excessive demands in return for the goods and services he provided.

As a gesture of goodwill, Percy gave the county and state one percent of his diesel up front. Percy would also provide a certain amount of food and fuel to each of the governments every month at no cost. That was his cost to avoid complete confiscation. Percy considered it close to extortion, but he bit his tongue and made the arrangements. He was getting something out of the deals, anyway. The additional arrangements he'd made gave Percy a few material things he wanted, and the jurisdictions received much needed extra food and the fuel to provide for the needs of the communities.

Sara would get enough fuel to do her job in her hybrid. Despite all the electronics, it had survived just fine in the garage of one of the cottages, shielded by the earth surrounding it.

They found a computer module for Andy's Jimmy and his friends used it on occasion, for a small fee. Andy seldom used it. He was almost always in one of the estate vehicles taking care of something for Percy.

By the time October rolled around, everything in the orchards and fields that could be harvested and used had been. There had been some losses to the ever-bearing strawberry crop, as there had the blackberry crop. But what did survive had sold for a premium price in town, despite Percy's intention to have it simply as the fruit portion of the food rations. After the initial purchase in the store, people began buying and selling from one another at higher prices.

The tree fruit crop suffered some, but not as much as other crops. There was quite a bit of additional handling of the fruit and the nuts. Percy insisted on double washing every single piece. Just as he did the strawberries and blackberries. Much of it was done in tanks, but the soft fruit was done by hand. The fruit and nuts, too, began to fetch premium prices in town.

Some of the fruit was far enough gone that, though edible, it wouldn't even stand a trip into town. It was made into juice, jelly, preserves, and butters, or dried. Percy had the equipment to do it all. The sisters were kept busy helping Mattie with it. And Mattie had a pretty thriving supplemental business selling fruit pies for a while. Mattie baked them and Susie sold them in town, sharing the proceeds with Susie and the girls.

One thing that Percy worried about was his bees. He'd moved all his hives into the bee barn and closed it up right after they'd put the berms at the other barns. He'd kept the barn closed and the sugar water feeders filled until the radiation had dropped way down. Still the bees were dying in droves. He checked all the hives with the survey meter. The readings were only marginally above the background reading in the barn.

October started off cold. As cold as November usually was. Jim and Bob were bundled up to their eyeballs when they drove the Jeep onto the estate October Third. The top was ripped in several places.

"Almost didn't get back," Jim said, as they sat around the kitchen table in the house, hands wrapped around bowls of Mattie's chili. Percy, Mattie, and Susie were clustered around, to hear the story.

"We got there just fine," Bob started off.

Jim continued. "Had mom convinced to come with us. Then it happened." Two pairs of sad eyes turned up to Percy.

"What you taught us," Bob said, "Saved us. But it was too much for Mom. She had a heart attack. We carried her to the hospital, but it was too late."

"Got a pretty good dose of radiation in the process," Jim interjected.

"Yeah. Got sick as a dog. They let us stay in the shelter they'd set up in the hospital. By the time we were well enough to travel..."

Jim took up the story again. "We felt like we owed the folks that took us in something, so we worked, helping the community get going again. We were still pretty weak at that point, anyway."

"Yeah," added Bob. "Still are. That radiation stuff is pure poison." The two exchanged a look. "The docs at the hospital said we'd have a much increased chance of cancer or leukemia and stuff in a few years."

"Yeah," Jim said. "But it was our Mom. We had to try. Anyway, we finally went back to the house and loaded up a few things we wanted to bring back. The Jeep wouldn't start, of course."

"The EMP thing, we figured." Bob was telling the tale now. "So we unpacked the computer you talked us into taking with us, Boss. Cost an arm and a leg when we bought it, but it sure was worth it. Money ain't worth nothing now."

"We had that silver you gave us," Jim said. "That saved our behinds a couple of times. People saw that date before 1965 and snapped 'em up. We managed to eat and fuel all the way back on those two rolls. Had to push a few times for a few miles at a time, between stops where we could get gas. Part of what took us so long. Didn't want to leave the Jeep, since it would run."

Bob grinned up at them. "And I tell you, every time we pushed, it was up hill."

"'Cept that time when the dang thing almost got away from us when we topped that little rise."

"Yeah. Anyway, we finally made it back."

"What happened to the Jeep?" Percy asked.

"Oh," Jim said. "That." Again the brothers exchanged a look.

"Yeah. Somebody tried to stop us. Fired right into the Jeep from an overpass. No warning or nothing. We floored it and made the guys jumping out from the edges of the overpass scramble to keep from getting run over." Bob shrugged the sweater he was wearing down. "Dude clipped me with a twenty-two round before we got out of range."

They saw the pink pucker on Bob's shoulder. "Jim was weaving and all," Bob continued, "but they either had somebody really good or really lucky."

"If they were good, they'd been shooting something besides a twenty-two and you'd probably be dead. I say it was our good luck and their bad."

"Can't argue with that, Twin. Anyway, here we be. With one hole in me and a few rips in the Jeep top."

"Yeah," Jimmy said. "I see you got some new hands, by the look of things." He was eyeing the two sisters that had come into the kitchen moments before. He looked up at Percy's face. "We still got a job, Boss?"

"Of course you do," Percy replied. "But not for a few days. I want one of the doctors to look you over and decide when you can go back to work and how much you can do at the moment."

"That's fine with me," Bob said. "I can't seem to ever get rested. A couple days with no responsibilities would be good."

CHAPTER THIRTY

The sky was clear and there was no fallout when Calvin and Nan suited up again two days later and headed to town. It was slow going through the thick layers of ash. It was drifted five feet deep in places. The rains had made it a heavy mess. But the U500 with front bucket easily cut a path. Though the ash was drifted in places, other stretches of the road had been blown clear before the rains wetted the ash down.

They were fearful of what they would find in town. The fear was justified, though there were many survivors. There were also many houses showing no signs of life. Their first stop was at the police station.

Chief Connolly was there with both the town's officers. "So you two are okay?" he asked.

They'd checked with the survey meter and the radiation at the station had faded to about the same level as at their home. Calvin and Nan had taken off their respirators when they entered the building. Calvin nodded. "We wanted to report we found the Andersons the other day. They must have been on the way out to our place. Both of them were dead."

Bill Connolly sighed. "I'll add them to the list. We've been meaning to do a census of the town and outlying areas, but just haven't had time."

Just then Nan noticed the slight wince the Chief made when he sat down at his desk and pulled over a notebook. "Chief, are you okay?"

"He got shot," said one of the officers. Neither Calvin nor Nan knew him, though they'd seen him from time to time. "I'm Officer Tom Perkins," he said, reaching out to shake both Calvin's and Nan's hands.

Stanley Smith, the other officer, said, "A small group tried to loot the store. We stopped them, but the Chief took a round in the thigh."

"Oh, my!" exclaimed Nan. "Are you all right?"

"I'm fine," Bill said. "It was just a scratch on the thigh. Betty Lou fixed it right up." His eyes took on a distant look. We need to get out there and see if they're okay."

Tom said, "We've only been out and about for a couple of days. Haven't had time to do much. Only rig we've found so far that will run is Jackson Clements old Ford." Tom sighed. "He didn't make it."

"Yeah," added Stanley. "He knew he wasn't going to make it and brought the car down and left a note for us to use it. We went to check on him when we found it. He was dead."

"And we need to do something with his body. And the others I know are out there," said the Chief. "I just don't know what."

Calvin and Nan looked at each other. "We might be able to help with that," Nan said.

"Yes," Calvin added. "With our equipment we can dig graves and haul bodies if we need to. Clear the ash where needed. But we have a pretty limited supply of fuel."

Nan looked at Calvin questioningly, but didn't contradict him on their fuel situation. It had occurred to Calvin that not everyone needed to know everything about them. Tom was eyeing their gun belts and holsters.

"That would sure help," Bill said. "I'm not sure what we're going to do. Only a couple of the town council made it. The mayor didn't. We've talked to state emergency management and they told us were on our own for a while."

Tom started to edge around toward the side of Nan and Calvin. "You know, Chief. We're basically in charge. We ought to think about commandeering their equipment if it works."

"Hold your horses, there, Tom," the Chief said. "And come back around here. What's the matter with you? They just said they'd help out."

Tom stopped flanking the two, but didn't move back. Calvin edged Nan slightly behind him and his right hand drifted to the gun belt, near the holster, his eyes narrowing as he looked at Tom.

"Well, we at least ought to disarm them. We don't need a bunch of guns around at a time like this. Look what's already happened."

"That's enough, Tom!" There was a distinct note of anger in Bill's voice. "We're not a bunch of jack booted thugs out to rule the town. We have a job to do. That's to protect and serve this community. I aim to use every resource I can, but we're not going to usurp the Constitution. Not on my watch."

"Come on, Tom," Stanley said. "We talked about this. It's going to take a community effort to get through this. Trying to strong arm people is not going to help."

"Well look at what happened to the Chief! He could have been killed. That was some of our upright citizens that did that to him. If I ever find out who shot at us, I'll..."

"You'll arrest them and they'll be tried," Bill said firmly. "We are officers of the law. Not a judge, nor jury, nor executioners. Some things are different now, yes. I don't want to hear any more about it. If someone is making trouble, we'll do something about it. But the Stubblefield's are already trying to help. I aim to let them."

The Chief looked over at Calvin and Nan. "Thank you for your offer. We'll see about supplying some fuel for you to use. When can you start?"

"With the radiation levels where they are, I don't think we should be out of shelter more than four hours or so. It takes us close to half an hour each way, so that gives us three hours a day to get things accomplished. We can bring the equipment in tomorrow and get started.

"I think it's best if you and the townspeople get together and decide what the priorities are. We'll provide the equipment and a little manpower, but it is up to you guys to provide the plan."

"Okay," Bill said. Tom seemed to be settling down.

"We just want to help where we can, without getting radiation sickness or shot or anything," Nan said.

"Nobody is going to get shot that doesn't deserve it," the Chief said. He looked a bit surprised when the other four suddenly laughed. It dawned on him then, what he'd said. "You know what I meant," he said with a chuckle. "Now," he continued, looking at Nan and Calvin, "Is there anything we can do to help you at the moment?"

Calvin shook his head. "No. I want to get back. We just wanted to see how things were going and if we could be of help. We'll be in tomorrow morning with the equipment and we can get started."

Bill stood up, with another wince, and shook Calvin's hand. "Okay. Sounds like a plan. We'll get with the others and come up with more of a plan for tomorrow."

For the next several days Calvin and Nan did some very unpleasant work. Those that had survived in and around town had begun to make themselves known. New council members and a mayor had been elected and they had wanted individual graves dug. Calvin was able to talk them out of it, with support from the Chief.

Calvin dug a wide trench and the bodies were laid in it side by side. Someone was marking down the exact location and markers would be set, sometime. It took several days, working only three hours a day, to get the work completed. But it was finally done, except for those that would die from radiation exposure. There were several that were very sick and would not get better.

It was a heart wrenching time and Calvin and Nan went home every day with tears in their eyes. Though there were no tears for the occupants of another trench grave that Calvin had to dig just after the last local had been buried.

The small grocery store had become the local meeting place. Calvin had used the Unimog to clear the parking lot of ash. The town council was allocating what resources were left, and people were trading and bartering for things in the parking lot, too.

Nan and Calvin were in town again, working with the city council and the Chief, planning a scavenging trip using the Unimog, one of the Stubblefield Jeeps, and a couple of old farm trucks that still ran, when a carload of outsiders roared into town. They stopped at the store and clambered out of the VW van, guns waving.

Other than the near riot at the store a few weeks earlier, there had not been any real trouble in the town. But Nan and Calvin, and the police force weren't the only citizens going around armed. Before they could think about it, Calvin, Nan, and the others returned fire when the group opened fire on the crowd as they moved into the store. It was a short battle.

One man from town took a round in the arm. The Chief got the first aid kit out of the old Ford that was their new squad car. Tom and Stanley checked over the marauders and found two of them alive. One man and one woman, both severely wounded.

"What do we do, Chief?" asked Stanley.

"About all we can do is bandage them up with what we've got and get old Broderick the vet to take a look at them. County says they're going to send over a doc to check everyone out, but that's going to take a while yet. I'll call it in and see what the county wants us to do with them in the meantime."

He looked over at the Ralph Clemens, the local that had been shot. "Ralph, too, I guess."

"What about right now?" Tom asked, as Sally, the woman that had bandaged Ralph, began to work on the two injured marauders. "We can't take them in to the county jail at the moment. At least we haven't taken out the old cells at city hall yet. Put them there, even injured?"

"Yep," replied the Chief.

"Just one, though," Sally said. "The woman just died."

Stanley went to get a stretcher from the ambulance shed for the man. Sally stood up to talk to the Chief. Of the five ambulance attendants in the town, Sally was the only one that had made it through the war. Two had been gone on vacation when things started, and the other two had each tried to shelter in place for their families. Neither had been successful.

Sally had become hardened to illness, injury, and death since the war, being the only one with anything other than advanced first-aid training in town that was ambulatory. There were three nurses, all employed by the county hospital. All three were down with injuries or radiation sickness. And Betty Lou hadn't been back to town since that first day.

"You all right?" Calvin asked Nan, seeing her watching the injured man being placed on the stretcher in preparation of being carried to the city hall jail.

Nan leaned against him and Calvin put his arm around her shoulder. "Yeah. I guess so. It's just that something like this seems so pointless. All we have to do is help one another. We'll make it. There is no real need for things like this to happen."

"I know," replied Calvin. "But you know as well as I do that there are people in this world that would rather take and not give in return."

"Yes," Nan said with a sigh, "I do. I just don't like it much. Let's go on back home. The plans are made for the trip tomorrow. Nothing more we can do here."

Nan was driving one of the Jeeps and Calvin the U500 the next morning when they returned to town. It was a bright, sunny day, and warm. The Chief and the Mayor met with them for a few minutes before the convoy of vehicles left town.

Besides Calvin and Nan, Stanley Smith was going along as official city representative. Two farmers, with older bob trucks that still ran, were coming along. Four people would ride the backs of the trucks, with an additional man in the cab of each truck. That gave them a total of twenty people.

Everyone was armed. Calvin had an M1A and his Glock 21. His load bearing vest and belt carried six spare twenty-round magazines for the M1A and four thirteen-rounders for the Glock, along with two one-quart canteens, first-aid kit, a utility pouch with a few odds and ends, and an M-6 bayonet for the M1A that was more for field use than its intended purpose.

Nan was similarly equipped, except she carried a Steyr AUG and a Glock field knife. The others were armed with a mix of weapons, mostly hunting rifles and the occasional revolver.

The police armory for the town was limited. Stanley was in uniform and carried his normal load out, including a Glock 17 9mm with high capacity magazines. About the only other options he had was a Remington 870 12-gauge pump shotgun or one of two M1 Carbines the town had acquired in the 1950's. He left the 870 for Tom in town and was carrying a carbine with a fifteen round magazine in it and four thirty-rounders in his pockets.

Calvin led the way, clearing the ash where needed, with the Unimog. They found their first vehicle about five miles out of town. It was locked and abandoned. Stanley used a key gun to get it unlocked. There was nothing in it of real use. "We found a few people just outside of town," Stanley said. "One or more of them were probably in this when the EMP hit." They siphoned the gasoline from the car's fuel tank and transferred it to a fifty-five-gallon drum in one of the farm trucks. Stanley took down the pertinent information and they moved on.

It went much the same until that afternoon. Nan and Calvin wore their load bearing equipment over their Tyvek coveralls. The others, except for Stanley, had some type of overall or coverall and jacket to protect themselves from the ash. Everyone had respirators or dust masks, as well.

When they found bodies, and they found many, in vehicles and afoot; Stanley recorded what information he could find. A few of the passenger vehicles had some supplies that were useable, and they were loaded onto the trucks. Not a one of the vehicles would start. They emptied any fuel that remained from each one.

The only major find was the delivery semi for the grocery store. It had been on its way to town with a full load for the store. They tried to start it, too, but to no avail. Everything was transferred to the smaller trucks. It was late afternoon and they decided to head back to town.

When they returned, they found the roadblock at the edge of town. The Chief and Tom had not been idle during the day. The town council had decided they did not want a repeat of the previous day and authorized the roadblocks on each road into town. They would be manned by armed local citizens until they were sure the threat was over. Each one would have a radio available so those manning the roadblocks could call the police force for assistance, if needed.

Calvin and Nan made a couple more trips with the townspeople, but became worried when they saw some signs that there was at least one group out there that was raiding for supplies. They had found one family massacred. A man, woman, and two children. The house had been ransacked. Anything and everything that might be of use to a roving band was taken. Everything else was trashed. It looked like the gang had stayed in the house for at least a couple of days.

After the find, Calvin and Nan stayed at home for a while. Partly to conserve their stock of fuel, but also for security reasons. The Chief and his officers had suspicions that someone in town was involved with the gang. If the gang got word from someone in town that the Stubblefield's were doing well in the aftermath, it would only be a matter of time before the gang descended on them. Calvin arranged with the Chief to have two way radio communications between their home and the police station, in case their home was attacked.

Calvin and Nan were careful to always go outside, either together, or with one covering the other from a good vantage point. They were working diligently in the greenhouses. The ash had pretty much destroyed the garden. The attack and the volcanic activity had them worried about the weather.

What little news was coming from FEMA, through the county and thus the town, was to expect a severe winter. Calvin's and Nan's gardening paid off. They had plenty of vegetables to can. They'd been able to trade for a half a beef from one of the locals, and a whole pig from another. Both had taken partial payment in gold and silver coins and the remainder in work on their farms with the Stubblefield's equipment. Mostly digging burial pits for the animals they lost.

Both had some working farm equipment, but very little fuel, despite the ongoing scavenging trips by those in area. Small amounts of fuel were coming to the town from FEMA, but only for emergency and protective services. Food shipments were also few and far between. The community had to fend for itself, for the most part.

With heavy snow starting in early September those that could, prepared for the forecasted harsh winter. Quite a few had moved to the camps that FEMA set up, hoping for the best. The rest hunkered down and also hoped for the best.

Except for that small handful that had no preparations, except for weapons. With a system that looked good to become an early blizzard, the gang finally attacked the Stubblefield home. Calvin and Nan had continued to keep their guard up. That included regular checks of the property.

"Nan," whispered Calvin into the Motorola FRS radio. "We've got company. Bad company from the looks of it. Get back to the house and up in the stairway cupola. You'll have 360 degree vision. I'll hunker down in one of the hidey-holes and hit them from the rear while you take them head on. But be sure to keep scanning all around."

"Okay," Nan whispered back, the tension in her voice obvious. She'd been following Calvin; about twenty yards back as his cover. She hurried back to the house, entered, and locked everything with the security system.

They'd talked about how to effectively defend their home, and having one of them outside in prepared defensive positions and one in the armored cupola was the only remotely effective method of repelling an attack of more than one or two people. At that, if there were enough of them, it wouldn't work either and Nan would have to bug out through the escape tunnel and join Calvin outside.

She took the time to call the police station and tell them they were coming under attack, then hurried up to the stairwell cupola. They had pre-positioned ammunition there, just in case. Nan removed the thirty round magazine in the Steyr AUG and inserted a one-hundred-round Beta C-Mag dual-drum magazine into the rifle.

Nan used the binoculars kept in the cupola and did a quick scan all around the property. The only place she couldn't really see was the area right in front of the house. She kept checking the other areas, but watched the area around the road leading to their place. She could see at least six men in the forest, and two walking up the road itself.

Calvin was watching, too. From inside a prepared fighting position. It was off the road, but where he could see parts of it. He waited a while as the group continued to move toward the house. Calvin checked the forest behind him. No signs of anyone else staying back to cover the group's rear.

When he was sure everyone was between him and the house, Calvin exited the fighting hole and move toward the men, to another fighting hole. He removed the cover, climbed inside, and pulled the cover back over him quietly.

Calvin could see all of the front of the house and a good section of the road, as well as much of the open space between the tree line and the house on the front, and well to each side of the bluff.

Those in the forest stopped, each one taking up a position behind a tree right at the tree line. One of those in the road threw his arm over the other one and hunched down slightly, faking a bad limp.

That settled it for Calvin. He had some question that the people had just wandered into the area and were being cautious. The deception proved otherwise.

"Hello the house!" the one supporting the limping man called out as they stopped out in the open area in front of the house. "My friend's been hurt! We need some help!"

They waited a few seconds and repeated the call. When they received no answer both men stood up, bringing weapons out from under their coats, and moved toward the house. The snow started to fall lightly. Calvin lined the sights up of the M1A on the center of the back of the man that had shouted. He squeezed the trigger.

As soon as Calvin fired, Nan began to fire on those that had just started toward the house when their two companions had brought weapons out began to approach closer. Calvin put another round in the man he'd shot, and then took out the second man, who was simply looking around uncertainly, his rifle at the ready.

Again Calvin fired two rounds, and then switched his aim to those still approaching the house. They had begun to bob and weave, but Calvin and Nan were both experienced shooters. It was some time before the group realized that they were being fired on from behind as well as from the house, and began to return fire at Calvin. They had been concentrating on the cupola.

Calvin tried not to think about the fire pouring toward his wife, despite the fact that she was well protected with concrete, steel, and thick Lexan. And the firing ports were just large enough to use, and no larger. He could tell she was taking out those most likely to get behind her first, letting Calvin take care of those around the front of the house.

It didn't take long for the gang to realize they were in untenable position. The survivors began to run back to the forest. Nan stopped firing, but when Calvin continued to drop assailants, she resumed, as well.

Those few still able to move had run out of sight. "Nan," Calvin called her on the radio. "Stay alert. We're not moving until I know they aren't coming back or the Chief gets here."

"Okay," Nan replied. She switched magazines, putting in another of the three C-Mags they had for the AUG, then set it down and picked up the binoculars. The snow was beginning to get heavy, but she continued to scan the area. At least that kept her mind off what had just happened.

Calvin was doing much the same, surveying the area all around him. He was beginning to get a little cold by the time the Chief and Stanley showed up thirty-five minutes later. Calvin waited until the two got out of the car and he was sure it was them before he came out of the fighting hole. "Nan," he said into the radio, "Keep watching. We're coming in."

As he approached and saw the Chief with the force's shotgun, and Stanley with an M1 Carbine, Calvin called out. "Over here!" He was holding the M1A down at his side so they wouldn't mistake him for an attacker.

Both continued to swivel their heads around as Calvin walked up. "Looks like you took care of it yourselves," Bill said.

"Maybe," Calvin said. "Some of them got away."

They walked over to the two bodies near the front patio. Bill looked at the bodies, and then gave Calvin a quick look. Calvin said nothing, but looked calmly back. The two men's weapons were lying in plain sight.

They went and checked each of the other bodies. Well, six bodies and three badly wounded live men. None of the three were able to move on their own. "What do we do, Chief?" Stanley asked.

"Well, I'm tempted to just put them out of our misery," Bill replied. Stanley looked shocked. "But we can't do that," the Chief continued. "We'll have to send someone out for them. It's really a county problem, you know." Bill looked at Calvin.

The snow was coming down harder. "You can't leave us out here like this!" one of them cried out.

Amidst groans and the occasional scream, the three were moved none too gently over in front of the house. "I'm not going to ask you to take them inside," Bill said, as they propped them up against the patio wall.

"Stanley," the Chief said then, "You stay here and guard them. I'll go back to town and see what I can do about getting a deputy and an ambulance out here." He looked down at the three men. "Don't be holding your breath, fellows. It could be a while." His voice was as cold as the weather was turning as the snowfall increased. Bill headed out to the old Ford.

One of the men had lost consciousness when the situation finally got to Calvin and he went inside to make them something warm to drink. He called Nan down from the cupola. She wouldn't be able to see anything now, anyway. With the snow falling, and the light fading, you could only see a few yards.

Nan took Stanley inside to use the bathroom while Calvin watched the men and tried to help them drink the warm beef broth he'd made for them. It was mostly a waste of time. The one was unconscious, one had chest and stomach injuries, so couldn't drink, and the third died of his wounds before Calvin could try to help him take a sip.

Stanley came back out carrying a cup of the broth to warm himself up, with Nan accompanying him. "Nan," said Calvin, "I'm going to get the Bobcat and drag the bodies over by the road."

Nan nodded. She swapped rifles with Calvin, taking his M1A and giving him her AUG. It would be easier to sling and keep handy while he worked, just in case. He didn't want to be out there with just his Glock 21.

The man with the chest and stomach injuries gurgled loudly one time, spasmed and died while Calvin was moving the bodies. By the time he'd moved the bodies from around the house, and the two on the patio, the third man had died. Calvin added him to the pile.

"Chief," Stanley said into his handheld radio. When the chief responded, Stanley said, "No need to bring the ambulance. All three of them have died."

Calvin and Nan both heard the reply, as did Stanley. "Just as well. County, through state, from FEMA, just put out a shoot on sight order for looters and marauders. We'd have had to hang them tomorrow. Anyone captured in the act is to be executed immediately. Only if there's reasonable doubt is anyone to be held and taken to the FEMA holding camps. I'll be there in a few more minutes to pick you up."

Calvin and Stanley took a quick trip around the tree line, checking one last time, before they went into the house to wait for the Chief. Nan started a fire in the fireplace. "How are you holding up?" Calvin asked her, putting his hand on her shoulder when she stood up.

She sighed, gave him a quick hug, and said, "Okay, I guess. But I'm going to need some serious crying time here pretty soon."

Calvin hugged her to him and held her for long moments. "I may just join you," he said softly.

Bill came in for a few minutes to warm up when he arrived. The heater in the Ford wasn't working all that well and the temperature had already fallen to below freezing. "We can't stay very long," he said. "The road is starting to get bad."

"You want to stay here tonight?" Nan asked. "We can lead the way in the morning with the Unimog, if you think it's too bad to go back tonight."

"No. We'll be fine," Bill replied. "But keep your radio on, just in case. I don't want to have to walk the rest of the way in if the car quits."

As he and Stanley bundled up to go out into the storm, Bill looked at Calvin and Nan. Calvin was standing with his arm around Nan shoulders. "You two did what had to be done," Bill told them. "Don't knock yourself out about it. That's the group that's been killing and raping and stealing from the survivors. When we catch up to the rest of them, they'll meet the same fate."

Bill frowned. "I hate to leave those bodies out there. Could be wild dogs get to them. They deserve to be dead, but I don't like to see bodies desecrated."

"Chief," Calvin said, "we haven't seen a single animal or bird since the start of this. I think the ash got what the radiation didn't. Oh, there's bound to be a few animals that made it, especially ground dwellers, but I doubt there's anything out there now that'll brave this storm.

"You could be right. Now that you mention it, there hasn't been much in the way of wildlife, except for domestic animals. And a lot of them died during this, too. Okay. We'll see you guys... whenever. I think you're safe for now, but keep being careful."

"Thanks, Chief. Thanks for being there when we needed you. You were right. We're really the county's problem."

"You may be the county's problem," Stanley said, "But we aim to see you stay safe. You and that equipment of yours. It's going to be a big part of saving the town."

When the Ford had disappeared into the snow and the darkness, Calvin and Nan returned to the fire, after locking the door. True to her word, Nan snuggled up against Calvin and began to cry softly as he held her.

CHAPTER THIRTY-ONE

Buddy and Charlene went out nearly every day, suited up. When they were actively decontaminating they wore respirators. If just getting some fresh air and sunshine, such as it was with the nearly constant volcanic haze in the air, they wore dust masks.

By then end of another two weeks the area around the shelter was decontaminated and they could go outside without the Tyvek suits. "Char," Buddy said, as he checked the city again with the binoculars, "I think I should go down and see what we can find in the city. We have food for a long time, but I'd like to get more. Some more ammunition. Some more supplies for you."

"When should we go?" Charlene asked.

Buddy took the binoculars down from his eyes and looked at her. "I think it should just be me."

"Oh, Buddy! That's too dangerous! We should both go. I'm comfortable with a gun now to be of some help, if something happens."

"I know," Buddy replied. "It's just... I'm worried it might be bad. And now that I have you, I don't want to lose you."

"Well, Buddy," Charlene said somewhat sternly, "I feel the same way about you. If you go down there alone and something happens, I would never know it. I couldn't stand that."

"It would be better if we both went. But then again... I hate leaving the place alone now. We've seen smoke a couple of times. There are other people up here."

"The chance of anyone running across us is slim. You said so yourself."

"I know. But I still worry." Buddy paused for a moment, and then added, "Okay. We'll go down together, but be prepared to take the place back if someone had found it. At least we've got some of the supplies cached, too."

"Do you plan to stay overnight, or go and come back?"

"We'll take things for an overnight stay, just in case, but I'd rather do a quick reconnaissance, pick up what we can find, and get back here. There's bound to be some people that made it. I want to find out what I can. The radio broadcasts haven't been that informative."

"Tomorrow?" Charlene asked.

"Tomorrow," Buddy said.

They moved the shielding from in front of the garage doors that after noon, in preparation of taking the truck out the next morning. They loaded up what they wanted to take with them, and then turned in early. It would probably be a long day, the next day.

They didn't see any signs of people until they got to the suburbs of the city. It took them most of the morning to make their way that far. The roads were choked with abandoned vehicles.

Tense with worry, Buddy cautiously drove up to the two men walking along the side of the road. Both stopped and turned to watch as Buddy approached. Both were armed, but left their rifles slung over their shoulders, though they looked ready and willing to bring them into play if needed.

"Hi," Buddy said. He had his window down and drove up to them on his side of the truck. "I see there are other survivors. I'm Buddy Henderson. This is Charlene Brubaker. We're up in the hills."

Buddy breathed a slight sigh of relief as the two men nodded politely. The first one, dressed in jeans and a flannel shirt said, "We figured there are a few of you up there. I'm Alan and this is Juan. We're headed in to the shelter to get supplies. Any chance of getting a ride? Aren't too many vehicles working anymore."

"We can tell you how to get there," Juan said.

"You understand, we have to be careful," Buddy replied. "The news reports..."

Juan patted his rifle. "Understood. We haven't run into anything yet, but we always go armed."

"Okay," Buddy said. "Climb in the back. But if I get a bad feeling about something, you'll have to get out. Okay?"

"Sure," Alan replied. "Any less walking is better than not any less walking." He gave Buddy the address where a shelter had been set up by FEMA. Buddy knew where the location was. There would be plenty of time to see if there was some type of ambush set up.

There were more and more signs that some work had been done on the roads as they got closer. A regular lane had been opened up in the worst of the traffic jams. It was another twenty minutes before they saw more people. They were all moving the same direction. There were children as well as adults. Perhaps ten percent were armed in obvious ways.

Convinced that the two men had been telling the truth, Buddy stopped to let a family of six, with small children, climb into the back of the truck, too. It was another fifteen minutes of slow driving before they got to the entrance of the compound set up on the parking lots of a Wal-Mart and a Sam's Club.

There were a handful of vehicles parked outside the compound. Juan directed Buddy over to them. When Buddy was parked, the others got out of the back of the truck and thanked Buddy and Charlene.

A National Guardsman walked over, M-16 slung, and said, "I'll log you in and your vehicle will be guarded until you return. Can I see your ID? You'll need to show it again to get the truck, in case I'm not on duty."

Buddy pulled his wallet out and handed his driver's license to the corporal. The Guardsman dutifully recorded the number on the clipboard, along with the truck's license number.

Handing the license back to Buddy, the man said, "You look new here. You need to see registration first off." He pointed to one of the tents near the entrance. There was a table set up in front of the tent. Next to the tent was a large board with many things posted on it.

When Buddy and Charlene got over to it, they could see that the postings were mostly messages from one person or group to loved ones, stating their condition and location. It wasn't too busy at the moment at the table, so Buddy and Charlene approached it.

"We just came down from the hills," Buddy said. "First time since the war."

"Fill these out and we'll get you on the census," the Guard Lieutenant said. "Are you healthy? Do you need a doctor immediately?"

"No," Buddy replied. "We're fine. We just wanted to find out what is going on." He was filling out the card as he spoke. "Should we put our old address or... Oh. Never mind. I see." Someone came up behind them, so Buddy and Charlene moved to one side and continued filling out the form.

A Sergeant took the form from them and went into the tent. A few minutes later she returned and handed each of them a laminated ID card. "You can show this to get rations and such. Be aware that the information is recorded in a computer and anyone found abusing the relief system will be dealt with harshly. You'll have to check your weapons, but you will get them back when you leave."

The Sergeant nodded over toward a tent a few steps further in from the registration tent. Half a dozen soldiers were taking and giving weapons as IDs were shown. Buddy looked back at the sergeant and said, "We were going to try to find some more food, but we're pretty well supplied. It looks like..."

"You'll need to speak with our Captain, Sir. There is nothing I can do for you. I have a specific job to do. Just tell Lieutenant James what you have in mind. She'll direct you to where you need to go."

Buddy nodded. Charlene had yet to say a word. When there was a break in the line, Buddy stepped back up to the Lieutenant's position. "Lieutenant, we're not desperate for food or anything. We're more interested in finding out what is going on."

"That's good to hear," she replied. "Go to the third tent in the cluster just inside and ask for Captain Hansen. He's the PIO. He can update you."

It wasn't quite a madhouse, but the place was busy. Buddy and Charlene followed some other people inside the delineated area and approached the tent. Several people were standing around. Buddy saw a soldier standing at the entrance of the tent and asked for the Captain.

"He's just getting ready to give an update, Sir. Just join the group there and you should be able to hear everything."

They listened to the Captain and learned the condition of the city, surrounding area, statewide and nationally. It wasn't good. Buddy and Charlene exchanged a look. Charlene started to say how lucky they'd been, but realized that luck had been only a small part of their good fortune. It had been Buddy's foresight and preparations that had allowed them to be in as good of shape as they were.

After the briefing, they hung around until the Captain could see them. "I don't really know what to do," Buddy said. "We've got a place in the hills. We're okay for the moment, but we'd like to get more food, fuel, and some ammunition. We heard about the marauders…"

"We can't help you on the ammunition. The food yes. Fuel we're using all we can salvage for official purposes." The Captain gave them a hard look. "As you mentioned, there have been some marauding. That includes looting. Now I know there are some areas of the country where that has been condoned as salvage and scavenging, but here in the city it will not be tolerated. Just keep that in mind."

Buddy nodded. "Like I said, we aren't that bad off, short term, as long as the marauders don't make it up our way."

"I don't want to sound too harsh," the captain quickly said. "You can barter, trade, or buy whatever someone has to offer, as long as it hasn't been looted. There are people that have. Most do not."

The captain's fatigue was suddenly obvious when he added, "Most of those out there now are not going to make it. Too much radiation exposure. It just hasn't caught up with them yet. But you didn't hear that from me. Shouldn't have mentioned it at all. But you folks look like nice people, trying to do the right thing.

"I'd suggest you share as much as you can, if you have supplies, but I'd be cautious. Resupply is going to be problematical. I'm afraid that is all I can tell you. Since you've said you have supplies we can't really give you anything, despite the fact that it is known that at least a few people are getting everything they can, even if they already have good supplies. Fear at work with all this talk of a bad winter coming on."

"I guess we should head back to our place, then," Buddy said. "I wouldn't be comfortable taking anything, anyway, with people needing that have nothing." Charlene squeezed his hand in agreement.

"I wish I could do more. I can make arrangements to see our commanding officer, though I don't think it would do any good. I'm not a policy person, as you know. I disseminate information." He managed to smile then. "And acquire it."

"No. That won't be necessary." Buddy shook the captain's hand when he held it out. "Thank you for the information."

"Good luck to you. Oh. If you do have a mind to trade, there is an area on the far side of the compound for barter and trade. It separate from the compound itself. You'll have to walk around."

"We'll check it out." With that, Buddy and Charlene left.

"What do you think?" Charlene asked Buddy as they made their way toward the entrance of the compound.

"Let's check out the barter area. What the captain said changes things a little for us. I thought we'd be able to scrounge things. I guess they are in places, but not around here. Though I bet some are. Some get caught, others are sneakier."

"Okay. Let's see what they have."

Buddy thought there was quite a bit available. But most of it was of no use to them. He and Charlene did make a note of things that were in demand. They would be able to do some trading if things continued much the same.

A few people were taking silver and gold coins, though many would only trade item for item. Buddy had brought some coins with him and used some silver to buy all the seed he could find. Gardens were going to be very important in the future. Even more important would be farms.

There was a different guard on duty at the parking area, but upon showing his driver's license again, and the new ID, they were able to get the truck and head out. Rather than turning back toward the hills, Buddy headed for Charlene's place first. She gathered up quite a few more things, and with Buddy's help loaded them into the truck. They did the same at Buddy's place.

Both their houses were in decent shape. They'd not been damaged much by the blast, other than losing some shingles. Neither had been looted. Buddy suspected that would just be a matter of time. He would try to find the parts to get the plumbing van going so he could move it and all his plumbing supplies up to the new place.

CHAPTER THIRTY-TWO

It wasn't until he got to the suburbs that Charlie saw any activity. What he did see was people all heading in one direction. He followed along slowly, keeping his distance from everyone. Part of the way was uphill and he was very tired when he came to what had to be a government camp.

Charlie pulled out of the way and thought about things for a long time. He really didn't like the idea of being in a camp, but they should have food and a safe place to sleep. Probably medical care. He must have stayed in the shelter long enough, since there were people here in the open. Still, he hesitated.

He noticed that people with transportation, the occasional motorized vehicle, several bicycles, and even one horse, were all going to one area and leaving their vehicles. There were also people coming back and getting the vehicles and leaving. That convinced him.

Showing the state photo ID when asked, Charlie asked several times if he would be able to get his belongings back and was assured patiently each time that he would. He went through the registration process FEMA had in place, and then sat down to a hot, filling meal.

Charlie got a change of clothes, since they were offered, and three days worth of food. "That wasn't so bad," Charlie said softly, as he pedaled away. Though told it was safe to be out of shelter now, if he hadn't received much radiation exposure, Charlie thought that since he had received enough to make him sick he should stay in shelter all he could.

But it was a long ways from the construction site to the FEMA camp. Charlie decided to try to find an abandoned house with a basement he could stay in until he decided what to do. He'd been told it was going to be a terrible winter. Deciding that a ritzy place was as good as a hovel, if it was abandoned, he headed for the upscale part of this suburban area.

He almost went past the house, but he saw the front door open and decided to investigate. The place certainly looked ritzy enough. Charlie looked around carefully, and then quickly pedaled the bike to the side of the house. He hid the bike and trailer near the back corner of the house, behind some landscaping bushes.

Taking his closet pole, minus the chains and buckets, Charlie waited a few minutes, then quickly went inside the house and closed the front door. "Hello!" he called, not yelling, but not so soft that it couldn't be heard.

It took a couple of hours to search the place. It was fancy, all right. And it did have a basement. There was even some food in the pantry. Fancy food. The food in the fridge and freezer was all bad. He found a few tools in the garage. Taking a shovel, he buried the stinking mess in the side yard.

When he went out into the backyard he noticed two big plastic looking disks some distance from the house, and a nice bird fountain with gazing ball, but didn't think much about them.

He'd tried a faucet. No water pressure, he noted, but remembered from the articles in the paper that there might be some in the hot water heater. He'd get to that later. He waited around until dark, to see if anyone showed up. When they didn't he brought his things inside the house. He brought the bike inside, but didn't want to open the garage door manually to move the trailer in. He left it hidden behind the bushes.

Charlie didn't fill the buckets very full, but he used the shovel to dig a pretty good size hole in the back yard, near the fence line, and put the dirt into several buckets. He would use it to cover the waste in the toilet bucket, and then bury the accumulation in the hole.

He was feeling the strain by the time he had the last two buckets in the basement. It had been a long day for him. The basement was semi-finished and included a family/game room, as well as a bedroom.

Sleeping in a real bed helped Charlie. He woke up refreshed. After he ate, he stashed some of his belongings in several places outside the house, and then hooked the trailer back to the bike and set off. Apparently water wasn't a problem at the camp. They let him fill all six of the buckets he had on the trailer.

Charlie took a rest after taking each of the buckets into the house. That was his drinking water. Water from the pool in the backyard would do for sanitation and bathing. The rest of the day he spent resting, inventorying items in the house and garage of use to him, and making plans.

CHAPTER THIRTY-THREE

Angela hadn't told Emily about the man staying in the house for the last three weeks. She'd seen him on the camera system in the back yard occasionally, digging and filling holes. He would also get water from the swimming pool with a pair of buckets on a pole. He seemed harmless, moving slowly, as if he were weak. Of course, he was out in radiation of over a Röentgen. He must be staying in the basement, for shelter, Angela had decided. She wondered what had brought him to that specific house.

Despite the man being there, they needed to get out of the shelter and take a look around. The information on the radio indicated FEMA and the National Guard had a camp nearby where they could get help and find out more about what was going on. They still had plenty of supplies, but the reports of a bad winter coming had Angela worried. And Emily was next to useless when it came to decisions.

Emily was content to let Angela call the shots. She made no protest when Angela strapped on the holster and 1911A1 pistol that had been in her fanny pack, and slung the Benelli over one shoulder, a bandoleer of shells over the other, and began climbing the ladder up to the shelter hatch. She'd checked the camera. The area was clear at the moment.

When she had the hatch un-dogged, she quickly opened it and clambered out, closing the hatch behind her. Angela ran over to the side of the house and looked around the corner, bringing the Benelli around off the sling and to the ready.

After checking the other side of the house, she tried the back door. It was locked. Angela had taken the precaution of getting Emily's keys from her before she left the shelter. Quietly she unlocked the door and went inside.

Things were in better shape than she expected. There was no sign of any ransacking. Deciding to leave the basement for last, she checked the rest of the house. It was obvious that some things had been disturbed, but there was no wanton destruction.

Finally, Angela tried the basement door. It didn't have a lock, but when she opened it the door knocked something down the stairs that made a loud clattering noise.

The noise from the early warning system woke Charlie up. He'd been taking a nap, one of several he took every day. He was regaining his strength, but it was coming slowly. He had to work at the camp for a couple of hours now, each time he went in to get food or water and he was tired much of the time.

He lay there quietly, not moving, in the darkness of the basement bedroom as he heard footsteps on the stairs after several long moments. Afraid he might get shot if the person or persons coming down the stairs were armed, and he startled them, Charlie finally decided to call out. They'd find him anyways. Perhaps he could talk his way out of this. He got up and went to the open door of the bedroom.

"Hello! What do you want?"

Angela stopped her descent. He was in the room that opened off the family/game room. "I want to know who you are and what you are doing here."

"Just crashing," Charlie replied. "Look. I'll get my things and go. I thought the place was abandoned. I don't want any trouble. I'll just go."

"Where is that big stick you carry?"

Charlie was surprised. "How'd you know about that?" he asked, but quickly answered anyway. "There by the sofa."

"Okay," Angela said. "Come out where I can see you. I have a shotgun. I'll use it if you try anything." There was enough light from the basement windows, set high in the basement walls to see adequately.

Charlie stepped out, his hands at shoulder level. "Don't shoot me. I'll be out of here so fast you'll never even know I was here. Can I take my stuff with me?"

When Angela saw Charlie she came down the last three stairs. "Is there anyone else here? And don't lie to me. I've been watching the place for some time."

"Just me. Honest."

Keeping the Benelli at waist level, but trained on the man, Angela took a quick look around. It was obvious the man was living in the basement. But he was living neatly. Still no signs of wanton destruction. "What's your name?"

"Charlie. Charlie Grayson."

"If you want to get out of this alive, Charlie, you'd better tell me the truth. Do you have a weapon?"

"Closest thing is the closet pole there." Charlie was keeping his hands up. He took a step forward and added, "Please. Just let me leave. I'm not out to hurt anybody. I just wanted a safe place to stay until I can head south. I have radiation sickness." Realizing that the woman might think it contagious he quickly continued. "But it isn't catching or anything."

Angela frowned. "I know that. How bad is it?" She kept the shotgun trained on him and made a small motion for him to stop moving. He did.

"Not too bad, but I'm not up to a long trip. FEMA says the winter is going to be tough. I aim to put together some supplies and go south. FEMA is handing out a little food for work."

"Yeah. I heard that on the radio." Angela shifted the gun slightly, raising the end of the barrel enough for it to point over Charlie's head. But ready to drop it again and fire if needed.

"You have a car or something? And fuel?"

Charlie shook his head. "No. Bicycle and trailer. Fuel is hard to get. There's people scavenging, though they aren't supposed to. You can buy it if you have whiskey, food, guns and ammo, or silver and gold. If you don't get caught."

"So there is trading going on," Angela said. She brought the shotgun barrel down and tucked the stock under her arm. "You can put your hands down. But don't try anything."

"I won't," Charlie replied. "Yeah. You can trade. A lot of people are. There is a lot of scavenging, despite the National Guard patrols. They aren't pushing it too hard as long as it doesn't get too flagrant. Or violent. They're really cracking down on violence."

"What are they doing to gun owners?"

Charlie shook his head again. "Nothing if you don't use it first. A lot of people go armed. Me, I just have my closet rod handy."

Angela started visibly when Emily called down from the top of the stairs. "Angela, are you okay down there?"

Looking up the stairs, Angela saw Emily standing in the doorway, John on one side, and Catherine on the other.

"Jeez, Emily!" Angela called up. "You scared me half to death! And I could have shot you. What are you doing out of the shelter?"

"Well, the kids wanted out and you've been gone a while and I wanted to see what was going on and... I know you told us to stay, but it's been such a long time and you were out... and I was afraid you might just take off... and... I don't know. I'm sorry!" Emily was starting to cry.

"Okay, Emily. It's okay."

"Someone has been here, haven't they?" Emily asked.

"Yeah. A man named Charlie. He's here now. He's been living in your basement for three weeks."

Again Charlie was surprised at her knowing that detail. She must have been watching from the start. That was creepy.

"Is he dangerous?"

"I'm not. Really," Charlie said quietly.

Angela frowned. "I don't think so, but we can't take any chances," she told Emily. To Charlie she said, "I'm going to let you go, with your stuff. But don't try anything."

"Thank you," Charlie replied, relieved. "I won't try anything. It'll take me a little while to move everything."

"I understand. Make sure it's far away."

Charlie's face fell. "I was just going to move to the next house," he said, the disappointment obvious in his voice. "I can't afford to get too far from the FEMA camp."

"Oh," Angela said. "But how do I know I can trust you not to try something?"

With a shake of his head, Charlie sadly replied. "I guess you can't, can you? Can I have a couple of days to move everything? I'll do it whenever you say."

Angela groaned when Emily called down, "Why can't he stay here, Angela? We're staying in the shelter. He can't do anything to us there."

"Emily!" Angela barked. Under her breath she muttered, "Tell all our secrets, why don't you."

It hit Charlie then. The big disks on the ground in the back yard must be part of an underground shelter. "You must be alone, then," Charlie said. Before he could continue, Angela spoke.

"What of it? I've got the gun. And I will use it."

"I understand. What I meant was that it's hard being on your own. I don't want to stay in the camp, but I'm afraid all the time that someone will catch me off guard and hurt me and take my stuff. Like you could have done, if you wanted to. Maybe I could be of some help to you. I don't want anything, but you're going to want to go to the camp and register. You can get food and water there. And information. I can keep an eye on things."

"Yeah. Like that's going to happen." Angela snorted.

Emily had come down the stairs several steps. She bent down and looked at Charlie. "Isn't that a good idea, Angela? We need to do that. Get registered. I'm sure the government will know what to do. But I don't like the idea of leaving the place empty."

Angela just shook her head. After a moment she said, "But we don't even know him. He could do anything."

"We have to trust someone," Emily said quietly. "Has he really done anything to indicate he's a danger? It doesn't look like he hurt the house."

"Well, no, not really. And he's got radiation sickness."

With that, Emily backed up the stairs and gathered her children to her. "Maybe it's not such a good idea, then."

"Emily, you can't catch radiation sickness from someone. Not if they've been decontaminated."

Charlie quickly interjected, "I have been. Clothes and all."

"Oh," Emily said. "That's different, then." Firming up her voice, Emily added, "I've let you make the decisions so far, Angela. But I've always been one to lend a hand. At least when Edward would let me. Which wasn't often. He's obviously a sick, homeless man. And he said he wants to help. We should help him if we can."

"Things have changed," Angela protested.

Angela was rather impressed when Emily stood up to her. "I must insist."

"Well, it is your house and shelter. And I'm not going to give up what you've shared with me, unless I have to, so what you say goes." Angela looked over at Charlie again. "I guess you get to stay." It was Angela's turn to harden her voice. "But you try the least little thing and I'll put you down like a rabid dog." She was surprised when Emily didn't protest.

"You aren't making a mistake," Charlie said. "Okay. What's next?"

"I want to see this FEMA camp of yours. Come on upstairs." Angela stayed cautious, but Charlie followed her up the stairs without any problems. They all took seats around the dining room table. Angela had the Benelli slung over her shoulder, but kept her hand near the Colt 1911.

"I'm reluctant for all of us to go at once," Angela said, when no one else spoke up. The two children headed up to their rooms to get some toys they'd been deprived of for the last two months.

"Maybe you and Charlie should go so you can check it out while I and the children stay in the shelter."

Angela was surprised again. It was what she was going to suggest. "Okay. That sounds workable. But you must promise me you will stay in the shelter with the hatch dogged until we get back."

Emily nodded. "When?"

"I was going in tomorrow for more rations and water," Charlie offered. Emily and Charlie both looked at Angela.

"Okay, I guess. Charlie and I'll go in tomorrow."

CHAPTER THIRTY-FOUR

Firewood became another major commodity as the weather turned wintry before the end of October. Percy had been coppicing his woodlands for years and had massive amounts of firewood stacked in several huge storage piles around the estate.

One of the deals he'd made when he'd gone into the city so many months before when he'd first become uneasy with the world situation and the weather patterns was the purchase of firewood from several establishments that sold it in the city. He'd bought a total of a hundred full cords and it had all been delivered, except the last two cords, by the time the war started.

He'd made quite a few deals since then, to obtain wood from others. A few people cut it and sold it to him. Percy wouldn't clear cut, so many people allowed him to send a wood cutting crew in to harvest selected trees for firewood. He took the entire tree, including branches. The good stove wood he began stockpiling at the hardware store. He'd found someone to manage it for him. They began selling the firewood, along with the remaining stock of items that Percy hadn't taken out to the estate.

After Percy had moved what he wanted there was plenty of room to stack firewood inside the store. There had been three house fires in the time since the war. There simply wasn't water available to fight them, nor equipment with which to do it. The town had a small pumper truck, but with only the two-hundred-fifty gallons of water it would hold, and no working hydrants to pump from, each of the three fires had been lost causes. Percy bought the houses, demolished them and stored the good lumber for later use. Wood not useable as lumber was added to the firewood piles, including furniture that wasn't exceedingly useful.

Many people were grateful for the source of wood. No one said much when the winter worsened and people began to tear down abandoned houses for the wood they contained. Tom and the city council finally just condemned several of the houses, demolished them and used the wood and furniture from them in stoves that Randy built to heat the rooms in the school for people to use as shelter when they couldn't heat their own homes adequately.

An opening was made in the outside wall of a room adjacent to the school's kitchen. A large water tank was moved in and a pump with a pressure tank connected to it. A generator was run twice a day to pressure up the water system and provide electricity for several purposes. Part of the diesel they bought from Percy was used to run the genset. A horse drawn wagon with a water tank in it kept the tank in the school supplied. A limited amount of hot water was obtained by circulating water through the radiator of the engine of the generator.

Percy wasn't able to make quite enough biodiesel to prevent using the stocks of the commercial fuel, but the use was vastly minimized. One of the things he paid a premium for were the chemicals needed to produce the biodiesel. The alcohol production was going well. Several vehicles had their engines converted to run straight alcohol, based on information obtained from books that Percy had in his library.

Gasoline was scarce. Percy had set up a buying program for gasoline the day he'd made so many other deals in town. He was buying gasoline from people that had cars that wouldn't run, but still had fuel in them. He got over a thousand gallons that way. Most of it he accumulated in a tank in town and sold in cans out of the hardware store. He also sold some biodiesel there, as well.

Plans were made to convert a couple of trucks with gasoline engines to run on wood gas. It was a project for the next year, when better plans for providing firewood would be made.

Percy kept the generators going at the estate on a limited basis. They ran only when needed, then were shut down to conserve fuel. The heaviest use was for supplemental grow lights in the greenhouses. Some of the plants began to show signs of distress when the weather stayed cloudy for days on end. The regular rains kept the panels clear, and there was increased UV, but the lights were needed in three of the greenhouses that had plants needing more light than nature was providing.

With what people were doing on their own, in town and on other area farms, people were able to have enough to eat, though many lost considerable weight. Many had it to lose. A few didn't.

Since it was easy to keep warm, one of the cottages was declared the new clinic. The equipment was moved from the clinic that had been built. Henry made regular runs into town and back to deliver small quantities of food, and shuttle people back and forth that needed a doctor or were paying off their labor barters to Percy.

Percy made it a point to feed everyone well when anyone worked for him. Many of them considered the hours of labor they'd already received some good, product, or service for, as a gift from heaven. They often got the equivalent again of what they originally purchased, as Percy provided everything, including their transportation.

Percy even insisted they see the doctor while they were at the estate and had an arrangement with the Doctors Bluhm to cover the cost so anyone working more than four hours for Percy had at least one comprehensive doctor's visit. They didn't have a real dentist, but Jock studied up, again in Percy's library, and began to do the work.

There'd been a dentist in town at one time. He'd left in a hurry with the IRS after him two years previously. He'd left all his equipment behind. It was one of the properties that the city council had declared town property. Percy bought the equipment and moved it to the cottage for Jock to use.

It was an austere Christmas for everyone, but most that were Christian were able to celebrate to some degree. Percy hosted a Christmas Eve party in the school auditorium and almost everyone in the area attended.

One of the reasons for the party, besides the Christmas aspect of it was to have half a dozen marriage ceremonies performed. It was easier for the one surviving minister to perform them. It was also easier on the couples. The reception was taken care of, and all the guests were pretty much guaranteed to be there.

Four of the couples were townspeople. One couple was Andy and Susie. The sixth was Percy and Sara. He'd asked her after their Thanksgiving dinner at the estate and she'd agreed. Mattie had helped her move her things from the gold bedroom to Percy's that weekend. Percy had the idea for the Christmas party and wedding when he'd asked her.

Percy provided all the food and drink for the party. It strained the production of the greenhouses, and put a noticeable hole in Percy's reserves, but he felt it worth it. Things were going well. The townspeople provided the decorations, except the tree. Percy provided it and contributed it to the firewood pile after New Years. Everyone brought an ornament. The tree decorating was the start of the party as everyone hung an ornament.

It was the best meal many of the people had all winter, except those that worked at the estate from time to time. Percy hadn't skimped. It was only partly due to the fact that not all the animals would survive the winter, though that was a factor. Two steers, four hogs, and thirty-six chickens fed the nearly three hundred and fifty people that attended. It was nearly the entire remaining population of the town and surrounding farms.

Even Sara's boss made it down to attend. He was down to consult with Sara on her progress evaluating the area's population and progress. He stayed for the party and left Christmas day to go back to the capital. There were many places, he said, that weren't celebrating. Of all the counties he dealt with, this one was doing the best, by far, of any of them.

There was no celebration for the New Year. The weather had been cold and snowy for Christmas. It was downright bitter the week after and got worse after New Year's Day. New Year's Eve night the low at the estate was forty-one below zero. There was four and a half feet of snow on the ground. The snow was dirty, mixed with the ash that continued to fall from time to time.

Those at the estate did fine. It took very little to heat the earth-sheltered structures to a comfortable temperature. The animal barn didn't need any heat. The animals kept it more than warm enough.

Percy always remembered the death toll in the town and surrounding area. There were forty-one deaths from the cold. The same number as the negative thermometer reading.

At least the bees had quit dying off. When Percy had checked the hives in the bee barn that night there were only the normal number of bee carcasses outside the hives. The fanners at the entrance of one of the hives looked like very young bees. Percy breathed a sigh of relieve. Bees were very important to a farm.

CHAPTER THIRTY-FIVE

"Okay, honey," Sara said, "I'm up. What is so important today?" Sara was standing and stretching beside their bed.

From the bathroom Percy said, "We've got to get a load into town today. It's your first trip driving one of the Unimogs with the snow blower on the highway. I want you to practice on the driveways before we get out on the highway."

"Oh, Percy! I'll do fine. You know you can have one of the others drive it if you don't trust me." The last was added chidingly.

Percy looked around the doorframe. He still had shaving cream on his face and the straight razor in his hand. Unlike most of the men, he still shaved every day. "It's not that I don't trust you. It's just... I worry about you. I finally have you in my life and I don't want anything to happen to you. Since the road became so bad, using the snow blower is tricky and dangerous. Especially at the stream crossing. It's really narrow there across the culvert we put in after the bridge went down."

"Oh, Percy," Sara said with a smile. She stepped up to him, put her arms around him and kissed him on the lips, shaving cream and all. "I love you when you worry. I love you a tiny bit more when you don't, but it's not that much different."

Percy wiped his wife's face clear of shaving cream with the towel from the vanity. "I love you too, all the time. No matter what. Now get your shower and get dressed. We are going to clean the driveways on the estate before we leave, whether its practice or just getting the job done."

When they went downstairs for breakfast, Andy was fussing in the kitchen, banging things with the cumbersome splint on his left leg. "Dadgum it," he half cursed. "I hate this thing."

"He won't sit down and let us do it," Amy said. Her sister nodded.

Susie came into the kitchen and put her hand on Andy's arm. "Come and sit down. Let them do their job. I keep telling you not to try to do things with that leg. Jock said you need to keep off it. That splint isn't quite as effective as a regular cast, but the one that will fit you is on Howard."

Andy frowned at his wife, but took a seat, out of the way. The sisters went on with the breakfast preparations. Mattie was sick in bed with a bad cold. "I wish I could go with you," he groused. It's my job to be doing things like this. Not you and Mrs. Jackson."

"Not when you're hurt, Andrew," Percy said, pouring them both cups of tea. The coffee that was left was kept for special occasions. There were four coffee plants in one of the greenhouses, but Percy wasn't sure they'd produce. Even if they did, they wouldn't provide much coffee. But some. Eventually.

"You've worked hard enough, and will again. You can monitor the radios, just as you've been doing. Each person has to do what he or she is capable of doing. You can do the radios and keep things on an even keel around here. And keep an eye on the other Dr. Bluhm. Dr. Bluhm has been saying she's doing too much, too."

"When are you going to start calling us Jock and Melissa?" Melissa asked. She elbowed Jock just a little. "What have you been telling them? I just realized that everyone has been trying all of a sudden to get me to take it easy."

"Well, it's your first child, and you've had some problems already."

"I've got the second best doctor in the state attending me. I'm fine and I will be fine, if Junior here ever decides to take a break from trying to kick my insides to the outside." Melissa's hands cupped her belly. It was February and she was almost eight months along. She was short and slender. Jock was tall and rangy. Apparently the baby was going to take after its father.

After a quick breakfast Sara, Susie, Jock, and Percy headed for the equipment barn through the tunnels. The additional berms had all been removed before the worst of the freezing weather had hit. Suzie fired up the Bobcat 5600T Utility Vehicle. She ran it over and connected the snow blower for it. Percy and Jock were raising the barn door to get out the vehicles.

Susie used the Bobcat to clear the accumulation of snow near the doors and headed toward the animal barn doors. Percy and Sara climbed into their respective Unimogs. The snow blowers for them were already attached. The box beds were installed the night before. The plows had been on for days. The two headed out of the barn, one blowing snow one way, the other, the other way.

It took only a few minutes to get the three feet of accumulation cleared from the area between the various barns. The rest of the crew would work on moving the fifteen foot high windrows of blown snow that resulted from the multiple snow blower passes away from the barns later. Right now they wanted to get the day's delivery to town. They were only making two runs a week now and people were waiting on the food.

Henry pulled the shuttle bus out of the equipment barn and followed the two Unimogs, now clearing the driveway toward the open gates. Percy took the lead and Sara dropped behind him, offset to clear an almost doublewide road. They turned toward Doc's first, and cleared the road to his place and his drive while Henry waited in the shuttle bus for them to return.

It didn't take long. Doc would be able to get out now if he needed to in Andy's Jimmy he'd started using when his old Dodge Power Wagon blew an engine. The engine was being replaced, but it would be spring before it was done.

The piles on either side of the road stood close to twenty feet high. The actual snow depth was over ten, but each of the last few trips to town the road had needed clearing. Not much of the snow blown to the sides of the road had melted.

Percy slowed appreciably when they came to the stream. The bridge, damaged some during the quakes, had become detached at one end and half fallen into the stream. Percy had moved a large culvert from the county maintenance shed and installed it in the stream. They filled over it and packed the fill down using the Unimogs and the Bobcats. A layer of compacted gravel completed the roadbed. The culvert was big enough around, but it was only twelve feet long. Not much margin of error when crossing the stream.

Percy eased onto the new stretch of road and cleared the single lane. He pulled back onto the highway on the other side, stepped out of the truck, and watched Sara cross the culvert. She did it easily and waved to him. She passed him and took up the lead position. Henry followed sedately behind, his passengers napping. Another crew would be coming back with him to work the labor hours with which they bought food, fuel, and firewood. Not a one begrudged Percy the work.

Reports coming in on the radio indicated that, as they had been at Christmas, their little community was thriving in comparison to others in the state. Down south it was better, but there was no guarantee it would continue to be so. Even the areas that weren't under the waters of the new, much larger Gulf of Mexico.

Much of the crowd at the school didn't really think it was so great. With the heavy snow accumulation, Steven's store had been abandoned, as had the hardware store. Everything centered on the school.

The main entrance of the school had been cleared with shovels, and there were the signs of a couple of paths leading somewhere. Percy and

Sara cleared the same large area cleared on the last trip.

People were waiting for the food delivery. Those scheduled to work the next few days eagerly helped unload the food and take it to the kitchen. Steven would distribute it from there. He, like several others that had remained fairly independent, had moved his family to the school when it became difficult to maintain heat in their own homes.

"Hi, Tom," Percy said. He noted that the Mayor was beginning to look haggard. The harsh weather was telling on his health. "What's the word today?"

"Fair, at best," Tom replied. "It's a struggle. Thank God for your help. Most of us never would have made it through without you. The reports from the feds and the state are indicating that the weather should be breaking in another two to three weeks.

"Still not much chance of aid. We're going to have to plan better for next winter. Or move south. That discussion starts every few days. I'm beginning to believe it may be a viable option. People are dying here, and I can't do anything to stop it."

"Tom, you're doing everything you can. Some of the people that have died just made bad choices. Estelle and Dwayne never should have tried to go back to their place after Christmas. It was too cold and snowy. And young Dale… Janice would have preferred to see him a few days after her birthday, rather than see him make the attempt to deliver her birthday present in the middle of a blizzard. It's tragic, but he made the choice to walk to the farm. It wasn't your fault.

"This is still a nation of individual freedom. We can't deny people the right to make stupid decisions. At least, not unless the decision will affect other people. Then there is some justification. Like when you prevented Jeb from storing fuel in his family's area here in the school. There would have been a fire, eventually. I know he blames you for the fact that the container was overturned and the fuel lost, but you still made the right decision."

"That man is upset about something, every day. I wonder sometimes if I object to moving the town south next spring, just because Jeb and Abigail are for it. And Wilkins. The three of them are still coming up with plans to try to get you ousted from the estate. Now, if just them, and a couple more I could name, would head south on their own, I'd be all for it. They're a constant thorn in the operation here.

"I mean, everyone is entitled to an opinion. The things we've done here have been group decisions, but they are always so negative. It just really gets me down."

"Tom, you're a good guy. The offer to have you come out to the estate and stay still goes," Percy said.

"I can't leave these people," Tom said slowly, looking around the auditorium where they were standing. Fortunately, unlike most such structures, the school's auditorium was an arched construction building. Basically a large Quonset hut. It took the snow load with no problem. The rest of the school was much the same. A large asterisk of Quonsets with dormer windows in the single floor sections.

"Not," Tom continued, looking back at Percy, "any more than you cannot help where you can. You don't have to be supporting this town with your resources."

"You know I'm doing just fine. I've pretty much got all the original value of gold and silver back in trade that I put up to help get things started. People had a little here and a little there. And when Alfonse set up his little assay, refinery, and mint operation to turn jewelry and other things with precious metal into coins, a lot more came out of the woodwork. There is a lot of gold and silver in things that I had no clue. Alfonse has been able to extract it for people and put it into useable form.

"For a fee," they both said together. It was a catch phrase now, heard often during discussion of bartering, trading, and requests for services.

"I know. But you really don't have to be doing all of what you do. You could sit back and live comfortably, supporting yourself for the rest of your lives at the estate, without all the hassles and work."

"It's just not in me," Percy replied. "I've worked all my life to get where I am. It didn't turn out the way I imagined, even with all the planning I did for such things. It is essentially what I set out to do, in the event of an emergency. Have what was needed to get by and help others if I could. I guess I never really believed it myself, that things would happen the way they did. I'm just glad I'd made the preparations I did. And I've made a good living in the process."

"A lot of people are grateful you did. Even some that used to make fun of you for your strange ways. And that equipment you bought. Who ever heard of farming with trucks and industrial equipment but you? And keeping working teams to actually farm with, not just have to march in parades, in the day and age of mechanized farming. Just you. I haven't really said it in a while, but thanks, Percy, for all you've done."

"Come on, Tom. You don't need to say that. I do what I do because I want to do it. It's an ego thing I guess. I like being prepared. I like having my toys. I never really needed all those six wheel versions of my vehicles. I just like them. They work great in these conditions, sure, but four wheel drives would be almost as good."

"Maybe," Tom said, "But if things ever get back to normal enough to allow me to obtain some of the same things you have, I'm going to. Those trucks of yours are amazing. And I can tell you, my four wheel drive SUV never would have made it across that stream the way your six-wheel-drive Suburban did when the bridge first went out."

"Hopefully things will get back to a semblance of what they were. The reports we're getting indicate there are many areas firing up again. Smaller scale, but to a degree."

"Yeah. Where the weather is still reasonable. You were right about the Gulf Stream. Apparently it did sink. The experts are saying that we're in for these kinds of winters for a long time to come."

"Just like Canada used to have. They dealt with it. So will we. And I agree with you. Those that want to go south should go. This area will easily support the same number of people that are here now, if they are people that want to be here and are willing to do what it takes to make a comfortable life. It's just a matter of adjusting to things. And a matter of scale."

"I know," Tom said. "There are a few taking to this like ducks to water. Others never will. Maybe we should plan on helping some go south this spring."

"I'll see what I can come up with," Percy said, grinning.

"No doubt," Tom said, his grin matching Percy's. "But before we get too maudlin, or too eager to get rid of people, let's get through the rest of winter."

"Good idea," Percy agreed. They went their separate ways then. Tom to see about an administration problem and Percy to get things ready to go back to the estate.

It was still snowing lightly, but there was no need to use the snow blowers on the way back. Henry got the current batch of six people settled in the bunkhouse as Sara and Percy parked the Unimogs and went to check on things in the house and the barns.

The snow had been moved, piled in a nearby open area. The dirty white pile was growing. "I know we need to keep this cleared, but why are you being so careful to keep it so organized," Jim asked Percy as they stood behind the barn and watched Bob put the last bucket load of snow on the pile using a Unimog.

"That ash mixed in with the snow will be very good for the fields. I want to work it in like compost next spring. Piling up the snow like this will leave the ash behind when it melts. Speaking of which, show me how the Ice House is coming."

"Another good layer," Jim said, leading Percy around the pile of snow, to a spot behind the utility barn. In the space between the barn and a section of the orchards was a growing mound of ice. Each morning when it was the coldest, water was sprayed on the mound, freezing as it flew through the air or when it hit the existing ice.

A light structure of wood had been built to form a cavity in the ice when the pile was first started. Now they just had an inverted U shape that was moved slightly each day to maintain a tunnel into the head high cavity. Flexible plastic tubing was laid in a spiral pattern inside the ice as the mound was being built.

Later in the spring, when they could no longer create more ice easily, the ice mound would be covered with straw bales to insulate it. The cavity would be used to store things requiring refrigeration. Water could be pumped through the tubing and used to cool things, too.

The entire mound was sitting on plastic lying on the ground. As the mound did melt, the runoff would be directed to one of the many underground water storage areas Percy had incorporated when he began the renovation of the place. That cold water could also be used for cooling purposes.

The storage areas were stacked interlocking panels consisting of four-inch high cylinders inside of pits with plastic liners. The stacked panels allowed a top liner to be laid down, and then the pit backfilled with eight inches of covering that would support vehicles. The panels took up only roughly four percent of the space in the cavity, leaving room for thousands of gallons of water in each one. All water diverted into the tanks ran through gravel and sand filters to remove debris.

Percy collected pretty much all the rain and moisture from snow that fell on the area comprising the estate building area. Since a generator had to run part of the time anyway for other needs, it was no problem to have a pump moving water from a well to make the ice mound.

A large tarp was drawn over the mound when the spraying was finished. Snow was blown over it to keep the sun from hitting the mound. Not that they got a lot of sun, but there was no reason to let any of the ice melt until it was needed. Plus, the snow that accumulated naturally was removed and added to the ash and snow pile Percy was building.

"Looking good," Percy said. "Thing might just last all summer, if we get it big enough. Though, from what the reports are saying, this summer may be as hot as this winter was cold."

"This'll be the place to hang out, if it is. Set up a lounge chair inside and just let the heat glow outside."

"Yeah. Right. Go find something to do." Percy laughed and Jim responded in kind. Percy headed to the house.

Melissa, Andy, and Mattie were commiserating with each other in the dining room as the sisters went about their work. Sara had started preparations for the household noon meal. She mostly supervised and the young women did the work.

"Burgers for lunch okay, Percy?" she asked.

"Sure," he replied. "Dr. Bluhm over in the infirmary with today's load?"

"Dr. Jock Bluhm is," Melissa called to him from the dining room. "This Dr. Bluhm is right here. I should have kept my maiden name for my work," she groused.

"I'm going to see how he's doing," Percy said, ignoring the pregnant woman's comments.

"Barbie didn't look too good this morning. We might have another inpatient for a while. Until that baby comes, too."

"I'd better go check on her," Melissa said. Andy stood and helped her get up from the chair.

"You be careful," Mattie admonished, wrapped up in her favorite blanket. Her voice was muffled from the congestion of the cold. "You're not in the best of shape yourself. Be sure to use the tunnel and don't go outside."

"Yes, Mother." Melissa quickly apologized for her sharp remark. "I'm sorry Mattie. It's not your fault. I just feel rotten. The tyke is kicking me something fierce."

"It's all right, sweetie," Mattie got out before she started coughing.

"Maybe you should go lie down, Mrs. Simpson," Andy said. "Susie will kill me if I let anything bad happen to you."

"Thank you, Andy. I think. And I think I will." Mattie staggered off to her room.

"I think I'll lie down, too," Andy said. "My leg is hurting." He went off to the bedroom he and Susie shared.

"We'll call you when lunch is ready. Andy paused, lifted a hand from the crutches to wave, and then hobbled on down the hallway.

"I guess it's just us for a while, ladies," Sara said.

Everyone seemed to be in a better mood by the time lunchtime rolled around an hour later.

"Makes me thankful I'm doing as well as I am," Melissa was saying as she, Jock, and Percy re-entered the kitchen to the smells of grilling hamburgers. The sisters were setting out plates and flatware, as Sara monitored the burgers.

"She's going to be fine," Jock said. "She's just having a lot of discomfort. It'll be over soon. The baby has dropped." Jock looked over at Percy. "Do you think Amanda would come out for a few days to help? You can up her pay a little. Take it out of my ration. I'd like an experienced nurse to help with the delivery. She's been doing fine in town since she showed up."

Amanda Gardner had walked into town one day before the weather had become so bad. She was headed to Arkansas from Wisconsin. She'd been carrying a huge backpack, pushing a mountain bike piled high with equipment, with a pipe strapped to the handlebars to steer it.

There was a two-wheeled deer drag loaded with additional equipment and supplies attached to the bike as a trailer. An inverted adult size snow sled topped the supplies. The sled had been converted to a pulka with plastic pipe and rope and could be used to carry the deer drag and bike in snowy conditions.

There were also a pair of cross-country skis, a pair of snowshoes, and a pair of alpine poles strapped to the equipment to allow winter travel.

When she arrived her intentions had been to stop for a day to rest. She agreed to stay and help with the medical duties for a share of food. She'd been invaluable to Jock, with Melissa able to do limited duty due to her pregnancy. When the thaw came in the spring, she'd head south again, with a fresh stock of jerky and dried fruits and vegetables. She was trading some labor for additional food stocks for her trip.

"I'm sure she will come out for that. And I'll absorb the additional cost. She wants as much food for her trip as possible." Percy was adamant about taking care of any additional barter Amanda might want.

As it turned out, Amanda was happy to do it. And it worked out well. Shortly after Barbie safely delivered her seven pound eleven ounce baby boy, Melissa went into labor. Melissa bore an eight pound thirteen ounce baby girl. Both babies were healthy. The happy news was transmitted to those in town.

The births seemed to be a turning point in the weather. It snowed more, but they were light snows, both in intensity and color. For the moment at least, the volcanoes to their west were behaving. There was still over two feet of snow when March rolled around, but it rapidly melted under the often seen sun.

The early rains began not long after the snows had melted away. Since they'd been able to decontaminate the fields the previous fall after stripping the fields for fuel production, Percy began turning the ground as soon as the horses and oxen could get into the fields safely.

Besides the moisture from the accumulation of snow that winter, the early rains, cold as they were, added another significant amount of moisture to the worked ground. The irrigation ponds and canals were also full. Percy was sure that the moisture and significant amounts of volcanic ash would result in bountiful crops. He expected a shorter than normal growing season, so pushed to get things planted as soon as it looked like the danger of a hard frost was over.

The federal government was doing its best to provide what help it could, and getting weather reports, both short range and long-range forecasts were a priority they had been able to do.

When the roads were relatively safe to travel again, Sara began the spring census of the area.

Percy had her take the Chevy pickup with the shell and plenty of emergency supplies. The first few weeks of her work there was still danger of a sudden blizzard. By the end of March, seasonal weather prevailed.

Most of the people that had worked their rotation had been trained in what they would do come spring if they worked at the estate. The preparation and then planting went well. Percy had always saved seed to plant and had more than enough from the prior years to plant everything he wanted, despite last fall's failed crops. There were a few other farms equipped to do horse farming and the small amount of seed left in the farm supply store was divided among them.

For the first time in his life, Percy deviated from the rotation plan for the fields and garden. He knew the ground was in good enough shape to plant every available acre to get a good harvest. The plan was to go back to the rotation the next year.

Since the weakest of the stock had been used for food during the winter, the stock that was left was in prime shape. Percy had only been using a fifth of the space in the animal barn before the war. The additional animals had filled it, though not to the point of overcrowding any of the animals.

All the animals seemed grateful to get outside the first time they were allowed to do so. They'd all been exercised regularly in the barn, but the freedom of the first pasture trip seemed to bring out the friskiness in all of them, including the chickens. The dogs had opportunities to go outside during the least severe of the weather, so weren't quite as excited as the other animals were.

Nature had taken its course, as expected, and all of the female animals began giving birth. Susie and Percy had a good handle on it, but Doc helped, as did the Doctors Bluhm. They only lost three piglets and one calf. Baring another disaster, there would be meat for the year.

With the crops in and being cared for by hand and by animal power, other projects began to come to the fore in people's minds.

CHAPTER THIRTY-SIX

Calvin and Nan were able to get to town a few more times before winter hit full force. They helped all they could; wherever they could, helping people prepare for winter. There wasn't that much they could do. They hauled as much wood as they could get cut, letting the town council allocate it. They were getting a small fuel allocation from the state for what they were helping with, allowing them to conserve their own fuel.

When October rolled around they made what would be their last trip until spring. It saw the end of the gang that had attacked them. They'd been caught in a house in town, the owner of which had been providing the information and shelter. When she traded a jar of homemade preserves to Sheila McGuire for a half pint of liquor, Sheila recognized the label on the jar. It had come from one of the families that had been massacred by the gang. The woman showed it to the Chief.

Calvin was with the group that surrounded the house. They never determined if the gang had heard about the no mercy dictate that had come down, but they surrendered without a shot. They were hanged the next day, including the woman, during another snowstorm.

Calvin and Nan didn't go outside much that winter. Only to take the occasional look around and to clean the solar panels of snow. The snow was fourteen feet deep at its worst. They could not have gone anywhere even if they'd wanted.

They checked with Bill from time to time on the radio he'd left them. Things were not going well in town, and from what little information Bill was getting, things weren't much better in the outlying areas like where the Stubblefield's were.

But Calvin and Nan did just fine. They barely touched their stock of LTS food, using mostly the home canned goods they'd put up the previous fall.

The snow was down to only five feet deep when they decided to try to make it to town. It took them a week of long days of work with the Unimog to get there. They worked three more days in town under Bill's direction, clearing the most important travel lanes.

Again Calvin and Nan helped in many ways, as spring came in with a whimper. The extreme winter had taken a heavy toll in life. Less than twenty percent of those that had survived the war survived the winter. The town itself lost proportionately more than the outlying areas.

Several of the farms, used to being on their own for long periods during normal winters had survived intact. Others had not.

Bodies were buried, including those that had been hanged the previous fall. They had been there the entire winter, it being beyond the capability of the town residents to dig their way to them, much less bury the bodies. The cold weather had preserved them.

One farm family survived the winter by moving an antique wood kitchen stove into their barn and living there with the animals for mutual warmth and support.

It was never said aloud, but there were suspicions of cannibalism at one farm. But everyone there died, anyway, so nothing was done about it. Nothing could be done.

The survivors pulled together to make it. Very little food and not much more fuel came to the town through the auspices of the state and FEMA. They got a little, accepted gratefully. Most of their supplies were scavenged, through a FEMA sanctioned plan, from those that had not made it through the winter.

Not all had starved to death. Many deaths came early in the winter when a storm plummeted temperatures to thirty and forty degrees below zero for days on end. Most of the deaths were caused by freezing, or asphyxiation when wood was burned in snow covered houses with not enough ventilation.

Once travel could be accomplished, most of the rest of the population of the town and countryside opted to go to relocation centers in the southern states. A hardy few, farmers mostly, chose to stay.

Calvin and Nan stayed busy berming up barns and houses for the next winter, and cutting wood for hire. They started the garden and continued to grow vegetables in the greenhouse. They talked about going south, but with some of the farmers sure they could endure the winters; there would be food for barter, trade, and sale. They decided to stay.

FEMA managed to keep a trickle of fuel coming in, and Calvin was able to refill his tanks before the end of fall, doping it with PRI-G and PRI-D to keep it stable, as he had the year before. They were still well stocked with propane.

It was going to be some difficult years, but with the hardy people that chose to stay behind and continue with their lives, and Calvin and Nan with their resources they were willing to use for the benefit of the community, in return for supplies, there would continue to be a human presence in the Black Hills. Even the flora and fauna began to make a comeback the following years.

CHAPTER THIRTY-SEVEN

Buddy was able to barter and trade for quite a few things the next couple of months as they prepared for the winter. He also bought a few things with silver and gold, but he was holding what he had left pretty closely. Though he was pretty sure it was some scavengers, he traded for almost three hundred gallons of gasoline over that time. It kept the truck running back and forth for their weekly trips, plus increased his supply slightly.

FEMA and the National Guard began allowing those with businesses to open them for a limited time each day. Buddy was able to get new ignition parts for the plumbing van. It took several trips to move it and all the supplies he had at the house to the shelter. He also moved the storage building and re-erected it beside the shelter.

Much of what he acquired he was able to trade his expertise as a plumber, and some of his supplies. He was one of six that plumbed water and sewer for the camp as it grew. The tradesmen had plenty of unskilled help to get the work done. Everyone that wanted to stay at the camp and receive assistance had to contribute some of their time.

Buddy knew the winter, no matter how bad it got in the city, would be worse, but he and Charlene both preferred to be where they were, rather than in the camp. He wasn't sure how well they would make out if the winter got as bad as the forecasts said it would.

And the Captain had been correct, the die-off continued, though more people were coming out of the hills, to the camp, as their supplies ran out. Despite the fact that the total population of the region was falling, the camp population was growing.

Those facts made some things more difficult. Others less so. One of the farmers that was ill and going to stay in camp made Buddy a good deal on two roosters, a dozen layers, and three brood hens. It took Buddy and Charlene several days to haul enough dirt into the shelter to make a spot for the chickens for the winter. The farmer had thrown in the old pen and coop. It was set up near the garden spot they prepared for the next spring.

Knowing what was needed, Buddy took the opportunities during the decent weather to make arrangements with several other farmers to help out on their farms in exchange for meat, vegetables, and other staples. None would give him anything in advance, and he couldn't really blame them for that.

But as the severity of the coming weather became obvious, Buddy, since he'd already made the contacts, was first in line to stock up on butchered meat as farmers culled the animals they had left to herds they could take care of during the winter.

Things like freezers were cheap. Buddy picked up two twenty-one foot chest type freezers for next to nothing and installed them in the shelter. He filled both of them completely full with meat. Hunting laws had been relaxed, or more truthfully abandoned. Game had already begun to disappear during the immediate aftermath of the war, due to the radiation, but also to hunters taking anything and everything they could to survive.

But there was still a little left, and hunters were out in force. Buddy bought as much fish, fowl, and game as he could to finish filling the freezers. He hunted some himself, on his property and added to the take.

That was when he ran into the only trouble they had in the aftermath. Buddy had Charlene with him, teaching her to hunt. They were looking for anything they could get so Buddy had the Savage 99, and Charlene was carrying the Stoeger Coach Gun. They were at the edge of the property nearest the road when they saw three men, who also appeared to be hunting.

Buddy had grown a bit careless since things had been going so well. He hailed the others, intending to see how their hunt was going. Their response was to fire at Buddy and Charlene. Fortunately all three missed, and Buddy and Charlene dropped below the slight rise they'd been coming up. It flashed across Buddy's mind that this needed to be taken care of right now. They couldn't allow any rogue hunters that were willing to shoot on sight to have access to the property.

"Charlene," Buddy whispered, guiding her to a rock outcropping. "Hide here, with the shotgun out. Give it a couple of hours. If I don't come back, make your way to the shelter, being really careful. Anyone comes up and it's not me, shoot first and ask questions later. I'll make sure you know it is me. If I call you anything but Char, you know they caught me and they think they are making me show them where you are. Come out shooting. I'll go down to give you a clear field of fire."

"Buddy, I'm scared!" Charlene whispered back.

"I know. So am I. But we have to take care of this now. We can't have them at our backs. They'll eventually find the shelter and kill us. You know that time I won't talk about much?"

Charlene nodded.

"What I learned then applies to this situation. Just stay quiet and keep a good watch. I'll see you in a little while. I love you." Buddy leaned forward and kiss her deeply, and then faded away into the forest.

Charlene set out several 12-gauge shells, and loosened the Glock 21 in its holster. She was as ready as she could be. She jumped once several minutes later when she thought she heard a shot. But she couldn't be sure.

She was gathering up the shells, in preparation to head back to the shelter, as Buddy's time limit of two hours was almost up, when she heard Buddy's strong voice. "Char," he said, "It's me. Everything is okay."

She lunged into his arms in the fading light. He held her for a few moments, and then said, "We need to get back to the shelter. One of them tagged me before I got him."

With a gasp, Charlene stepped back and looked at Buddy in alarm. Then she saw the blood on his pants. "It's not serious," he said quickly. "But it hurts like the dickens and it's starting to get dark."

Despite not needing it, Buddy finally accepted Charlene's shoulder as support as they walked back to the shelter in the fading light. She cleaned and dressed the wound at the shelter, without another word, and then just held Buddy silently, until he fell asleep.

The next morning there was a foot of snow on the ground, and it was coming down heavily. Buddy got dressed, grunting and groaning a bit, over Charlene's objections. "I have to, Honey. It won't take too long, but those three had some things we can use."

"Well, I'm coming with you!" she insisted.

"Are you sure you want to? It's not a pretty sight."

Charlene gulped slightly, but she nodded. "I insist."

Buddy suggested they forego breakfast, and Charlene was glad he had. Stripping the equipment and then the clothing from the first man made her stomach churn. The second and third time weren't as bad. Buddy had made clean headshots, so there wasn't much gore. Just the fact they were handling dead bodies.

Buddy had insisted they wear their Tyvek suits, with rubber boots, gloves, and respirators. There was some type of bug going around and he didn't want to chance that the men might have it.

It was an amazed looked on Charlene's face when Buddy led her to the county road and she saw the truck there. They threw the gear in the back of the pickup truck, on top of three deer carcasses and half a dozen turkeys.

The truck was a small Toyota four-wheel-drive pickup that had seen better days, appearance wise. But someone had loved the truck at one time, Buddy pointed out, opening the hood. The engine was immaculate and it started right up.

Buddy was hurting by the time he finished dressing out the game. There wasn't room in the freezer for it so he hung it in the storage shed. It would be plenty cool enough now for it to keep until they used up some of it and made room in the freezer for the rest.

They didn't get off the property until the following spring. When they got to the city they found a virtual ghost town. Whatever had been going around the previous fall had been deadly. FEMA and the Guard had pulled out when only a few survived. What supplies were left were adequate for the few people that chose to stay behind.

They only knew that because the one person they found in the camp had kept a journal. It was still in his frozen hand when Buddy and Charlene found him. They loaded up the remaining supplies over the next three days and took them to the shelter. They used it to trade with those few on the surrounding farms that had survived.

Buddy fulfilled his promise to help on the farms that had people that made it through the winter and received enough supplies, in addition to their own garden, to make it for at least two years.

By that time the area began to recover. FEMA moved back in and began to help those that were left. Buddy and Charlene needed little actual help, but welcomed the fact that fuel and supplies were again available on a limited basis. Life would be hard for a while, but they would make it.

CHAPTER THIRTY-EIGHT

"Are you sure you want to do this?" Angela asked Emily.

"Yes, I do. Sure, the shelter got us through the fallout and stuff, but we can't live in it forever. I know you think I'm making a mistake, but I'm afraid we won't make it far enough south before winter sets in. FEMA and the National Guard won't let anything bad happen to us. Everyone that wanted to go south left two weeks ago."

"I know," Angela said, "But Charlie just wasn't ready. We still have time. The authorities have said there are places to stay once we get there. And we can work. With the rest of the food from the shelter, and those bug-out bags that were there, we'll have what we need to get south. Are you sure you want to give all that stuff to us?"

Emily nodded. "If it hadn't been for you, I and the children would never have survived this. And Charlie has been a big help since we found him. It's the least that I can do."

"Well, I'm not going to turn it down," Angela replied. She hugged Emily and both children, and Charlie did the same. Charlie and Angela watched as the three turned and walked into the FEMA camp, to take up residence.

"Come on, Charlie. Times a'wastin'. "

"You sure like to push an old man around," Charlie groused. He wasn't one-hundred percent, by any means, but he'd recovered remarkably during the summer months. The fact that he had a safe place to stay, and someone to watch his back, had allowed him to get more rest in a shorter period of time than he had for years. The food he got from FEMA wasn't in great quantity, but it was enough for him to recover.

In the weeks, then months, after they'd made connections, Angela had come to look upon Charlie as an uncle she'd never had, and to trust him completely. Charlie's feelings were reciprocal. He came to appreciate Angela's resourcefulness, knowledge, and skill. She had been the one that guided the small group through the last months. It was she that insisted they go south. Charlie had been ready to go into the camp at one point, but Angela had talked him out of it.

When they got back to the Baumgartner's, the trip going faster than it used to, now that Angela had a bicycle, they began to make their preparations for leaving. They had traded a few things from the house to a couple that were going into the camp for it. Like Charlie's, it was a good mountain bike.

They had also acquired an old pickup that still ran, and a trailer. Angela had traded her car for it. It had taken a while to get it out of the traffic jam. They'd been collecting gasoline for a long while. It wouldn't be enough to get them as far south as they wanted to go, but it would get them a long ways on the journey.

It took them three days to pack up everything they were going to take, including the remainder of the LTS food, the weapons, and removable equipment from the shelter. Once Angela had decided they were moving, and Emily had approved the action, they used what they weren't going to take for barter, to get the rest of the things they needed to take with them to ensure the success of the trip.

Charlie had rigged larger and better trailers for the bikes, and modified four of the packs that were part of the ten BOB's that had been in the shelter to fasten to the bikes that they would push, rather than ride, when they ran out of fuel for the truck.

A farm family heard about their plan to go south a day in to the preparations and asked if they could travel with them in return for some fuel. They had a two-ton farm truck with a trailer of gasoline. They were still trying to find more food when the group left.

Angela readily agreed. That would let them take all the food from the shelter with them. Enough to share, with plenty left over for their first days in the south.

Angela had to admit, whether he had planned to or not, Edward Baumgartner had prepared well. They were a well-equipped, though small, expedition that set off for greener pastures and better climate that day.

It was no easy trip, but with the goods they had, and the arms they had to use twice, they made their journey. They were even able to cache everything that wouldn't fit on the bikes and trailers when they ran out of fuel after parting ways with the Stanford's, who were headed for relatives about three quarters of the way to where Angela and Charlie were going.

Once they established themselves, Angela and Charlie returned and retrieved the caches. It was enough to see them through the winter at the farm they found that needed willing hands.

Emily and the children didn't fare well that winter. The two children froze to death one bitterly cold night, and Emily died a few days later, from malnutrition, cold, and grief.

It was experienced farmers and survivalists that owned and ran the farm where Angela and Charlie took up residence. Unlike Emily, John, and Catherine, Angela and Charlie would make it.

CHAPTER THIRTY-NINE

Some of the first were the plans of those that wanted to go south to avoid another winter like the one they'd just endured. Sara's census indicated there were three hundred twenty one people in the area that included the town and the estate. One third were children. Almost half the adults wanted to move if it were possible.

Reports had come from the area of the new Memphis Bay of the Gulf of Mexico that they had fared well. Memphis had snow most of the winter, but it was one or two feet at a time, not four or five or six or more, and not nearly as often. They'd had two periods when the snow was gone for a few days. It was a much different kind of weather than before the war, but reasonable to the minds of the town folk. More like what they were used to.

The area around the Gulf had suffered even more than the town had, because no one in that area was even remotely prepared for that type of hard winter. The death toll had been high, according to the reports Sara was getting. There were places available for people that wanted to go there. They would be welcome.

Everyone at the estate attended the town meeting set to discuss moving. Percy hadn't wanted to bring up any of the projects he had in mind until the issue of moving was settled. It didn't take that long.

Sara had reported that there would probably be a big change in the population soon when she turned in her preliminary report in March. Both the state and federal governments were represented at the town meeting. When it was clear that so many people wanted to move, the government representatives asked to be allowed to speak.

Sara's boss spoke first. "We don't like to lose citizens, in ordinary times," he said. "These are extraordinary times. The way the future looks, winters like this past winter will be the norm for many years. The state lost many of her citizens, between the war and the weather. Our services, such as they are, are strained to the limit. I doubt if you have noticed, since things have gone so well here."

There were some murmurs and restlessness from the crowd at that. Howard Broadfield lifted his hands for a moment. "I know. I know. Everyone here suffered. But believe me, compared to most you really did have it easy. I lost three toes myself to frostbite and that was in the state's shelter at the capitol.

"Be that as it may, we have been helping people in other locations to the best of our ability. Many of them also want to leave and go south. It would ease the strain on the state's resources and speed our recovery. The state will help with this project, to a limited degree. We can discuss the details after you've conducted your meeting."

The federal official took the podium next. She was a representative of FEMA. "Howard is right," she said. "As long as some move south, and not all, everyone will benefit. The south was hit even harder than you here." Again came the murmurs.

"Believe me when I tell you, twenty below in Memphis is ten times worse than forty below here. People were not prepared for anything except a dusting of snow, perhaps once each winter, and temperatures below freezing only a few times a winter. Estimates are that in this area we lost fifty percent of our population directly to the war, and sixty percent of what was left to the winter weather, combined with the results of volcanic and seismic activity. Twenty percent survived.

"Down south, the death toll from the war was about the same. The weather, complicated by severe earthquake damage and flooding, caused a ninety percent death toll on the war survivors. Only about five percent of the people residing there are still living."

That brought more murmurs, but these were of dawning realization that perhaps they had fared relatively well.

Claudia Robertson continued. "Despite the damage from the earthquakes and floods, life will be easier there. There are buildings left standing that can be repaired for use, including homes as well as businesses. We... the federal government... have a stronger presence there, also due to the less severe weather. There are more remaining resources, though, like here, organized scavenging will need to take place. There are rules in place to compensate people for losses, but everything remaining, just like here, will be used.

"Your bartering system has worked so well here, as word of it spread similar systems were instituted in many places with government assistance. That's not to say that people weren't doing anything similar. They were. This was just the most advanced and well thought out plan."

Nearly every resident of the area looked over at Percy. He turned red.

"You won't be going into a strange environment. People are doing similar things to what you're doing here. FEMA wants to see the relocation succeed, just as the state does. We do not want any more deaths that can be avoided. If some of you move south, I think we can save lives."

Claudia smiled. "Chancing being booed again, I must say that there has been very little lawlessness around here. Now, it was nothing like books and movies late in the last millennium depicted, but there have been cases of lawlessness in other areas. Highwaymen and such. Because of that, Federal troops can be assigned to accompany the wagon train, so to speak, to the south. That is, if this area can provide at least four men of appropriate age to add to the forces for at least two years. The military is just as shorthanded as everyone else and we need recruits. From what I understand goes on here, it'll pretty much be the same deal. Room and board, with a little spending cash for luxuries. In silver. Again, two year commitment, but everything will be provided for your services as soldiers."

"What about women?" a woman called. "I was in the army a few years ago. I still got what it takes."

Claudia was shaking her head. "It's too difficult to maintain the facilities necessary in the field for mixed gender units. You can certainly reenlist, but you would be transferred to a base operation. Probably north of here."

There was some laughter at that and the woman replied, "I'll pass, thank you. My sights are set on the south."

Several men were speaking up and Claudia interrupted them. "The trip is not dependant on whether men sign up. We just won't be able to provide an armed escort for the trip. You would be expected to help in the defense, of course, but a group of ten troopers would accompany you, commanded by a Lieutenant. Four locals would be joined by six experienced people. Training for the four would begin immediately, from the time they joined.

"Now, only a limited amount of supplies will be contributed. They will be for the troops to get there and enough to get back. The only thing we can supply for you is a water truck and treatment plant to supply safe drinking water. You will need to take everything else with you, to get you there. As I said, there are some resources already there. You won't have to worry about immediate housing when you get there. Final quarters you'll work out with the local authorities. If you contemplate running some sort of legal business, you'll want to take whatever it is with you.

"I'll be available, like Howard, after the meeting, for questions. Thank you for allowing me to speak."

There was polite applause, and then Tom and the members of the city council took seats around the conference table. People looked over at Percy expectantly. Tom looked at him too. "You might as well come up here. We're going to need your help and input on this, anyway."

Sara gave Percy a slight shove to get him started. Red in the face again, Percy went up and took a seat at the table. "I don't plan on moving," Percy said. "I don't really know what I can contribute. I just wanted to find out how many would be going. And when."

Tom looked a bit alarmed. "But you will help us with supplies and such, for the trip, won't you?"

"Well, of course I will. But that'll be a straight forward barter, just like always."

"Sure," Tom said with a relieved smile. "You'll need to be involved in this so you will know what'll be needed."

The open meeting lasted until almost ten that night and was tabled until the next morning, only a few of the details worked out. Essentially the same people showed up at ten the next morning to resume the discussion. The state and federal representatives were actively included in the discussions. There had been no problem having enough volunteers for military service. There would be four going on the trip, plus a couple more going to base duty, including one woman. Not the woman that had asked about it.

There was a plan in place by that evening. Percy was playing a much larger part in it than he had anticipated. He'd found himself volunteering to do this, then that, provide a few things, and supervise some of the preparatory activity. By the time the plan was finalized three days later Percy found himself leading the trek, though he would return, with the military contingent, with the people he was taking to help on the way.

He was thanked many times for agreeing to participate, over the next few days, as preparations began. Many of those going were farmers from the outlying areas. They had a hard time surviving on their farms during the winter. Many had moved in to the school, though not all. While they were discussing what would be required for the trip, Percy realized that while there would be housing, and even some ready food supplies when they arrived, many of those wanting or needing to go would be hard pressed to come up with the quantity of supplies required.

It wasn't that Percy couldn't supply the items. He could. The problem was that for the time before they left the people wouldn't be able to work off the debt, and very few had enough hard currency to pay him. He couldn't just give his products away to those that needed them. It would cause too many problems with those that were paying.

It hadn't been in his mind initially, but Percy warmed to the idea he came up with. He talked it over with Sara, then a few key people at the estate. Percy began trading the supplies that were needed, for peoples' property. When it was property he really didn't want, he was able to help set up equal trades with other people to get the land adjacent to his.

Percy also took in trade homes and property in town. Many just thought he was being kind to those not able to pay any other way. Which was okay. He would take property even if a person could barter labor, goods, services, or hard money.

Percy tried to get people to understand that he did have reasons for what he was doing. He wasn't that kind. People nodded, but thought what they wanted. Sara finally told him to quit worrying about it and just take care of business. He worried a little about stripping the estate of too much, but Susie assured him the plan was more than workable.

Susie would stay behind, in charge of the operation, with Jorge Ramirez as foreman. The cadre of already trained farm hands would be able to do everything needed with the equipment they would have. Mattie, Jock and Melissa would also still be at the estate. Andy would be going on the trip, as would Sara.

It would be a wagon train indeed. Not only was their group going, but also when it became known that Percy was leading the trip, many of the other communities and individuals asked to join the group. They were providing their own supplies, but wanted to travel with a large group. Percy sighed and agreed when Howard and Claudia approached him with the idea.

"We knew a lot of people wanted to go, and planned more than one trip, but a large group, while there are problems with it, will get more people there faster and more safely than two or three small groups. It also doesn't strain us helping nearly as much either," Claudia said.

"One of the biggest problems," she continued, "is safe drinking water. And our purification system is more than capable of handling the larger group. It was really overkill for just a hundred sixty odd people, but it is the smallest unit we have. It'll handle the daily needs of at least a thousand. Still a bit overkill for the five hundred or so that looks like will be going."

"Five hundred!" Percy exclaimed. The idea gave him shivers. It turned out that there would only be four hundred eighty-nine. Percy still shivered when he heard the number.

Most would be taking handcarts of some type on the trip. Some would be walking with backpacks. A few had cars and enough gasoline to go that far. Several from the town were taking the cars that had been converted to run on alcohol. Percy would be taking the tank trailer with a split load. Diesel, gasoline, and alcohol.

In addition to the fuel tank trailer, the Kenworth tractor would be pulling a second trailer with a fifth wheel dolly. It was one of the reefers, to keep food fresh on the trip. It would save on time since they would not have to wait for much of the food to be dried. They'd be able to leave in late June.

Three of the Unimogs would go on the trip, as would the pickup with the bed shell. Percy was leaving behind the Suburban. He was taking the Kenworth based motorhome he referred to as The Beast. It would be towing a box trailer on a fifth wheel dolly. It would carry much of the other supplies that needed to go. Behind the box trailer would be the barge trailer.

Also going would be the Kenworth service truck. It would be towing a second box trailer on a fifth wheel dolly, with more equipment and supplies. It, like the Kenworth Tractor, would pull a second trailer, also on a fifth wheel dolly. It was the flatbed.

The flatbed would carry equipment too, mostly camp gear, which the military had agreed to furnish since there were so many going, including twenty soldiers instead of ten. Since their rate of speed would not be high, the flatbed trailer would be equipped so people could ride on it. Most of the people that didn't have horse drawn wagons or operable cars would be walking, though it was expected that those with vehicles with space would make arrangements to carry as many people as possible.

As for the military detachment, there would be a Lieutenant in charge, as before, but there would be an additional sergeant and two corporals in the small command making twenty-four in all. The detachment was set up as four squads, each led by a platoon sergeant, with a corporal, and two private-first-class soldiers. They'd have five Hummers, each pulling a trailer. Two of the trailers would be fuel trailers.

Though they had the military Hummers, Percy decided to take the Indian with its sidecar to use for scouting, along with two of the Rokon's.

Each of the three Unimogs would be pulling trailers. One Unimog would go with a flat bed, loaded with equipment, with front-end bucket attached. It pulled a trailer carrying several potentially useful implements useable by any of the Unimogs. The implements included the backhoe and a dozer blade, among several others.

Another Unimog was also equipped with a flatbed. It carried equipment on the bed and towed an equipment trailer to carry the pickup, Indian, and the Rokon's. The third Unimog was equipped with a box bed to carry the equipment for Percy's group, and would have a large flatbed trailer that carried yet more supplies and equipment.

In addition to the horses being ridden and pulling wagons, there were at least another twenty that would be herded along. Besides the horses, three bulls, and thirty head of cattle, mostly heifers, were going with some of the farmers. There were several pigs going, but they were all being transported in wagons or trailers.

With people walking, and the stock, Percy figured they'd be able to average ten miles a day. They expected to travel almost seven hundred miles. It would take over two months. The trip back was expected to take less than two weeks.

"Place looks like pictures of Independence, Missouri when it was one of the departure places for the westward migration," Howard told

Percy as they walked through the bustling town. It was bustling because of the dozens of families and large number of individuals preparing to head south toward the outskirts of Memphis, Tennessee, which was now a port city on Memphis Bay of the Gulf of Mexico.

"And I feel like Ward Bond in a bad episode of Wagon Train if there ever was one. This is not quite what I expected when I agreed to do this."

"You'll do fine, Sweetie," Sara told him. She was walking alongside him, her arm linked with his as they checked the various voyagers' sets of equipment.

"Some of these people are not going to get there with what they started with," Percy said.

Claudia, walking with them, chuckled and said. "I thought you watched Wagon Train. Of course some of them won't make it with what they started with. And I bet hard cash that a few drop out before you get there, but that you'll wind up gaining a few on the trip."

Her smile faded when she added, "And the condition of a few of them... you may lose a couple, too."

"I know," Percy said. "It would be nice if Jock could go, but he and Melissa are both needed here. I want things set up to have a real clinic and at least a makeshift hospital before winter hits. And they'll be overseeing the new homes going in on the estate."

Many of those staying behind would be stripping the town of everything useful, including dismantling many of the buildings. The materials would be used to build housing on the estate property east of the barns.

Though not domes, all the new structures would be earth sheltered. There was plenty of material to build the walls heavy enough to carry roofs heavy enough to carry the earth they would be covered with. They would be rather smaller than what would have been built before the war and climate changes, to make them easy to keep heated in the harsh winter.

There were five compounds planned, each a large U shape, almost rectangular, with a central courtyard area that the dwelling spaces would face. Each of the dwellings would house four people easily. Larger families would use two units. There were to be ten dwellings in each compound and four units that could be used for storage and for cottage industry.

Like Percy's dome structures, the earth roofs would boast walled patios over the entire U, providing much additional space. There would be a gap in the nearly closed U to allow access to the courtyard. The compounds would be side by side, the closed ends of the U's facing the north and the open end the south.

A sixth compound, similar in construction would be used to house animals. Again, like Percy's compound, a tunnel would connect the individual compounds, though it would not be built by the simple expedient of setting sections of pedestrian underpass into place in a trench.

Instead, a slightly tapered tube would be constructed of planking and sheet metal, on top of a sheet of plastic. The resulting pipe would be six feet high, five feet wide at the bottom and four feet wide at the top. The sheet of plastic would then be wrapped up and over the pipe and the trench backfilled.

Only two of the housing compounds and the animal compound would be built that summer.

"Amanda," Percy said, "is going, much like her original plan. She'll be of great help. I plan to keep her on the payroll until we get there. She's done such a good job this winter. I'd like to see her set up shop when she gets there, and it will be easier if she has a few assets."

Sara patted her husband on the shoulder, but said nothing about his remark. They came to the group of military men and Sara excused herself. She needed to go talk to one of the new groups and give them some advice about their vehicle. It would never make it the way it was packed.

"Lieutenant Pastolori," Claudia said, "This is Mr. Jackson. He'll be in overall command."

Pastolori saluted, and then reached out to shake Percy's hand when Percy held it out. "I'm sorry I'm late, sir. My men and I will get up to speed as quickly as possible. There was a group of bandits preying on two of the communities that had quite a few people come down here. We wanted to take care of the situation before we left. We are the most mobile force in the area."

"I'm glad you took care of it first, Lieutenant," Percy replied, looking over the group assembled before him. There was a wide spectrum of men, young and old, several different races, all different sizes and shapes. Eight of them definitely looked like recruits. The rest of the command looked exceeding competent. Percy was confident the new soldiers would be brought into the fold quickly and easily. They wanted it, and those doing the training obviously knew what they were doing.

Percy continued, "I take it you have the equipment and supplies you need?"

"Yes, sir," the Lieutenant replied. He smiled then, showing even white teeth in his rather dark face. "We are looking forward to the fresh rations you have so graciously offered to share with us. I hear that this is the best eating outfit in ten states."

"I don't know about that," Percy said, turning red again. "But we do okay. I have good hands that see to it."

"Yes, sir, and we will do our best to make sure everyone makes it there safely, and those of us coming back, safely as well."

Percy never did get Lieutenant to call him anything except Sir and Mr. Jackson. He learned to live with it. Unfortunately, in his eyes, most of the rest of the civilian group began doing the same thing. His people more as an inside joke, because it bothered him a little. The rest out of respect generated from that shown him by the military and the local townspeople. And it was reinforced over time by his actions.

Worry lines wrinkling his face, Percy, two days later, gave the order to move out. The worry lines were justified that first day. They made barely five miles. Three small groups changed their minds and turned back. Two more had vehicles that broke down. Another two ran out of fuel. Despite all the information that had been distributed, they thought fuel was going to be furnished, gratis. Their vehicles, a pair of pickups using gasoline, were huge fuel hogs.

Percy had determined to be firm before they left. He was not going to be a pushover for every little problem and ailment. He needed to get the people to Memphis and get back in plenty of time for the harvest. He knew the projects would go okay without him there, Susie and Jock would see to it. He still wanted to inspect them before winter set in.

Percy had fuel calculated to get everyone there and his group back with a good safety margin. The military did the same. Percy would not cut into the safety margin to provide fuel for these two vehicles. They had no way to pay for it, even if Percy had been willing to allow it. He left it up to them to find someone that would provide them with transportation. He would give them enough gasoline to get back to their home, if they couldn't convince anyone to take them.

Both pairs of men did find someone willing to allow them to travel with them, in return for labor around the camp. Both were families with small children and only the mother and father to care for them and do all the camp work.

Percy was a bit surprised, but the arrangement worked all right. The trucks were abandoned, pushed well off the road. Percy allowed the men to stow their gear on one of the trailers, as he'd made the same arrangement with several others short of space. The four men would take turns helping Percy's group with their chores in return for the use of the space.

It was nearly midnight when the camp finally was assembled and settled down to Percy's satisfaction. Despite the lateness of the hour, the orders were to rise at daybreak, and be prepared to travel by seven the next morning.

They were late starting, with some similar confusion about breaking camp, as there had been the night before on setting up the camp. It was almost nine before the Lieutenant's Hummer led the way. Despite the later than preferred start, they managed to make their goal of ten miles.

The camp setup went much more quickly and the camp was secure by nine. There'd been a few gawkers along the route. Word had traveled ahead of them and it became common to see people along the roads, watching the group pass.

And they did stay on existing roads for the most part. Only when bridges, overpasses, and underpasses were out, or the road was blocked in some way, did they leave the pavement. Some of the pavement was in relatively poor shape after almost a year of no maintenance, but the roads had received very little traffic during that time, either.

The Unimogs and their implements were of great value when a road needed to be cleared, or approaches from and to the roads had to be made when they did need to take a detour.

As Percy had expected, some of the vehicles gave out quickly, despite staying on the pavement most of the time. He'd allowed for some of it, and with the example of the out-of-fuel vehicles, arrangements were quickly made for those whose vehicles could go no further to continue on the trip.

As time passed, they managed to pick up a couple of useable vehicles along the route, by bartering. Percy helped out by trading out some goods with the group needing the vehicle so they would have the resources to make the trade.

Percy was pleased, that despite the time it took to ferry everything across the rivers that lacked useable bridges by using the barge trailer, they were averaging more than the ten miles expected. They chose places to camp at night that had plenty of forage for the animals, so they didn't slow much during the day to graze.

The military water purification system worked as they were told it would. They even treated the water for all the animals, just in case. The food was holding out well. Percy had allowed for some bartering along the route. They were trading to those that needed it about as often as those that had extra food bartered it to them, primarily for gold and silver, though once in a while, they wanted something else.

Percy always gave first chance at the barters to the group of people moving. He would trade only if no one else wanted the particular trade. Not that he took every trade offered. There were things being offered for trade in which he had no interest. Apparently word was traveling ahead of them by radio that a wealthy band was on the way. People were people. They would get what they could, when they could.

Only once in the first three weeks of travel were they bothered by any form of banditry. They had been warned in one small town they passed through that a band of about ten people were waylaying people traveling the route Percy's group was taking. Lieutenant Pastolori and his men were ready for the attack when it came.

They'd sent some of the more or less normal vehicles ahead, driven by the soldiers. The Hummers held back, out of easy sight. When the lead car radioed that there was a roadblock ahead, the Lieutenant ordered the Hummers ahead at full speed, top mounted machine guns and grenade launchers ready to fire.

When the bandits saw the cars stop and the Hummers approaching at high speed, they began to fire, but quickly broke away and ran. Three of the bandits were killed outright, another three injured and taken captive. The others got away.

"How many in your group?" asked Lieutenant Pastolori of one of the captives being treated by Amanda.

The man was totally dejected. He was drawn and thin, weak with hunger. "Thirteen of us. Picked up a couple of kids wanted the easy life just a few days ago. Tried to tell them this was no easy life. Slim pickin's. And now we got the Army convoying people. It ain't rightly fair. What'cha going to do with us?"

"Legally, martial law is in effect. We have the right to execute looters and bandits caught in the act. But what I'm going to do is treat your injuries, give you enough food for yourselves and the rest of the group that survived, and tell you to go straight. We're coming back through here in the near future. We hear you're still active and we'll hunt you down and execute you. You understand me?"

"I unner'stand," the man replied. "Billy Joe ain't gonna like it, but me, I'm agonna do it. I think the others will, too. More power to you if you kill Billy Joe. He's a mean un', even afore the war. The rest of us... we just kinda fell into it. Bad mistake. My wife, God rest her, is probably turning in her grave."

The three men stood along the road by the barricade that had been pushed out of the way by the Unimog with the front-end bucket. Those in the convoy looked on curiously as they passed the three.

The three stood openmouthed as the full impact of what they'd attempted hit them. "We nary stood a chance," said the one that had been questioned. "Look at them rigs. Billy Joe said they was a rich outfit, but Lordy, I never seen nothing like it. Even without them soldier boys we'd'a lost. Them folks sportin' more guns than the soldiers."

The man was right. Though they kept them out of sight for the most part, nearly every group making the move was carrying arms of some type. That included Percy and his crew. Percy, Andy, Jim, and Bob stood near the former roadblock with their HK-91 rifles held at the ready until every last person, vehicle, and animal was well past it. The Indian and the two Rokon's had been offloaded from the trailer and were parked near the Hummers.

When everyone was past, Percy climbed into the sidecar of the Indian, Andy took the controls and they headed to catch up to the convoy again. Jim and Bob straddled the Rokons and joined them. The Lieutenant left in the last

Hummer, bypassing the convoy and taking up the lead again.

CHAPTER FORTY

The group began to see signs of the serious damage caused by the giant earthquakes caused by the nukes set off along the New Madrid fault system and related faults. Very few bridges remained standing and the pavement of many of the roads was wavy or broken in many places.

Only the presence of the barge trailer allowed them to cross the Missouri River near Hermann, Missouri. They were getting rain every few days and the river was swollen with the runoff. Fording anywhere near the path they wanted to travel was out of the question. Aerial surveys done after the war by FEMA showed not one intact bridge between St. Louis and Jefferson City.

They were ahead of schedule by at least five days, so Percy ordered a camp set up. The majority of the group would rest for two days while the barge trailer was rigged as a tethered ferry. Then everything would be shuttled across, a group at a time.

The Kenworth Service Truck was taken across the river under the power of the two big Mercury outboard motors on the barge trailer. When it was across a Unimog was taken across with the implements needed to get the south side of the crossing set up. They were able to use the remains of the bridge approach to anchor one end of the cable that had been brought along for the purpose.

The north side was anchored similarly. Heavy pulleys were fastened to each end and the middle of the west side of the barge. A Unimog was fastened to each end of the barge with cables long enough to reach all the way across the river.

Three days after they'd reached the river the first ferry trip began. They moved the animals first, to get them onto fresh graze. On the north side the Unimog would put tension on the barge to hold the ramps against the shore.

When everything was loaded the Unimog on the south shore would pull the ferry across, with the heavy cable running through the pulleys keeping it from drifting down stream. The south side Unimog would hold the ferry against the south shore until it was unloaded, then drive toward the river as the north side Unimog pulled the ferry back across. It took them less than half a day to get everyone and everything moved.

They stayed the night on the south shore of the Missouri, and then continued their trek the following morning. Now experienced travelers all, including the stock, it took less than an hour each morning to strike camp after breakfast and a little over an hour to set it up each night.

Summer was upon them and they were able to travel for almost ten hours a day. They were able to manage twelve to fifteen miles a day, depending on how many streams and rivers they had to cross. They were carrying three bridging sections they made after they found three forty foot long aluminum I-beams at a building site on the way. Four-foot wide platforms were built on each beam.

In places where the crossing was less than thirty feet and there was no easy way to ford the stream, the work crane on the Kenworth utility/service truck was used to set the beams in place to make a temporary bridge. It was much faster than rigging up the barge trailer each time.

Percy wouldn't allow them to span more than thirty feet, even though the panels were forty feet long. He was afraid of collapse. For gaps wider than the thirty feet the barge trailer was unlimbered and everything was shuttled across on it. Often as not the barge only had to move a few feet to make the crossing.

In those cases, as they'd done at the Missouri, the Unimogs would pull the ferry back and forth, only without the stabilizing cable, since the Unimogs could stabilize it, with the much lighter downstream flow of the smaller streams.

Since the barge was over forty feet long, it often could bridge the gap, on the water, and not need to be moved. It couldn't support the weight of the equipment across an open span the way the I-beams could. It had to be in water to support the weight, so the backhoe on the Unimog was used to actually widen the stream at the point of the crossing to get the entire barge trailer in the water. The barge trailer had tow bars at each end, so it could just be crossed by everything and then pulled out on the other side. The larger rivers, they used the same technique that had been used at the Missouri.

Though they did find an occasional crossing that could be used, their average travel distance dropped slightly due to the number of crossings they had to make, and the much worse roads in the southern half of Missouri, caused by the earthquakes.

They continued traveling generally southeast and finally picked up Interstate 55 north of Cape Girardeau. The road was in poor shape, because of all the earthquakes that had shaken it. There was not a single overpass standing, or underpass that wasn't blocked. The pavement was offset in many places by up to dozens of feet.

The ground had also shifted vertically in places, both by shearing and in waves. There were places where the pavement was a few inches to a few feet higher on one side of an uplift. The waves generated by the earthquakes had pulled the pavement apart at the joints in places.

But the route itself still existed. They changed their procedure of staying on the pavement most of the time and went to running along the shoulders or median. Sometimes in the ditches or along the edge of the fences where the ground itself could be smoothed by the equipment Percy had brought along.

A Unimog with the dozer blade led most of the way from Cape Girardeau, smoothing the path for those following. It was not unusual to have to pull a stuck vehicle from clinging mud, since the rains continued, off and on, heavier than they'd been further north, due primarily to the proximity of the rather larger Gulf of Mexico.

It was outside of Osceola, Arkansas that the group had their only pitched battle with bandits. Percy and the Lieutenant had information, both from the government and from locals that a band hiding in the Mississippi bottoms were raiding both river traffic and road traffic. They were reported well led and well-armed.

But the members of the group were seasoned travelers now. They knew what potential ambush sites looked like. Lieutenant

Pastolori had all five Hummers leading the way, and checked every potential ambush site. They found the bandits along a stretch of relatively good road. Each end of the particular stretch had a fallen overpass blocking it. Both blockages had been cleared, but the material was still piled precariously alongside the road.

Percy and the Lieutenant studied the situation from the basket of the aerial lift on the Kenworth utility/service truck. They'd lifted themselves just to the tops of the trees at a ridge a mile from the first overpass.

"This has to be it," Pastolori said. "The road is pretty good, but the ditches are wide and deep. You go through the first cleared overpass... They shift the rubble to block it and the one on the far end. You're trapped on the stretch of road. They have clear fields of fire from the forest on the one side, and probably some emplacements out in that field.

"I'm sure they are there, though I have to admit, I can't spot them. I think the reports are right. These guys know what they're doing. We would have checked this out, but we'd have sent someone through if Charlie hadn't spotted the movement at this first overpass."

"So what do we do? I have no problem backtracking a ways and going around. Take some time, but we have it."

"That's the safest approach," Lieutenant Pastolori said. "And that's what I recommend we do if you don't want to do the plan I'm about to explain to you. I'd like to put these bandits out of business. You're in overall charge. I can't order you to have your people go into a fight. But I think we can take these guys with minimal, if any casualties."

"I don't like the idea of knowingly risking any lives. We'll lose three days, but we should go around."

"And if they have people watching and move their ambush?"

Percy frowned. "You think that is likely?"

"I'm not sure likely, but definitely possible. We're reasonably sure the bandits are here. Even if they've had someone watching us, they really can't have a true idea of the capability of your equipment. It wouldn't take long to rig some shields on front of your trucks. They have the capability to take to those fields at speed.

"The Hummers with their firepower can take those that would be at the tree line. They may or may not know about the grenade launchers. Their people have to be right at the edge of the trees. Once they fire, we can direct deadly fire right onto them. "I don't think those in the fields would be able to stand up to a charging wall of fast steel with concentrated fire coming from it behind barricades.

"We would come up like we would normally, but would stop and pour fire into the area where those that are to block the road would be. The Hummers would advance on the woods, and your team, with soldiers behind the barricades, would attack those in the fields, if there are any. I have to be honest. All the attackers might be in the woods, but I suspect there are some in those fields."

Lieutenant Pastolori fell silent and waited for Percy's comments. "The country can't afford to tolerate banditry. I say we do it, but I'm going to be careful who goes and doesn't."

"Of course," Pastolori said.

Percy lowered the aerial basket and the two of them began to detail the plan to the group. Percy was more than a little amazed at the outpouring of rage toward the bandit's plan.

Tom said it best perhaps, when he commented, "They would murder women and children in an attack like that. I, for one, don't want them doing that to anyone, not just us. If we go around, they will prey on others. From what we've seen on this trip, there will be others following us. I don't want the knowledge that I could prevent something from happening and didn't do anything about it."

"I'm not going to lie about it," Lieutenant Pastolori said. "There is a significant chance of casualties on our side. And we will be killing people. I will give them a chance to surrender, but I imagine they'll just laugh. Killing people is not easy. It stays with you the rest of your life. Anyone that doesn't think they can handle that should stay in the group that stays back."

The consensus was to attack the bandits as the Lieutenant had suggested. The timbers from the bridging sections were quickly removed and attached to the fronts of all three Kenworths and the three Unimogs, leaving only small view ports for the driver to see through. Secure platforms for two riflemen were incorporated on each vehicle, with firing ports for the riflemen to use.

Percy would not let any family men participate, including Tom. They had sharp words over it, but Percy told Tom that he wanted Tom in charge if something happened to him. It was just as difficult to get Sara to stay behind, too. She wanted to drive The Beast, which was where Percy would be with his HK-91. He finally convinced her, too. Other than him, at one of the gun ports on The Beast, all of his people either stayed with the bulk of the group or were driving the vehicles.

It went even better than Percy had hoped. Like the other attack, many of the bandits broke and ran when the firepower of the group became obvious. There were six trapdoor hidey-holes in the fields along the road. Each had two riflemen. The rest of the bandits, twenty-three more they learned later, were in the edge of the woods.

There were three bandits at each of the overpasses. The ones at the first overpass were all killed almost instantly when the withering fire erupted from thirty weapons when the lead vehicles stopped and everyone in them opened up with rifles.

The Hummers charged toward the edge of the woods, drawing fire. As soon as a bandit fire point was identified, the Hummers used their machineguns and grenade launchers to good effect to silence them one or two at a time. By the time the first half a dozen bandits were dispatched by the gunners in the Hummers the others turned tail and faded into the woods.

The bandits at the far overpass were seen running for vehicles that disappeared quickly down the road. It was an absolute rout in the barren fields. The three Kenworths, on their high flotation tires didn't even slow down when they left the road. They hit the fence that bordered the first field.

Only a couple of rounds were fired from the first hidey-hole. The sight of the six onrushing trucks panicked every one of the bandits in the fields. They all climbed out of their holes and began running. But there was no place to run. A few rounds from those holding on securely behind the barricades on the trucks and, to a man, the bandits threw down their weapons, stopped running and lifted their hands into the air.

Percy was a little concerned that the twelve men might just be shot by his people, but a few words about turning them in to the authorities in Memphis would do more good in the area than their executions would, calmed the situation.

The soldiers went into the woods a little ways on foot, but there was no sign of the rest of the bandits, besides the eight they'd killed in the first few minutes of the short battle. That was a total of eleven killed, including the three at the first overpass. With the twelve captured, Lieutenant Pastolori was sure the bandits had been broken up as a force. One of those killed at the overpass had been the leader of the band. The second in command had been killed in the woods. Their third in command was one of the captives.

From what the captives told Lieutenant Pastolori, those that survived were not very likely to be of any great danger. That end of the line in the woods had been the least experienced of the group, and those at the other overpass had been mere kids.

With the amount of supplies that had been used up there was room to take the captives with them the rest of the way to Memphis. The hunters in the group had managed to take a few game animals as they traveled in the bottomlands along the now even mightier Mississippi. There was enough food to feed the prisoners, though there were calls to let them go hungry until reaching Memphis. Percy made sure they were fed.

Interstate 55 had actually washed away in a few places, where the river was much larger due to the influx of the Great Lakes waters at Cairo, Illinois. The going slowed slightly more with the conditions.

The Corps of Engineers had a pontoon bridge in place across the Mississippi, just above where it emptied into the new Memphis Bay. The group was able to cross with no problems, though only a few at a time were allowed to cross. It was the largest group that had needed to cross since the bridge was installed after the others had all dropped during the first earthquake.

They met the Memphis FEMA representative and he directed them to the housing the group would use until each family group picked out the area were they would settle permanently. Percy had intended to turn around and head back immediately, but the horse trader in him wouldn't allow it.

Percy and those going back with him spent two days in and around Memphis, with Percy making several deals. A few were immediate, but several were long term deals, having to do with sea based products now available with the changes in the Gulf of Mexico. As it was, they froze half a trailer load of seafood in the reefer trailer and took it back with them to the estate. The fish tanks at the estate in the animal barn provided fish protein, but the seafood would be a welcome addition to their diets while it lasted.

Percy was able to buy a few hundred gallons of diesel in Memphis. There was some coming by way of the Gulf from Texas. One refinery was back in operation. Most was going to the military, but coastal communities were getting some distribution. One of the things he'd hoped for, and managed to get, were significant quantities of the chemicals he needed to continue and increase his production of biodiesel.

He was also able to pick up more seed, including a quantity of hemp seed from the Ag department of Memphis State University. He'd had quite a bit from having done a pilot project for the Iowa Department of Agriculture. Percy had not been allowed to grow it on a production basis the way he wanted, but those restrictions no longer applied. At least, he didn't intend to follow them. And from the source where he got the seed, quite a few other people weren't either. Hemp was too important a source of too many products not to start growing it again.

They started back toward the estate the last week of August. With the work they'd already done on sections of the road, without the stock, and with everyone going back riding Percy's vehicles, the trip went quickly, as Percy knew it would.

They said goodbye to the military in a town that looked rather different from what it had when they left. There were still plenty of buildings, but there were very few mostly wooden structures left.

Tom, and the handful of other townspeople that had gone on the trip to help, went the rest of the way out to the estate with Percy and his people. Like the town, the estate looked markedly different. The work on the new housing was well underway. The fields were showing good stands of crops. The snow and ice was all gone, except for Percy's insulated mound.

Percy noted the fervor with which the twins were welcomed back by the Statler sisters. Amy and Sandra had decided to stay on, while the rest of the family headed for Memphis. Percy was sure it primarily due to the fact that Jim and Bob were both staying.

Andy and Susie disappeared quickly, but discretely after the welcomes were exchanged. Sara and Percy were left in the house, with Mattie and Tom and his wife Marie, whom they'd picked up in town, as everyone else went out on their own. Mattie was quickly filled in on the happenings of the journey. She began filling them in on the progress that had been made at the estate.

"Things are going well, Boss," Mattie said. "All the hands had pretty much learned what they needed during the winter. With my talented daughter at the helm, and Jorge's help, the care of the fields has gone just fine. The animals are doing great. You could see how far the building has gone. Everything is ready to put up the wall for the greenhouse enclosure. The clinic and hospital is almost done.

"The storms keep raging through, and there is some loss to the crops, but we all knew there would be. But we have enough people and hoes to keep the weeds down the horse drawn equipment can't do. The hemp, especially, is doing great. The shipments to town are going fine. We had some trouble with the methane thing, but they got it figured out from your written instructions and the books in the library. Every tank we have that can be used for waste oil is full. You should be able to make several batches of biodiesel in a row, without any problems."

"Good," Percy replied. "I was able to get enough hemp seed to do another eighty acres next year, even if there is a problem with this year's crop. But if it goes well, we can have at least one hundred sixty, if not two hundred forty. I take it the special seed plants in the greenhouse are going okay, too?"

"Yep," Mattie replied. "I check those myself every few days. They're coming along great. I'm not sure how much seed each one will produce, but every plant is doing well."

Percy smiled. "Plenty. I probably didn't need that other seed, but I'm glad I got it, just in case. Now, how are the Doctors doing?"

"We're doing fine," Melissa said, coming into the kitchen, Jock on her heels. "And the baby even better. Welcome back, by the way."

"Thanks. Can I hold her?"

Sara looked at Percy in surprise. They couldn't have children, of course, and Percy had never said a word about particularly liking children. He'd always done fine with the ones they came into contact with during the last few months, but he seemed truly anxious to hold the baby and see how it was doing.

As he took the baby, Percy was asking, "How have you two been? Mattie tells me the clinic and our mini-hospital are about done. How's the health of everyone, here and in town?" Percy was looking down at the baby in his arms as he listened to their responses.

"Barbie's little Michael is doing just fine. Barbie is doing okay. She needs to continue to take it easy. She is really struggling to keep it together. Losing Mike this winter hit her really hard. She's still struggling with the idea of being a single mom in these times."

Percy only nodded, and Jock took up the report from his wife. "As you can see, Melissa, Junior, is doing just fine. As is her mother, as you can also tell." His arm was over Melissa's shoulders and he gave her a loving squeeze.

"Mattie finally got over that cold, but only recently. She is going to have to take it easy this winter, too."

"I'm fine, thank you very much," protested Mattie. Rather less forcefully than her normal protestations. She was beginning to feel her age.

"Everyone else," Melissa said, "is doing fine. Just the usual minor things. No more broken bones but a few scrapes and things from the various projects. Nothing at all related to the farming."

Percy looked up then. "And in town?"

"Not as good there," Jock replied. "A couple of people haven't recovered very well from illnesses from the winter. And there are reports coming in now of outbreaks of human anthrax and really bad smallpox.

"I don't know if you heard it from the military while you were on the road, but it was confirmed that both biological and chemical weapons were used. We haven't heard too much about the chemicals from the weekly report from the Feds. We were informed that Wisconsin and Michigan were both hit with anthrax.

"It's just speculation, but they think they wanted to infect the dairy herds as well as people. I don't think they were expecting the terrible winter. They've lost most of the herds north of us. Quite a few survived, of course, in isolated events, but the big dairies couldn't get most of their herds into enough protection to save them."

Melissa spoke up again. "We're really going to have to watch things carefully, with the additional inter community travel. If an epidemic gets started, in the close confines like we have here, and had at the school and city hall last winter, the entire population of any given group could be wiped out. Epidemics turn pandemic quickly in these types of conditions."

Again Percy looked up and nodded. "Anyone in town need any special consideration?"

Jock answered again. "Those that are still weak will need plenty of good food, especially protein. Everyone else needs are similar, just not as critical."

Percy stood up and handed little 'Lissa back to Melissa. "They'll get it." He looked at Mattie and continued. "I want you taking it easy. Let the sisters do the work. Just supervise." He looked at Melissa then. "Tell Barbie we're going to need someone to help with the smaller children here at the estate when we have families here. She was planning to be a teacher. As soon as she is up to it, she's in charge of the littlest ones. She's now on the fulltime estate payroll. Make a note, Sara."

He looked over at Jock. "Print up some flyers with things people need to watch for this winter, including the signs and symptoms of the pox and anthrax. Anything else you think important.

"I'll talk to Susie about starting a real safety program. We've always tried to work safely, but I want people aware of dangers. What might have been a minor annoyance in the past, can be life threatening now. I'm going to go look over the construction. Anyone want to come? Sara?"

"I'll be out in a bit," Sara replied, smiling at Percy. "I've a couple of things I want to do here in the house first."

Percy gave her a quick kiss on the lips, grabbed his hat, and headed for the door.

"Whew!" Mattie said. "He was on a roll, there."

"It was this trip," Sara told the others as the Bluhms took seats. Sara took the baby when Melissa offered her.

"He's seen the effects of no organization. Many people we saw really did have it a lot worse than we did. Right, Tom?"

"Sara is right," Tom replied. "Some had as much in the way of resources as we did in some of the cities and larger towns. But a lack of cooperation and coordination of resources, like Percy did here, caused as much damage as everything else."

"Don't limit your contribution," Sara quickly said. "You were the main other half of what happened here. Without your leadership in town, much of what Percy did would have been wasted."

"Maybe you're right, but less than half of us would have survived, except for what Percy had been doing for years. He did it on purpose. It was like it was a mission for him. But think about that one barn we saw. It wouldn't have taken much to have bermed it up and used it for shelter for animals and people. People died for a lack of forethought."

"Percy has more than his share of forethought," Sara said.

"Yeah," Mattie replied. "I've been here a long time, and I've learned that he seldom does anything for a single reason. Most things that he buys have multiple uses, just like those ugly trucks. And those bikes of his. He uses one to cultivate the garden sometimes. Whoever heard of gardening using a motorcycle?"

The others smiled.

"He takes the responsibility he's taken onto himself very seriously. He did before, but even more so now."

"I know how he feels," Tom said softly. The others looked over at him and smiled. Then they all noticed how much more gray hair he had than they could remember. The little group broke up then, Sara and Tom going out to join Percy on his inspection tour.

The work was coming along nicely. Sara could see that Percy was pleased. The structures would be completed by October first, with the rest of the estate's equipment now back. That had been Percy's goal. The weather would be turning bad by that time, but Percy was confident the finishing touches could be put on the structures and people moved in before the worst of the expected bad weather hit.

"Tom, are you, Marie, and the kids planning on moving? You know you have a place here anytime you want it."

"I know," Tom said. "But as long as we still have a town that is a town, I feel like I should be there. Some of us are going to finish fixing up the city hall and live there this winter. There and the school, with the improvements that are being done to it, should house anyone that doesn't want to live off by themselves.

"I know quite a few people are going to take you up on the offer to stay here, at least during the winters. Now me… I was thinking… well… Never mind. It'll be a couple of years probably before I could do anything, anyway."

"What?" Percy asked. "You have a plan of some kind?"

"Actually, I'd like to get back to farming. It's even more important than it used to be. I was a farmer for a long time before I went into the insurance business. You know that. I was leasing out the three hundred acres I had. I've been thinking about trying to farm it again. It's just pretty difficult to get geared up again. In a couple of years, maybe."

"You're still concerned about the town. What about continuing to live there and start farming right there. With all the vacant lots now, you could start with them and then start working your acreage when you have things the way you want them."

"Percy," replied Tom, "You know I can't afford to buy up those lots. I don't want to trade my current land, even if someone would take it. I want my kids to have at least some legacy. And before you offer, I won't use your property without paying for it, and I can't."

"We are going to need all the food and other organic products that can be produced. There are other arrangements that can be made, besides outright purchase. Such as lease purchase and farming on shares.

"If you want to use the arable land in town that I own, you can, for ten percent of what you produce. I'll provide what you need, that you can't acquire on your own, and you can pay it off over time with another one percent of production until everything is paid off. How about that?"

Tom looked thoughtful.

Sara urged him, "Talk it over with Marie, Tom. It's a good deal, and the more substantive farms we have going in the area the better. Even with the weather, there's rebuilding to be done. And it will be done. With the discussions going on in Congress, flat rate taxes payable by hard currency or goods, products, and services will provide the means for a full recovery eventually.

"Not everyone has the ability to inspire others to do their best, the way you and Percy do. If you have an ongoing estate, even if it starts small, our little area of Iowa will be a model for other communities."

"You make it sound like a responsibility I can't shirk," Tom replied.

"It is, in a way. Everyone that can contribute should, each in his or her own way. You've already been doing it, with you duties as mayor. I'm not suggesting you haven't been doing your share. You have. It's just that if this is something you want to do, anyway, it's just one more way of helping the community."

"What? Did you two rehearse this? You aren't really leaving me much choice, the way you're both putting it. I mean, it's too late to start now, except for prep work, but it does sound like a good deal." Tom paused, looking off into the distance for long moments. "Look. Let me talk it over with Marie and the kids. See what they say. They'll be a big part in the success or failure. If they really don't want to do it, I'm not going to make them."

"I'm confident," Percy said. "Marie's like you, and your kids are your kids. They've all done more than their share. I suspect they'll want to do this, too."

They did. During the evening radio contact with town, Tom said as much. They would work out the arrangements over the next few days.

CHAPTER FORTY-ONE

The harvest of the early crops was beginning and Tom ran a harvesting crew for Percy, as part of their arrangement. Two crews were still working on the housing, but most of the rest of those that could labor were working in the fields. Everyone else was providing a support function of one type or another.

The weather cooperated, at least part of the time. The indications were, as feared, that it would be another severe winter. Equipment had finally been rebuilt to access the few satellites still in orbit, including a few of the weather satellites. Naval ships were a large part of the reporting network providing global weather information.

There would be no moderation of the North Atlantic weather systems with the warm waters of the Gulf Stream now traveling deep under the fresher waters of the ocean between North America and Europe and North West Africa.

Cold snowy winters and cool, wet summers would be the norm, counter to the normal weather cycles when the climate turned colder. Cool climate eras tended to be dry eras. There was less evaporation and much of the available moisture was locked up in ice and snow.

Warm climate eras tended toward lots of rain. With the higher rates of evaporation and the huge amounts of moisture in the atmosphere, the rain, drain, and evaporation cycle was constant. With warmer oceans overall, storm system after storm system would develop.

With the effects of the massive amount of ash and nuclear created dust that had entered the atmosphere, that would take years to eventually settle, temperature drops were worldwide. Less so in the southern hemisphere, though even there many more nukes had been used than most scenarios had foreseen. And many had been tectonic plate attacks, activating many volcanoes. The southern hemisphere, though with slightly clearer skies, still had significant temperature drops.

Instead of the world going into another little ice age, the nuclear reactions that were still going on under the oceans and seas in several places continued to pour heat into the system in isolated spots. These were creating huge storm systems one after the other, carrying large amounts of moisture, counter to the general cold era climatic trend.

Normally, when a reactor lost its cooling system, it would quickly go critical, usually blowing the reaction vessel apart by steam explosions, which scattered the reactive material and therefore stopped the reaction.

In the cases of the nuclear powered ships and submarines that had gone down more or less intact, the cooling system had failed, of course. However, a more than suitable one was immediately available. The ocean or sea itself. The nuclear fire continued to burn, moderated and cooled by the salt water surrounding it.

A few of the reactors that went down still operating were nearing the time when fuel would need to be replenished. Most had anywhere from five to ten years of fuel remaining, under ordinary operating conditions. The reactors, controlled only at the level they were in when the sinking happened, and moderated by the seawater, would probably run for considerably less time as the sea took its toll on the equipment. In any case, it appeared that the particular distorted climate that the war and nature together had created would exist for at least another three to five years.

After that, nature would take its course. What that would be; only time would tell. For the moment, Percy's and Tom's concerns were planting, tending, and harvesting crops during the shorter growing seasons the current climate was producing. Tom was able to get some help from the Iowa state government, and the federal government. State governments, as well as the Federal government, were much changed, but still in place and beginning to offer real help again.

People were willing, for the most part, to pay their taxes, since they were payable with other than money, of which people had very little. Gold and silver were circulating again, but much of the trade that was going on was still for tangibles. With the government accepting them to provide much of the support required to do their work, the work was getting done. The economy was still running on a value base; gold and silver; but much of the actual transfers were in goods, products, and services, though valued on the gold and silver standard.

One of the highest priorities was the housing and feeding of the remaining population. So farmers got as much help as could be. With much of his reserves still intact, Percy traded most of the assistance offered to him to the few other farms still in a semblance of operating condition, including Tom's in-town efforts.

As the town had done, county, state, and the federal governments took possession of property not legally claimed by anyone. They were honoring deals and trades, such as those Percy had entered in to with the former legal owners. Those simply claiming property because it was abandoned lost it to an appropriate government entity.

Towns were entitled to property within their pre-war city limits. The counties, states, and federal government divided the rest. Counties got twenty percent for their use, the state fifty percent, and the federal government controlled the other thirty percent.

Some of it was sold outright, to people like Percy that had the resources to buy it. Most was leased out for use to generate the income needed to accomplish other tasks. In Tom's case, a few city lots were rented from locals that still owned them. Most of what he was preparing to put into production were lots that Percy had bought from people leaving the area.

The war and its aftermath had changed Camden Dupree. After Percy had started using the bank as his central exchange, and other people did the same, Dupree, with the profits of his handling of the accounts, had begun doing things much the same way as Percy. He acquired some property, not just because he could, but also because it could be put to good use. In no way a farmer, the lands he bought he leased at the same types of rates that Percy started to do. A share of the production. But it let people get back to productive work, and put land into production that would have lain useless otherwise.

It wasn't always farmland, either. He began financing cottage industry, too, just as did Percy. When Percy and Tom realized what Dupree had been doing, they met with him and set some long-range goals, and instituted cooperative plans to get them done.

One of the people that took Percy up on his new housing at the estate was Randy Phillips. He took one of the community housing units and one of the commercial ones for his use. His former welding service was now essentially a blacksmithing operation. He was converting some existing farming equipment to horse drawn, as well as building new, there at the estate, using scavenged and recovered materials.

That wasn't to say that only animal-based farming was taking place. With a few refineries going again, each state was getting an allotment for fuel for emergencies and for food production. The government would not provide fuel for other types of farm products. Since much of Percy's production wasn't food, he got very little of the fuel so allotted.

Tom, when he'd retired from farming and begun leasing out his land, had sold his equipment. One of the items Percy had taken in trade the previous winter that he really hadn't needed, was a Kubota estate tractor. While it wasn't suitable for large-scale farming, it was ideal for Tom's city lot farming. The family that had owned it had been using it to mow their large yard, and for a garden.

Percy, though he had no need for it, and because of the Kubota's utility, had kept all the attachments the family had for it intact. The tractor and implements were enough to set Tom up for the town farming. Partly because he simply didn't want to get everything from Percy, on general principles, Tom made other deals for a pair of horses and a wagon, though they weren't really needed for the ground prep work. The tractor would get done what he planned that fall.

Though he worked one day each week at Percy's, as did Marie, Tom Junior, and Shirley, the rest of their time, other than town council time, was spent preparing several of the now houseless town lots for the spring. Remaining piping and such was taken down below ground level and carefully capped for possible future use. Then available manure from the animals being kept in town was spread and turned under. With the ground in furrows, it would accept all the moisture it would be getting through the rest of fall and throughout the winter.

At Percy's urging, Tom prepared several basements that existed on some of the properties to hold water in the rare chance of a drought. Having seen the utility of Percy's ice mound, he set up a system to make ice blocks to stack in a few of the basements that would then be covered with straw at the end of winter. The ice would be used the following summer to help keep some of his products cool until they could be sold.

People had learned a lesson the previous winter. Insulation was an important survival tool during the severe winters to be expected. Every acre of tall grass that grew naturally or had been sowed was used. Mostly for feed, but much of it found its way into, onto, or around buildings as insulation. Because of the great danger of fire, wherever possible it was covered with earth or a fair grade of adobe made from the local clay soils.

Tom converted one of the remaining large buildings into an insulated barn. With his team and wagon he moved some of the grass bales Percy baled up in order to insulate the barn. More were stored for feed and bedding for the winter for the wagon team, a riding horse, two brood sows, half a dozen piglets to be used for food that winter, two fresh cows, and two dozen chickens.

Part of the deal he'd made with Percy was for additional feed for his animals. It would be oats, some of the protein rich cakes left after pressing various plants for their oil, and some of the mash from his stills after the alcohol had been extracted. It would be enough to supplement the regular high-grade hay and the grass hay that Tom would buy. The extra milk from the second cow would not be needed for the family's use. It would be sold or used as feed for the other animals.

The snow began to fall before Tom was finished, but all the weather critical work was done. The rest could be done at his leisure. The one thing he asked Percy for some help with was additional firewood. He simply had not had enough time to get enough together to last the winter, even with the much better insulated housing.

Percy had been careful of his wood harvesting. He maintained the harvesting rate of his coppicing woodland that encircled his estate and was part of the fencerows between the forty-acre fields that made up the arable land. Quite a bit of the land he'd acquired had some trees. Even those he allowed only limited cutting.

Many people were cutting anything and everything. Percy wouldn't. There was quite a bit of scrap wood from dismantled buildings. It would be used. Percy would be making paper and cloth from the hemp he was growing eventually, but at the moment, at least this winter, the hemp straw that wasn't used otherwise, would be available for burning.

Percy was raising tree seedlings in one of the new greenhouses that had been built that summer. The seedlings would be planted the next spring on some of the property that Percy now owned adjacent to the estate. The seedlings would be heavily mulched the following winter and each winter after that until they were large enough to survive without it.

With the tree spades Percy had; a medium sized one for the Bobcats, and a larger one, for the Unimogs; the trees would be transplanted to their final growth spot. Most of the trees were ash trees and would be harvested over and over again, through the coppicing process. It would just be a few more years before the first harvest. But Percy knew it was important to get the process started with getting the trees into the ground initially. With other fuel sources available for the meantime, Percy held fast on his tree cutting restrictions.

With the alcohol production going well, Percy was selling some of it to people who had bought the simple alcohol stoves that Randy was making and selling.

Two of the other sources for firewood were state and federal lands. They allowed selective cutting, supervised by a state or federal employee. Percy had enough time and resources to send teams in to purchase and harvest all the governments would allow.

He was permitted to take more than most, since he offered, and fulfilled, a promise to give ten percent of the firewood harvest to the governments for their use, and leave another ten percent with the governments for the governments to sell with no labor or fuel investment of their own. Percy added the government wood to the stocks he made available for sale to those unable to obtain wood on their own.

Steven Gregory's grocery store had evolved into a bartering center serving the entire area, not just the estate, town, and immediate surroundings. Like Camden Dupree, Steven took a small percentage of each transaction from those with ongoing goods, products, or services to barter. He had an arrangement with the town to provide those that weren't bartering on a constant basis, like Percy and several others, the facility for a small fee.

Once it became the primary place for the region to barter, the counties, state, and federal governments kicked in a little to support the operation. Most of the things the government agencies acquired wound up going through the Steven's Barter Store. Like Tom and Percy, Steven acquired some additional property, including the stores adjacent to his store. He had a place to store goods and products that people brought in to barter on consignment.

Also, like Tom, he made arrangements to have ice made that winter and stored for use the next summer to make shipping some of the more perishable items feasible. People were learning how to deal with the situations that the war and climate had presented to them.

With the preparations complete that had been planned to endure the winter, those at the estate, in town, and at isolated locations elsewhere, put their lives into winter living mode. Only one trip per week was required to get enough of the estate's products to the town to serve their needs, and keep Steven Gregory's store supplied.

People stayed relatively healthy and happy. The Doctors Bluhm had a great deal to do with the first, and a little with the second.

Percy had a great deal to do with the second. One of the things he'd acquired while in Memphis was another large screen high definition monitor and home theatre system. The town had not had a theatre for years, but each

Saturday night everyone that wanted could watch a movie in the gym at the school.

People had liked the fact that Percy had working video at the estate in one of the activity rooms of the bunkhouse. Now everyone could see some of the huge collection of movies that Percy had, in addition to those that people brought from their own collections. The town's contribution to the community night was the power from the generator for the electronics. On Saturdays the generator was run and all the other things that needed power were taken care of at the same time the movie was shown.

As during the previous winter, Percy threw a huge Christmas party, providing mostly everything except the decorations. While there'd been a few outsiders the previous time, quite a few people managed to show up for the party. The invitation with RSVP had gone out through the radio network in the area, now kept manned daily. Several government officials attended, from various jurisdictions.

The news coming in that winter was much better than that they'd received the winter before. Theirs was not the only community doing better than it had the previous winter. One final blizzard dragged on until April the next spring. There was a short break, with the snow beginning to melt, when the rains started. They were not alone in the devastation wrought by raging floods. The estate and the town fared well, but the roads suffered tremendously. There had been some maintenance the previous summer and early fall, bringing the road system to a slightly better stage of repair, making for an easier mode of travel.

The rains and the floods wiped out many of the repairs and created much new damage. Percy used the bridging sections they'd created during the move south to span the stream he'd put a culvert in the year before. The culvert had been washed away. The parts of the bridge that had not been salvaged shifted and dammed the stream. This caused the stream to find a new route for a half mile before it merged into the old streambed again.

It took some time, after the initial rains had ceased for a while, to get a permanent low water bridge put in, using concrete rubble from the old bridge, plus rock and gravel from the nearby gravel pit. It would be washed away, probably, in another storm like the first one of the spring, but things were set up to rebuild it relatively easily and quickly.

Percy and Tom got their crops in all right that spring. Percy conserved much of the seed he had stockpiled and used the seed provided by the federal government, through the Iowa

Department of Agriculture, which was one of the biggest government departments in the state now. The federal government had rescinded the laws restricting the production of hemp. Percy no longer had to grow it in violation of the law. Those in power had finally recognized the importance of the crop to the recovery of the nation, much as it been instrumental in the early days of the republic when it was a crime to not grow hemp.

Percy went back to his plan of rotation of his land. With the additional acres he'd acquired adjacent to the original estate, he was able to bring a full six hundred forty acres under cultivation, leaving three times that much each lying fallow, being built up with compost and manure from the much larger animal population, and having nutrient building cover crops planted.

Assuming reasonable harvests, there would be an excess of every product, even after harvesting for seed and local use.

THE END

EPILOGUE

Seven years later Percy was still able to retire early, at age sixty. The estate was being ably run by Susie and Andy. The new regional hospital was nearing completion at the site of where the clinic was to have been so many years and events before. The old town site was now one large farm, as productive as the estate, owned by Tom and run by his children and their spouses.

New vehicles were seen on the freshly paved road that ran on the south edge of the estate. The new town had grown up on the other side of the road. Percy's estate was now in town and Tom's place was five miles outside of town.

The statistics were showing between a four and five percent increase in cancer type diseases. A few of the locals that had survived heavier doses of radiation in the days after the war were beginning to show signs of the diseases brought about or hastened by radiation exposure. Only three children out of twenty-seven born in the years after the attack had shown any signs of abnormality. Only one of those cases had been severe.

There had been slightly more than an average number of naturally aborted pregnancies, some of which were attributed to the radiation. The area was about average for the nation. Some places the problems were worse, others less severe.

From all appearances every reactor sunk during the war had finally failed to function. The climate wasn't getting any warmer, but it was getting drier. People were prepared for it now.

The anthrax and smallpox pandemics in the United States had finally run their course. They cost the country another twelve percent of the population surviving after the first year after the war. Whole communities had been wiped out by both smallpox and anthrax. Apparently the Enhanced Bubonic Plague that had been used as a weapon in the United States had been destroyed by nukes from other countries that hit New York, Los Angeles, and Chicago. Unfortunately the same could not be said for Europe, most of Africa, and much of China. The New Black Plague took over half of those that survived the war itself. Countries were making progress, some much more than others.

The Unimogs and Bobcats were still doing their work running on plentiful hemp biodiesel and so were the Kenworths. Sara and Percy were ready to do a little sightseeing of this rejuvenated nation. They were up to it and so was The Beast. The barge trailer had been expertly modified over the years. The Suburban and the Harley could now be carried both trailered and on the water with The Beast.

Percy finally decided to use up some of the rations he'd put aside in the preparation days before the war. Some of that freeze-dried and dehydrated food was pretty good.

AUTHOR'S NOTE

This has been a cautionary tale. I have tried to paint a picture of what life might be like for those that have chosen to prepare for natural and man-made disasters. I make no claim that this is exactly what would happen if something like the events in the story were to take place. This story was written so people would think about the so-called unthinkable. It must be remembered that it's not that Chemical Weapons, Biological Weapons, and Nuclear Weapons cannot be used because they've all been used during wars in the past. As a matter of fact, all three were used in World War Two alone. Chemical and biological weapons have been used several times since then. Human beings have always and will always seek progress. It is part of human nature. They even seek progress in warfare. It is simply a matter of time before weapons of mass destruction are used again.

Jerry D. Young

THANK YOU FOR READING
"PERCY'S MISSION"

By

Jerry D. Young

LIKE THIS BOOK?

See more great books at www.creativetexts.com

"SIMPLER TIMES"
"BUGGING HOME"
"THE SLOW ROAD"
"LOW PROFILE"
"RUDY'S PREPAREDNESS SHOP"
"CME: CORONAL MASS EJECTION"
"HOME SWEET BUNKER"
"THE HERMIT"

& MANY MORE GREAT
POST-APOCALYPTIC FICTION
& OTHER TITLES

THANK YOU!

www.ingramcontent.com/pod-product-compliance
Lightning Source LLC
Chambersburg PA
CBHW050608110726
47899CB00001B/19